IN THE COMPANY OF MEN

CAROLYN FINCH

IN THE COMPANY OF MEN

By: Carolyn Finch

In The Company of Men

By: Carolyn Finch

Editors: Alex McGilvery and Julie Sherwood

KDP ISBN: 978-1-7772999-5-8

(Ingram spark) ISBN 978-1-7772999-6-5

(e-book) ISBN 978-1-7772999-7-2

This is the third revision/edition, published June 2021

Canadian Certificate of Copyright 2020

Registration number: 1171888

❀ Created with Vellum

CHAPTER 1

*E*tta Lynne's heart sank as she sized up the competition in front of her. In the waiting room of the Manitoba Teachers' Federation, every woman needed this *one* job in Oakland—desperately.

Etta carefully pleated her skirt so the tattered edge wasn't so obvious. A young teacher across the hallway watched her, and when their eyes met, Etta saw sympathy there.

Finally, Miss Little appeared in the hallway and called Etta in.

Plastering a big, insincere smile on her face, Etta followed her into her office. Together, they sat down and reviewed the requirements for the position.

"This job opening, this offer, is not the kindness you think it is." Miss Little fixed Etta with a fierce look of concern, cleared her throat, fidgeted with the pearls at her neck, blinked and continued. "When Miss Ford left in a flood of tears, we chalked it up to the theory she was young and inexperienced. Now, Rose Ellice has disappeared. Without a trace." Miss Little's voice dropped ominously. "All her belongings are still in Oakland, and the police can't find her…"

"I have a family to feed." Etta leaned forward and cut her off. Her gaze locked with Miss Little's. "I just admitted my mother to the hospital, and if I don't get this job, I can't afford her care."

1

Etta remembered a flood of guilty shame as the doctors said she should have sought treatment earlier for her mother's advanced pneumonia.

"My sister is seven months pregnant. She lost her husband to the Spanish flu, and her pregnancy is delicate, but she still works as hard as she can to make ends meet. We have sold the house to pay for the doctor's bills." Etta choked on the partial truth.

Even now she couldn't say the truth about the house.

The house was bad enough, but selling all of her precious art supplies had opened a chasm of despair Etta couldn't crawl out of. Whatever had compelled her to pick up a pencil and draw, or mix oils together to paint, had smoldered and died as the man at the pawn shop turned up his nose at the brushes and gave her an insulting price.

That derisive sniff at the bristles caused something inside Etta to snap. As he bundled her paints and tossed them behind the counter, her heart broke into pieces. Cali had held her hand tightly, murmuring that as soon as Mother was well, they wouldn't have to pay doctor's bills, and they would have enough to buy them back.

Etta knew, deep down, they would never have enough. She had kept the letter of acceptance to the Toronto School of Art, a letter she had carried with her since before the war started, even though she was certain there was no possibility of school now.

No, just endless teaching to catch up for the mess their father had left for his daughters and wife. Her body trembled with worry as she thought of facing Mr. Santini, her landlord, without enough rent money. She couldn't afford both the rent and hospital fees.

She would have to owe the hospital because Santini's stakes were much higher.

Shaking those thoughts away, her eyes sharpened as she looked at Miss Little across the desk.

"Between the war and the flu; it left us with nothing." Etta's voice darkened.

Not even our dreams.

"I am very sorry. I know things have been difficult." Miss Little spoke with sincerity.

Etta rubbed her forehead in an attempt to calm down.

"I wanted to be clear about the risk. I have not forgotten the kindness... your word... that... saved me..." Miss Little dropped her voice, worried someone would overhear.

"Miss Little, please." Etta shook her head and took a deep breath. "That was a different world, before the Great War, a different time. I have forgotten all about it."

"I never will. I have to be sure you understand; the work environment in Oakland is less than ideal." Miss Little's lips tightened as she spoke. There was more to this than she was letting on. Etta wondered whom she was protecting. "As I mentioned... Mrs. Ellice... a seasoned veteran of a teacher... well..." Miss Little's voice trailed away.

Etta lost the last reserve of her patience.

"What do you know?" Etta demanded.

"Mrs. Ellice..."

"Never mind Mrs. Ellice. What did Miss Ford say? The first teacher forced to quit." Etta cut straight to the point. A back-breaking shift in a laundry on Pacific Avenue started in an hour. She had to be at work within the hour or they would dock her pay.

"She would only say some men on the board were... how should I put this delicately... well... not kind." Miss Little dropped her voice for the last two words.

Etta rolled her eyes and shook her head. "Good grief."

"As in, quite inappropriate..." Miss Little dropped her voice further as if someone might overhear. "She felt that one of the board members was too harsh and demanding. A trustee was upset that she wore a purple skirt."

Etta shook her head. "The code is clear; teachers aren't to wear colour. What was she thinking?"

"She was used to the city, I think."

"Well, Oakland is hardly a city." Etta shook her head. "She is twenty?" She tried and failed to take the contempt from her voice.

"Nineteen."

"Young and inexperienced," Etta declared. "I'm twenty-eight with eight years of experience; I can handle a nasty school board. Nothing I haven't seen before. I'll nip it all in the bud and get it sorted. I'll send you a full report." Etta's tone frosted with impatience.

Miss Little fidgeted with the perfectly stacked papers on the desk. "Etta, please remember that whatever happened with Mrs. Ellice, sadly, *she* did not contact the Manitoba Teachers' Federation, or they prevented her from doing so. Don't make that mistake. Even though the Federation is only months old, we are here to help."

"If I get the position, you mean." Etta dared to hope.

"You are up against Mr. Merritt." Miss Little's voice dropped.

"Well, this is a waste of gas, then." Disappointment dropped Etta's heart to her feet.

"I have it on good authority that Mr. Merritt was just hospitalized with shell shock." Miss Little arched an eyebrow. "While I am not unsympathetic to Mr. Merritt, it is to *you* I owe a favour. You will be the only one they are interviewing on Friday."

Etta took a deep breath and let it out slowly. "I don't know how to thank you."

"We're even then?"

"You never owed me. I expected nothing for telling the truth." Etta straightened up. "You were innocent of the charges."

"You and I both know, sometimes that doesn't matter." Miss Little's jaw tightened. "I've been waiting a long time to clear this debt to you."

"A debt only in your head, but I'll take it and thank you." Etta held her hand out to Miss Little to shake it before she left.

Miss Little stood up and took the proffered hand. Miss Little's felt small and dainty, soft in her own.

"Miss Little, I appreciate this very much."

"There is one last thing."

"Oh?" Etta's eyes searched Miss Little's.

"The school board... a Mr. Jackson Nash, who is on the board, and the mayor... well..." Her voice was so high she squeaked.

"Well what, Miss Little?" Etta crossed her arms over her chest.

"Yes. He... just a moment, I can read the letter." Miss Little cleared her throat. "I will just read the part that applies..." Her eyes flicked up to Etta's and then dropped down again. "The war is over. Two female teachers leaving in one year is unacceptable. We have no time or patience left for hysterics. Send us a soldier — forthwith!"

"Hysterics! Forthwith!" Etta's jaw dropped at the rudeness of the mayor of Oakland. She stiffened her spine and clenched her jaw as she thought of how to handle this new threat to a job she desperately needed.

"They need the position filled immediately. You will get it, and you will do well." Miss Little spoke with a confidence neither of them felt.

"Right." Etta tried to agree but failed to sound sincere.

"Mr. Merritt is not going to show up. You'll get it." Miss Little's eyes softened in sympathy as she repeated herself.

Etta turned the door handle to put an end to the meeting. No time for pity and regret. She had work to do and a job interview to prepare for.

"Hysterics." Etta snorted. "Mayor Jackson Nash better be battle ready. I will do this job, and I will do it well. I will not leave in tears."

Miss Little swallowed hard. "You might find you catch more flies with honey than vinegar..."

"I don't want to catch flies, Miss Little. I want to provide for my family." Etta's eyes blazed with intensity.

Miss Little looked at her in alarm.

"However, thank you for this. I appreciate it very much." Etta forced her tone to be gentle since Miss Little looked as though she were on the verge of tears.

"Before you go, Miss Lynne... do you have anything... well... anything to wear?" Miss Little asked delicately.

Etta's face flamed with humiliation. This dress was her very best. Cali had spent an hour mending and taking it in. Unfortunately, the hem was so badly tattered it couldn't be taken up.

"Of course," Etta lied through her teeth. "I will wear something more appropriate."

"Hang on." Miss Little scurried around the desk and pulled open a trunk near the door. "This is a donation." Her eyes flicked up as if checking for evidence of pride in Etta's stance that would show offense at being offered the charity. "I grabbed it in case a teacher needed a new cloak. Maybe your sister could work her magic."

Etta took the caramel-coloured worsted wool from Miss Little's hands. With her one last ivory lace blouse, she might look presentable.

"Thank you," Etta said simply. "Since the letter says send a soldier... will you send word that I'm not a man? Or how do we proceed?"

"I have sent your application as E. Lynne." Miss Little bit her lip. "I am banking on the fact that when no one else shows up, they will have no choice. I couldn't think of any other way to get you an interview."

Etta's jaw tightened.

"You must charm them," Miss Little implored her. "If anyone can, you can."

"I appreciate what you are trying to do here, Miss Little." Etta placed the length of fabric under her arm. "But, sadly, I'm fresh out of charm."

CHAPTER 2

Oakland's mayor, Mr. Jackson Nash, scowled up at the darkening sky. The clouds threatened rain or snow every day, adding to the rising floodwaters threatening the town.

He shook those thoughts away. Weather was a constant battle on the prairie, and he couldn't do a thing about it. There were more pressing matters demanding his attention.

Marching his way down Crescent Street, Oakland, Manitoba, he nodded to merchants as they prepared for the day.

Three problems tumbled in his brain, torturing him constantly.

First — where in the world was Rose Ellice?

His jaw tightened in worry. A female teacher disappearing was unheard of.

Completely, absolutely unheard of!

Now that the wretched war was over, life should return to normal. Not this madness!

For days, they thought for sure she would send word, or her family would send a notification that she was safe with them, no harm done. Just a misunderstanding, maybe? Who knew what set women off!

Nash had called in the Mounted Police, and Detective Kane was due to arrive today. He intended to interview everyone who knew her or had contact with her. Surely she would show up somewhere! Someone had to have seen something! Nash tried to stop worrying about what happened to her and leave the job to the police. Constable Lark was inexperienced and set Nash's teeth on edge, but Detective Kane was a battle-scarred and experienced investigator. He would get to the bottom of it! Nash resolved to put the matter out of his mind.

Easier said than done.

Nash obsessed about a lot of things, including the second pressing matter needing his full attention today — who was E. Lynne? Miss or Mister? Nash's eyes narrowed at the thought of anyone being so sneaky as to send a résumé without showing the gender of the applicant. E. Lynne, if she was a woman and not the soldier he had requested, was about to get a piece of his mind!

Nash rounded the corner of Crescent and Main. Mr. and Mrs. Hartwell were flipping the open sign on their joint design firm Hope in Oakland. Nash knew Mrs. Hartwell designed gowns and fripperies for most of the brides married in Manitoba. Women came from as far as Winnipeg to see her latest creations. They had never had children. Prior to her death, his late wife had informed him that Mrs. Hartwell had some woman trouble that Nash had promptly informed her he didn't need to know about.

Woman trouble was for women to discuss. No need for men to have anything to do with all that!

He nodded to Mr. and Mrs. Hartwell and kept moving.

Across the street, he watched with amusement as Mr. Ballantyne, the surveyor, and Mr. Ballard, the jeweller, carefully avoided speaking to each other. They barely nodded to one another as they put keys into door locks and opened up their respective storefronts for the day.

Both men had their eye on the massive building between their premises — a beautiful brick building with a booming café and generous living quarters upstairs. Word among the men, who met for coffee every day, was that the café was coming up for sale. The back of the building had a large balcony of sorts that looked out over Elizabeth Park. The old men speculated that Mrs. Hartwell had been talking about expanding her operation into the building, but who knew? Small towns generated more rumours than one could shake a stick at.

The last thing Oakland needs is another place for women to congregate and gossip!

There was more than enough of that happening at Lady Harper's 'at homes.' Nash's eyes narrowed at the thought.

Three people wanted the cafe. If Mrs. Hartwell wanted the building, Mr. Hartwell would intervene. If not, Ballard and Ballantyne would sort it out like men, and there was no need for the council to get involved.

He tipped his hat to Mrs. Carmichael, who looked wistfully at the building the men were fighting over and kept moving. Mrs. Carmichael was highly emotional, entirely too high-strung. Nash didn't have the fortitude to deal with her high-flown suggestions while he was still bracing himself for the day.

Nash's mind whipped back to E. Lynne. Why not Mr. Lynne? Why only E? Nash hated surprises. E. Lynne — gender unknown — and Mr. Merritt, a soldier — gender clearly known, thank you — were both being interviewed today for the teaching position suddenly vacated by Mrs. Ellice. Nash's mind eased, as he was confident that Mr. Merritt would put an end to this never-ending teaching crisis.

Nash knew about spinster battle-axes *of a certain age.*

They were known to send correspondence to the board peppered with demands and exclamation points. If E. Lynne were indeed a woman, *E.* would be dismissed—forthwith! Nash straightened his shoulders. He braced himself to battle a woman who was likely sixty years old, and a sour old spinster who simply needed to be put in her place, and he was *just* the man to do it.

Stopping in quickly to pick up the mail, he tried not to be detained by Mr. Hackle, the postmaster.

Tried and failed.

"There's a vehicle I don't recognize outside town hall." Mr. Hackle's very long eyebrows rose in speculation.

Nash wondered why Mr. Hackle didn't purchase a small pair of scissors to mow down his offending eyebrows.

He works with the public, for heaven's sake!

"Is that so?" Nash didn't make eye contact, unable to handle those horrific eyebrows this early in the day. He took his envelopes and turned on his heel to leave.

"I saw a woman get out of the motor car and enter the office." Mr. Hackle wiped the counter closer to Nash, baiting him into a reaction.

Nash paused; he straightened his shoulders but didn't react. "Hmm. Maybe someone is lost and looking for directions, Mr. Hackle?"

"She marched into the office like she had a *purpose*." Mr. Hackle's eyes narrowed as if he knew he was being lied to.

Nash stopped flipping through the envelopes in his hand and turned to face Mr. Hackle. "Well, I guess I better get to work and find out what's what."

"Terrible thing, that girl teacher gone missing." Hackle's tone wheedled for more information, and Nash began to think some men of this community were bigger gossips than the women.

Nash shot a tight smile at Mr. Hackle that showed he had no intentions of continuing the conversation. He wished, as he did every single day of his life as mayor, that he could get his mail without an interrogation.

Mrs. Daindridge and Mrs. Carr slowly crept their way toward their mailboxes; canes clattering and mouths nattering, eyes peeled for information they could speculate about at home. Nash tipped his hat and made a move for the door. If they got their claws into him, they would pounce, trying to wring out any information they could about Rose Ellice that they could chew on for weeks. Nash politely slid by them. Since their husbands had died, the widows had lived together to save on expenses. Unfortunately, they chose Mrs. Daindridge's home, directly across the street from Mrs. Lemon's.

Nash's third and final pressing problem — Mrs. Lemon. The war widow on his council agenda today lived under their noses and couldn't buy jam without them having a conversation about what brand. In Mrs. Lemon's current financial situation, she wouldn't be buying jam at all.

Worry for Mrs. Lemon snaked through him.

He hated the thought of a war widow being destitute. Russell Lemon had been a respectable and reliable man. How he could have died in the war without making provisions for his pretty young wife was completely beyond Nash. So, it fell to the men of Oakland to see that she was taken care of. She wasn't the only widow they worried about, but she was the only one slated to lose her house in October.

If only she would marry her brother-in-law, Lester Lemon! This suggestion, made to Mr. Holt, the deputy mayor, was promptly shut down. Mr. Holt's wife —Lily Holt — was a firecracker who needed her wings clipped. Nash shook his head in disapproval. Mr. Holt could battle anyone but folded like a cheap suit when it came to his wife. At any rate, Holt informed Nash that the women of Oakland would have his guts for garters if he so much as whispered the suggestion of marriage as a solution.

No mention of marrying Lester, under any circumstances, *no matter how much sense it made.*

Nash sighed. Women were tricky to navigate; he never knew what would set them off.

He gave Mr. Hackle a curt nod before he carried on.

"Good day, sir." Mr. Hackle nodded and returned to his uncategorized envelopes.

Nash took a moment to pause as he stepped outside the post office. He took a deep breath of fresh air and let his eyes sweep over the great, empty bowl of natural prairie where a group of boys were roughhousing on their way to school. Snow still drifted in the park – April was such an ugly month — but soon it would disappear. After a brutal and viciously cold winter, he longed to see the deep green of the oak leaves make their appearance. He yearned to leave the burdens of the day and slip over into Elizabeth Park and walk the trails overlooking where the creek met the river like he had as a child.

Nash remembered with great happiness a simpler time when women like Mrs. Lucy Lemon were not on the verge of losing their homes because of a war that had ravaged every family in Canada. He thought back fondly to a time when a woman teacher would *never* have gone missing.

He fervently hoped E. Lynne was a man and they would have two candidates for the position. It would just make everything much easier. Nash's jaw clenched in frustration.

Until they knew exactly what had happened to Mrs. Rose Ellice, no woman was safe in her vacated teaching position. A man taking over the job would ease Nash's fears. He could not, in good conscience, put a woman's life at risk. He had enough on his plate.

While he was hoping for a man —a soldier who had returned from war— unfortunately there was a disturbing trend of men coming back from war shaking like leaves on a poplar tree. Nash wasn't unsympathetic. He'd been to the front — he would never truly recover.

He woke in the night, sweating and shaking; sometimes he found it difficult to cope with the aftermath of the war. His memories snuck into his dreams and tormented him.

They said something about 'shell shock'. The war had been a trauma and a tragedy; he had done his duty and came home changed. He had lost his wife and son in childbirth two years before the war started. A part of him was glad she hadn't had to live through it. Nell had had a gentle spirit he had loved; she would have been utterly devastated by the war.

The war had stolen some of the best young men in their community and broken the hearts of the women. What the war hadn't taken, the Spanish flu had swooped in and added insult to injury.

Nash straightened his shoulders at the thought. There was no time to wallow.

Moving along, he nodded to Mr. Rood at the mercantile. He stopped to help Dr. Barrett with his awning at the pharmacy and clinic. As they adjusted the awning, he noticed Mrs. Spicer walking toward them. Poor Mrs. Spicer looked downcast as she made her way past the men. She didn't look comfortable in their presence, trying to shrink into her heavy coat. Nash stepped aside politely as she entered the clinic, not the pharmacy.

Dr. Barrett took a deep breath and let it out slowly as his eyes followed her inside.

"Mrs. Spicer looks like she's been dragged through a knothole. One wonders if that..." Nash tried to find an appropriate word to describe Mr. Spicer and couldn't, so he cut straight to the point. "Is she all right?" Nash asked Dr. Barrett. "Every time I see that woman, her eyes are permanently on the floor. Like someone broke her spirit."

"She fled from Russia just after the war started with no family support, no help. Her English is poor, and who knows of the tragedies she faced in her home country." Dr. Barrett spoke quietly as he fiddled with the edge of the awning. "It would be nice if she would reach out to the women of this community for support."

"She's married to Herman Spicer, which compounds the tragedy," Nash remarked.

"I really need to have this replaced." Dr. Barrett ignored the statement as he examined the seam on the edge of the awning.

"Does he hit her?" Nash squinted as he watched her.

"I'm a doctor, and I don't discuss my patients." A warning note in Dr. Barrett's tone told Nash to back off. "You want to know what is going on with Mrs. Spicer, I suggest you ask her." Dr. Barrett picked at the tattered awning and then dropped his hand.

Nash watched with sympathy as Mrs. Spicer sat down, placed her handbag on her broad lap, and waited. Pieces of her hair fell forward as she bowed her head. Nash noticed her hair was not thick enough to hide the sadness on her face.

Nash had seen this look before in the men's eyes when they had been too long in the trenches. Devastation and hopelessness had eroded her features. He saw it in his own face when he woke up sweating and shouting late in the night.

He shook those maudlin thoughts aside as he tore his gaze away from Mrs. Spicer and turned his attention to Deputy Mayor Holt. After bidding Dr. Barrett good day, together he and Holt turned the corner to cross the street, and sure enough, an unfamiliar motorcar, a Tin Lizzy if ever there was one, was waiting at the curb. Nash hesitated for one moment with his hand on the door handle of the Town Hall.

"May as well face this," Holt encouraged Nash.

"We asked for a soldier," Nash reminded Holt.

Nash turned the handle and opened the door.

A woman, late twenties, stood up and faced them head on.

"She doesn't look like a soldier to me," Holt murmured under his breath.

No indeed!

At first glance she looked delicate and vulnerable, with big blue eyes and blonde hair piled high on her head. She wore a long linen car coat over her caramel-coloured wool skirt, a white lacy blouse, and a blue cameo at her throat. Didn't matter that he couldn't see an inch of skin, her dress didn't hide that she was far too thin. She was so pale she seemed almost transparent. She peeled off her gloves — her driving goggles still perched on her forehead — then pulled a pair of eyeglasses from her handbag and put them on. She blinked at the men.

Nash's eyes narrowed, and he groaned as he realized this woman *had* to be E. Lynne.

When I was a student, teachers didn't look at mayors with such an impertinent expression!

Nash cringed as he thought about how long ago that day was. At forty years old, he hadn't set foot in a classroom in over twenty years.

"E. Lynne, I take it?" Nash frowned at her.

"Mayor Nash?" Miss Lynne's eyebrow arched as if she were accusing him of something.

Already!

"That's me," Nash growled.

"Mr. Nash, I am early because I was hoping I could have a word with you before I meet with the board." Her clipped tone cut straight to the point. Nash knew with every fibre of his being that any letter from her would be *peppered* with exclamation points.

"I'll stop you right there. There has been a mistake —Mr. Merritt is interviewing today, so…" Nash held his hand up to stop any further discussion. To his dismay, she ignored it.

"No one else is here. There has been a slight misunderstanding, which is why I would like a moment of your time. If I may…" Her face flushed red.

"You may not," Nash snapped back in a tone he didn't soften. "I am a member of the board, and the rest of the board needs to be present."

"I know you were expecting a man—they informed me of that just yesterday. I would like to plead my case if I might…"

E. Lynne needed to be put in her place.

He said no.

He meant no.

"Miss or Mrs.?" Nash tilted his head to the side as he waited for her answer.

"Miss." Her tone frosted with ice.

"Miss Lynne, you may not." Nash narrowed his eyes at her. "Please, have a seat. The board will arrive in fifteen minutes. I can assure you, we will hand you your walking papers, so don't get too comfortable."

Miss Lynne opened her mouth to speak and then promptly shut it.

"What was that?" Nash challenged her as he opened the door to his office.

"Nothing." Her chin lifted with defiance.

"That's what I thought." Nash turned his back on her. "Mrs. Delaire, coffee in my office."

He shut the door firmly behind him.

CHAPTER 3

*D*orothea Delaire tried and failed to tear her gaze away from the blonde-haired and blue-eyed E. Lynne. She recognized a threat when she saw one. Even with the glasses, E. Lynne with her delicate features could turn a man's head.

Why isn't she married? Does she know Mr. Nash is single?

Dorothea scurried into the coffee room to make Mr. Nash his morning coffee exactly the way he liked it. She knew deep down inside — she had to act fast. They were at odds now, but what if that changed?

She needed Mr. Nash's head turned permanently to her.

Dorothea despised deskwork with every fibre of her being. She should be engaged to Mr. Nash by now! She couldn't wait to spend her days picking out drapery colours, packing a lunch for his daughter, Grace, and then having friends over for coffee in the afternoon. She survived the tedium of office work by dreaming about what their lives would be like once they were married.

Soon, she promised herself.

Very soon.

She watched out of the corner of her eye as Miss Lynne got up to read minutes from the previous council meeting that were pinned to the board. Then she sat down on a chair by a room with a closed door. Dorothea's eyes narrowed as she added a scant teaspoon of sugar to Mr. Nash's coffee cup. She tilted her head to the side as she thought of how to disarm E. Lynne before she met with the board.

Dorothea added cream to Mr. Nash's coffee then checked her reflection in the mirror. Her pretty lips curved into a grin. Miss Lynne was pretty, certainly, but Dorothea knew she looked better. Masses of black hair and clever green eyes gleamed back at her. Squaring her shoulders, Dorothea pinched her cheeks, picked up Mr. Nash's coffee, and quickly made her way across the crowded office. She knocked politely on the mayor's door before entering.

Dorothea paused at the door, hoping Mr. Nash would look up and see her new sweater that showed off her curves.

Mr. Nash's nose was buried in a file.

Dorothea fought the rise of frustration as it built inside her. She placed his coffee on the desk at his right hand.

"Who does she think she is? Sending an application as E. Lynne!" Mr. Nash grumbled as he took a sip of coffee without saying thank you. "What is this world coming to?"

"It is not aboveboard at all, sir." Dorothea pounced on the opportunity to agree with him.

"Why isn't she married? Why aren't all these women getting married and getting on with it? The war is over. It's time for things to go back to normal. Uh… except in your condition as a new widow." Mr. Nash's eyes flicked up to Dorothea and then back down to his papers.

"I wouldn't say *new*." Dorothea spoke cautiously; she never contradicted him.

Mr. Nash, or Nash as everyone who knew him as a friend called him, was very old fashioned. Dorothea *pretended* to be old fashioned too. She played the game to the very best of her ability.

"However, with this Miss Lynne… I completely agree," Dorothea said breathlessly. "Here, this will help. I brought you some cookies. I made them myself last night." Dorothea leaned forward to put a plate of fresh-baked cookies on the desk by his hand. Her locket clattered to the desk beside the plate.

"Oops!" Dorothea grabbed the locket and fiddled with it.

"Could you… would you be able to squeeze this latch closed? It keeps coming loose. I'm not strong enough."

Mr. Nash adjusted his reading glasses and reached forward to take the clasp in his fingers. Dorothea nearly swooned as the hardness of his knuckles brushed against her sweater. He quickly squeezed the clasp and returned to his rant.

"You really must get that fixed. It falls off too often," Mr. Nash reprimanded her. "You will lose it one of these days."

"Yes, sir." Dorothea bowed her head.

"Honestly, even this Mrs. Lemon." Mr. Nash's forehead furrowed with frustration. "Lester Lemon is a perfectly good brother-in-law ready to do the right thing! Will she marry him? No! Can I even suggest it? No. Mrs. Holt would shoot me out of a cannon. How do we get these women to see sense?"

I don't care about Lucy Lemon, Mrs. Holt, or E. Lynne! Why can't you see that I am perfect for you? See me! Marry me, and take me out of this drudgery!

Dorothea stopped listening to him as she thought about what kind of ring they would pick out. She wanted Mr. Nash locked into matrimony, so she never had to calculate tedious accounts ever again!

Dorothea ignored his rant about Mrs. Holt as she delicately edged the cookies toward him.

Mr. Nash ignored the cookies.

"Oh, I know. It's a serious problem." Dorothea tisked with disapproval as she kept her eyes lowered. "I completely agree."

Mr. Nash harrumphed.

Beneath her lashes, Dorothea allowed herself to look at Mr. Nash just a little longer than necessary. A handsome man with a commanding presence about him, he made her heart pound with excitement. He stood nearly six feet tall, with a broad chest and *all his hair*. An experienced barrister, he ran the mayor's office efficiently.

Everything her dead husband wasn't— powerful, ambitious, hardworking, and decisive. So commanding, her entire body tingled with desire as he berated Miss Lynne.

Ronald Delaire, her dead husband, had been a melted cream puff compared to the gorgeous, hard-as-nails Jackson Nash.

Dorothea's eyes skimmed over Mr. Nash's powerful shoulders as he reached for his coffee. She ached to stand behind him and rest her hands on the hard line of his shoulders, to let her hands slide down to the solid plane of his chest. She snapped her attention back to the conversation at hand.

"I want the current school budget on my desk before the board arrives."

"Of course," Dorothea agreed quickly, her knees weak at the sound of his deep voice. "I'll get that for you right away, sir."

Mr. Nash turned his attention to another matter while Dorothea quickly scurried away to find the file he had requested.

She smiled to herself. She was exactly the woman a man like Mr. Nash needed.

He just didn't know it yet.

After finding the budget, she placed it on his desk near the cookies.

"Thank you, that will be all. Let Mr. Spicer know I would like to see him before we meet with this teacher."

"Right." Dorothea closed the door to his office and returned to the coffee room.

Fresh cup of coffee in hand, Dorothea made her way across the office to stand by Miss Lynne. She noticed her white lacy blouse and caramel-coloured skirt.

This wouldn't do. She looked fresh as a daisy in the combination. Wasn't there a rule about teachers wearing colour? Wasn't caramel a colour?

Miss Lynne looked up at her warily.

Dorothea smiled down at her sweetly.

"Oh, honey, don't mind Mr. Nash. He was expecting a man, a soldier actually. We have a bit of money set aside for the applicants they turn down." Dorothea directed the comment to Miss Lynne, delighting as she caught the hint of desperation in her eye. "I can give you the gas money to get home. Where did you come from?"

"Brandon." Miss Lynne held her gaze.

Dorothea's stomach churned with anger as Miss Lynne

addressed her as an equal. She didn't like how Miss Lynne replied with a clipped tone.

Who do you think you are?

Dorothea wrestled her emotions under control. "Oh! Such a long way. Here, sugar, take this coffee. It'll help settle your nerves before the men show up." Dorothea plastered a fake smile of friendship on her face.

"No, thank you." Etta shook her head.

"Suit yourself." Dorothea took a side step, deliberately tripping on the floorboard and upending the entire cup of hot coffee, all over Miss Lynne.

Miss Lynne yelped as the coffee burned her through her clothes.

"Oh! Oh my goodness! I am so sorry!" Dorothea's gaze met Miss Lynne's; she smirked.

"Never mind, I am fine." Miss Lynne brushed Dorothea away.

"I am just so clumsy!" Dorothea gushed insincerely. "Oh, honey, I am so sorry."

"What is going on?" Mr. Nash pulled open the door to his office and stuck his head out.

"I was just bringing Miss Lynne some coffee, and I tripped on this pesky floorboard! I feel terrible." Dorothea's eyes filled with tears. Dorothea saw in Mr. Nash's eyes that he believed her. It was so easy to manipulate men.

So simple! Present their ideal, and you could do what you want. Apologize and weep when you get caught. As long as you could pull off the breathless, silly, weak woman routine, you could get away with anything.

Miss Lynne pulled the soaked fabric away from her skin as best as she could.

"Fetch her a cloth to clean up," Mr. Nash barked as he turned on his heel and returned to his office.

Dorothea raced to the staff room, grabbed a dirty tea towel and returned to Miss Lynne.

"Again, I am just so sorry. All this way from Brandon for a job intended for a man." Dorothea pressed the tea towel into Miss Lynne's hand. She noticed with glee that coffee grounds dropped off the tea towel and clung to the lace of Miss Lynne's blouse. "This must be just devastating for you." Dorothea's tone dripped with sweet syrup. "I wonder if they will even bother to interview you once Mr. Merritt shows up?"

"I'll be fine, thank you." Miss Lynne sopped up the coffee with the dirty tea towel. Once she was done, Dorothea took the tea towel and took a step back. Confident she had done all in her power to disarm Miss Lynne, Dorothea returned triumphantly to her desk and got back to work.

A moment later, as Dorothea looked up from her tedious work of calculating taxes, Miss Lynne caught her eye and held it. There was a glint of determination in Miss Lynne's gaze she had only seen once before — in her own.

CHAPTER 4

*N*ash looked up as the skinny, slippery, Brylcreemed-
to-the-nth-degree secretary treasurer, Mr. Spicer,
slithered into his office and sat down. Everything about
Herman Spicer was cold and calculated, even the way he
crossed his long, thin legs and folded his narrow hands on his
lap. Nash wondered how the man could be entirely monochro-
matic, but all six feet of him was dressed in a beige suit
and shirt, which matched his freckles— also beige. His skin was
like the underside of a toad. The teeth marks from the comb
were still obvious in Spicer's sparse, slicked-back hair. When he
checked the time, he had to move the face of the watch as it had
slipped under his wrist.

Nash had never, ever liked Herman Spicer. He didn't like
him when they were kids in school, and he liked him even
less now.

Nash remembered his mother had tried to help him realize
that Herman Spicer came from a troubled home. As a genteel
lady who never gossiped about other women in town, she only
made general statements about Mr. Spicer's mother. Nash, out
of respect, never actually asked. However, he learned later Mr.
Spicer's mother had acted in an appalling manner. He had it on
good authority that the senior Mrs. Spicer was known to take a
drink... quite a few drinks. She embarked on other outrageous

behaviour, leaving Herman at home to fend for himself. Nash's mother, who had never touched a drop of alcohol in her life, had been appalled. Nash had not been permitted to visit Herman at home, lest he be led astray. No loss, as Nash and Spicer had been locked in conflict their entire lives.

Nash knew now, Herman had rebelled against his mother by resolving to be top of his class and leave her behind. When his mother needed care later in life, Nash heard it on good authority Herman had ignored her cries for help. She had perished as a vagrant in Winnipeg, according to local gossip-monger Mrs. Carr. It was anyone's guess what had happened between Mrs. Spicer senior and young Herman. In truth, Nash really didn't care. The result was the man sitting across the desk from Nash.

Mr. Spicer was a fanatic about chastity and virtue. The Manitoba Teachers' Federation code of conduct was ridiculously strict, but he enforced it with zeal. Mr. Spicer particularly loved the part of the code that forbade any female teacher from being in the company of men after 8:00 pm. Nash knew Mr. Spicer spied on the teachers they hired in Oakland, ready to enforce that line of code to the letter. All the more reason to hire a man; Mr. Spicer had created a difficult work environment for the female teachers. They hadn't known it when he had originally been chosen for the school board because he was well known for demanding and insisting the teachers push young men into university.

With the good came the bad.

Spicer seemed terrified that an underdressed female teacher could lead the girls of the school astray and young boys might lust after an inappropriately dressed older woman.

Dealing with Mr. Spicer was a tedious operation.

All this insanity had escalated when Miss Ford worked for the school in Oakland. She had worn a purple skirt to school. Spicer called an emergency meeting where he humiliated her in front of the entire school board. Nash remembered wanting to slug him to shut him up, but sadly, in a civilized society, that behaviour was frowned on. Miss Ford had run in the night, and now Mrs. Ellice was missing.

Nash's eyes narrowed as he wondered if Spicer had something to do with her disappearance.

Nash was certain of one thing. The man sitting in front of him mistreated his wife. Mr. Spicer's insatiable need for dominance and control had to be behind these teachers not fulfilling their obligations.

The women were not strong enough to stand up to Spicer and bring their concerns to the authorities. Nor should they be. It was up to men, specifically the men of the school board, to protect them. Nash wanted to drag a confession out of Mr. Spicer himself.

Desperately.

With his fists, preferably.

But, as with all things involving Spicer, you could never deal with something head on. You had to out-manipulate him. The school board had real problems, and Nash was weary of one trustee being a *constant* concern.

Nash knew the feeling was mutual because Spicer had run for mayor against Nash and lost.

Nash sighed and consulted the budget in front of him.

As an accountant, Spicer was the natural pick as secretary treasurer for the school board. Nash couldn't stand the thought of being on the same board, but he didn't have a choice.

Since the war men were in scarce supply, so Nash forced a polite smile on his face and asked if he would like some coffee.

"No. No thanks." Spicer checked his watch again.

"This budget is still out?" Nash ran his fingertip down the columns. "Has that three hundred dollars turned up?" Nash mentally added up the sums to double check the final loss of three hundred dollars.

Mr. Spicer reached into his breast pocket and pulled out a wad of cash. "Yes. My wife claims it fell behind my desk when she cleaned my office. She must have knocked it off by accident."

Nash took the bundle of cash and counted it, verifying that there was indeed three hundred dollars all accounted for. He longed to hold it to the light to be sure it was real money.

Spicer shifted in his seat, and his hand shook a bit.

Nash was certain Spicer was hiding something.

"I have an adjusted budget." Spicer handed Nash a new budget and moved to snatch the old budget out of Nash's hand.

Nash kept the budget that revealed the missing money out of Spicer's reach. His eyes skimmed the new budget. No mention that the money had gone missing.

"This budget has no mention of the missing money." Nash watched Spicer's face carefully.

"The money has been found and promptly returned. Why retain record of the missing money? Rate payers would worry that we had mishandled funds. What purpose would that serve?"

Nash heard a slight tremor in Spicer's tone that made him wonder what had actually happened with the money. He didn't trust Spicer. Not at all. His gut said to keep the evidence that Spicer had mishandled the funds. He tried to put the thoughts away, but they niggled at him.

"It's the honest way to proceed." Nash looked over the new budget and then back to the old one.

Spicer's jaw tightened, and he leaned back in his chair. "Whatever you think." Spicer shrugged. "If you want to cause the public to lose faith in our ability to handle their money, so be it."

He's a bit too nonchalant...

Nash carefully tucked the old budget away, making a note to put a copy in two safe places. Here and at home. Something was off or nothing was off, Nash just couldn't put his finger on it. But his lack of trust made him cautious.

Nash changed the subject.

"How do we get rid of this E. Lynne, Mr. Spicer? We all agreed we need a man to fill this position. The job will go to Mr. Merritt, right? I just wish we knew why he hasn't shown up yet!" Nash shook his head.

Spicer's hand shook a bit as he fiddled with his watch. Nash wondered if he was imagining it.

"He is in hospital. Nerves," Mr. Spicer said coolly.

"Nerves!" Nash blustered. "What do you mean, nerves?"

"Shell shock. He thought he was up to the job, but he can't cope." Spicer's tone was not judgmental either way.

Nash rolled his eyes. "That's a fine kettle of fish."

Spicer shrugged. "Difficult times."

"Until we know what happened to Mrs. Rose Ellice, we all agreed we needed a *soldier*, Mr. Spicer. We have lost two female teachers, and we cannot lose another. I will make that perfectly clear," Nash growled. "One woman running away and one disappearing in one school term is outrageous."

"We can't leave the position unfilled any longer. We will let her know right up front that we will not tolerate any inappropriate behaviour from her. If she is insubordinate or if she doesn't fulfill her role, she will lose more than her job. The next teacher that leaves in the night will lose her career. That should stop *that*." Spicer's eyes gleamed with anticipation. He leaned forward in his seat; his breath quickened.

Nash shot Spicer a sharp look to see if he were speaking in jest. He seemed too eager to have another woman in his employ to boss around.

Nash knew with certainty Spicer was serious.

"Maybe Mr. Merritt will get out of the hospital in time to interview. We can try to put it off."

Spicer shook his head slowly. "Not according to my sources. Shell shock, and a bad case of it. Poor man is completely incapacitated with nerves."

"There is no one else?"

Mr. Spicer shrugged and checked his watch again. "All the men have jobs since the beginning of the school year. We are scraping the bottom of the barrel."

Nash sighed. "Since we will discuss Mrs. Lemon after we sort out Miss Lynne, what is the situation there?"

"Lester Lemon has asked her to marry him, and she is refusing."

"I heard." Nash's jaw clenched in frustration.

Spicer snorted with derision. "Mrs. Lemon is a hysterical female. She's being nostalgic and ridiculous. Lester Lemon would look after her needs, and he would also get the family home back. It is in everyone's best interest if she would just agree. The willfulness of women is on the increase, and it must be stopped. Lucy Lemon needs a reminder that a young widow needs a reputation that is *above reproach*. Working as a cleaning woman at the hotel is very *compromising*. Is she truly cleaning?"

Fury pounded through Nash at Spicer's implication that Lucy Lemon was not chaste and virtuous. Nash couldn't take the anger out of his tone as he spoke. "Mrs. Lemon's virtue is above reproach. I better not hear any murmurings of her morality being questioned. Anyone who suggests such a thing will answer to me." Nash leaned forward.

Spicer swallowed hard as Nash placed his hands, clenched into fists, on the desk.

Nash despised the way Spicer's Adam's apple bobbed in his narrow throat.

Not wanting to discuss women with Spicer any further, Nash got to his feet. "Shall we? I believe the board is here."

Together the men entered the council chamber, where the rest of the board was waiting.

Lord Harper, as chairman, sat at the head of the table. He sat in the chair Nash used as mayor.

Lord Harper irritated Nash on every level. His own children were in a private school, a very fancy school called Appleton that cost a *fortune*. A high-flown place where the citizens that had built the surrounding community considered themselves English gentry. Indeed, they were, but this was Canada, and no one gave a toss about that now. No one cared but Lord Harper.

Yet not only did he want to be on the board, he ran for chairman!

Nash tried to push his negative thoughts aside... he tried and failed. Was Harper here for his own interests? To ensure that they would educate the peasant class, his future employees, sufficiently to handle matters in this town? Or was he here for the children of the town? Nash didn't like his thoughts about Lord Harper. At all. The man was insufferable if he didn't get his way.

To Lord Harper's right was Mr. Spicer as secretary treasurer. The rest of the trustees were Mr. Bennett, Mr. Holt, Mr. Ward, Mr. Carr, and Nash.

Spicer picked up a pencil to take notes.

Nash shot Mr. Carr a look and knew that every minute of

this meeting would be relayed to his mother, Mrs. Carr, who lived with Mrs. Daindridge— the two biggest gossips the town of Oakland had to endure.

"Mr. Nash, please ask Miss Lynne to join us," Lord Harper directed Nash.

Nash fought his inward frustration as he got up, opened the door, and escorted E. Lynne into the council chamber.

CHAPTER 5

$\mathcal{E}$tta looked down at her ruined dress in despair. It was bad enough to meet with a board that had requested a man, but being forced to walk in there with coffee all over her dress made her painfully self aware. She pulled her file out of her bag and stood when Mr. Nash opened the door to the council chamber.

Taking a deep breath, she preceded him into the room.

"Take a seat, Miss Lynne." The man at the head of the table indicated she should sit at the foot.

"Thank you for meeting with me today." Etta took her seat so the rest of the men would sit down as well.

Mr. Nash sat down at her right and briefly introduced all those present.

Etta's heart pounded so hard she worried they might see it beating through the fabric of her ruined blouse.

"Miss Lynne, we are all curious as to why you sent an application as E. Lynne. Were you aware we were expecting a male teacher?" Lord Harper, the man at the head of the table, shot her a dark look.

"My friend, Miss Little, found out about this job posting and sent the application on my behalf. I am sorry about the confusion. She was wrong to be misleading. However, I am here, and

I need this job. I am ready and willing to start today if that would help things."

"Today!" Lord Harper gasped.

"Sir, my sister is with child. Her husband fought in the war, made it safely home and then died of the Spanish flu. She is working, but her condition is delicate. We cannot depend on her wage. My mother is sick, and we have admitted her to the hospital with pneumonia. The hospital bills are more than we can pay unless I get this job. I am not being melodramatic, but if I return empty-handed, it will devastate my family." Etta's eyes fixed on Lord Harper's; she refused to look away.

Lord Harper cleared his throat, looked at the paper in front of him and then spoke. "What is your experience?"

"I have eight years of experience in various schools in the city of Brandon. I am..."

"The city allows their female teachers a little more latitude than we do, Miss Lynne." The man seated next to Lord Harper, Mr. Spicer as she recalled, cut in and spoke forcefully. "We have had to dismiss female teachers in the past for being in the company of men." Spicer's tone was ominous. "I trust we won't have that same problem with you."

"No, sir! You won't have any trouble." Etta met his gaze and noticed a glint of fury in his. He expected her to drop her eyes as a show of submission. She told herself to, tried to make her eyes drop, but she couldn't. Her spine stiffened, battle-ready for this new threat—Mr. Spicer.

"You know of the code of conduct we require of female teachers?" Spicer broke eye contact as he pulled a paper from a file in front of him.

Etta's stomach twisted as she watched the Manitoba Teachers' Federation code of conduct get passed from man to man until Mr. Nash handed her the paper.

She knew the code— the ridiculous, oppressive, vicious code. The code was loosely applied in cities, but strictly adhered to in religious communities. Oakland was neither, however, here it was in front of her. A warning— a reminder.

"As I mentioned, I have eight years of experience; I am well aware of the code." Etta's jaw tightened.

"We will ask, anyway." Mr. Spicer leaned forward. "Are you courting a man?"

"No." Etta's stomach soured as anticipation gleamed in his eyes. She could tell he enjoyed asking personal, intimate questions and delighted in her discomfort. Little did he know, she ate, slept and worked; there was no time for any shenanigans.

Men only let you down, anyway. If you couldn't trust your father, who could you trust?

"Do you promise to remain single until the end of the school term?"

"I do." Etta's throat tightened.

"You know that you have to ask permission to leave the town limits." Spicer tilted his head to the side like a bird of prey as he waited for her answer.

"Yes." Etta immediately worried about that clause. According to the doctors, her mother might not make it. She would have to leave if her mother died.

Surely they would be reasonable in that instance?

Etta determined to cross that bridge when she came to it.

"Are you pregnant?" Spicer asked.

Etta gasped in shock. "Of course not!"

"Mr. Spicer!" Lord Harper snapped at him. "She is a single woman! That is quite enough!"

Spicer's eyes narrowed at her. "It's been known to happen."

"Next question." Lord Harper shot him a look of warning.

"Miss Lynne, we take the virtue of our female teachers seriously. The young men and women of our society will look up to you." Mr. Spicer's eyes narrowed.

"I understand." Etta nodded.

He loves to humiliate women. I am not comfortable with this man as my superior, but I don't have a choice.

"Do you agree to wear two petticoats?" Spicer's eyes slid over her.

"That's enough," Nash boomed from her side. "Lord Harper, if you can't get Mr. Spicer under control, I certainly can."

Etta looked at the mayor in shock. Of all the men at the table, she hadn't expected him to stop this interrogation. She watched as Spicer fumed at Mayor Nash.

Oh gracious, they despise each other!

"I warned you, Spicer. That is all the questions you are permitted to ask. Honestly, what will you come up with next?" Lord Harper shook his head. "Miss Lynne, if you would step out, we'll vote."

Etta got to her feet. Nerves made her mouth dry as she addressed the board. "May I say one thing?"

"You may not." Mr. Spicer crossed his arms over his narrow chest.

"Now, now." Lord Harper shot a look of reprimand to Mr. Spicer. "What is it?"

"I understand the frustration of trying to hire teachers when two have left." Etta's voice started out quiet, but as she remembered the doctor's bills that were piling up every single day, her spine stiffened. "I assure you, I have no intentions of leaving if you hire me. Not only will I finish this term, but I will be available for the next school term. I *alone* am responsible for the welfare of my family. We do not have a man to provide for us, and our situation is desperate, sir."

I am not above begging.

"Please, I need this job. I will follow the instructions in your code of conduct to the letter." Etta stopped speaking. Her eyes met Mr. Nash's, and he held her gaze. The sympathy she saw in his eyes was reassuring. A quick glance over the rest of the men showed similar sympathy in all but Secretary-Treasurer Spicer's eyes.

His eyes looked hard as nails, and yet there was something else. She met his gaze and held it. His eyes narrowed at her.

He hates women.

Etta shivered at the realization.

He's one of seven.

"Yes, well…" Lord Harper cleared his throat, likely not comfortable with emotion. "We'll vote and let you know. Please, step outside."

"Thank you, sir." Etta gathered her file and held it against her body, trying to cover the worst of the coffee stain.

She turned on her heel and left the chamber.

CHAPTER 6

*E*tta thought the clock ticking on the wall would drive her mad.

Her pulse raced as she waited an entire fifteen minutes for them to decide. She wished for a pencil so she could draw while she waited but didn't want to give the mean secretary the satisfaction of declining her request. A sudden clatter at the front door startled her.

A man staggered into the town office, and from the smell, he was clearly drunk.

Etta gasped in alarm.

The drunk stumbled over to Mrs. Delaire's desk. His hand slid across her meticulously piled papers. Mrs. Delaire's jaw dropped in shock, but she said nothing, the fear he would attack her obvious on her face.

"Jackson Nash!" the man bellowed into the office.

Mrs. Delaire recoiled from him as far as she could.

Nash came flying out of the council chamber. "Angus. You're drunk!" He frowned in disgust.

"You stole my field! You stole my field, and you are giving it to a bunch of women!" Angus took a swing at the mayor.

Nash sidestepped him.

Etta's hand flew to her throat.

"Do that again, and I will hit back. This is your first and final warning," Nash growled.

"You stole my field!" Angus howled as he stumbled closer to Nash.

"Show me the land title, and we will return the field to you," Nash said patiently.

From the way he was handling Angus, Etta knew this was not the first time they had battled over whatever field this drunk and disorderly man thought he owned.

"I don't have it," Angus slurred.

"Bill of sale?" Nash suggested politely.

"We had a spoken agreement, and you know it!" Angus roared at Nash and then burped.

Etta gasped as Angus took another swing at Nash.

If I were Nash, I would hit back!

"The field has been planted, the proceeds going to the widows and orphans of Oakland. We have been over this many times before. You have no proof of sale. That means the proceeds go where the council decides. This matter is closed!

"Leave here and don't return. The next time you come into this office drunk and screaming about a field *you do not own,* I will have you arrested. Are we clear?" Nash grabbed Angus by the lapels and held him steady as he barked the instructions into his face.

Angus jerked back out of Nash's grip.

"You're a dirty thief! I know it— everyone does." Angus swayed on his feet.

"Angus, I will have you arrested if you do not leave this office!" Nash bellowed at him.

The men from the council chamber gently nudged Etta back out of harm's way as they came out to see what all the fuss was about. Mr. Bennett and Mr. Holt stood directly behind Mr. Nash, ready to assist him in removing Angus from the town office by force.

Mercy!

"Miss Lynne, kindly wait in the council chamber. A lady shouldn't witness such boorish behaviour; our apologies." Lord

Harper waved to the open door, indicating she should go back into the room the men had vacated.

Etta stepped into the council chamber and then peeked out as Nash held the front door open so Angus could leave. Mr. Bennett and Mr. Holt said nothing as Nash closed the door firmly behind Angus.

The men filed back into the chamber and took their seats.

"I told you that field would cause trouble," Spicer spat at Nash.

Etta's eyebrow arched as Nash scowled at Spicer.

"I won't have women starving and losing their homes in Oakland, Manitoba! Not on my watch!" Nash roared at Spicer, patience clearly spent. "Splain is dead. His land was up for tax sale. The town owns it. We will harvest it and split the proceeds with the widows and anyone less fortunate in this town, and if you don't like it, Spicer, you can—"

"There is a lady present!" Lord Harper reprimanded the men from the head of the council table.

Etta watched Mr. Nash out of the corner of her eye. He looked as if steam would pour out of his ears at any moment.

"My apologies, Miss Lynne." Mr. Nash's movements were jerky with anger as he nodded to her curtly and sat down in a huff.

"No apology necessary, Mr. Nash." Etta bit her lip as she began to look at him differently.

The proceeds of a field to be given to the women and orphans from the war was incredibly generous.

"We can table the unfortunate interruption of Angus and get on with this job interview." Lord Harper brought the meeting back under control. "Miss Lynne, Mr. Merritt was to interview today, but he is detained. We have no other option but to hire you. You should know that you would not be our choice for this position. The previous female teacher is missing without a trace. We are very concerned for the safety of our female teachers until we can verify what happened to Mrs. Ellice. We ask that you are cautious and contact us if any situations with students or parents make you uncomfortable. We do not wish you to come to any harm, miss."

A prickle of fear raised the hair on the back of Etta's neck as she watched Mr. Spicer's face as Lord Harper spoke of her safety.

What about board members who make me uncomfortable?

"Could you start Monday?" Lord Harper asked politely.

Etta's heart soared at the news. "I *can* start Monday, yes."

"We have a few details to arrange here. As the regular billet cannot take you in, we have a war widow in town who is looking for some extra income. If that is all right with you, we will arrange to have you stay with Mrs. Lemon. We will expect you at 4:00 pm sharp on Sunday evening. Mr. Nash and Mr. Spicer will show you the classroom and then make sure you are settled at Mrs. Lemon's. We will expect you full time starting Monday morning."

"Thank you, sir." Etta came around the table to shake Lord Harper's hand.

Lord Harper and the rest of the men scrambled to their feet. Lord Harper blinked at her in surprise as he took her hand in his own. "You are welcome."

"You won't be disappointed. I guarantee that the rest of this school year will go as planned." Etta beamed at the men around the table.

"We'll hold you to that promise," Spicer growled at her.

"I hope that you might consider me for the next year. If my work is satisfactory."

"Let's not get ahead of ourselves. You *will* have to prove yourself." Mr. Spicer held his bony hand out, and Etta couldn't avoid shaking it. He gripped her hand harder than necessary, hurting her. The bones of her hands ground together; she refused to wince, refused to let him see that it hurt. Etta wouldn't give him the satisfaction. She finally tugged her hand out of his grip. She shook Nash's hand last; his grip was firm, but not so hard as to hurt.

"We'll meet you Sunday at the school. I'll see you out." Nash held the door for her. He waited for her to pull on her linen driving coat, her gloves, and her goggles.

Together they made their way past the clerk to the door of

the civic office. Etta shot a triumphant look at Mrs. Delaire, and sure enough, the look she sent back was filled with venom.

Once on the street, Angus shuffled toward them.

Etta tensed in worry that Angus would take a swing at Mr. Nash again.

Mr. Nash immediately put his body between Etta and Angus as Angus weaved closer to her.

When the drunk stumbled by, Mr. Nash was careful to keep her protected.

"Sorry about that interruption. I can assure you, that is not the norm here in Oakland," Mr. Nash said to Etta. "Angus, take off before I lose my temper," Mr. Nash warned the man.

Etta placed her hand on the crank of her car.

Mr. Nash put a hand on her arm to stop her. "Let me."

"I can handle it," Etta shot at him.

"You can, but I'll do it," Mr. Nash insisted.

"I can assure you, I am used to looking after myself." Etta bristled.

"Maybe so, but I insist." Mr. Nash took her by the upper arms and physically moved her aside.

"You are very high handed," Etta muttered as she snapped the goggles down over her eyes and hoped with every fibre of her being that her car would start. Humiliation raced through her as Mr. Nash cranked and the car refused to come to life. One more crank, and the engine began to rumble. Etta let out a long sigh of thankfulness.

"You'll get used to it." Mr. Nash smirked at her.

"I assure you, I won't!" Etta slammed the driver's door shut, stomped on the gas, and prayed her car would get her out of eyesight if it died.

Etta roared out of Oakland as fast as her tires would take her.

CHAPTER 7

*M*rs. Daindridge looked around her kitchen before adding her secret ingredient to the pastry flour. Mrs. Carr, who was reading the newspaper at the dining room table, wasn't watching. Mrs. Daindridge, confident her secret would be safe from Mrs. Carr as she was distracted by her news, reached for the tin of baking powder, scooped out a teaspoon full, and carefully keeping her back to Mrs. Carr, she sprinkled baking powder into the flour of her prize-winning pastry. Her never-fail, take-the-recipe-to-the-grave pastry. Quickly, she put the tin back on the shelf as a shiny black Model T stopped in front of Mrs. Lemon's house.

"Mrs. Carr!" Mrs. Daindridge called as she moved to the window.

Mrs. Carr was slow to get to her feet, her hip clearly hurting her. She shuffled across the kitchen and picked up the second set of binoculars.

Mrs. Daindridge slowly slid the lace curtain aside, just enough that they could watch what was happening at Lucy Lemon's house.

"Is that Mayor Nash?" Mrs. Carr gasped. Her eyesight had failed in the last year, but what she couldn't see, Mrs. Daindridge *could*, with eagle-eyed vision. Mrs. Carr also had a hard time hearing, but Mrs. Daindridge could hear a fly drop to the floor two rooms away. Together, they pooled their strengths, and nothing got past the widows on Willow Avenue.

Binoculars pressed to the wavy pane of glass in their joint kitchen, they watched Mayor Nash get out of his car and knock politely on Lucy's door.

"That Jackson Nash..." Mrs. Daindridge sighed as she let her eyes travel the length of him. "The very cut of his father. From behind, you would think they were the same man."

Mrs. Carr rolled her eyes. Mrs. Daindridge had been sweet on Steadman Nash from the get-go. Most inappropriate!

"An eligible bachelor like Mr. Nash needs to find a wife and settle down. His poor daughter, Grace, being raised without a mother..." Mrs. Carr shook her head and squinted so she could see him clearly. "She needs a woman in her life."

Mrs. Daindridge wasn't concerned about Grace. She just couldn't tear her eyes from Mr. Nash. "He melts my butter," Mrs. Daindridge said breathlessly. "Look at him, he still has all his hair, Mrs. Carr! Tall, broad, dark, and handsome. If I were twenty years younger..."

"Twenty!" crowed Mrs. Carr, ever the realist. "Try forty, please, Mrs. Daindridge."

They held their collective breath as Mrs. Lemon opened the door to her home.

"Is she crying?" Mrs. Daindridge asked as she adjusted the little wheel in the centre of her binoculars to focus on Mrs. Lemon's face with better clarity.

"She should be," Mrs. Carr snapped. "She has a perfectly good offer of marriage from Lester Lemon, who, I have heard on good authority, offered to pay all the taxes and take care of her. Instead, she is working as a cleaner at the King Edward Hotel, of all the places in the world. No respectable woman would be caught dead cleaning in a hotel!"

"Mr. Nash needs a wife, too." Mrs. Daindridge's lips pursed in disapproval. "I don't know what he's waiting for."

"Well, I can report..." Mrs. Carr spoke conspiratorially.

"What?" Mrs. Daindridge and Mrs. Carr put down their binoculars and turned to face each other. Mr. Nash had stepped into Lucy's foyer, and neither of them could see through the windows.

Mrs. Carr's eyes gleamed as she spoke. "I have it on good authority, Mrs. Daindridge, Mrs. Delaire has her eye on Jackson Nash, and *nobody* better get in her way."

"No!" Mrs. Daindridge gasped at the thought. "Her husband is barely cold in the ground, Mrs. Carr!"

"Yes!"

"Where did you hear that, Mrs. Carr?" Mrs. Daindridge sputtered in surprise.

"I have my resources." Mrs. Carr's mouth snapped shut as if it pained her to gossip about a neighbour.

"Mrs. Carr, we have the same resources." Mrs. Daindridge narrowed her eyes, worried that Mrs. Carr knew a speck of information that she hadn't shared.

"Well, my son is on the school board..."

Mrs. Daindridge stiffened. Mrs. Carr having access to a member of the school board gave her inside information that she meted out to Mrs. Daindridge slowly.

Very slowly.

It irritated Mrs. Daindridge that Mrs. Carr filtered information. She always suspected she held things back...

"My son was checking on Mrs. Ellice's work before she disappeared without a trace... but that is another story... and he overheard Grace say to a friend that Mrs. Delaire had dropped off a pie, and it was *very good*." Mrs. Carr shook her head.

"Dropped off a pie!" Mrs. Daindridge gasped. "How *forward!*"

"Widowed only a few months." Mrs. Carr tisked and placed her binoculars on the counter carefully. She avoided the flour that dusted the surface.

"Something doesn't sit right about all that." Mrs. Daindridge's eyes narrowed to slits. "They say she met the doctor and the undertaker in her *unmentionables*."

Mrs. Carr shook her head. "Well, suffice it to say, Mrs. Delaire has staked her claim. I believe the pie was *cherry*, which we all know is Nash's favourite. So, now we wait to see if he picks up the hint. However, this is most unusual, him calling on a war widow this time of the day, especially if he *is* somewhat spoken for by Dorothea Delaire."

"If only all the widows were as considerate as us." Mrs. Daindridge shook her head. "If we hadn't moved in together, what sort of burden would we be to this community?"

"I agree, Mrs. Daindridge. A big burden for sure. Like this Mrs. Lemon and all her high-flown requirements for a new husband. We've lost so many good men — we have to make do with what we have."

"These young girls today." Mrs. Daindridge shook her head in disappointment. "They are willful. They want their way no matter what."

"I agree with you there." Mrs. Carr went back to her chair.

Mrs. Daindridge shot one last hard look at the empty front step of Mrs. Lemon's house and returned to her pastry.

* * *

NASH IGNORED the lace curtain moving in Mrs. Daindridge and Mrs. Carr's kitchen window as he stood on Mrs. Lemon's verandah. He knocked politely at the front door and waited.

Finally, Mrs. Lemon came to the door. She trembled in front of him. Her eyes darted past him down the street. Her hands shook with fear. "Mr. Nash, sir, I thought I had until October to pay my tax bill." Her eyes filled with tears that threatened to spill down her cheeks.

Nash's heart went out to her.

"Mrs. Lemon!" Nash exclaimed. "No! Please don't cry. I'm not here about that at all."

She took a deep shuddering breath and then burst into tears.

"Mrs. Lemon, please." Nash held his hands out in supplication. "Please, don't cry."

"I don't know what I will do!" She turned on her heel, retreated back inside her house and collapsed onto a settee.

Nash entered the house awkwardly. Men did not just burst into distraught women's front rooms uninvited and unchaperoned, especially with dreadful Mrs. Daindridge and Mrs. Carr watching from across the street. He stood awkwardly by the threshold of the door as she wept into a cushion.

"Mrs. Lemon. I am so sorry to stop by unannounced and without asking permission first... I had a question of a desperate nature to ask, and I really couldn't wait." Nash spoke as gently as he could.

Mrs. Lemon sat up and dried her eyes. "You'll think me silly." She shuddered on the settee. "I married Mr. Lemon when I was seventeen, and I never dreamed I would be a widow this young." Mrs. Lemon's eyes filled with tears again. "Russell handled all the finances, and he... I just don't understand how he could have let the taxes get to this state!" Mrs. Lemon wrung her hands with worry. "I just don't know what happened. How could he have left me like this?"

Nash shifted from foot to foot. "I am so sorry, Mrs. Lemon, I didn't know him well."

"You aren't coming to take my house today, but you will, won't you?" Mrs. Lemon reached for a handkerchief from beside the settee. "This is all too much for me, Mr. Nash. I can't cope. I can't stop crying, and I don't know what to do. I am working at the King Edward Hotel as a cleaner, even though that terrible Simon tried to get me to..."

"Get you to what, Mrs. Lemon?" Nash's eyes narrowed at the thought of creepy, blowhard Simon Treleaven propositioning this poor, distraught, vulnerable woman.

"He wanted me to be a barmaid," Mrs. Lemon whispered in shame. "He said I would make more money. Me! A barmaid! I couldn't hold my head up!"

Nash let his breath out slowly. If Simon Treleaven had propositioned this lovely, vulnerable woman, he would go to the hotel and readjust him, and he really didn't have time...

"I am trying my best, but the council won't see that..." She put her face in her hands.

Nash wished the earth would open up and swallow him whole. Weeping women disarmed him; he would rather be up to his knees in mud in a trench on the front line than standing in front of a sobbing woman.

"Mrs. Lemon, we see how hard you are trying, and that is

why I am here. We have a new teacher in town. She requires a place to be billeted. Could I impose on you to billet her? We will pay you..." Nash pulled the offer out of his breast pocket and handed it to her.

Mrs. Lemon read the offer quickly. Her head snapped up. "That much! Just to stay here?"

"Yes. So I immediately thought of you, Mrs. Lemon." Nash spoke gently in case she bristled at the obvious attempt at charity.

"Oh, thank you, Mr. Nash." She pressed her narrow hand to her heart. "I was not sure how I would pay the coal bill from winter, and this will pay it." Mrs. Lemon threw herself into Nash's arms and squeezed him hard.

Nash hadn't held a woman in his arms since his precious Nell died. He hadn't taken the time to court anyone, but Mrs. Delaire *had* sent a pie around. He hoped that didn't mean they were courting. In the labyrinth of social graces one must navigate as a bachelor, he had a sneaky suspicion it meant there was some unspoken understanding. If that were true, he needed to sort that out immediately. Nash put Mrs. Delaire from his mind as he held Mrs. Lemon, who trembled and wept against him.

"There, there." Nash patted her back awkwardly, hoping Mrs. Daindridge didn't press her binoculars against Mrs. Lemon's living room windows and then bang on the door, demanding to know what was going on.

"I'm so sorry." Mrs. Lemon leaped out of his arms as fast as she had flung herself into them. "I don't know what came over me. I am just so distraught, and you have offered me a way to pay a bill I didn't know how to pay."

"There is more, Mrs. Lemon. You remember the field we have designated to the war widows in our community?"

Mrs. Lemon shot him a puzzled look.

"You were to be informed by Mrs. Delaire..." Nash prompted her memory. "By letter?"

"I didn't receive a letter." Mrs. Lemon shook her head in confusion.

"Well, let me inform you of this good news. Hecktor Splain had planted a field of winter wheat before he passed. He has no one to leave his field and farm to, so the men of Oakland will harvest that field and give the proceeds to all the widows, and anyone else who needs financial support."

Mrs. Lemon wiped her tears and blinked up at him.

Nash noticed for the first time that her bright-blue eyes were rimmed with a wide black rim.

Never mind her eyes!

"That is so kind, I don't know what to say." Mrs. Lemon bit her lip.

"It's early, obviously, but we wanted you to know that the resolution *has* passed, just today, and you can count on some money before your taxes are due. Closer to the day, we will ask the women of the community to provide the meals for the men who are harvesting. The field is near Bennett Farm, so we are using Mrs. Bennett's kitchen, but we would not like the responsibility of all the meals to fall on her. If you want to contribute, please stop by the town office and let Mrs. Delaire know what you would like to bring."

"Oh, I would be thrilled to contribute. Please let me know in advance so I can ask for the days off. Oh, Mr. Nash. I don't know how to thank you." Mrs. Lemon breathed a sigh of relief.

"I'm glad that is settled, Mrs. Lemon. Miss Lynne is to meet us at the school Sunday afternoon, and we will escort her here, if that would be acceptable to you. If you would have supper for her, we would appreciate that." Nash checked his watch.

Mrs. Lemon's face fell. "Oh, Mr. Nash, it is so embarrassing… I don't have money for meat…" Mrs. Lemon's eyes filled with tears. "Never mind, sir. I can ask Mrs. Daindridge… sorry. I can figure something out…"

Nash's heart plummeted as Lucy Lemon stammered in shame about her obvious poverty.

No one should have to grovel to Mrs. Daindridge for anything!

"I will pay her first week's rent with a little extra." Nash pulled out his wallet and peeled off three bills. Mrs. Lemon looked at him as if he had hung the moon. "Is that enough, Mrs. Lemon? To care for Miss Lynn's needs and indeed your own until you receive her first week's rent?"

Mrs. Lemon's eyes filled with tears again, and her voice cracked as she spoke. "I will never forget this kindness, sir."

"There now," Nash replied gruffly. "There is hardly any reason... I am sure anyone would do the same... in this... uh...." Nash stammered as he watched her carefully fold the money and reach for a fresh handkerchief. "Mrs. Lemon, I apologize again that you didn't receive notification that would have set your mind at ease." Nash tucked his wallet back in his breast pocket. "Very odd Mrs. Delaire didn't inform you. I will look into that at once."

"Well, there was a war on and a flu epidemic to deal with," Mrs. Lemon said dully as she wiped her eyes.

"No excuse." Nash went to the door and rested his hand on the door handle as he turned around to speak to her. "If I can be of further help in any way, please let me know."

Mrs. Lemon walked to the door to see him out. "You aren't going to tell me to marry Lester, are you?" Mrs. Lemon squared her shoulders as if bracing herself for whatever Nash would say.

"No, Mrs. Lemon, I have been advised by a higher authority not to bring up Lester Lemon with you under any circumstances," Nash said reverently.

Mrs. Lemon tilted her pretty head to the side and blinked. "By God, Mr. Nash?" Mrs. Lemon's eyes widened.

"No. Not God." Nash chuckled. "Mrs. Lily Holt and Mrs. Ada Bennett. They have forbidden it."

Mrs. Lemon chuckled with him. "They are my dear friends."

"I'm glad. I will say good day, Mrs. Lemon. I will see you on Sunday with Miss Lynne. Thank you for taking her in. I appreciate it."

"Thank you, Mr. Nash." Mrs. Lemon tucked a piece of hair behind her ear and smiled up at him.

"One last thing, Mrs. Lemon. I don't want you to be alarmed. Detective Kane is coming to Oakland today to look for Mrs. Ellice. We know she was seen walking in the park the week before she disappeared, and since you live so close to the park entrance, Detective Kane might stop by with questions for you."

"Oh, of course, he is welcome to ask me anything." Mrs. Lemon's face creased with concern. "Surely there is a reasonable explanation. She was such a recent widow... isn't it possible that she just couldn't cope? Maybe she is in a doctor's care? In a facility for people who can't manage?"

"Maybe, but she has not informed her family. Her mother is concerned, as are we. She did lose her husband suddenly, but she assured us that she was well enough to work."

"Yes, but she may have just said that to be able to keep a roof over her head." Mrs. Lemon's face fell. "These are desperate times, for all of us who lost men to the war or to the flu."

Nash didn't allow himself to point out that Lester Lemon would ride to her rescue with the slightest encouragement. He didn't dare. Mrs. Holt would be on his doorstep, haranguing him, within the hour.

"Thank you for your time, Mrs. Lemon. Please take care. I will see you on Sunday." Nash quickly exited Mrs. Lemon's home, and after he cranked his car to life, the lace curtains in the joint residence of Mrs. Daindridge and Mrs. Carr twitched. Nash waved at the window and winked at the women on the other side of the glass. The lace immediately hung straight. Smiling to himself, he took one last look at the river and creek behind Lucy Lemon's beautiful house. He liked the big weeping willow trees that lined the river beside it. He left Willow Avenue and headed back to work. Back to his office, where Detective Kane was surely waiting to meet with him.

The light went out of his day at the thought.

CHAPTER 8

*E*tta placed the last of her luggage into the old Ford Model T and returned to the tiny apartment for her handbag.

She looked around the hovel they called a home. All of her paintings and drawings covering the walls of the apartment didn't take the gloom from the room. It still stung her heart that they had lost the house to pay for her father's gambling debts. She took a deep breath and pushed that out of her mind. Nothing she could do about it now. She sighed at the vast amount of laundry strung up to dry. Somehow Cali kept track of who owned what. The sisters were constantly shrouded in differing degrees of damp and drying laundry. The apartment had one room where they had put their mother until finally taking her to the hospital. Laundry dried in there, too. The air hung heavy with the damp smell of wet starch.

"Pray that rickety car gets me to Oakland." Etta grimaced at Cali.

"I really hope this works out." Cali's eyes filled with tears. "I'm worried, Etta. I feel like Mother and I are the world's biggest burden." She dropped her voice.

"Without you, I wouldn't have this beautiful new suit. You are a huge help. But I already have an enemy in that Mrs.

Delaire. Anyway, I still think we should have kept the fabric in case we needed it for you. Once you don't fit…"

Cali brushed Etta's concerns away. "Never mind. I'm stuck at home doing washing and ironing; I can wear a flour sack."

Etta smiled at her fondly. "How are you feeling? That was some fast seamstress work this weekend."

"I enjoyed the challenge." Cali grinned.

Etta wondered how Cali could keep grinning amidst all the depressing laundry. Beautiful pieces of lacy undergarments seemed to mock their grinding poverty. Tomorrow, Cali would painstakingly iron every piece and then deliver the packages to the rich who lived two blocks away. Etta and Cali marvelled at how, after crossing onto Ontario Avenue, there were streets of mansions with so many rich women who hired outside help. They hired Cali because she could mend and do alterations.

Etta brushed a piece of lint from her new skirt and then straightened up. She pressed her fingertips against the blue cameo at her throat, a cameo that had belonged to their great-grandmother. A piece of jewellery they couldn't bear to part with. Etta and Cali vowed that they would keep the cameo no matter what. Even as they promised, they knew if something happened, it would cover one month's rent.

Cali stood behind Etta, and together they checked her appearance in the mirror over the sideboard. Etta's blonde hair was a sharp contrast to Cali's dark chestnut, but their blue eyes were the same. Etta always felt like a washed-out dishrag, her features were so pale against Cali's vibrant colouring.

"The cameo is the same colour as your eyes, E, and it's a perfect contrast against the caramel-coloured wool. You look beautiful." Cali tilted her head.

"You should keep this to pawn in case you need some money for Mother." Etta started to unfasten the delicate clasp.

"We have to have something to remember her by." Cali placed her fingers on Etta's, stopping her. She took her hands in her own. After taking a deep breath, Cali let it out slowly.

"She might turn a corner." Etta squeezed Cali's hands in hers.

"I think you and I both know that she won't." Cali's eyes

filled with tears. "She is so sick. I will go to the hospital tomorrow."

"Don't cry, Cali. You can't cry alone, and I can't be blotchy... Oh, listen to me! So vain! Please, don't wear yourself out." Etta carefully wiped the tears from Cali's cheeks.

"I won't." Cali sighed sadly.

"I better get on the road." Etta straightened her shoulders.

"You will be brilliant, as always." Cali smiled her encouragement.

Etta's eyes swept over the cramped apartment, and her throat tightened with unshed tears.

This must be a nightmare, and I must be on the verge of waking up. The war can't have happened, this poverty... this unrelenting poverty can't be real. My brother is coming home. My father hasn't lost every penny to bookies...

"At least you'll have a bed." Cali grinned at Etta. "No more sleeping on a broken settee."

She's trying to cheer me up...

"If anything changes with Mother..." Etta bit her lip.

"I'll send word." Cali's eyes softened in sadness. "You can't be back here often. I know that. Don't worry about me, Etta. Really. Don't. I will be just fine."

Etta's eyes locked with Cali's. "I will always worry about you. Always. It's the curse of big sisters! Please, take care of yourself. If something happens to you, I am lost. It's too much... I can't live without you."

Cali reached forward to stop the sad words. She hugged Etta hard against her. "I love you."

"I love you, too." Etta squeezed her as hard as Cali's pregnant belly allowed.

The sisters tried to pull apart and couldn't. Finally, they wiped their tears away and forced themselves to step away from each other.

"I hate leaving you." Etta smiled at her.

"I hate it, too. I always have," Cali replied honestly.

"This is ridiculous. I can come back..." Etta shook her head at their emotional outpouring.

"We will be fine." Cali smiled her brightest smile.

Etta nodded, knowing in her heart things were changing for them, and there wasn't anything she could do about it. Her mother's care was out of her hands. Etta parted the dry laundry on her way to the door.

"Listen, Cali, we don't know the cost of doctor bills. If you can't work, sell this." Etta unpinned the cameo and pressed it into Cali's hand. "I don't like how Santini looks at us. I worry if we don't have the rent on time… I am terrified of what he will do." Etta bit her lip at the thought of leaving her sister alone in this terrible apartment. "Cali, this is no time to be sentimental. We have to be practical. If anything happens, if Mother gets sicker, you will need money."

Cali shook her head, and her face darkened. "I can take on more work." Cali followed Etta out of the apartment to the hallway.

"No, Cali, you can't." Etta turned to her. "Sell it if you need to. I will get a paycheck soon."

With one last hug, Cali's eyes filled with tears as she re-pinned the cameo at Etta's throat and refused to take no for an answer. Cali waved at her as she stood on the threshold of the hovel they called a home.

Etta's steps quickened as she made her way down the hall. She slipped down the two sets of stairs to the front door.

She heard footsteps behind her, and she picked up her pace. Her hand rested on the door handle of the apartment building when the man behind her caught up to her and grabbed her upper arm.

"Leaving before the end of the month?" Santini dragged her back from the door.

Etta let out a yelp of fear as he pulled her down the hallway.

"Take your hands off of me!" Terror made Etta's heart pound in her ears. She yanked her arm out of his grasp.

"Where are you going?" Santini leered at her.

"To work." Etta took another step back.

"With luggage? You think you can run off and not pay this month's rent?" Santini moved forward to speak directly into her ear. "I will get paid."

Icy-cold fear raced through Etta. "I have always paid you!"

Santini moved closer. Etta wanted to gag as the smell of his hot, smelly breath washed over her face. "I hear you can't afford this month's rent, and you lost your job at the laundry."

A soldier at the end of the hallway cleared his throat.

Santini immediately backed up.

Etta scrambled to get away from him.

"Everything all right here?" The soldier straightened his shoulders, narrowed his eyes at Santini and moved toward them.

"Yes. Yes, sir. I was just leaving." Etta pounced on the door handle and bolted out the front door. Her heart pounded in fear as she quickly cranked her motorcar to start. She leaped into the cab and slammed the door shut. Her hand trembled on the gearshift. Etta raced out of Brandon.

Worry for Cali pulsed through her. She thought about going back and packing her up... but someone had to be able to visit Mother in hospital. Etta bit her lip with fear that Santini might threaten Cali.

She put the thoughts from her mind. There were many soldiers in her building, and the majority were like the man who stepped in to help her before she left. Surely Cali was safe with so many men roaming around, prepared to do the right thing.

Her heart rate slowed down to normal by the time she reached Oakland. She noticed as she drove to the school that the river and creek had risen in the few days she had been away. She parked in front of the Oakland School. Etta's hands tightened on the wheel of her car — her father's car — the next thing after the cameo to sell if her mother's cough got any worse.

Worry about money spiralled into new fears.

What if the doctors put Cali on bed rest?

Etta tried to put all the concerns out of her mind. She failed. Finally, another Model T turned down the street and came to a stop at the front of the school. Mr. Spicer walked down the street to meet her as Mr. Nash got out of his car. Etta took a deep breath and let it out slowly.

Mr. Nash and Mr. Spicer met her on the steps.

"Well, Miss Lynne, please follow us, we'll show you to your classroom." Mr. Nash spoke with kindness.

Etta followed the men into the silent halls of the school. It smelled of chalk dust and old books, as all schools did. Up another set of stairs, they opened a door into a classroom for thirty pupils.

Etta took it all in at a glance. She walked to the bookshelves to see what sort of titles the students could choose from. Classics like *Jane Eyre* soothed her jangled nerves. She picked up the book and opened it, frowning as she noticed someone had written in the margin.

Blasphemy! How dare they write in this precious book!

Etta shook her head and noticed in the book beside *Anne of Green Gables*, a little piece of paper sticking up like a bookmark. Curious, she reached for the book and opened it.

'Three hundred' was scratched in black ink on paper that had been torn off something.

Maybe an invoice?

Etta frowned and wondered what on earth 'three hundred' meant.

Maybe someone just used this scrap paper as a bookmark.

Etta removed the note, shrugged, and then tucked the book away. She placed the note in her handbag as she turned to address the men in the room.

"Is this sufficient, Miss Lynne? Do you see anything you might require?" Mr. Nash asked politely.

"I need a record of where this class has left off, so I can prepare a lesson for tomorrow," Etta requested.

Spicer's eyes were fixed on her handbag, where she had placed the note. Her gaze met his, and she didn't look away.

"Is there something in your handbag, Miss Lynne?" Mr. Spicer took a step forward.

"Someone left a scrap of paper in a book, and I keep my classroom very tidy." Etta took a tentative step back.

"I'll take that scrap of paper." Mr. Spicer held his hand out.

"I'm sure that is not necessary. I'll dispose of it at home." Etta straightened her shoulders and lifted her chin, prepared to defy him if necessary.

This paper is important to him. Why?

"I'll take the paper," Mr. Spicer demanded.

"That's enough, Spicer." Mr. Nash stepped in.

Etta felt her heart pound in her throat at the look on Mr. Spicer's face. She knew deep down that if Mr. Nash wasn't there, he would have taken the note she found by force. Etta clutched her handbag closer to her side.

"Mrs. Ellice disappeared suddenly, so we really have little to go on. This is the class list for the four grades." Mr. Nash pulled a file from Mrs. Ellice's desk and handed her the file.

Mr. Spicer's eyes were cold and black as they slid over her in a way that made her feel exposed.

"Have you heard from Mrs. Ellice yet?" Etta croaked as she turned her attention to Mr. Nash, thankful that she wasn't in the room with Mr. Spicer alone.

Etta turned her attention to the file, where Mrs. Ellice had documented their grade averages to the right of their names. She tucked the file into her bag to check over when she had time and privacy.

"I'm sure that is none of your concern," Spicer snapped at her.

She looked up at him and held his gaze. She watched as fury darkened his eyes.

He hates a show of strength. If I want to keep this job, I have to pretend to be submissive — fearful even.

"We had it on good authority that she was *in the company of men*." Spicer's eyes narrowed. "Maybe something happened."

Etta burned with fury at his tone. "A serious accusation."

"Yes. One we hope isn't repeated." Spicer straightened up.

Etta heard the warning in Spicer's voice.

"I assure you, it won't be." Etta snapped the folder closed and met his gaze again.

"I would like to remind you that if we see any inappropriate behaviour, the reaction will be swift."

Nash stepped closer to Etta. "If you're all set then, you can follow me to Mrs. Lemon's. She has supper waiting for you."

"Thank you. Yes, this all looks in order." Etta nodded even as she suppressed a shiver at the intensity of Mr. Spicer's gaze.

Following the men back to the front door of the school, she prayed her car would start.

Nash insisted on starting it for her.

Etta clenched her jaw as he carefully moved her out of the way and then had to crank it more than once before it finally groaned to life.

"I think it's time for a mechanic," he suggested.

"Yes, I'm sure it is." Etta slipped behind the wheel.

Etta followed Nash through the town of Oakland to Willow Avenue, where a beautiful three-story yellow house sat proudly on the bank of the river. With the river on one side and a pretty creek at the back, the house was stunning. A veranda spanning the entire front of the house was bare now, but the skeletal remains of a Virginia creeper enclosed the whole west end of the veranda, where a pretty white porch swing swayed in the early spring breeze, ready for two lovers to hop on and chitchat in private.

No need to think of lovers on porch swings!

The river and creek at the side and back of the house were rising. Nash opened her car door, and she got out of the car promptly.

"Something to warn you about." Nash took her two bags from the back seat. "Across the street, in that little cottage there, are two of the town's biggest gossips. Notice the lace curtain is moving? They're watching our every move. The widows, Mrs. Daindridge and Mrs. Carr, will notice everything you do on Willow Avenue."

"Duly noted. I assure you, Mr. Nash, if they are watching my life that closely, I will bore them to tears." Etta rolled her eyes as she followed Nash to the veranda. He didn't even have time to put the bags down before the door was swung open by a very young, pretty Mrs. Lemon.

"Oh! Come in! I am so excited to meet you. Please, come right in." Mrs. Lemon's face broke into a smile.

Every surface of Mrs. Lemon's house gleamed. The smell of lemon furniture paste and roast beef caused an inner peace to settle on Etta.

"I made my specialty! I just know we will be fast friends!" Mrs. Lemon dragged Etta into a tight hug.

Etta's heart warmed as she looked at Lucy Lemon with her toffee-coloured hair, big blue eyes, and a few freckles on her nose. Mrs. Lemon smiled brightly at Etta, and for the first time in a long time, Etta felt an easing of stress. The fear between her shoulders began to loosen. Mrs. Lemon was a natural nurturer. She herded Etta and Mr. Nash up the stairs to the master bedroom.

"Oh, Mrs. Lemon, this is too grand. A spare room would be sufficient!" Etta breathed as the door opened on the master bedroom.

The windows looked out over the river and creek. No leaves were on the trees yet, and the grass at the edge of the river was still brown and grey, but it didn't matter; the view took Etta's breath away. No laundry piles in varying degrees of dampness. The early spring sun was weak but poured into the room nonetheless. A bed! White-and-yellow candlewick bedspread, pretty lace curtains drawn back so as not to distract from the view. A writing desk held a vase of dried roses that looked like a bridal bouquet, but Etta couldn't be sure. Her heart was touched at the thoughtful gestures. Mrs. Lemon had even placed a stack of fresh stationery ready for letters home.

A cozy chair and lamp sat near a stack of books.

Etta's throat tightened at the generosity of Mrs. Lemon. "You are too kind."

"Miss Lynne, you are my guest, so you get the best room in the house. Please, take your time. Supper is at six. Mr. Nash, are you and Grace joining us?"

"Thank you, but no, I will leave you two to get acquainted. Another time for sure." Mr. Nash checked his watch.

Together they returned to the front room.

"Thank you for everything." Mrs. Lemon smiled at Nash.

"You're welcome." Nash smiled back.

Etta took a deep breath and let it out slowly. "This place is more than I would have dreamed. I promise you, the school is in good hands. All will be well."

"We'll see." Nash frowned as he checked his watch again. "I

really must run. I have a meeting with Detective Kane. If you need anything, you know where to find me. I'm at the town office during the day."

"I won't. I can assure you of that."

"Miss Ford left in tears, and Mrs. Ellice is missing without a trace. I mean it when I say to contact me if you feel that you are in any danger." Nash's face darkened as he spoke. "We requested a man because we are concerned for the safety of a woman teacher here. We don't know what is going on, and until we do, I am asking that you are very careful."

Etta swallowed hard. "I will be."

Nash nodded and left.

Mrs. Lemon closed the door behind him.

Together, the women sat down at the dining room table. Just as Mrs. Lemon handed Etta the platter of beef, there was a knock at the door.

"I asked a few of the women to come to meet you." Mrs. Lemon jumped to her feet. "I hope that is all right!"

"Oh, Mrs. Lemon, that is lovely." Etta smiled up at her.

"Good. It's just a few of my closest friends." Mrs. Lemon wiped her hands on her apron and hustled to open the door to three women.

"Mrs. Holt, Mrs. Bennett, and Mrs. Hartwell." Mrs. Lemon introduced the women to Etta.

"Pleased to meet you all. Please join us, we were just sitting down to supper."

"This is late, isn't it?" Mrs. Bennett asked.

"Well, I had to meet with Mr. Spicer and Mr. Nash, to get my files and then get settled, so yes. I have held up supper for sure." Etta placed her napkin on her lap.

"Well, we've eaten, but you sit, Lucy. I'll make tea," Mrs. Bennett offered.

Mrs. Bennett put a kettle on, and Mrs. Holt placed teacups on the table.

"First of all, welcome to Oakland!" Mrs. Holt said as she settled across from Etta at the table.

"Thank you." Etta smiled warmly at her.

"Is there any news about Mrs. Ellice?" Mrs. Bennett asked

Mrs. Lemon as she set the teapot down on the dining room table.

"There is nothing to report. Detective Kane is meeting with Nash and Harris right now at the town office. I am very concerned. I think it is very clear that Mrs. Ellice has come to harm. It breaks my heart, she lost her husband so suddenly, and now this." Mrs. Holt shook her head. "I can't bear to think about it."

"We don't know yet." Mrs. Bennett pressed her lips together. "Please make sure Mr. Holt knows if they want to conduct a search, we can supply food for the searchers."

"He's been advised of that for sure. He's very worried now. He thought maybe a doctor had admitted her to a sanatorium for nerves, but the police have exhausted that thought. No Mrs. Ellice—anywhere."

Etta shivered.

The women were silent, thinking about where Mrs. Ellice might have run to.

Mrs. Bennett was the first to speak. "She was working with my adopted daughter, Ivy. We were paying for her to do advanced math with Mrs. Ellice. She really loved her and is worried to death about her."

"I am so sorry." Etta cut the Yorkshire pudding and slathered gravy over it. "Is she ready for university? Is there anyone to take over her advanced studies?"

"Mrs. Ellice told us that she is more than qualified to start university in the fall." Mrs. Bennett's face lit up as she spoke of her adopted daughter.

"We are here because we are hoping that Grace Nash can go with her." Mrs. Holt poured tea into Mrs. Bennett's teacup. "As you may have noticed, Grace is a tremendously gifted student."

"I actually haven't had a chance to look over the files of the students yet. I was going to do that tonight before bed." Etta's chest tightened. The women seemed to be on a mission, and she feared what they were going to expect from her.

"The only fly in this ointment is her father. Mr. Nash believes that she is too young to go to school so far away, but she is wasted here. She is bored, and since she lost her mother, we feel that she has lost her greatest advocate." Mrs. Bennett truly cared about Grace as if she were her own. Etta could tell from her tone. "We are here to speak for her."

"What would you like me to do? I presume you have spoken to him and he has said no." Etta tilted her head to the side.

"We were waiting to hear if the University has a seat for her. You'll think us meddling old women, I'm sure." Mrs. Holt tinkled a laugh. "But that battle-axe Miss Winthrop wouldn't pass correspondence on to us if it would benefit Grace. We need you to find the acceptance letter."

"You are not meddling. It appears that you care about Grace." Etta looked from Mrs. Bennett to Mrs. Holt and wondered if her life would have been vastly different and much improved if older women like this had advocated for her dream of art school.

"The correspondence from the University of Toronto should be here this week. Once we know for sure that Grace is accepted, we want to speak to Mr. Nash again. If you get a chance to advocate for her, we would appreciate that."

Etta pressed her handkerchief to her lips and held her hands up. "I am in a difficult situation here. I can't advocate for anyone, I am so sorry. I need this job. If I make an enemy of Mr. Nash, I won't be here next year, and my family will be on the streets. Surely Grace can wait until she is old enough..."

"We are all from England, and sending children to boarding school is hardly anything to bat an eye at. Nash is just being stubborn! Grace has lost her mother, and she and Ivy are like sisters. It seems cruel that she would have to lose Ivy too. Do you know what it's like to have a sister you are close to?" Mrs. Bennett asked Etta.

"I do. I can sympathize. However, *my* sister will be homeless if I can't work here. She is pregnant, and her husband died of Spanish flu. I am supporting her, and I am in very difficult straits, Mrs. Bennett." Etta's tone hardened. "But I will find that correspondence and pass it on."

"Thank you." Mrs. Bennett nodded.

"Well, that's settled. We've done what we could. We'll keep working on Nash." Mrs. Hartwell's eyes smiled at the women

58

from over her teacup. "I am thrilled that you are here, Miss Lynne. I hope you are still here to teach my child," Mrs. Hartwell said slyly.

Mrs. Bennett gasped. "What do you mean, your child?"

"It's so early. No one knows. Even Matt doesn't know... but I am so excited and hopeful this time. Everything feels different. I am sure this pregnancy..."

"You must see Dr. McDougall at once. Have you seen her?" Mrs. Bennett sat up straighter.

"I have an appointment next week." Mrs. Hartwell smiled at Mrs. Bennett.

"You be careful, young lady!" Mrs. Bennett said firmly.

"Young lady! I haven't been called that in years!" Mrs. Hartwell laughed.

"You're only forty." Mrs. Bennett smiled at Mrs. Hartwell.

"Forty is old for a first baby. But, when this baby is born, I want the best education for her." Mrs. Hartwell turned her attention back to Etta.

"Her?" Etta asked.

"Yes, I need someone to train." A smile played at Mrs. Hartwell's lips.

"Mrs. Hartwell runs a very successful dress shop known as Hope in Oakland," Mrs. Bennett interrupted. "She designs gowns for brides as far away as Montreal!"

"One bride, one time, from *Toronto*, Mrs. Bennett." Mrs. Hartwell rolled her eyes.

"It was the talk of the town, I tell you. Such a glamorous affair!"

"Anyway, we wanted you to know you are welcome here." Mrs. Hartwell sipped her tea. "I didn't mean to take over, but we *have* been waiting for this baby for a very long time."

"Who is Shannon?" Etta asked politely.

"Dr. McDougall, her first name is Shannon. She is a dear friend of ours who is a women's doctor in Brandon. She lived here briefly when we were starting a hospital in Oakland. Gracious, when was that? Oh, yes, 1904. Time flies! Anyway, she will be delighted at this news. She is coming on the weekend for supper. They are staying at the carriage house at Harper's, she and Cole, just like old times. I will have more news Friday night. I can't believe I have to wait almost a week, but I am sure. It all feels very different this time."

"Shannon and Cole back with us, it *is* like old times!" Mrs. Bennett beamed her approval.

"Yes, she will examine me, and I will have a better guess at the due date. She wanted to save me the drive to Brandon."

"That's so kind of her, but not a surprise. Shannon is one of the kindest women I know." Mrs. Bennett's eyes softened as she spoke. "She is the reason we have Ivy. When Shannon realized that Ivy's parents weren't able to manage her care, she intervened. In the end, we kept Ivy. Mr. Bennett suggested we find a family to place her with, but the first night I cuddled that child, I found her hiding food. I resolved to keep her. She needed the safety of us and our farm, and I would do it all again in a heartbeat. She and Grace have been close since grade school. Since they have both suffered the loss of a parent, it seems to have brought them closer and cemented their friendship."

"I will do what I can," Etta promised the women.

"Well!" Mrs. Lemon said brightly from the head of the table. "That's settled. Stay for dessert! I have some lemon sugar cookies. Please, everyone, let me refill your teacups. Mrs. Hartwell, how is Miranda working out?"

"Well ... early days." Mrs. Hartwell spoke cautiously.

"Miranda is my sister-in-law, who is working as an apprentice with Mrs. Hartwell in her dress shop, Hope in Oakland," Mrs. Lemon explained to Etta while she put more cookies on a plate.

Etta noticed Mrs. Hartwell's mouth tighten as Mrs. Lemon spoke of Miranda.

Maybe Cali could work for Mrs. Hartwell if Miranda Lemon isn't working out...

Mrs. Holt turned the conversation to happy things. Etta let the chatter from the women wash over her. It had been a long time since she had heard women visit without drying laundry dripping on their heads. A niggle of guilt fluttered around her heart as she thought of how much Cali would have enjoyed the company of these women. However, Cali, as the youngest child, had grown up with less responsibility. She had never had her mother take her aside and pile pressure on her. Groomed to be a wife and mother, Cali had been happy in that role. Etta felt a stab of envy. While they encouraged Cali to depend on her husband, they expected Etta to look after everyone in the family who couldn't look after themselves. Even before the war, she knew she couldn't depend on her brother. Her stomach twisted with the memories.

"You must be a teacher... your father can't cope... you must do the right thing by us."

She could still hear her mother's words, a heavy burden at the tender age of eighteen. Her acceptance to the Toronto School of Art didn't matter!

Her mother dragged her back to reality, placing an application to Normal School on her desk.

"Art is not a sure thing... Your father has those periods where he can't cope... your brother is not motivated... we need you," her mother stated with finality.

The conversation was over.

Anger and regret at her mother's words loomed over her. Looking back, that had only been the beginning. She had never dreamed that her father would gamble away every penny. Her mother had known and said nothing. As the shock wore off, waves of devastation washed over her; the knowledge that her father didn't care. He had loved gambling more than he had loved them. Frustration boiled inside her as she thought of how her mother didn't even try to stop him. There was nothing now. One blue cameo and a beat-up old Model T Ford was all they had left of the life they had shared.

Etta picked up her teacup. She resolved to enjoy the peace and tranquility of Oakland until June 30th, when she would be back to Pacific Street and a room full of laundry — and a screaming baby.

Etta bit into the world's best lemon sugar cookie and resolved to tackle one problem at a time. She firmly placed her negative thoughts out of her mind.

"What is sprinkled on top of this cookie?" Etta's eyes

widened with surprise as sweet sugar and sour lemon danced across her taste buds.

"Oh." Mrs. Lemon blushed. "That's an old family recipe. It's lemon sugar, Miss Lynne. In my experience, lemon sugar makes everything better."

Etta's heart warmed at Mrs. Lemon's kindness. She took another bite and hoped Mrs. Lemon was right.

CHAPTER 9

The next morning, bright and early, Etta cranked her car to start and left for school. The town of Oakland was already bustling. The men were leaving for work for the day, Crescent Avenue merchants opening up their shops, and friendly faces smiling at her from every direction.

Etta parked her motorcar on the street across from the school. She picked up her big satchel with the file that indeed documented that Grace Nash was brilliant. Multiple teachers had written that they hoped she would go onto university early as there was nothing further to teach her and she was becoming despondent. There was no way to challenge her as she was far beyond grade twelve already. Mrs. Ellice had placed a copy of her letter to the University of Toronto in Grace's file. As Etta read it, her heart had warmed to the missing teacher. She clearly had her students' best interests at heart.

Etta added her lesson plans for the day into her satchel and then looked up to see Mr. Spicer walking by.

A shiver of fear slid down her back as he stopped to talk to her.

Please, just keep walking.

Mr. Spicer stood by her car, and she had no choice but to quit stalling and get out of the driver's seat.

"Miss Lynne." Mr. Spicer nodded.

"Mr. Spicer." Etta straightened as he stepped nearer.

"Is that one petticoat or two?" Mr. Spicer's eyes swept over her.

Etta's pulse pounded with fury.

How dare you!

"How many petticoats? According to the code, you need two. Are you wearing two petticoats?" Mr. Spicer crossed his arms over his chest as he demanded an answer.

Etta swallowed her pride and lifted her skirt above her ankle to show him that she was wearing two petticoats.

"I assure you, I am well aware of the code, Mr. Spicer. I am wearing two petticoats, for sure." Etta dropped her skirt, and her body stiffened as Mr. Spicer's dull beige eyes slid up her body to lock his gaze with hers.

"Take care of the tone you use when you speak to me. I will not tolerate any disrespect from you." Mr. Spicer's eyes narrowed at her. He stepped closer, forcing her to look up at him. He stood so close, he violated her personal space.

"No disrespect intended." Etta lifted her chin.

Humiliation pounded through her. In a power struggle with Mr. Spicer, she would lose.

Every time.

To do this— to force her to prove her adherence to an oppressive code in front of her students, degrading her before she could even set foot in the classroom— infuriated her.

Her heart pounded with indignation, and her palms slicked with nervous sweat.

Mr. Spicer's eyes narrowed to slits as he examined her face, looking for defiance there.

Etta never backed down, but as she thought of her sister and her mother, she mentally added up the doctor's bill she needed to pay. The number in her head worried her; she quickly forced her eyes to drop in a show of submission.

"That's right, Miss Lynne." Mr. Spicer's breath caught. "You should lower your gaze when you speak to a superior."

Etta's stomach twisted in revulsion.

He hates women, he hates strength, he hates me... Did he do something to Mrs. Ellice? Is he the reason she is missing? Did he threaten her and chase her out of here so badly that she had to run far to save her career? Or is she missing because he wanted something she wouldn't give? Has Mrs. Ellice met a terrible end at his hands?

"You take special care to be sure you treat me with the respect I deserve. I have had enough of female teachers getting away with accusations and falsehoods. I won't tolerate it from anyone, including you." Spicer's words bit into her.

Etta's body stiffened as she tried to be calm.

"You should speak when spoken to." Mr. Spicer's tone dripped with contempt.

Etta's hands clenched to fists, and her heart raced with humiliation. "Yes, sir, I understand. I'm here to do my job to the best of my ability."

"Women who flirt and carouse are damaging to everyone. We won't have that here." Mr. Spicer stepped away from her.

Etta took a deep breath and let it out slowly. "Yes, sir."

"See that you remember that." Mr. Spicer turned on his heel and marched down the street to Crescent Avenue.

Gathering her last shattered nerve, she looked up and down the street, worried about who had witnessed this horrifying display of degradation. Her gaze met the eyes of Mrs. Spicer, who stood at the end of the driveway of her home. Etta raised her hand to wave at her but stopped at the raw pain in Mrs. Spicer's eyes. Etta bit her lip as she saw the defeat and sadness in the woman's eyes before she dropped her gaze. Mrs. Spicer finally turned her back and shuffled back into her house.

* * *

Mrs. Vera Spicer watched the pretty, young, blonde teacher – 'Miss Lynne,' Mr. Spicer had called her — lift her skirt to show her husband her ankle. Her heart broke in despair as her eyes swept over the teacher, her fine bones, her pretty face.

He is attracted to her. She is beautiful, and I am worthless. Every day he makes sure I know the truth of that.

Mrs. Spicer watched as the teacher dropped her skirt and looked up at her husband. She couldn't tell if that was a smile, a smirk, or a look of reproach.

Mr. Spicer complained about women chasing him all the time. He spoke of how shameless the teachers were as they flirted with him. How if the school board wasn't vigilant, the female teachers would run wild.

Vera's heart broke as she realized the new teacher had shown him her ankle, but her husband hadn't turned away. He had spoken to her. He had looked at her.

She could likely give him what Vera hadn't been able to.

A son.

Vera's heart ached at the thought. She tucked a limp strand of hair behind her ear. She picked at the frayed wool on her sweater.

Vera's entire body bowed under the sadness.

If I had a son, maybe I would be good enough for Herman Spicer.

That thought pounded through Vera's head every day of her life.

Every month when she reported that she hadn't conceived, the same contempt was in his eyes.

"The only thing a woman is useful for, and you can't even do that." Herman's words cut to her core every month.

Vera stifled a sob as she turned from Miss Lynne and started walking back to her house. She placed her hand on her abdomen, on the swelling there, and she paused. Looking up at the trees with their brave new buds, she thought about what was budding inside her.

Mr. Spicer didn't know.

No one knew.

Mrs. Spicer took a deep breath and let it out slowly. Her secret would come out, eventually.

CHAPTER 10

*W*alking up the stairs of the school, Etta made her way to her classroom. She rested her hand on the door handle as she tried to gather her thoughts before facing her students. Taking a deep breath, she let it out slowly. Feeling settled, she opened the door and stepped in to meet her grade eleven and twelve English class.

Etta looked over the students already sitting and waiting for her. Rows of bright and excited eyes beamed back at her.

"I am Miss Lynne. I am here to replace Mrs. Ellice. Can I get your names?"

The boys were less thrilled with her, but the roll call revealed Ivy Bennett and Grace Nash; Etta liked both girls on sight.

"Is it true, Ivy, you are going to university in the fall?"

"Yes, ma'am." Ivy's white-blonde hair was pulled back with a big blue bow to match her clever eyes. Grace's dark hair had the same bow, but it was dark green to match her skirt. Etta smiled at them fondly. Realizing life wasn't giving them the sister they wanted or needed, they chose each other. Etta's heart warmed to them immediately. They had big dreams and big obstacles, and Etta hoped she could help them without getting into trouble.

"And Grace, what about you?"

Grace opened her mouth to speak when a rude shout from the back answered for her. "She wants to go to university, too."

"Really?" Etta's heart sank as she watched Grace's face shine with excitement at the possibility.

"Yes, Miss." Grace beamed at her. "I would like to go with Ivy. We chose each other to be sisters."

"Wow!" Etta couldn't help but smile at her enthusiasm.

I wish I could help you. I know what it feels like to want an education you picked yourself...

"Ivy gets extra lessons. I wondered if I could tag along?" Grace tilted her head to the side.

"Mom said you can't do advanced math, but that you might be able to meet with me to discuss some of the books I'm supposed to read. You are more interested in art and literature, she said." Ivy's eyes lit up with excitement.

"I would love to talk about books with you!" Grace clasped her hands together.

"Absolutely! That would be fun." Etta, swept up by Grace's engaging smile, spoke without thinking. Silently, she cursed herself as she thought of what Mr. Nash would say about that. "As long as Mr. Nash says that's all right."

The mention of her father caused Grace's sunny smile to dim. "We're best friends. We do almost everything together."

"I'll speak to your father," Etta promised.

Surely he can't object to discussing books with her friend!

The morning raced by. At noon, after the children ate, they all filed outside. Etta retired to the small room with the other teacher in the school. Miss Winthrop looked up from her lunch; she was sixty if she was a day.

"I thought you were supposed to be a man," Miss Winthrop said in a crotchety tone.

"Sadly, they admitted the man who applied for this job to the hospital. It turns out he has shell shock and can't cope." Etta's back stiffened. "So, it forced them to hire me."

Miss Winthrop took a bite of her dill pickle spear. "Terrible business, Mrs. Ellice disappearing! Makes all women teachers look bad."

"Have they heard any news yet?" Etta asked politely.

"My guess, she's run off with a man. A married man." Miss Winthrop's lips curled in derision.

"Why do you think that?" Etta gaped at such a poisonous accusation. "She's a widow! I understand she lost her husband just weeks before getting this job!"

"Well, apparently he died in a car accident. She didn't seem too shook up, I tell you that. She said she had grown accustomed to him being gone with the war on and all. But she can't live on her pension, so she begged for this job."

"But why accuse her of being with a married man? That seems like such a vulgar thing to accuse anyone of." Etta couldn't stop herself from snapping at Miss Winthrop.

"I see things." Miss Winthrop's eyes narrowed with condemnation. "Such things like when a teacher is sick every single morning, it causes eyebrows to rise. I see terrible things, Miss Lynne. Women who take terrible risks and then must face the consequences."

"What sort of consequences?" Etta's mouth went dry at the vicious way Miss Winthrop spoke of Mrs. Ellice.

"Pregnant, alone, destitute. The usual consequences when one flouts the rules we are to live by."

"You're just guessing and judging her! If she was pregnant, it's possible the baby belonged to her husband...she was married..."

"Hmm. Well, I didn't notice her getting sick in the morning until a while after she had started to work here. What do you make of that?"

"I'm sure there must be a reasonable explanation." Etta pressed her lips together, wishing she could end the very uncomfortable conversation.

"Well, she didn't like Mr. Spicer. She said he was too restrictive. She didn't know her place, Miss Lynne." Miss Winthrop shifted in her seat.

"Many people think the teacher's code is far too restrictive." Etta didn't like the gleam in Miss Winthrop's eyes.

"Many of us don't think the code of conduct for teachers is restrictive at all!" Miss Winthrop snapped, clearly in the latter camp. "Do you feel restricted by these rules? Are you one to seek male attention? Flashing an ankle by any chance?" Miss Winthrop's eyes narrowed. The whiskers on her upper lip quivered as she waited for Etta to answer. "Pretty girls like you get into trouble all the time. It is a disaster for the teaching profession."

"I can assure you, I have no intention—"

"Oh. You can *assure me* all you like, but I've seen it all before." Miss Winthrop took a bite of her sandwich.

"I warned Mrs. Ellice she needed to be chaste and virtuous. It fell on deaf ears."

"Did you report her?" Etta's mouth went completely dry at the thought of one teacher setting up another teacher to fail.

"No." Miss Winthrop peeled one piece of bread off of her egg salad sandwich and shook a bit of salt on the filling. "Nature has a way of exposing women who get into trouble better than I can."

A sickening curl of concern crawled up Etta's back.

Who is the father of her baby? What happened here?

"So, Mrs. Ellice was pregnant, and you think the father is one of the men of Oakland?" Etta asked outright.

"Exactly." Miss Winthrop's eyes narrowed at Etta's tone.

"Who though..."

"No idea." Miss Winthrop shook her head. "I have heard that Mr. Nash was very, very attentive. I knew her to show her ankle to Mr. Spicer, a man she didn't like. Imagine..."

Worry pooled in Etta's stomach and twisted it to knots. She had just been forced to show Mr. Spicer her petticoats. To anyone walking by it could have looked like she was flirting! Her body pulsed hot and cold with humiliation and worry. What if someone misinterpreted that!

Gracious!

"It's impossible. She lost her husband just weeks before she started working here... it's not even possible that she would flirt with Mr. Spicer." Etta's voice cracked in surprise. "This is gossip, Miss Winthrop. Vicious gossip."

"I don't gossip, Miss Lynne," Miss Winthrop snapped at her.

What do you call what you have been doing all along!

"All I know is Mrs. Ellice was pregnant, and Mr. Spicer was

here a lot. Mr. Nash was very attentive. What happened between them, I would never speculate," Miss Winthrop said piously.

"Mr. Nash was very attentive?"

"Yes." Miss Winthrop's eyes lit up as spoke. "Of course, that would infuriate Mrs. Delaire."

"Oh?" Etta wished the ground would open up and swallow her.

"Yes, Mrs. Delaire, now, she's a case. They say that she gave her husband an overdose of morphine to get rid of him so she could have a chance with Mayor Nash."

Etta's jaw dropped in shock. "I'm sure that's not true!"

"Ask your friend Mrs. Lemon. Or your neighbours, Mrs. Daindridge or Mrs. Carr. They spoke of it long and loud to anyone who would listen until finally Mrs. Carr's son said she must be silent on the matter since the police dropped the charges."

"Well... if they dropped the charges..."

"There are many reasons a man would drop the charges if a woman is *scantily clad*," Miss Winthrop sneered. "That's what I heard anyway. Meeting with the doctor in her unmentionables..."

"Miss Winthrop!" Etta gasped in shock. "This is all speculation and gossip! We must not speak of this!" Etta despised Miss Winthrop with renewed fervor. To change the subject before she lost her temper, Etta grasped for neutral ground. "I don't know Mrs. Delaire, and I'm sure there is a plausible explanation... Miss Winthrop... Is it true Mrs. Ellice did private tutoring?"

"Yes. Ivy Bennett is going to university. Really, such foolishness! Mr. and Mrs. Bennett spoil her." Miss Winthrop shook her head in disapproval. "It surprises me as Ivy is not their natural child."

Etta's blood boiled at the mean-spiritedness of Miss Winthrop. "I think the Bennetts are to be commended and admired for taking in a child and raising her as their own. I can't think of a more beautiful gift..."

"Hmm," Miss Winthrop grunted in disapproval.

"Isn't it good to encourage our students to attend university, Miss Winthrop?" Etta opened her lunch and wished she could eat at her desk in her classroom. No way to do that now, she couldn't be rude... although Miss Winthrop was a terrible battle-axe!

Her throat tightened with emotion as she noticed a note from Mrs. Lemon to have a wonderful first day. Lucy had packed her a roast beef sandwich in wax paper, a little jar of pickles, a flask of hot tea, and two lemon sugar cookies. Etta couldn't remember the last time someone had packed her lunch. Mrs. Lemon was caring and nurturing. Etta didn't even know she needed a friend like Lucy until she landed in her life.

"Those young girls are foolish. They can't be let loose in Toronto, who knows what sort of trouble they'd find themselves in. Silly little country girls, both of them."

Etta tamped down a rush of frustration at Miss Winthrop's tone. "You disapprove of university?"

"Wholeheartedly."

Of course you do!

Etta ate her lunch with lightning speed, keeping her tea and cookies for her classroom away from Miss Winthrop and her archaic, mean spiritedness.

"At least Mr. Nash has sense. He's not letting Grace go to school. It is a waste of time and money." Miss Winthrop sniffed as she picked at her sweater.

"Miss Winthrop, you are missing a button," Etta pointed out, desperate to take the attention off of the thorny subject of Grace going to school and the legions of people who disapproved. A missing button *had* to be safe and neutral ground.

"Yes. The mornings are so cold, this is my heaviest sweater, and since these buttons are yarn covered, I can't replace it." Miss Winthrop frowned at the missing button on her cardigan.

"Maybe you could take them all off and put on all new buttons. Not yarn covered," Etta suggested helpfully, anything to stop this terrible conversation. Etta didn't want any further insight into Miss Winthrop's thinking.

"I could." Miss Winthrop shrugged.

Etta stood up and walked to the window of the room to

check on the children playing. On the ledge was a stack of mail addressed to Mrs. Rose Ellice.

Etta glanced at Miss Winthrop to see if she was watching. Distracted with her lunch, Miss Winthrop didn't look up as Etta picked up the mail to quickly snoop through it. Memories of holding her acceptance letter to the Toronto School of Art spurred her on.

One big envelope had 'Grace Nash' on the first line but 'care of Mrs. Rose Ellice' on the second line.

Etta's heart beat hard with anticipation.

This was the letter the women of Oakland were waiting for!

Etta folded the big envelope in half and tucked it in the fold of her skirt.

"Grace Nash is a brilliant girl."

"Humph. It won't do to encourage that child. You will only make an enemy of Mr. Nash," Miss Winthrop warned Etta.

"Oh, Miss Winthrop." Etta smiled brightly at her bitter, wrinkled face. "He's already an enemy. I assure you."

Miss Winthrop opened her mouth to speak and then firmly clamped it shut.

CHAPTER 11

*E*tta fled to her classroom to get away from vicious Miss
Winthrop. She tucked Grace's letter away so she could
give it to her after class.

Later that day, as Etta assigned free reading time, she pulled
on the bottom drawer of the desk. The drawer refused to budge.
Frowning, she leaned down and pulled harder, thinking it might
just be stuck.

The drawer didn't budge an inch.

Odd.

Kneeling down, squinting to see better, she looked closer to
find the key snapped off inside the lock.

Very odd.

As one class left the room and her grade eleven class entered,
two male students roughhoused their way to their desks, dragging her attention from the drawer. Quickly, she stood up to
reprimand them. As she ordered the boys to sit down, thoughts
of the stuck drawer fled her mind.

The day slipped past quickly, and as she left her classroom
to go home she noticed Grace and Ivy's heads bent over a
book. She yearned for her sketchpad and charcoals. They made
such a pretty picture of genuine friendship she itched to
capture it. At once, she remembered the correspondence in her
handbag.

"Grace! I am so glad to catch you. Are you on your way home?" Etta walked toward them swiftly.

"Yes. But we are just finishing this chapter." Ivy placed her finger on the paragraph they were both reading.

"You could each get your own book, I am sure." Etta chuckled at the two girls reading together. "What are you reading?"

"*Anna Karenina*." Grace smiled up at her. "Our favourite! We've read it six times, but we read it together so we can talk about it."

Etta's heart melted at their bent heads over one of her favourite books. "I have a spare book of *Anna Karenina* in my classroom. You are welcome to borrow it." She had seen it when she had found the scrap of paper with 'three hundred' written on it. Thoughts of Tolstoy fled as an icy shiver gripped her at the memory of Mr. Spicer's reaction. Surely it was a note used as a bookmark and nothing more. Etta smiled at the girls, putting her fears surrounding Mr. Spicer away.

"Have you read *Wuthering Heights*?" she asked them.

"No."

"Well, it's my favourite, and I have a copy. I will lend it to you, and once you have both read it we can meet to discuss it."

"Oh, Miss Lynne, we love to read and discuss books. That sounds so great." Grace beamed at her.

"I love to read and discuss books, too, and it's hard to find kindred spirits when it comes to book selections." Etta's heart warmed to the two girls even more.

"That's from *Anne of Green Gables*." Grace smiled at her.

"Yes. It is." Etta grinned back. "I know a kindred spirit when I see one."

"So do we," Ivy and Grace said at the same time.

"Grace, I have something for you. This letter is addressed to you." Etta held the envelope up for Grace to see it.

"Oh! Miss Lynne. Is this what I think it is?" Grace gasped in excitement. She leaped to her feet to take the correspondence from her.

"I'm not sure exactly." Etta couldn't stop the excitement from creeping into her voice. She remembered getting mail from the

Toronto School of Art. Her pulse had quickened, and she hadn't been able to open it for two days until her nerves calmed down. When they accepted her, she nearly fainted.

Ivy and Grace looked at each other. "I'm too nervous. You open it."

Ivy took the letter from Grace's hands. "If this is a yes..."

"It doesn't matter. My dad won't let me go."

A curl of defiance stiffened Etta's back as she heard the defeat in Grace's voice. "Did he say why?"

"He just says no and to stop thinking of it."

Ivy tore open the letter and read it eagerly. "You have a seat at the University of Toronto." She handed the letter to Etta so she could read it.

Grace's eyes filled with tears. "He'll say no."

Etta yearned to reach for her and assure her that she would speak to her father, but she reminded herself not to get involved. A mental picture of her mother in hospital and Cali having a baby with all the expense that would bring made her shut her mouth.

"Unless, maybe you could speak to him on my behalf?" Grace turned to Etta to plead with her. "It might mean more if it comes from you."

"Oh, Grace." Etta bit her lip. "It's not so simple."

Grace looked up at Etta from the floor. Etta's conscience compelled her to step in on behalf of the child. Her bright hazel eyes blinked as she implored her to intervene.

"I'll see what I can do." Etta's heart sank as she promised to try.

"Thank you, Miss Lynne." Grace threw herself into Etta's arms and hugged her so hard Etta nearly lost her balance. They laughed as Grace's excitement was so bright it was impossible not to be swept up in it.

"Your father is here right now to pick you up," Ivy said to Grace.

"Oh! Come with me." Grace grabbed Etta's hand, intending to drag her to the motorcar.

Etta groaned inwardly, picked up her satchel, and followed Grace out of the school to speak to Mr. Jackson Nash, the world's most old-fashioned fuddy-duddy, about his daughter, his young daughter, going to Toronto to be educated.

Etta dragged her feet.

I can't afford the hospital bills now...

Grace bounded in front of her.

"Dad, this came in the mail!" Grace tucked a lock of hair behind her ear and beamed up at him.

Mr. Nash took the letter from Grace, and his face fell as he read it.

"Isn't this just the best news!" Etta knew Grace was pressing her luck, but Grace refused to back down. "They accepted me. Did you read the part about how my marks are really good?"

"Listen, Grace. I spoke to Mrs. Ellice about this. She wasn't to get your hopes up. I don't think going to university at this time is in your best interests..." Mr. Nash spoke gently, but Etta heard the underlying iron in his tone. He wasn't going to change his mind.

"But I qualify! They are inviting me — even at my age!" Grace cried.

"Grace, we'll discuss this at home." Mr. Nash folded the letter and tucked it back in the envelope.

Etta's chest tightened as she watched Mr. Nash crush his daughter's dream.

"Mr. Nash." Etta tried to stop herself from getting involved.

Tried and failed.

Visions of laundry hanging in her hovel of an apartment flashed in front of her. She brushed the memories aside. She couldn't live with herself if she didn't stand up for Grace, whose eyes were filling with tears. Etta moved closer to her and slid her arm around her. At the gentle, tender show of kindness, Grace burst into tears, burying her face in Etta's shoulder.

"Is it possible that you would reconsider?" Etta's jaw clenched in fury as she patted Grace on the back.

"There is nothing to consider." Mr. Nash shook his head. "I'm not sending my daughter to Toronto. It's not safe. Anything could happen to her. She's only fifteen!"

"I'll be sixteen before I get there to start class!" Grace lifted her head from Etta's shoulder so she could plead with him.

"Mr. Nash, we have nothing to teach her... she's brilliant and..." Etta held Grace in her arms as Grace wept.

Mr. Nash's face darkened with anger.

Frustration pounded through Etta, stiffening her spine.

"Grace, that is enough. Into the motorcar, please." Nash held the door open for his daughter.

"Miss Lynne, please make him see sense. This is my dream." Grace wiped her eyes with the heels of her hands.

"Grace," Mr. Nash growled. "We've been over this."

"Mr. Nash." Etta tamped down her anger and faced Mr. Nash with every speck of self-control she could muster.

"Yes, Miss Lynne." Mr. Nash shot her an irritated look.

"The women of Oakland are concerned about her wasting her talents... they have planned..."

"The women of Oakland are not her parents." Mr. Nash's tone hardened in warning.

Taking a deep breath, Etta continued. "This is a *massive* opportunity. You can't just say *no*. I urge you to reconsider. This is a..."

"This is a fantasy, Miss Lynne." Mr. Nash cut her off bluntly. "She is still a child." Mr. Nash slammed the door shut on Grace's sobs.

"Would you at least promise to read the letter from the university? Please." Etta begged on Grace's behalf.

"This is not your concern. I made a final decision." Mr. Nash shook his head. "I am her father. I don't need to discuss my decisions with you. I am not required to seek your approval."

Etta saw red as hot anger pooled in her stomach.

"Your daughter's dream is not a fantasy." Etta's temper slipped its reins. "Her dear friend Ivy is going to Toronto— they *could* go together. Grace lost her mother, she can't lose her best friend too. They call each other chosen sisters. It is too much loss..."

"Ivy is an orphan, and she will have to make her way," Mr. Nash said bluntly. "Grace is not traipsing to Toronto. No."

Etta stared at him in shock.

"Furthermore, Ivy is not fifteen years old! I don't care if Grace will be sixteen by September. It is still too young to be in

78

a city the size of Toronto with no parents. No. The answer is no!"

Etta tried a different tack. "I understand they have found suitable accommodations for the girls— young women."

"Miss Lynne, I have already told Mrs. Bennett and Mrs. Holt of my decision. I will thank you to keep your high-flown ideas to yourself."

Etta bristled at the harshness of his tone. Her fingernails bit into her palms as she tried and failed to calm down. How he could completely disregard Grace's dreams brought back every bad memory from her past. "But they are best friends! They are like sisters! You can't separate them!"

"My daughter is *not* going to Toronto, under any circumstances." Mr. Nash crossed his arms over his chest.

"I can't believe you would... I can't even believe you won't *consider* this!" Etta's jaw dropped. "I don't think you quite grasp how brilliant she is!"

"Listen, Miss Lynne. I understand you want to be an advocate for Grace. It's very nice of you."

"Nice!" Etta blasted Mr. Nash.

"She's too young. I am aware that she has exhausted the school system here, that she is brilliant, but she's *young*."

Etta worried that steam would pour out of her ears at the condescension in his tone.

"The very notion of young girls running off to big cities to be educated—it just isn't safe. It isn't proper. It is not the natural order of things! This is a flight of fancy because her friend is going. She will be fine."

"Mr. Nash! I have never in my life met anyone as... as..." Etta grappled with herself to keep her tone respectful when she wanted to shout at him.

"As what, Miss Lynne?" Mr. Nash leaned forward, his head tilted to the side.

"The English send their children to boarding school all the time. Couldn't you think of it like that?"

"No, Miss Lynne, this is all for the best. I didn't have a child so that someone else could raise her. I would request that you don't encourage this nonsense any further. I am a very busy man. I must get going. Good day, Miss Lynne." Mr. Nash's tone indicated his thoughts on the matter were final.

Mr. Nash tipped his hat to her.

Etta burned with fury at the show of respect.

Mr. Nash cranked his car to start and hopped in the driver's seat. He nodded at her as he put the car into gear and drove off.

Etta's heart fell to her feet as she watched the car leave her behind. A wave of helplessness gutted her.

Poor Grace, I know how you feel.

Etta stalked to her car and cranked it until it started. She huffed as she got into the driver's side and tossed her satchel into the passenger seat.

Etta looked up and saw Mr. Spicer making his way home. She threw her car into gear and drove off before she had *another* altercation with him. Her temper was up, and she was terrified of what she might say to Mr. Spicer. She started to see why Miss Ford had fled and Mrs. Ellice had disappeared.

The men of Oakland are impossible!

CHAPTER 12

*E*tta tidied her desk on Friday afternoon, relieved that her first week was over. As the sun streamed in through the window over the bent heads of her grade ten English class, she looked up in surprise to see a man of medium height, dark hair, and dark eyes watching her before he spoke. She slipped across the classroom when he indicated she should meet him in the hall.

"How can I help you?" Etta's pulse beat hard in anticipation.

"I apologize for interrupting your class, Miss Lynne." He took out a notepad and pencil from his breast pocket.

"That is all right."

"I am Detective Kane. I am investigating the disappearance of Mrs. Ellice. I understand you don't know her, but I am interviewing everyone. Have you heard of where she might have gone?"

"No, I haven't. She does have a pile of mail in the room where we eat our lunch, though." Etta nervously scratched her eyebrow.

"And where is that room?"

"Down the hall and to the left." Etta pointed to the room where she no longer ate her lunch with the dreadful Miss Winthrop.

"Thank you. If you see anything, and I mean anything, I want to know about it. You can reach me at the barracks. Do you know where those barracks are?"

"Yes, sir." Something about his commanding presence made Etta stand up straighter.

He turned to walk down the hall when Etta called out to him. "There is one thing."

"Yes?" He turned to speak to her.

"I found a piece of paper in a book with 'three hundred' written on it. It is probably nothing, but the bookshelf in my room is used by all of the teachers. It just struck me as odd. When I found it, Mr. Nash and Mr. Spicer were in the room, and Mr. Spicer demanded that I give it to him."

Detective Kane's eyebrow arched. "But you didn't."

"No. I kept it. I had a funny feeling about it. I'll get it for you."

"I'll put it in the file and interview Mr. Spicer immediately. Might be nothing, might be everything."

A chill raced down Etta's spine as she entered her classroom and went to her satchel to retrieve the note.

She emptied the contents on the desk and rifled through it.

"Oh. I am so sorry. It's not here now." Frantically, she searched through everything in her bag.

"Have you left your bag unattended?" Detective Kane asked.

"Yes... I leave it by my desk... when I check on the children at recess I don't take it with me, and my door is not locked during the day." Etta's mouth went dry at the thought.

Detective Kane's eyebrows drew together as he wrote down three hundred and then underlined it.

"Anyone could have taken it, then. What colour of ink?"

"Black." Etta's hand flew to her throat; a sickening feeling of violation overcame her. Someone had gone through her handbag... Mr. Spicer? How would he sneak in and steal it? Did he get Miss Winthrop to?

"Did it look like female or male writing?" Detective Kane's hand was poised to write down her answer.

Etta snapped back to attention. "How would I know if it was male or female writing?"

"Sometimes women's penmanship has a bit of a flourish..."

Detective Kane didn't look like he'd ever added a flourish in his life. If, as the saying went — curved was the line of beauty and straight was the line of duty — he was straight as an arrow.

Etta thought about it before she answered. "It was just numbers, and there was no flourish."

"I see."

"There is one other thing, but it is gossip." Etta placed her belongings back in her satchel.

"Follow me, please." Detective Kane led the way past the students, and they shut the door behind them.

"It is likely a vicious smear campaign. Honestly. I am not sure, but Miss Winthrop thought Mrs. Ellice was pregnant." Etta fidgeted with her collar, uncomfortable about the implication of that accusation.

Detective Kane's head snapped up in surprise. "Thought?"

"Apparently, Mrs. Ellice was ill in the mornings."

"That could be other things. You can't work as a teacher if you are pregnant..."

"Exactly. So, it's likely just a jealous old woman..."

"Jealous is an interesting word. What would she be jealous of?" Detective Kane's clever eyes bored into Etta's as if searching for a reason why she used the word jealous. "From what I heard, Mrs. Ellice was a widow, and she lost her husband suddenly. Facing eviction, she applied to teach here whether she was ready or not. So what is there to be jealous of?"

Etta's eyes widened in surprise. "Have you met Miss Winthrop?"

"No. Not yet. She's my next interview."

"The Miss Winthrops of the world despise the Mrs. Ellices of the world. Younger women who are..." Etta stopped speaking to gather her thoughts.

Detective Kane waited patiently for her answer, as if he had all the time in the world. "Yes?"

"Beautiful, youthful, their lives ahead of them. Jealousy is an ugly thing." Etta bit her lip as if she had said too much.

"Is she jealous of you?" Detective Kane asked.

"Oh. No." Etta's face felt hot as she blushed. "I don't think so."

Detective Kane tilted his head to the side as a silent invitation to say more.

"Anyway, apparently Mr. Spicer was attentive to her, as was Mr. Nash, according to the viper Miss Winthrop. That is all I know." Anxiety tightened her chest as she gave Detective Kane, who never blinked, never missed anything, the names of two men who would now be suspect in this disappearance. She shivered.

"Viper. Such a strong word." Detective Kane's voice deepened.

Etta knew he watched her reaction carefully.

Etta shrugged. "I dislike gossip and slander. Women should help other women, not spread lies about them."

"Anything else?" Detective Kane didn't drop his gaze.

"Nothing I can think of." Etta's throat tightened.

"If anything comes up in conversation, I would like to know." Detective Kane put his notepad in his breast pocket.

"Of course. I will let you know right away."

"Thank you, Miss Lynne. Sorry to interrupt your work, but I suspect that harm has come to Mrs. Ellice. I would like to remind you to be safe. I suggest you don't leave your home after dark, and if you must be out after dark, I really must insist you aren't alone, miss."

Etta nodded. "Right. Thank you."

Detective Kane nodded back and headed toward the break room.

Etta watched him stride down the hallway, his sharp eyes watching for anything out of place. After returning to her class, she dismissed the students for the day. She then picked up the two carefully wrapped parcels in her satchel and found Ivy and Grace sitting off to the side of the school. Grace's face was twisted as if in pain. Etta's brow furrowed with concern as she made her way over to them.

"Girls, I brought you a gift."

"Thank you, but Grace is not well." Ivy looked up at Etta, worry in her eyes.

"What is it?" Etta pressed her hand to Grace's forehead, checking for fever.

Grace curled into a ball of pain.

"Gracious! Whatever is the matter?" Etta's eyes swept over them both with concern.

"It is a feminine complaint." Ivy shot a worried look at Etta. "This is her first time."

"First time, oh, honey. I'll drive you home. Come on. Aspirin and a hot water bottle, and you'll be just fine. Do you have any supplies?" Etta asked.

"Mrs. Bennett gave me a package, but it's at home. I didn't really know what was going on. I didn't feel well this morning, but I thought it was just a headache. I didn't know." Tears gathered in Grace's eyes.

"That's all right. Let's get you into the car, and I'll pick up some aspirin at the chemist shop. Come along." Etta helped Grace to her feet.

Ivy's blue eyes clouded with concern. "But she doesn't want her father to know about this."

"Oh, Miss Lynne, please don't tell my father. This is so embarrassing!" Grace wiped her tears on a handkerchief Ivy handed to her.

"I think Mayor Jackson Nash would be the last man on earth to trouble with a feminine complaint, for sure." Etta sighed, a sigh that started at her feet and worked its way up. She didn't want to tangle with Mr. Nash again; she couldn't control her temper. Just the sight of him made her entire body stiffen with wrath.

"All right. Let's get you home, Grace. Ivy, is your ride here?"

"I'm having supper with the Hartwells tonight. I am to stay with Grace until this evening."

"Oh! Right, the Hartwells and the Harpers are hosting the lady doctor, right?" Etta remembered Mrs. Hartwell's excitement at having her friend confirm her pregnancy and tell her the due date.

"That's right. My parents are going as well. Grace is staying with me and meeting them for supper. Maybe I should stay with her if she's not well."

"You must ask your parents. Let's get you home to bed, young miss. I have my motorcar here, and we'll get you all sorted out before your father gets home. I'll tell him something that won't embarrass you or him. You will be right as rain in no time."

"What will you tell him?" Grace moaned with embarrassment.

"I'll say you have a headache. Would that work?" Etta's heart went out to her.

"Sure." A sheen of sweat broke out on Grace's forehead as she stood up and made her way to the motorcar.

"Thank you. I wasn't sure how to get her home." Ivy flashed Etta a bright smile as she helped Grace to her feet.

After a quick trip to the chemist, Etta let Ivy direct her to Mr. Nash's home. He owned a big brick home overlooking the river and swinging bridge.

Etta and Ivy set to work to make their patient more comfortable. Etta put a kettle on to boil as Ivy helped Grace get settled into a nightgown.

At five minutes past five, Mr. Nash bustled into his home and stopped dead in his tracks.

Etta bristled as she stood at his oven.

Mr. Nash's jaw dropped. "Can I help you, Miss Lynne?" Nash sputtered in shock.

Etta drew herself up to her full height.

"Your daughter is not well, Mr. Nash. I brought her home, and I am just settling her."

The blood drained from Mr. Nash's face. "Does she have a fever? I can take her to Dr. Barrett right now."

"No, not a fever." Etta screwed the top onto the hot water bottle.

"What then?" Mr. Nash frowned in confusion.

"Well, I told her I would tell you it is a headache, which is the code for a feminine complaint." Etta dropped her voice so they wouldn't be overheard.

Mr. Nash's face blushed red. "Say no more, I'd rather not know…" Mr. Nash shook his head. "Thank you for helping her. I'll leave you to it."

"Very mature." Etta frowned. Her decision to tiptoe around

him was forgotten as she stood up for Grace. "She is crying and in pain."

Mr. Nash slumped down at the kitchen table and dragged a hand through his hair so it stood up.

"Is she all right?" Mr. Nash asked quietly.

"She's not feeling well, and it embarrasses her that you will find out, and now I can see why." Etta shook her head in disappointment.

"I'm a man, a soldier. This is not my field!" Mr. Nash sputtered, as if to defend himself.

"She's your daughter, and it is your job to make it your field." Etta's eyes hardened in judgment.

"Mrs. Bennett talked to her... I thought that was the end of the matter." Mr. Nash's jaw clenched.

"She lives with you!" Etta scolded him. There was an air of vulnerability about Grace that pulled protective instincts out of Etta.

Mr. Nash ran his hands through his hair again. His face went from red to white. "What should I say?"

Etta thought about it. "Don't say a thing about it being a feminine complaint. Just say you hope she is feeling better soon."

"This is a nightmare," Mr. Nash groaned.

"You could have your lady friend see to her needs this week if you are too delicate to handle this situation." Etta couldn't keep the frost off her tone.

Mr. Nash blinked. "What lady friend?"

"Mrs. Delaire. I have it on good authority she brought a pie by." Etta wiped the drips of water off the side of the hot water bottle.

"Yes, my... well. I don't know exactly what we are. One wonders how to proceed sometimes." Mr. Nash crossed his arms over his chest.

"You don't know if you are courting Mrs. Delaire?" Etta asked. She couldn't stop the surprise from sharpening her tone.

Mr. Nash's eyebrows shot up in surprise. "Courting? Gracious, I hope not."

Etta rolled her eyes. "Are you or are you not courting? Mrs.

Delaire should have known to speak to her and check up on her. She's fifteen...many girls have already started by this point..."

Mr. Nash's face reddened. "She brought a pie by. I don't know exactly what that means."

"You're courting," Etta said succinctly.

"I suspected as much." Mr. Nash sighed in defeat.

"Listen, I'll talk to her." Etta softened. "I'll be back straight away. I have more to say to you."

Etta turned on her heel, and as she walked away, she could hear Mr. Nash groan from down the hall.

Etta opened the door to Grace's room and watched Ivy tenderly stroke hair back from the young girl's forehead.

Grace's room was pink with a pink bedspread. The wallpaper was a spattering of dainty pink roses and pale-green vines. Etta looked around and frowned. Did the late Mrs. Nash pick this wallpaper for her little girl? If Grace was her daughter, she would help her redecorate the room to suit her tastes and the time of her life now.

Ivy looked up at Etta. "The aspirin seems to be working. Poor thing."

Etta's forehead creased with concern. "A hot water bottle will work miracles."

"Such a delicate situation," Ivy murmured in sympathy.

Etta sat on the bed, and Grace curled up against her. The poor child was starved for female love and attention. Etta's anger toward Mr. Nash reared up again. "The medicine will work soon, darling. I'll stay until the pain stops." Etta rubbed Grace's back gently as she curled around her hot water bottle. Stroking Grace's hair back from her forehead, Etta worried about the slight temperature she detected.

"You're going to Hillcrest for supper?" Etta whispered to Ivy. "I wonder if you should go now so you are not late. Time is flying. I think this girl will be fast asleep at any minute."

"I was hoping to stay with Grace." Ivy got off the bed and picked up her books. "The grown-ups are very boring."

"Try to enjoy it." Etta pulled another blanket over Grace as the aspirin took effect and she started to drift off.

Etta tucked her in and smoothed her hair away from her

face. "Sleep well."

Ivy dropped her voice so as not to disturb Grace and so Mr. Nash could not overhear. "Have you had time to talk to Mr. Nash about her going to school?"

"Ivy... I tried. I will try again, but it doesn't look very promising." Etta got off Grace's bed.

"Grace thinks you can win him over." Ivy bit her lip.

"Don't hold your breath!" Etta frowned. "His mind is made up. She is very young... I don't know what will change it, honestly. Could Mrs. Bennett speak to him? Maybe Mrs. Holt?"

"They have both tried." Ivy's shoulders slumped. "By the time September is here, she'll be sixteen, and I so *badly* want her to come with me. We feel like sisters, Miss Lynne. Do you know what that feels like to leave your sister?"

Etta's heart broke at her tone. "I know exactly what it feels like. We have until June. I will keep trying where I can," Etta promised.

Together, they returned to the kitchen. Mr. Nash's broad back was to her as he stood at the counter, buttering a piece of bread.

"I'll go now. I am expected at Lord and Lady Harper's for supper. I hope Grace is all right." With that, Ivy slipped out of the Nash residence and left Etta to deal with Mr. Nash alone.

"Would you like salt and pepper on your chicken sandwich?" Mr. Nash turned to ask Etta.

"You're making me supper?" Etta's mouth dropped open in shock.

"Listen. I think we have gotten off to a rotten start. How about a truce? Please? I am out of my depth." Mr. Nash gestured to her to sit at his table. He placed a sandwich on a pretty plate in front of her.

"I didn't take you for the sandwich-making kind." Etta looked at the food on her plate in disbelief.

Mr. Nash sighed. "A few years ago, I couldn't do much, and I still don't understand how to run a household. That was entirely Nell's domain."

"I see." Etta poured tea into his teacup and then her own. She looked at Jackson Nash with new eyes. He looked tired and stressed, as if the weight of the world were on his shoulders.

"Just as this... well, this situation with Grace would have been... entirely up to her. I am a soldier. I am absolutely not cut out for this, and I can't..." Mr. Nash's face burned red with embarrassment.

Etta cut her sandwich in half and took a deep breath.

"She has what she needs. Mrs. Bennett spoke to her, but it was a while ago. I'll answer any questions she has and handle this whole situation. She's embarrassed enough, adding you to the mix would be too much."

Mr. Nash swallowed hard. "I should have known, and I should have made arrangements."

"Honestly, maybe I was a bit harsh, Mr. Nash. If you spoke to her about this, she would have died of embarrassment." Etta took a bite, surprised that the sandwich was delicious. "Which is unfortunate because it's a fairly natural process that half the world deals with, and yet it is..."

Mr. Nash held up his hands, cutting her off mid sentence. "Yes... well... presumably you can manage all this with her, and we can let this subject drop?"

"Of course." Etta desperately wanted to roll her eyes at him but didn't dare.

Mr. Nash seemed oblivious, but so concerned, it was endearing.

"She is a lovely girl," Etta said as she sipped her tea. "Ivy is a delight, too. They are very good students, so easy to teach."

Etta slyly brought up the matter of education on neutral ground.

Mr. Nash narrowed his eyes in suspicion. "Yes, Ivy is a credit to Ada and John. They adopted her... hmm... she was very young. Around the age of three."

"The women of Oakland told me a bit of her story. Ada Bennett is a tremendous woman."

"No child would be abused in Ada's presence." Mr. Nash nodded in agreement. He took a bite of his sandwich.

"I enjoyed meeting her."

"If all women were like Ada, we would have almost no problems in this world." Mr. Nash put down his sandwich and took a sip of tea.

"Almost no problems?" Etta arched her eyebrow, inviting him to continue.

"Well." Mr. Nash dropped his voice as if he were revealing something alarming. "Mrs. Bennett, Mrs. Holt, Mrs. Hartwell, those ladies that have been speaking to you about Grace, they were all involved in temperance, and they had lots of hard opinions."

"Oh, no." Etta gasped with sarcasm. "Well, I'm surprised you didn't squash *that* when you had the chance."

"I wasn't mayor then," Mr. Nash said as if the mayor at that time had fallen down on the job. "Holt was mayor, and whatever Mrs. Holt wants, she gets. She is a firecracker. It is extraordinary! It's not like Holt isn't a tough-as-nails negotiator, but where Mrs. Holt is concerned, he's soft." Mr. Nash shook his head in disapproval. "It's concerning. Sometimes I wonder who exactly is running this town." He shook his head as if women running a town would be a fate worse than death.

"I am a staunch temperance…" Etta stammered in defiance.

"Of course you are." Mr. Nash shot her a big grin. He picked up the delicate pink teapot; it looked out of place in his broad hand.

"I believe in temperance because, as a teacher, I have seen the suffering of alcohol abuse on families…"

Mr. Nash put the teacup down and leaned in to listen to her.

Etta's heart hammered in her throat. Mr. Nash, bigger and stronger up close, looked at her suddenly as if she were the only woman in the world. It was disarming.

"Yes?" Mr. Nash tilted his head to the side to listen.

"Listen, temperance was to give women some protection from violence in the home. That is not the battle between us, Mr. Nash. I am pleading with you to listen. I've heard Grace speaking to Ivy about school. This is not a flight of fancy. Yes, she is only fifteen. I understand that, but she will be sixteen in September, and she will be under the care and supervision of Mrs. Rallings. I understand she was from Oakland. She *guaran-*

tees their safety." Etta met Mr. Nash's gaze and watched with dismay as his eyes glazed over.

Mr. Nash let out a very long sigh.

"Why not let her *try* and see," Etta begged. She hated that he reduced her to this. "She is so brilliant we have nothing for her to do in school. She's surpassed the grade twelve students…"

"No, Miss Lynne." Mr. Nash shook his head no.

Etta's spine stiffened.

"She is brilliant, Mr. Nash. I looked over her transcript. I've never met a student that skipped two grades and then started advanced studies…" Etta clamped her hand over her mouth.

"What advanced studies?" Mr. Nash's eyes narrowed.

Etta's heart pounded, her throat tightened. "She is so incredibly smart!"

"I'm not talking about her brilliance," Mr. Nash reprimanded her.

Etta opened her mouth to retort and then promptly shut it.

"I know she is smart enough; that is not the problem. She is too young, and I'm not able to let her go. I lost my wife in childbirth. I lost the years I was at war… I can't let her go. I am not ready…"

"You would stifle her due to your own selfishness?" Etta gasped. A curl of fury unleashed in her. Her mother's words pounded through her head.

Art school is not a sure thing. I need you here… your brother can't cope…

Selfishness!

Mr. Nash was a selfish as her mother. Putting their needs before the needs of their child. To grow, to learn, to reach for new heights…

Etta forced the painful memories down and hoped her tone was respectful. "She has her heart set, and she can do it! She needs to move on and grow. All these plans in Toronto are in place to help her because of Mrs. Hartwell and Mrs. Bennett! They have worked hard to help her realize her dream! They feel that your late wife would have wanted her to go. Please, you can't say no!"

At the mention of his late wife, Mr. Nash's eyes flashed with anger. "I can say no! I *have* said no!" Mr. Nash lost his temper.

Etta's heart pounded with rage at his dismissal.

"But what if not getting this chance in life causes her to be desperately unhappy?" Etta's teeth clenched together hard enough to break.

The look of frustration on Nash's face caused Etta to lose her temper completely; she stood up and faced him over the table.

"I won't have her in Toronto, in school!" Mr. Nash stood up and met her head on. "Not now. Not yet."

Etta lunged for the door. "I think I best leave before I say something I regret. I will speak to Grace at a later date. I have left aspirin and set out everything she needs on the dresser. We never need to speak again, Mr. Nash. This is the last you have heard, from me, on this subject. I bid you good day."

"Listen, Miss Lynne…" Mr. Nash followed Etta to the front door.

She whirled on him.

Mr. Nash stopped dead in his tracks.

"I don't like you, Mr. Nash. But I have to get along with you to do my job. So I'm leaving before this fight escalates."

"We're not fighting," Mr. Nash growled. "We are discussing."

"I am not continuing to speak to a close-minded, selfish man like you a moment longer." Etta gasped at her outrageous comment. "Oh! I can't believe I said that out loud! I am…"

"Sorry?" Mr. Nash tilted his head to the side as if inviting her to apologize.

"No. I can't lie." Etta glared up at him, and her eyes narrowed. "I am not sorry. I meant it. You are wrong. Utterly wrong. I just wish I hadn't said it out loud. I need this job. Let's just part here before I lose my temper."

"Probably for the best," Mr. Nash agreed.

Etta sighed. "Look, about the feminine complaint, I'll pop in and check on her tomorrow. Learning about it and experiencing it are different things. That way you don't have to bother your long list of ladies." Etta couldn't stop herself from one parting shot.

"Really not a long list," Mr. Nash said dryly.

"Oh? I don't know about that. I wore an entire cup of coffee for a day when Mrs. Delaire thought I was getting entirely too close."

"She would never... intentionally..." Mr. Nash seemed genuinely shocked at her suggestion.

"I think she wants to be the next Mrs. Nash, and for that she has my deepest sympathies!" Etta's eyes narrowed as she left the house and made her way across Mr. Nash's front lawn.

Mr. Nash followed Etta to her motorcar, and then he made a move to crank it to start. Etta stopped him with one hand up. "I'm quite able to manage my car myself! You, sir, are no gentleman! No need to pretend! Don't touch my crank!"

"Miss Lynne, I'll start your car," Mr. Nash barked at her.

"You will not, under any circumstances, take one step nearer to that crank handle!"

"Miss Lynne, there is no need to get hysterical." Mr. Nash shook his head.

"Hysterical!" Etta roared at him, forgetting to keep her mouth shut to protect her job and career. "I can't believe you! I am not hysterical! I am frustrated by your arrogance and your ignorance!"

Mr. Nash tugged her out of the way so he could crank her car started.

Etta resisted the urge to beat him to death with her handbag.

The car cranked to life, and Nash straightened. Etta stood toe to toe with Jackson Nash, furious that his size forced her to look up at him. The smug look in his eye made her wild with anger. She tried to shut her mouth and couldn't do it. "I won't bring this up to you again, but I should warn you. I am forced to tell the women of Oakland that you are standing in her way."

"You will not." Mr. Nash's lips thinned, fury flashed in his eyes.

"Or what?" Etta's eyes tightened in anger.

"You listen to me." Mr. Nash took a step closer, so Etta was forced to look up at him again. "I will not be harassed into sending my daughter to Toronto. She can go to school when she is old enough, here!" Mr. Nash roared at Etta.

Etta stiffened her spine. "She has a seat in the University of Toronto! You are clipping her wings, and she will never forgive you! You are selfish!"

"I am a realist, Miss Lynne," Mr. Nash shot back at her. "A realist! You would do well to remember that."

"Oh, you're something all right. I'm not sure I would call it a realist." Etta's body shook with frustration.

"You involve the women of Oakland, and I will tell them what I told you, and then I will remind their husbands to get them in line. She is my daughter and I will raise her the way I see fit. Good day, Miss Lynne." Mr. Nash dismissed her.

"Get their women in line!" Etta gasped in horror. "You, sir, you are…"

"Yes?" Mr. Nash turned to address her. "Mayor? Trustee of the school board? What do you want to say? Just say it."

Etta's entire body trembled with anger. "How *dare* you throw your authority at me? How dare you try to intimidate me with your titles? You can have me fired. I understand. You can destroy my life. Fine! You have all the power, but I will tell you this." Etta jabbed her finger into his chest. "You are wrong. You are very, very wrong, and this is a mistake that will haunt you for the rest of your life. Grace will never forgive you, and neither will I. You are one hundred percent *wrong*." Etta's heart pounded hard as she brushed past him, yanked open her driver's side door and got into her motorcar. She ground her gears in her haste to leave Mr. Nash standing on the street with his hands on his hips.

CHAPTER 13

*E*tta pulled her pillow against her body as she settled into bed for the night. She tossed and turned as she tried not to think about Mr. Nash and his hard-headedness. A fist of hot tears lodged in her throat as she thought about Grace's future and how Grace's dreams were dashed, just like her own.

Watching Grace open her acceptance letter reminded her of her own acceptance letter. She remembered the sense of fulfillment she had felt just by being accepted. To be so thrilled to be chosen only to have it dashed due to a parent's decision was heartbreaking... In her case, parents who couldn't cope. In Grace's case, a parent so selfish he couldn't see past his own nose. Mr. Nash was putting his needs before his daughter's. In Etta's mind, in her heart, this was unacceptable. Etta bunched up her pillow three different ways and still couldn't get comfortable.

Finally, just as Etta drifted off to sleep, she heard a pounding on the front door loud enough to wake the dead.

Both Etta and Lucy scrambled into their robes and hurtled down the stairs to a white-faced Mr. Nash.

"What is it?" Etta gasped.

"Grace's calling for you. She won't let me near her. Will you come?" Mr. Nash didn't wait for her to answer. He took her by the upper arm and led her to the car.

"Of course." Etta tripped, lost a slipper on the front lawn and left it. Her foot froze and hurt from treading on icy-cold stones as she raced to keep up with his long strides. She ignored the threat of Mrs. Daindridge and Mrs. Carr seeing her flee into the night wearing only a nightgown and one slipper. She didn't care. Leaping into the car, Mr. Nash closed the door behind her.

Mr. Nash ground the gears as he roared across the bridge to his house.

"I'm no expert, but I think it is something other than a... well... a feminine complaint." Mr. Nash's jaw clenched in worry. His knuckles were white on the steering wheel. "The pain seems rather serious." His eyes were wide.

"Why not take her to Dr. Barrett?" Etta pulled her robe tight around herself as the icy April air chilled any exposed skin.

"She won't let a man near her. She is embarrassed. She only wants you." Mr. Nash stopped at the curb and leaped out of the driver's seat. He dashed around the motorcar and held open the door for Etta.

"There is a woman doctor at Lord Harper's carriage house. Maybe we could take her to see her?" Etta suggested as she ran up the sidewalk to Mr. Nash's house.

"At Lord Harper's, you say?" Mr. Nash flung open the front door. Together they ran to Grace's room.

"Yes."

Mr. Nash's entire body stiffened when Grace moaned in pain. "That would be best then."

Etta went to Grace's bed where she lay, pale and sweating, and took her hand. "Where does it hurt?"

"On my side."

"Just one side?" Etta smoothed Grace's hair back from her face.

"Is it supposed to hurt like this?" Grace's voice escalated in panic.

"No, it shouldn't. Would you see Mrs. Bennett's friend, Dr. McDougall?" Etta held her hand as Grace wept in pain.

Grace's cries of pain intensified.

"Mr. Nash, we're taking her to Dr. McDougall. She's a woman doctor. She'll have a peek and see what's going on. This is not normal," Etta directed as she slid her hand over Grace's abdomen on the right side, causing her to scream in pain.

Mr. Nash scooped up his daughter and carried her to the motorcar and settled her into the back seat.

Etta climbed in beside her and cradled her head in her lap.

"Oh, darling, we will get this all sorted out straight away." Etta soothed her as she rubbed her back.

Grace wept against Etta's knee. "I can't bear this pain."

"I know, love. We're almost there." Etta caressed her face.

"Don't leave me." Panic and pain caused Grace's voice to shake.

"I won't." Etta held her hand in hers and stroked her hair. "I am right here. We will get you all fixed up in no time."

Mr. Nash's worried eyes met Etta's in the rear view mirror.

Etta bit her lip.

Mr. Nash drove faster.

* * *

DOROTHEA DELAIRE'S eyes narrowed as she watched Mr. Nash and Etta race into Mr. Nash's house.

Hmmm. Miss Lynne does not take a hint well.

A cold finger of worry traced down Dorothea's back.

I'm losing him.

She paced around the parlour, watching through her window as Mr. Nash carried Grace to the car and Miss Lynne jumped in right beside her.

As if she were already her mother.

A slither of fear shivered through Dorothea. The thought of losing a man like Mr. Nash to the likes of Miss Lynne — never!

I'm prettier than her. I'm better than her. How could he be attracted to her? She is in his car, dressed only in a robe and nightgown.

Dorothea's eyes narrowed to slits as she watched Nash's car disappear into the night.

CHAPTER 14

$\mathcal{I}$n the backseat of Nash's car, Grace wept in Etta's arms. "It hurts so much!"

"Is this normal? This pain?" Mr. Nash demanded an answer from Etta. All niceties tossed aside, he screeched to a halt in front of the carriage house where Dr. and Mr. McDougall were staying.

"I don't know," Etta sputtered as she held Grace close.

"How do you not know? You are a woman!" Mr. Nash exclaimed.

"It's different for everyone," Etta shot back at him. "This is her first time, maybe that's why…"

Grace buried her face in Etta's lap and wailed harder, from embarrassment or pain, Etta wasn't sure which.

"We're here, darling. We are here," Mr. Nash said as he opened his car door. "I'll ask if she can see Grace."

"Good!" Etta adjusted Grace gently against her. "I'd rather not be seen in this nightgown!"

Mr. Nash shot her a look. "Yes, the fewer eyes on that flannel atrocity, the better."

Etta opened her mouth to retort and then clamped it shut. She smoothed Grace's hair back from her face.

Mr. Nash left them in the car as he ran to the carriage house. He raced back to the car within thirty seconds. He gathered

Grace in his arms, and together the three of them went into the carriage house.

"I'm Dr. McDougall. If you gentlemen would give us some privacy, I'll examine her, and we'll decide how to proceed here." Dr. McDougall was professional even as she stood in a night-gown herself. A pretty nightgown, if Etta could tell under the robe. She knew Dr. McDougall and Mrs. Hartwell were great friends, so likely it was a Hope in Oakland creation.

There was no time to talk. Grace screamed in pain.

"Don't leave me, Miss Lynne." Grace grabbed Etta's hand.

"I'm not going anywhere, darling." Etta squeezed her hand in hers as Nash and the doctor's husband, Cole, left the room.

"I'm Etta Lynne, the new teacher," Etta said to Dr. McDougall.

"Shannon McDougall, the old doctor." Dr. McDougall chuckled.

"I've heard of you, and thank goodness you are a woman!"

"Not words I hear every day, I can assure you." Dr. McDougall laughed outright. "Let's take a look, shall we?"

Grace screamed in pain as Dr. McDougall made a careful examination.

"Pain in right side; this is appendicitis, not cramping. She needs surgery tonight. We can't wait." All jesting aside, Dr. McDougall shot a concerned look at Etta. "We'll take her to Dr. Barrett, he has an operating room, and I will do the surgery right now."

"Don't leave me." Grace gripped Etta's hand hard.

"Good work. If you hadn't brought her tonight, she would have died." Dr. McDougall called her husband into the room.

"I want my mom." Grace wept.

"I won't leave you. I promise." Etta put her arms around Grace and held her as she wept into her shoulder.

Mr. Nash stepped into the room and stood by the other side of Grace. Etta looked up into his tortured eyes. She knew looking at his face; he had heard her crying for her mom.

"I want my mom. I want my mom," Grace wailed as pain made her incoherent.

"Darling, I know." Etta looked away from the pain in Mr.

Nash's eyes. She stooped down and kissed Grace on the fore-head. "I know. I'm not your mom, but I will make sure they take care of you. I won't leave you."

"So, you will do the operation now?" Mr. Nash asked Dr. McDougall in surprise.

"Yes." Dr. McDougall placed a few drips of ether on a mask and placed it on Grace's nose and mouth. "This will help right away."

Grace's hand relaxed in Etta's.

"This will be a long night," Dr. McDougall said softly. "We'll keep her sedated, so the pain isn't as bad."

"I'll stay, Dr. McDougall, if it is all the same to you. She has asked me to, and I think it is the least I can do." Etta stood closer to Grace as Dr. McDougall slipped the mask off.

"Poor dear. Was this her first menstrual period?" Dr. McDougall asked Etta.

"Yes," Etta confirmed.

The blood drained from Mr. Nash's face.

"Mr. Nash, I am sure you have done your best, but this can't be easy." Dr. McDougall spoke kindly to Mr. Nash.

Etta noticed how Dr. McDougall had a way of maintaining everyone's dignity as she discussed a sensitive subject. She thought she might be less judgemental going forward.

Mr. Nash nodded. "Thanks, you're right, I am at a loss."

Mr. Nash crouched over his daughter and stroked her hair back from her forehead. "You will be fine, darling. I will stay with you, and everything will be good. The pain will go away."

Watching Mr. Nash, Etta saw a whole new vulnerable and tender side to him. This was a man who would do anything to protect his daughter. A well of heart-warming emotion opened in Etta as he reassured Grace until she drifted off to a deep, ether-induced sleep.

"Let's get this pesky appendix out, and she will be healed up in no time." Dr. McDougall smiled at both of them. "You did the right thing. In future, Mr. Nash, this pain is not normal. You were right to be concerned."

"Thank you for seeing her on such short notice." Relief

washed over Mr. Nash's face as Dr. McDougall started getting things arranged for the surgery.

"Let's go." Dr. McDougall spoke in a tone that brooked no arguments.

"Dr. Barrett is expecting you, Shann," Mr. McDougall said from the doorway.

"Thank you, Cole." Dr. McDougall smiled up at him.

Etta's heart skipped a beat as she saw the obvious love between them. He carried her doctor's bag as she slipped her hand in his.

Mr. Nash gently scooped Grace up into his arms and carried her to the front door.

"Once we settle her, I'll take you home. Is that all right?" Nash's face was white with fear.

"Of course." Etta opened the door for him and followed him to the car. She crawled into the back seat. Nash carefully laid Grace down with her head on Etta's lap.

Once Grace was in the operating room, Nash and Etta sat together in the waiting room. They could hear a clock tick on the desk where Dr. Barrett's nurse met with his patients.

Guilt and worry pounded through Etta at how close they had come to losing Grace. Her throat tightened as she spoke. "I need to apologize to you, Mr. Nash."

Mr. Nash's eyebrows shot up at the word apologize. "For what?"

"I believed she was struggling with cramping. I never dreamed of anything else being wrong." Etta pressed her hand to her heart. "She could have died, and it would have been my fault. I am so sorry." Etta's eyes filled with tears. She dashed them away. "What if the surgery is too late, and something happens to her? I will never forgive myself." Etta's heart ached at the thought of how close they had come to losing her. "I'm so sorry."

"There is no need to apologize." Mr. Nash's eyes softened with sympathy. Mr. Nash took Etta's hand in his. "Please, don't be upset. How could you know? I am so glad she felt comfortable enough with you to tell you what was wrong." Mr. Nash shook his head. "She couldn't come to me, and I hate that. When she was calling for her mother..."

"Oh, Mr. Nash, you can't feel bad about that. You are a hard-working parent who loves her. You are doing your best. You are a great father. It's just daughters need mothers sometimes... it is not because you aren't a good parent." Etta wondered at the twist of fate that had her screeching at him in the street about going to school in Toronto one minute and then comforting him in a waiting room not even twenty-four hours later!

"Everyone said I should have gotten remarried by now." Mr. Nash shook his head. "If I had a wife..."

Etta shook her head and cut him off. "No. I don't think so. You have a community of women who love her and you. You have everything you need." Etta squeezed his hand hard in support. "Don't feel bad. The last person on earth I would have discussed a feminine complaint with was my father. Don't be too hard on yourself." Etta felt awkward suddenly. Looking down, she noticed the difference between their hands. Where his hand was very big, hard, and broad, hers was slight and delicate in comparison. Never in her life had she held the hand of a man she wasn't related to. She patted his hand and then drew hers away. "Just so you know, as long as I'm here, I will do what I can for her."

"Spare no expense, Miss Lynne," Mr. Nash said simply. "Give me a bill for whatever she needs and your time."

"She's my student." Etta waved the thought of payment away. "I would never dream of charging you. I am happy to do it. She is a darling girl, and I am a little flattered that she took to me so quickly. Maybe she could tag along at Ivy's tutoring session. We are going to discuss books since I can't help Ivy with advanced math."

Mr. Nash shook his head as a grin tugged at his lip. "You are quite a negotiator."

"It's just reading and discussing books." Etta grinned back.

"I think she would like that. Just don't fill her head with all your high-flown ideas," Mr. Nash growled in mock disapproval.

"I'll try to dampen my enthusiasm." Etta's grin turned into a beaming smile.

"Miss Lynne, you will not win every battle with me. Be clear on that," Mr. Nash warned her.

"We'll see." Etta lifted her chin with impertinence.

Mr. Nash and Etta smiled at each other in the dim waiting room as a fragile peace developed between them. Just as Mr. Nash was about to speak again, Dr. and Mr. McDougall entered the waiting room and interrupted their conversation.

"I kept the incision as small as possible, but this will be a painful recovery. Dr. Barrett has informed me that his nurse has taken ill, so we think it would be best if I take her to Brandon with me, and she can stay in my ward. I removed her appendix, but she requires round-the-clock care. I fear infection in a case like this."

"All right." Mr. Nash's face was white with fear again. "Thank you. I really can't thank you enough."

"You are welcome to come and see her, of course, and we can figure out when she will be ready to return home at a later date. You best get Miss Lynne home before she gets into trouble." Dr. McDougall winked at Etta.

"Of course." Mr. Nash shook Dr. McDougall's hand.

"I shall see you tomorrow then?" Dr. McDougall asked Mr. Nash.

"Can I follow you tonight?" Mr. Nash asked. "Make sure she is settled in?"

"She won't be coherent until first thing tomorrow." Dr. McDougall smiled at him. "You are very welcome to stay by her bedside tonight. That is a lovely thought."

"I'll take Miss Lynne home and then go straight to the hospital," Mr. Nash said.

"Please, tell her I stayed until I couldn't anymore. I can't leave the jurisdiction without permission," Etta explained. "Mr. Nash, let her know I couldn't come. I want her to know how much I care."

"I will." Mr. Nash nodded. "I think she knows."

Together, Etta and Mr. Nash said goodbye to the McDougalls and climbed into his motorcar.

"What time is it?" Etta tried and failed to stifle a yawn.

"Two in the morning." Mr. Nash checked his watch.

"I came here with no intentions of getting into trouble, and yet here I am at two in the morning, in a nightgown and... in the company of men! There is nothing worse! I've broken three rules just tonight," Etta moaned.

Mr. Nash chuckled beside her. "Technically just one man, not in the company of men, which sounds so much worse. Regarding nightgowns, I don't think anyone would call that a nightgown... I've seen nightgowns..."

"Remember yourself, sir!" Etta gasped in mock outrage. "It's not funny. I could lose my job!"

Mr. Nash chuckled beside her. "You won't lose your job. I'll vouch for you. This was an emergency."

"Mr. Spicer makes me very nervous." Etta wasn't joking now. Her voice shook. "Mr. Nash! Don't turn down Willow Avenue! I'll walk... if your car wakes up Mrs. Daindridge or Mrs. Carr! Mrs. Carr's son is on the school board, and if he finds out..."

"Listen. You are wearing *plaid flannel.*" Nash squinted as he drove past the entrance to Willow Street to hide his car. "No woman in the history of the world would wear a getup like that to seduce a man. I'm not letting you wander around Willow Street half dressed in the middle of the night. Especially not *now* with Mrs. Ellice missing. No, I'll escort you."

"Absolutely not." Etta tried to fight her rising sense of panic.

"You're being melodramatic." Mr. Nash frowned at her.

"I am not."

"You are. No one is up. I'll walk you safely to your door, but we'll leave the car here, so the headlights don't wake up you-know-who."

"Back door in case one of the gossips is getting a glass of water, please." Etta shot him a look of pure fear.

"Sure. If that makes you more comfortable," Mr. Nash conceded.

Etta let out a sigh of relief.

Mr. Nash parked in the shadows and then quickly slipped around to open the door for Etta. She looked up at him in the moonlight as he held his hand out to her. Tentatively, she placed her hand in his and stood by him on the sidewalk.

"You don't have any shoes on!" Mr. Nash gaped in surprise.

"Shhh!" Etta hissed. "Would you be quiet? You'll wake up the whole street!"

"Your right foot is bare, Miss Lynne! You'll catch your death!" Mr. Nash ignored her reprimand. He grabbed her and swooped her up into his arms.

Etta gasped in alarm as she was standing one moment and the next was cradled against the hard wall of his chest. "Mr. Nash! This is inappropriate! Put me down this instant!"

"Your foot is bare, and there is ice and snow everywhere." Mr. Nash ignored her and started walking down the street.

"You can't carry me all the way there…" Etta hissed at him.

"I can. There's nothing to you. Hang on." Mr. Nash dismissed her whispered pleas to put her down.

"If Mrs. Daindridge and Mrs. Carr see this, they will…" Etta's voice trailed away as they neared the widow's house.

"Miss Lynne. Your poor foot." Mr. Nash shook his head. "When did you lose your slipper?"

"When you came to get me. It's on the front lawn. You must get it and hide it."

"I am *not* catering to two old gossipy women." Mr. Nash carefully maneuvered around the shrubs so she wouldn't get scratched.

"*You* don't have to maintain a reputation. You can tomcat around, and no one would even blink."

"Not true," Mr. Nash protested.

"We don't have the same rules, and you know it," Etta whispered. "By the way, do you carry people around often? You are quite good at this." Etta watched his profile in the moonlight as his eyes darted around, watching for patches of ice.

"Yes, in the war. I had to drag a few friends out of dangerous areas."

"Like this?" Etta's jaw dropped open.

"No. Over my shoulder." Mr. Nash laughed. "They were grown men… you don't carry grown men like this!"

Etta couldn't stop a chuckle, even if it sounded slightly hysterical due to the circumstances. As she got a mental image of him carrying one of his fellow soldiers in such a fashion, she laughed harder. "Well! I didn't think so."

His arms were iron hard around her. Etta had to admit to herself that the feeling was not at all unpleasant.

"Would it have been easier to toss me over your shoulder?" Etta wondered out loud.

Mr. Nash laughed. "No! That might hurt you! We already have one nearly burst appendix, we certainly don't need two!"

"Well. Thank you for carrying me. My foot was rather frozen. But I fear we will be on the front page of the paper tomorrow," Etta said dryly. "I can see the headlines now. Mrs. Daindridge and Mrs. Carr dead from a heart attack after watching a scandalous..."

"Miss Lynne, please calm down. Whatever fallout there is, I'll handle it." He shifted her in his arms as he picked his way around a mound of snow that had piled up against a fence to get to the back of Mrs. Lemon's house. Once up the steps, he opened the door.

"This door is unlocked! Miss Lynne, make sure you lock this door behind me! You shouldn't have any unlocked doors! Detective Kane is almost certain Mrs. Ellice was last seen in the park near the river," Mr. Nash reprimanded her.

"Really?" Etta bit her lip in fear as their house was the closest to that area.

"Yes. Doors locked — at all times," Mr. Nash insisted as he carried her down the hall.

He set her down carefully in front of the coal heater. He piled more coal on the small flame. Etta held her frozen foot up to the fire as it crackled in the grate.

"I am more worried about my nosy neighbours than a killer. They'll get me fired. I'm sure of it." Etta flexed her foot as it started to thaw out.

"This entire night was my fault. Not yours. You have nothing to worry about," Mr. Nash assured her as he handed her a blanket to wrap around her shoulders.

"I've always worked in cities. I am not used to the code being so strictly enforced." Etta pulled the blanket around her tighter.

"Mr. Spicer is a fanatic, Miss Lynne." Mr. Nash tucked the blanket around her tighter, wrapping her feet so they would warm up. "Fanatics are dangerous because you can't reason with them. You will never win in an argument. You will never make him see sense. Be very careful around him." Mr. Nash's eyes burned with intensity as he spoke. "He doesn't really want you fired—he thrives on power. He wants to dominate you. I have tangled with men like that before, and while they tend to back down to men, they delight in oppressing women. I suspect it is because of how he was raised, but I don't know. I just want you to know that I won't let him hurt you."

Etta blinked at those words.

"He is one voice on that school board, and I am one voice. The rest of the men are reasonable." Mr. Nash adjusted the blanket at her feet again. Etta wondered if he was stalling.

"But what if you are not on the board?" Etta fidgeted with her collar.

"There is no reason to remove me." Mr. Nash shrugged.

"That's the second time today I was warned about Mr. Spicer." Etta bit her lip.

"Who else warned you?" Mr. Nash's gaze locked with hers.

"Detective Kane was at the school, and he said to be very cautious."

"Good, you should be." Mr. Nash nodded.

They watched the fire for a moment in silence, as they were both lost in their thoughts. Etta thought of the teacher last seen in Elizabeth Park only a week ago. She wondered what Mr. Spicer was capable of. Or was it someone else? Mrs. Ellice was pregnant... by her husband? Or another man who wanted her to be silenced? Who wanted Mrs. Ellice gone?

"Well, good night, Miss Lynne. Let's hope tomorrow is uneventful." Mr. Nash smiled at her in the darkness of the room, only the streetlight illuminating the parlour.

"Just remember, if anyone asks, you never saw me," Etta reminded him.

Mr. Nash chuckled. "Be sure to lock the door before you retire for the evening. You should take a hot water bottle to bed. I'll fill it for you."

"No, no. Go to your daughter. You must be worried sick. I'm fine." Etta got up to follow him to the kitchen, still draped in the blanket.

Nash rested his hand on the door handle of the back door and turned to her. "Miss Lynne…"

"Yes?" Etta looked up, startled.

"You didn't bring up Grace going to university, again. Are you losing your edge?" Mr. Nash teased her.

"I was saving that lecture for tomorrow," Etta shot at him impertinently.

Mr. Nash laughed, and Etta grinned.

"Good night, Miss Lynne." Mr. Nash's warm eyes crinkled as he smiled at her.

"Good night, Mr. Nash." Etta's heart skittered in her chest.

As Mr. Nash disappeared into the night, Etta carefully locked the door behind him.

A warm glow filled her as she set the kettle on the stove for some hot tea to warm her up. She peered out at the river and the creek. The ice was breaking up. She stood still as she noticed a movement in the shrubs by the riverbank.

She shut the lights off in the kitchen. Sure enough, there was a figure in the yard. Her breath caught in her throat as she saw the light from a lantern be quickly snuffed out.

Terrified, her heart beating hard, she raced to the front door and checked it. It was locked tight.

She held her breath as she watched the person, trying to discern if it was a man or a woman. There was no way to tell. Whoever it was left Mrs. Lemon's property and slipped over the bridge into the park.

Terrified, she grabbed her hot water bottle and raced up the stairs. She knocked on Lucy's door.

"Lucy," she hissed.

"What is it?" Lucy called back, her voice muffled by the closed door.

"There was someone in our yard. With a lantern! I saw him…. Or her… I don't know! I locked everything…" Etta shook with fear.

"Come in at once!"

Etta opened the door and slipped into Lucy's room, where Lucy was sitting bolt upright in her bed.

"This is ridiculous, I know… but can I sleep here?" Etta asked frantically.

"I was just going to say the same thing." Lucy pulled the covers back and made room for Etta to crawl in beside her.

Etta locked the door to Lucy's bedroom and clambered into bed with her friend. She placed the hot water bottle at her frozen feet, and then they both lay down and pulled the covers right up to their chins.

"Who do you think it was?" Lucy trembled beside her as she whispered in the dark.

"I don't know. I couldn't even tell if it was a man or a woman." Etta pressed her toes to the heat of the hot water bottle. "I'll tell Detective Kane in the morning."

"Was it Mr. Spicer?" Lucy asked.

"I don't know." Worry snaked through Etta.

"Did Mrs. Delaire see you when Nash went to get Grace? Was she here, trying to trap you together?" Lucy's voice shook.

Etta, remembering the vicious look in Mrs. Delaire's eyes as she threw hot coffee on her, bit her lip in fear.

CHAPTER 15

*D*orothea let the lace curtain fall back into place as she watched Mr. Nash pull his car up in front of his house and get out. Miss Lynne and Grace were not with him. Within minutes, he was back in his car with two bags.

I wonder if something has happened to Grace?

Dorothea pleated the lace curtain with her fingertips as she thought of how much easier it would be to slide into his life without a daughter scowling at her. Everyone knew daughters hated stepmothers.

Her mind raced to formulate a perfect plan. The thought of losing Mr. Nash as a suitor was inconceivable. There were so few prospects in this town that would do. No blue collar for her, never again. Mr. Nash had power and authority, which would become hers by extension when they married.

Dorothea's heart raced as she considered how to remove Miss Lynne as a threat. She dragged the covers back on her empty bed. She lay down and pressed her fingertips to her eyebrows, hard, to ease the tension there.

What was the best way?

Slowly, the tension in her forehead relaxed as she realized what *was* in her power. As an idea took root in her mind, Dorothea's lips curved into a smile.

It was almost too easy.

* * *

MR. SPICER MARCHED into the civic office early. He looked up with alarm as Mrs. Delaire entered behind him. He narrowed his eyes as he watched her place her light coat on the back of her chair. He thought her clothes were too tight, but she wasn't in his employ; there was nothing he could do about it.

A few moments later, Mrs. Delaire appeared at the open door of his office and tapped on the doorframe. "Mr. Spicer, I wondered if I could have a word?"

Spicer tensed for a confrontation.

What could she possibly want? She never gave him the time of day. In fact, he was certain she was repulsed by him.

"I have a busy day ahead of me, Mrs. Delaire." He kept his tone clipped to indicate he had no time for her.

"I won't take a moment of your time. I'm just not sure of whom to turn to with this information, about Miss Lynne." Mrs. Delaire's breath caught as though she were worried about saying the wrong thing.

Spicer's head snapped up. He motioned that she take a seat and then quickly closed the door to his office.

He noticed her shudder as he passed her to close the door. A shiver of power pulsed through him as he realized she was afraid of him, of his position.

He sat back down across the desk from her and waited. He watched as her pulse quickened in the hollow of her delicate throat.

She's terrified of me.

She should be.

"I saw something last night that I am not sure what to do about." Mrs. Delaire tilted her head to the side.

"Oh?" He narrowed his eyes slightly as he anticipated her next words.

Mrs. Delaire pulled the cardigan around her shoulders tighter.

A knock at the door interrupted them.

"Yes," Mr. Spicer called out, his eyes never leaving her.

The door opened.

"I'm so sorry." Mrs. Spicer placed a lunch box on Mr. Spicer's desk. "I wasn't well this morning, and your lunch was not packed in time. I'm so sorry."

She tucked a stringy, lank piece of light-brown, graying hair behind her ear; her eyes remained lowered to the floor.

"I have business to attend to." Mr. Spicer dismissed his wife without a thank you.

Mrs. Delaire shot Mrs. Spicer a look of contempt. Mr. Spicer caught it and held her gaze. Mrs. Delaire dropped her eyes.

Good, you know your place.

"As I said, I am very busy." Mr. Spicer leaned forward.

Mrs. Spicer slipped out of his office, closing the door behind her.

"This is just so awkward. I saw Mr. Nash and Miss Lynne in his car last night at around midnight." Mrs. Delaire bit her lip to make her I'm-worried-to-get-anyone-into-trouble routine convincing. Mr. Spicer recognized the manipulation in her eyes. "Maybe I shouldn't say anything, but I do think female teachers are not supposed to be with men at night in their nightgowns.... Isn't that correct?" Mrs. Delaire's eyes widened.

"Nightgowns!" Mr. Spicer's head snapped up in shock. "No. Not out at night, and certainly not in a nightgown. Was it a revealing nightgown?"

"Well... I couldn't really tell..." Mrs. Delaire bit her lip and fidgeted with her locket.

"Completely inappropriate." Mr. Spicer's lips thinned.

"I thought, perhaps, you would know what to do," Mrs. Delaire simpered.

"I do indeed, Mrs. Delaire. Please, leave that with me." A curl of anticipation slid around his heart, making it beat faster.

She's pretending to be innocent. She wants Nash for herself.

"Certainly." Mrs. Delaire nodded and kept her head slightly down in a sign of respect.

"Let the Federation know we want a replacement to take the place of Miss Lynne when she is fired for these actions. We'll need a teacher for Friday. Send that letter today. I can make that request without alerting the entire board. Then contact the board and book the board room for tomorrow night."

"Oh! Fired?" Mrs. Delaire gasped. "Oh, my goodness! I haven't gotten her fired, have I? I would never forgive myself!"

"Mrs. Delaire, type me a note that she is to meet us tomorrow night in the boardroom." Mr. Spicer stood up. "I'll deliver it myself."

"Oh. This is not what I had envisioned at all!" Mrs. Delaire pressed her hand to her heart.

Mr. Spicer met her eyes, and she quit acting.

"If you ever see any other inappropriate behavior, you are to come to me at once." Mr. Spicer picked up his briefcase and moved around the desk.

Mrs. Delaire shrank away from him.

He held the door open for her to complete the duties he had assigned.

"It would be best if you kept this to yourself for now. No need to alert Mr. Nash, as he is implicated in this accusation." Mr. Spicer saw her eyes light up at Nash's name.

"I can keep this quiet." Mrs. Delaire bit her lip. "You won't say it was me, though? I would hate for Mr. Nash to think I am keeping secrets..."

"Mrs. Delaire, maybe you could do a favour for me, and I will do a favour for you." Mr. Spicer pulled his door shut and took a step toward her.

Mrs. Delaire's eyes widened in panic.

"There is a budget in Mr. Nash's possession. It is an incorrect budget. The date on that budget is March 25, 1919. I need that incorrect budget in my possession. It has been replaced with the current correct one."

"Oh. Well, would that get me into trouble?" Mrs. Delaire bit her lip in worry.

"No! Of course not. It was a preliminary budget that only Nash and I ever saw. My worry is that it is confusing. Taxpayers panic when there is a hint of money missing. The money is returned, and there is no reason to alert anyone. Since only Mr. Nash and I know... it's a simple matter to just destroy it."

"Why would he keep it then?" Mrs. Delaire's hand fluttered to her throat. She toyed with the locket there. A locket designed to drag a man's eye to her neck or farther down.

This woman is a tart!

"Mr. Nash and I have had ... shall we say ... personality conflicts over the years. I believe he is keeping this budget to accuse me of something later. It's devious and inappropriate behavior between colleagues. It will be in his files. Once I see that budget, I promise, Mr. Nash will never know you said a word against him."

"All right, I will find that budget," she stammered.

"Perfect. I will return in an hour, Mrs. Delaire. You will have that correspondence ready and the budget on the desk when I return."

Mrs. Delaire swallowed in fear.

You are used to charming men to get what you want. You picked the wrong man.

"Mrs. Delaire, we will keep this between you and me." He took a step back. "Don't cross me. It will not end well for you if you do."

Mrs. Delaire's breath became ragged as he stepped back again and opened the office door once more.

Mr. Spicer suppressed a twisted sneer of contempt as she fled from the room.

By three o'clock in the afternoon, they had mobilized the school board; all but Nash, as he was in Brandon, dealing with his daughter's health crisis.

Better if he is not here, anyway.

Spicer left the note to meet on his desk, knowing full well he probably wouldn't get back in time. They had a majority to decide.

Spicer picked up the summons for Miss Lynne and made his way to the school. Leaving the note on her desk, he smiled as he thought of how she would feel tomorrow morning. Seeing this note, knowing her career and her future was in the palm of his hand.

An accusation of being in the company of men past eight o'clock in the evening was a death knell for her career, as it should be. Women like Miss Lynne, and Mrs. Delaire, were shameless, tempting, and left to their own devices, they would cause havoc in society. Like that Mrs. Ellice.

Pregnant! A new widow and pregnant!

Mr. Spicer burned in fury at the thought. How irresponsible. No thought to the life a child faced with a mother who had such a loose moral character that she would find herself in such a position! Weak... like his own mother. These women needed to know their place, and he intended to remind them. For the good of society, someone had to enforce the rules, or there would be absolute chaos!

This accusation would devastate and destroy Etta Lynne. He would crush her, and there wasn't a thing she could do about it.

It was almost too easy.

CHAPTER 16

The next morning, Etta jogged up the stairs to get to her classroom. Detective Kane waited for her at the door.

"Good morning, Miss Lynne." He got straight to the point.

Anticipation prickled through Etta as she tried to read his face and couldn't.

"Good morning, sir. Is there something I can help you with?"

"Yes. Two things, actually. Where could we speak privately?" Detective Kane looked around, trying to find a place where they could speak.

Etta's heart started to hammer.

Stop being a ninny!

"We can speak at the end of the hall, sir."

Together they made their way to the quiet space. Etta looked up at him and waited.

"I want to apologize. I think I gave you a scare last night, Miss Lynne. I was searching the riverbank. We have heard that Mrs. Ellice was last seen at Elizabeth Park. I thought of knocking on your door to let you know it was only me, but thought you might…"

"Oh! Detective Kane!" Etta pressed her hand to her heart in relief. "I am so glad it was you! If you had knocked on my door, I would have died of fright."

"I suspected as much. There was an address for an apartment

in Winnipeg in the mail I retrieved from the staff room. I am off to Winnipeg right now to investigate that lead. I wanted you and Mrs. Lemon to know that I have been patrolling your yard at night."

"Why?"

"Sometimes a murderer will return to the scene of the crime..." Detective Kane's voice deepened.

"Murderer!" Etta gasped in alarm.

"We can't rule it out. Mrs. Ellice should have turned up by now. I am hoping there is something in the apartment that will indicate what happened. If she was pregnant and the baby belonged to another man, not her husband..."

"That seems improbable!" Etta shook her head.

"Miss Lynne, at this point, I have to follow every lead. I should be back in a day or two, depending on what I find out. Constable Lark is to patrol near your home and in the park. Let Mrs. Lemon know because I don't have time to brief her. Keep your doors locked at all times. Likely, Mrs. Ellice is in a facility in Winnipeg for nerves, but if she was murdered ... well, we will take all precautions." Detective Kane tucked his notepad back in his pocket.

Etta swallowed hard. "Yes, sir."

After Detective Kane left the school, Etta unlocked the classroom door. Her heart stuttered as she noticed a piece of paper sitting on her desk. Panic pulsed in her throat as she read the summons to meet with the board that very evening.

Her heart sank with fear, and she fought back tears all day. Finally, she could escape back to Lucy's.

Lucy sat her down at the dining room table and poured her a cup of tea. She took the note from Etta's hand and read it swiftly.

"They are accusing me of something." Etta's heart pounded with dread. She longed to pace around the dining room.

"Maybe they just want to commend you for the good job you are doing." Lucy's eyes widened.

Etta twisted a linen handkerchief between her hands. "Mr. Spicer despises me. No good can come of this."

Lucy sipped her tea. "Don't take it personally, Etta. Honestly,

Mr. Spicer is not nice to women. He just isn't. His poor wife. I don't know how she stands it."

Etta's nerves tightened her stomach into knots.

"What is his problem?"

"His mother was… I'm not sure how to put it delicately… widowed at an early age, and she… well… had a reputation…" Lucy dropped her voice ominously.

"Gracious! Is that why he's determined every woman is on the verge of…"

"Yes." Lucy nodded.

"I have never been inappropriate! What happened to innocent until proven guilty?"

"Oh. Etta." Lucy's eyes clouded in worry. "Is Mr. Nash going to be there?"

"I don't know." Etta's stomach clenched with worry. "He stayed with Grace last night, and I don't know if he came back today."

Etta pushed food around on her plate. She couldn't eat a bite and felt guilty about leaving food when they had so little.

"Detective Kane said that he believes either Mrs. Ellice is in a care facility or the worst has happened. He fears she is not missing — he worries that she has been murdered. Do you think it might be Mr. Spicer? Was he inappropriate with Mrs. Ellice?" Etta asked Lucy finally.

"I don't know. I work so much, I am out of the earshot of any speculation." Lucy leaned forward. "Listen, don't borrow trouble. This might be nothing. It might be about Grace. Maybe they just want to remind you that Mr. Nash is not agreeable to her having extra lessons."

"Lucy, you don't gather an entire board together to reprimand a teacher about tutoring. I'm losing my job tonight, and if that happens, what will I do? My mother has to have care. Cali is seven months pregnant… I can't…" Etta stopped talking as fear and worry closed her throat.

"I'll come with you." Lucy reached across the table and held Etta's hand.

"That is very kind, but I *have* to do this alone. There are good men on this board. I have to trust someone will take a stand on my side."

"Whatever happens, we'll get through it together. I promise." Lucy squeezed her hand tight, but Etta saw worry and fear in her eyes.

* * *

ETTA'S HANDS slicked with sweat as she sat in the empty board-room, waiting for the members to enter. Deep voices and sharp outbursts rumbled in the hallway. She dreaded the door opening at the same time as anxiety made her pulse quicken. If she had to wait much longer, she was certain she would have a heart attack. Etta smoothed her hands on her skirts and braced herself for the confrontation.

How will I pay Mother's doctors' bills?

She slid the palms of her hands on her skirt again. She smoothed the fabric, trying to calm her heart.

Finally, the door opened, and the men took their seats, facing her. She nearly wept with relief as Mr. Nash entered with them. His face, granite hard and unreadable, didn't change as he looked at her.

She took a deep breath and let it out slowly as relief loosened the panic tightening her throat. Mr. Nash would vouch for her virtue.

Lord Harper stood and addressed the room. "Thank you for meeting with us, Miss Lynne. How has your first week been?"

"I have enjoyed my first week here. I am happy to say, I feel as though I have fit in well, and the students are delightful." Etta gilded the lily a bit, but no need to be negative about a job she wanted to keep. Some students were delightful, some were not. That was teaching.

"We'll get straight to the point," Lord Harper said. "Mr. Spicer, I will give you the floor."

Etta's mouth went dry as Mr. Spicer stood up.

"Miss Lynne, we have had a concerned citizen come to us and accuse you of being in a motorcar with a man, not your father or brother. What say you?"

120

Etta nearly sighed with relief. Surely the board would be reasonable when a medical matter was at stake! "I have a very good reason." Etta hated that her voice shook even though she spoke of an innocent situation. She cleared her throat and spoke again, more firmly. "Grace Nash became ill in my classroom. She was so sick she couldn't walk home, so I took her home to Mr. Nash's house."

"Did you leave immediately?" Mr. Spicer attacked her.

"The illness Grace was suffering from was one of a feminine nature. I felt it was prudent to stay and alleviate her symptoms to the best of my ability."

"We do not allow female teachers to be in the homes of single men in this community unchaperoned." Spicer's vicious tone ripped into her.

Etta gathered her courage to defend herself. "I stayed because at times, it is more comfortable for a young woman to speak to an older woman about such a delicate matter. I was not intending to overstep Mr. Nash's authority as her father, but I felt I was in a better position to assist than he was." Etta watched the men in the room look at each other. They were satisfied with the answer.

"Are we to assume, then, you were still assisting Miss Nash with a feminine complaint at midnight that same night? In a nightgown?" Mr. Spicer tilted his head to the side as he continued his onslaught.

The men in the room gasped.

Mr. Nash stood up. "I will answer for that, as the rest of the night is entirely my fault."

"I assure you, we will hear your side of the story when we have heard from her," Mr. Spicer snarled as he attempted to dismiss him.

"No!" Mr. Nash moved to stand in front of Etta. "That's enough, Mr. Spicer. I won't watch you attack her. She's innocent, and you know it. If this will be a bullying session, like the purple skirt incident, I won't have it. We can take this outside and settle it like men."

Etta's mouth dropped open as Mr. Nash stood in front of her, and she went from addressing the entire school board to being silenced by Mr. Nash. She couldn't see around his shoulders.

"I am not in the habit of having a woman answer for my actions and conduct. You direct any further questions to me." Mr. Nash's voice deepened, his stance broadened. Etta wondered for one fleeting moment if Mr. Nash and Mr. Spicer *would* step outside and beat each other to a pulp.

"What say you?" Mr. Spicer sneered at Mr. Nash.

"As Miss Lynne already mentioned, Grace, my daughter, was suffering from a feminine complaint, and in my ignorance, I had not made sufficient preparation for this. She was in increasing pain and wanted Miss Lynne to assist her. She trusted Miss Lynne, and I felt that Miss Lynne was in a better position than I was. As any of you can imagine, a young woman would naturally request the help of a woman, not a man. Her pain was unbearable, and aspirin was not helping. I did not know if this was normal, or if we needed a doctor to intervene."

"Why *didn't* you take Grace to a doctor?" Lord Harper asked quietly.

Etta's heart seized in her chest at his tone.

"Grace was embarrassed and refused to see a male doctor. I thought it was very foolish, but she was screaming in pain, and I would do anything to help her at that point. Anyway, she wanted Miss Lynne, and I wanted her to be well. So I went to retrieve Miss Lynne at midnight that night."

"You are her father. You could take her to any doctor you chose. This is just ridiculous. A teacher instead of Dr. Barrett!" Mr. Spicer shouted as he banged both fists down on the table.

Etta jumped at the sudden noise.

"You will *lower* your voice and conduct yourself professionally, or I will make you, and I daresay I will enjoy it," Mr. Nash growled as he warned Spicer. "My daughter was so distraught and in so much pain, she was embarrassed. I would have flown her to the moon if she needed it." Mr. Nash took a step forward, finger pointing at Mr. Spicer.

Etta moved slightly so she could see around Mr. Nash. The men in the room rubbed their chins. Etta knew they were thinking about Mr. Nash's statement and they found it reasonable. As Etta watched the men respond to Mr. Nash, a bloom of hope rose in her chest.

"Grace doesn't have a mother, as you know. She wanted her teacher to be with her, and it is entirely my fault I didn't make preparation for this. *I take full responsibility.* Miss Lynne knew of a female doctor staying at the Harpers' carriage house, and Grace had her appendix out at one in the morning. My daughter is in Brandon Hospital under Dr. McDougall's supervision."

"I can attest to the fact that Dr. McDougall was in my carriage house and she mentioned this to my wife before she left." Lord Harper's tone indicated that there should be no further argument.

"After the surgery, was Miss Lynne in your motorcar, with you, no chaperone?" Mr. Spicer lowered his voice but didn't take the contempt out of it.

"What man here would send a woman to walk home in the *middle of the night* with no physical protection when one teacher has already gone missing, and she is presumed dead?" Mr. Nash challenged the men to use their reason instead of being whipped up into a frenzy of moral outrage by Mr. Spicer.

Etta could imagine Mr. Nash in court; he would be very convincing.

"You were in a car together. No chaperone, late at night." Mr. Spicer's face twisted in fury.

"That is correct." Nash crossed his arms over his chest.

Mr. Spicer drew himself to his full height. "In the company of men, past eight, that is grounds for dismissal."

Etta's heart pounded so hard she worried that it would stop.

"Mr. Spicer, I am to blame. It was my family crisis that precipitated the events. If we dismiss anyone, it will be me. Not her." Mr. Nash refused to back down.

"She was alone with you in a motorcar. You are not her brother or her father," Mr. Spicer shot at Mr. Nash.

"These were extenuating circumstances," Mr. Nash growled.

Etta could hear in his tone, his patience was slipping.

Mr. Nash took a step back and moved so his body continued to block Etta from Mr. Spicer's view.

Never in her life had a man defended her to this extent. He intended to save her job, her career, and her reputation.

"I asked a question and didn't get an answer," Mr. Nash snapped at the room in general. "Who would allow a woman to walk home in the middle of the night, alone?"

"No one would," Mr. Bennett said firmly. "They did not intend to *persecute* women with this code, Mr. Spicer. Miss Lynne is innocent. There are extenuating circumstances. If my wife finds out we fired this innocent woman on silly charges like this, Mrs. Bennett would evict me out of my home until I came to my senses. I would agree with her."

Mr. Holt nodded in agreement. "Mrs. Holt would have my guts for garters."

The tension twisting Etta's heart into knots started to ease.

"Just because your women are out of control does not mean this violation shouldn't come with a penalty." Mr. Spicer refused to give up.

Etta's heart skittered again.

Mr. Holt stood up, nose to nose with Mr. Spicer. "What did you accuse my wife of?"

Etta couldn't see Mr. Spicer, as Mr. Nash's broad back was in the way, but a silence fell over the boardroom.

"Is there a code of conduct or not? Female teachers influence our young women! How long before every young girl in this community throws caution to the wind and is in the company of men, in motorcars with no chaperone! Do you want that on your conscience? Our job is to enforce the code. You are suggesting we toss it aside. This is a slippery slope." Mr. Spicer's voice took on a whining tone.

Where the majority disagreed with him previously, the mention of their daughters being in motorcars without proper chaperones was not acceptable in any context. Etta peeked around Nash's shoulder and watched as half seemed to agree with Mr. Spicer. If they voted, it could go either way.

Straightening her shoulders, she moved to stand at Mr. Nash's side. She could feel anger vibrating off him in waves. Other than Mr. Holt and Mr. Bennett, the men seemed worried that it would look like they were supporting immorality.

"Fire me." Mr. Nash lifted his chin. "Do what you want to me as a trustee, but you will not interfere with Miss Lynne's job here. Fire her instead of me, and I will take every one of you to the Manitoba Teachers' Federation myself."

Etta's jaw dropped in shock.

That was a big threat to a school board! A mayor taking an entire board to the Federation!

The men shuffled. They clearly didn't want to lose Mr. Nash to save Etta, but they believed they didn't have any other recourse. A hard line had to be drawn.

"I'll make it easy for you. I'll save you the vote. You will have my resignation tonight. I will step down from school board trustee, *if* you promise that she will remain in this position until the end of June. As we have seen no reason to fault her teaching, I step down with the understanding that she will finish this term and be considered for a position here next year." Mr. Nash stood solid and immovable as he faced Mr. Spicer.

Mr. Spicer tilted his head to the side. Etta noticed his lip twitched in a small smile. There was triumph in his eyes.

Mr. Nash has played into his hands! He didn't really want me gone. He wanted Nash to resign! Why?

"We'll tender your resignation tonight and fill your spot right away." Mr. Spicer's eyes swept over Etta again. "We cannot guarantee Miss Lynne's job until the end of the term. It depends on how closely she adheres to the code of conduct that we reminded her of when she started this job. I *can* guarantee you, Miss Lynne, without Mr. Nash on the board ready to jump to your defense, the next accusation will find you fired. Immediately. We take the conduct of our teachers seriously. You are no exception. The girls of our community look up to you, and your conduct must be flawless. I dismiss you." Mr. Spicer sneered at her.

Etta opened her mouth to speak and caught Lord Harper's eye. He shook his head slightly to silence her. So she clamped her mouth shut.

Etta pulled her big satchel over her shoulder and stalked from the room. She swept out of the town office and cranked the shaft of her car until her hand hurt.

"Let me." Mr. Nash gently peeled her hands off the crankshaft.

"Leave me. They are watching." Etta's jaw clenched, her body stiffened as Mr. Nash took over the crankshaft.

"I don't care." Mr. Nash cranked the car, and it didn't start — again. "I'll start your car. Just get in."

Etta leaped back out of his reach. "You just let them fire you to save my job. They'll think we're courting. Now you are starting my car." Etta's hand clutched at her throat. "Why did you do that?"

"Because this is wrong, and I'm not in the habit of letting women pay for mistakes they didn't commit. It was my fault. I paid the price. It's one less thing on my plate, anyway." Mr. Nash shrugged.

"But what about... what will people say?" Etta looked back at the window of the boardroom fearfully. "You are the mayor, and you resigned, but the gossips will assume they fired you! It is shameful! Your reputation..."

Mr. Nash cranked her car hard. "I don't really give a toss about what people say. I never have."

"What if the community says we are courting? What then? Mr. Carr will run straight back to Mrs. Carr!" Panic edged Etta's voice.

"Well, we aren't." Mr. Nash lost his patience and growled at her.

Etta's back stiffened at his tone, hurt replacing the crippling anxiety she had just endured in the boardroom. Wounded, she tossed her satchel into the front seat. "If any rumours come of this... I have too much at stake here, Mr. Nash."

Her car *finally* rumbled to life.

Etta breathed a sigh of relief.

"Listen, that was harsh and unnecessary." Mr. Nash looked up at a few of the men watching from the window of the boardroom, like male versions of Mrs. Daindridge and Mrs. Carr.

Etta got in her car and slammed the driver's side door shut but wound down the window so she could still speak with Mr. Nash. "I think Mr. Spicer wanted you gone. This wasn't just about me."

Mr. Nash didn't seem to notice that she was upset. "I think you're right. Any idea why?" Mr. Nash frowned at the men and then pulled his attention from the window of the boardroom to her.

"No. Have you fought with him?"

Mr. Nash sighed. "I'm the mayor, and he is not. He ran against me and thought he would win. Mr. Spicer is, and always has been, a sore loser."

"Well, it looks like you'll finally get your wish. I think it will be a soldier here next term." Etta started rolling her window up.

Mr. Nash put his hand in the way and pressed down so hard, she couldn't crank it up any farther. "That was before I knew you... knew your situation. I'll try to get Lord Harper to keep you on."

"Listen. I appreciate you trading your job for mine. I really do. But I think it best if you stay away from me from now on. I have too much at stake here. My mother is dying, and I need this job, this money." Etta's throat ached as she held back tears.

"Etta." Mr. Nash kept his hand stuck in her window. Etta swallowed hard and looked up at him. "Etta Lynne."

"Yes."

"Stop this at once," Mr. Nash demanded.

"Don't you dare speak to me like that!" Etta frowned at him as she tried again to roll the window up. He pushed down harder so she couldn't. Pitting her strength against his was futile; she gave up with a huff.

Mr. Nash bent down to look her straight in the eye as he spoke. "Whatever happens, you are a teacher in this community. We look after our own here. I will make sure you have what you need for your mother and your sister. I promise it."

Etta's eyes widened. "How?"

"Remember the field Angus was screaming about? Well, the proceeds from that field are to alleviate the financial concerns of the women and widows of this community. I kept the terms surrounding the field loose enough that the council can add any additional women to the list of community members needing help. I'll put you on the agenda to be added to the list at our next meeting." Mr. Nash's eyes met hers. He didn't look away.

"You can't add me," Etta hissed at him. "They'll say we're courting."

"I'll get Holt to add you." Mr. Nash kept his gaze level with hers.

"Thank you, but I hate being a burden like this. You don't understand." Etta shook her head. "I should say thank you. I should be grateful. I just want to make an honest wage and pay for my way in life. This isn't over. If they find a reason to fire me, and they will… with their henchman Miss Winthrop watching every move and Mr. Spicer counting my petticoats. It's only a matter of time."

"Counting your petticoats?" Nash's eyes darkened and flashed in fury. "What are you talking about?"

"Oh. You didn't know?" Etta's voice choked in anger. "He did a petticoat inspection on the street, in front of the students. A way to let everyone know he has all the power, and I have none."

"What do you mean, Miss Lynne?" Mr. Nash's face darkened further.

"I had to lift my skirt above my ankle to *verify* that I was wearing two petticoats." Furious and humiliated, Etta tried to roll up her window again. She gave up as Mr. Nash pressed down harder.

"Let me go." Etta shot Mr. Nash a look of desperation.

"How often does he do this?" Mr. Nash's tone sounded strangled, as if he were holding himself back from exploding.

"It happened once. I avoid him now. I wait until he has passed the school grounds, and then I park my car. Or I park in a different space, away from the sidewalk." Etta couldn't look at Mr. Nash; humiliation causing a fist of hot, salty tears to tighten her throat, tears she could no longer gulp down. "He did it to Mrs. Ellice, too. I know because Miss Winthrop saw it and falsely thought she was flirting with him. She thought I was flirting, too. I think she is attracted to him. She seemed jealous… I don't know. I don't want to talk anymore. Let me go. Please."

"Miss Lynne, I am very sorry." Mr. Nash took his hand from the window and took a step back. "That is humiliating and a gross misuse of power. I am going back there right now to handle it."

"He'll accuse me of lying," Etta said dully. "His word against mine, and he is a secretary treasurer, and I am just a teacher. He will win. The board almost always wins."

"I'll fix this. I promise it. This won't happen again, Miss Lynne. I apologize on behalf of the board. This should never have happened. Ever."

Etta nodded, his kindness softening her. "All I know is Mr. Spicer is treating me the same way he treated Mrs. Ellice, and I am scared. Detective Kane suspects she was murdered, and now I am terrified it's not just my job on the line. I see how he looks at me. I know he hates me." Etta resented that her throat tightened in fear as a tear escaped to slide down her face.

"I'm sorry. We will make sure you have protection," Mr. Nash promised gently.

"How? You are not on the board now." Etta looked up at him in alarm.

"I can offer that protection myself, and I don't need a board to allow it." Mr. Nash's jaw clenched hard. "I fought a war. I can keep two women alive until we sort this out."

Etta opened her mouth to protest, and Mr. Nash shook his head as he read her mind. "You leave Mrs. Daindridge and Mrs. Carr to me. Yes, if I am around keeping you two alive, they'll talk, but I will deal with them."

"You'll charm them?" Etta accused him.

"Always." Mr. Nash's face broke out into a smile.

Etta took a deep breath and let it out slowly.

"Mr. Spicer lays a hand on you, I will put two fists on him..." Mr. Nash spoke ominously.

Tears gathered in Etta's eyes. She couldn't stop them.

"I am very sorry that this happened, Miss Lynne." Mr. Nash's gaze locked with hers.

"Me too." Etta pushed down the clutch, put her car in first gear and peeled out of the parking lot.

CHAPTER 17

*E*tta slunk out of the school, grateful it was Friday, determined to hide in her room at Lucy's for the entire weekend. Out of sight, away from the gossip roaring through Oakland at the news Jackson Nash had resigned due to a scandal involving Etta Lynne.

There were whispers and rumours about nightgowns at two in the morning, which was a nail in the coffin for her career. Mr. Nash could gallivant any time of day or night; no one would bat an eye, but Miss Lynne!

The residents of Oakland were shocked, appalled, and completely scandalized.

Everyone wanted to know what had happened.

No one knew exactly.

Stories erupted and were dissected and gossiped about, nonetheless. Where they lacked information, they made it up.

Etta wanted the ground to open up and swallow her.

There was no such luck. As she returned home after her last class on Friday, she saw three cars parked on her street.

As Etta let herself in through the front door, Lucy looked up from the company of women in her parlour—battle ready, lips thin with disgust at what had happened.

Mrs. Holt, Mrs. Bennett, and Mrs. Hartwell poised to come to her defense.

"We heard." Mrs. Holt stood up and crossed her arms over her chest. "Mr. Holt told me everything, and we are wild with fury."

"Thank you, but I think it is best to just let this all die down. I won't speak of it. I will finish my time here and return to Brandon in June. I will be very careful." Etta's shoulders slumped in defeat.

"That won't do," Mrs. Holt sputtered. "Mr. Spicer is a bully, and we must stop him."

"Yes, he is," Etta agreed cautiously. "But it will not be me that helps you stop him. I have already told you, I have a family to support. I am not in a position to battle him. You have husbands on the school board. I suggest you speak to them. I am a teacher, nothing more. I am powerless. They can fire me, and there is no recourse. There is nothing I can do."

"This is preposterous. There has to be something!" Mrs. Hartwell shook her head; she looked from Mrs. Holt to Mrs. Bennett for a solution.

"There isn't." Etta held her hands up to stop a tirade from Mrs. Holt. "This isn't the first time. It won't be the last. My only hope is that Miss Little can find me a new post in September, preferably in Brandon so I can help my sister with her baby."

Mrs. Hartwell rubbed a hand absently on her abdomen. "These are difficult times. We wanted you to know that we know you are innocent of any charge of being in the company of men. It is preposterous."

Etta nodded and gratefully accepted a cup of tea from Lucy.

"I just wish my stomach would calm down. I can't keep food down at all. The thought of people gossiping and slandering me behind my back is awful."

"That's why we're here," Mrs. Bennett said gently. "We're sorry there is not more we can do."

Everyone jumped when a gentle tap at the door interrupted their conversation.

"If it's Mrs. Daindridge and Mrs. Carr here to pick at me, I will hide under my bed," Etta vowed as Lucy got up off the settee.

Lucy excused herself and then returned to the drawing

room. Etta caught a look of concern in her eyes. "Etta. There is a telegram for you."

The women all held their breath as Etta took it from Lucy. As she read it, her eyes filled with tears.

"My mother has taken a turn. Cali has asked me to meet her at the hospital." Etta's heart broke as she said the words. She placed the telegram on her lap and covered her face with her hands.

"Oh, Etta." Lucy moved closer. "Oh, I am so sorry."

The women in the room moved closer to lend support. As Etta wept, Lucy kept her arms around her tightly.

The women of Oakland reached out and placed their hands on her as Lucy rocked her like a little child.

"Listen." Lucy wiped Etta's face with a clean handkerchief. "You need to go this minute. I'll drive." Lucy let go of Etta. She dashed for her purse. The rest of the women nodded their approval.

"How will I leave town without permission?" Etta's eyes filled with new tears.

"We'll sneak you out." Mrs. Holt's eyes gleamed with anticipation.

Etta looked from Mrs. Holt to Mrs. Bennett.

"We'll bring the car to the park. You'll get in the back seat, lie down, and Lucy will drive you out of town. Come on. We need the excitement." Mrs. Bennett leaned forward as Etta considered the idea.

"All right," Etta agreed. "I can't face this board again. I just can't go another round. Nash won't be there to speak on my behalf. Your husbands tried. They really did. But without Nash, there is no majority…"

Mrs. Bennett, Mrs. Hartwell, and Mrs. Holt's eyes narrowed in fury on her behalf.

"Come on." Lucy took her hand and pulled her up out of her chair. "I'll drive and then catch the train home so you can have alone time with your sister and your mom. Or I can stay. Whatever you want."

"Thank you. You're a dear friend." Etta blinked back her tears.

"Stay the weekend, and I will deal with the board on this matter," Mrs. Holt promised.

"What if they…"

"You leave the board to us." Mrs. Bennett said as she took a stand by Mrs. Holt.

Etta nodded. "All right."

"Come on." Lucy tugged at her. "Let's go."

CHAPTER 18

$\mathcal{L}$ucy stopped the car in the parking lot of the hospital. Etta took two deep breaths and let them out slowly. She was thankful that she was back in Brandon, where she had anonymity and no prying eyes to worry about.

Lucy reached for her hand. "Whenever you are ready."

"I still have a mother, Lucy. Let me hang onto that for a minute. Once I go in… once I know for sure… it's over, I fear I can't bear it." Etta gripped Lucy's hand tight.

"We will get through this, together," Lucy murmured softly.

Etta took a deep, shaky breath.

"What if I fall apart?" Etta's voice shook.

"Then I'll catch you and piece you back together." Lucy patted her back. "I am right here. We will bring Cali home. That's what we will do. We'll take this one tiny step at a time."

Etta let Lucy's calm words wash over her. Tears splashed down her cheeks and soaked her collar. She curled forward as emotional pain swamped her. Etta's tears fell on their joined hands. "Lucy, I feel like my heart is breaking apart. My brother, my father, and now…"

Lucy interrupted Etta's downward spiral. "You are not alone. You are part of this community, and we care for one another. I've seen it. So let's find Cali." Lucy's words calmed her.

"All right." Etta wiped her tears away. She took two deep breaths and let them out slowly, trying to slow her racing heart.

Together, Lucy and Etta got out of the car and walked into the hospital. The front desk nurse looked up.

"I'm here to see Eleanor Lynne." The words dragged out of Etta as she braced herself to see her mother in her final stages.

"She's in room 38, down the hall to the right."

"Miss Lynne! Mrs. Lemon! What a surprise." Mr. Nash made his way across the waiting room to stand in front of them. "What is going on?" Mr. Nash's forehead creased with concern as he noticed the eyes of both women. "You've been crying."

"My mother has taken a turn. I am just going to her." Etta took a deep, ragged breath. "I don't know how she is. I just got here." Etta thought about bolting out of the hospital and running as fast and as far as she could, but she didn't.

Mr. Nash followed behind Etta and Lucy.

Etta's chest ached with unshed tears as she saw Cali sleeping in a chair near the bed beside her mother.

Etta took in the scene at a glance; she slumped on the door frame. She struggled to get her emotions under control. Her eyes filled with tears. Cali couldn't handle this. Etta couldn't handle this.

Etta tried to gather her courage; she had to pull herself together for Cali. The weight of responsibility was so heavy that she felt as though she was drowning.

"Let's see if we can find the attending doctor and find out what exactly is going on. We can create a plan," Mr. Nash murmured quietly so as not to disturb Cali.

Etta blinked up at him.

Cali startled awake as Mr. Nash left the room to find the doctor. Quickly, Cali scrambled to her feet. Etta grabbed her and hugged her hard.

"I came as soon as I could. Are you all right?" Etta asked Cali.

"Oh, Etta. I am so glad you are here." Cali's face crumpled in tears. "I saw the doctor. He doesn't think Mother will last the night. This is all just the worst news. She's not getting better, and I can't stay with you as she suffers. I am suppose to be on bed rest." Cali's voice escalated in panic. She pulled away from Etta and began to wring her hands in worry.

"I can stay." Etta tried to sound braver than she felt. "Oh, and this is Lucy Lemon, I live with her. She was kind enough to drive me in."

"Since you are on bed rest, I think you should come home with me. We'll settle you in, and that way you aren't paying rent at that apartment." Lucy reached out to Cali and hugged her.

"There are still some deliveries for my work. I put addresses on the packages, but I can't deliver them." Cali's eyes widened. "Oh, Etta. I don't want to leave you alone to handle this, but I am so scared I will lose this baby."

"You won't." Etta spoke with more confidence than she felt. "Let me discuss this with Lucy and Mr. Nash. We can figure this out."

Etta looked at her mother, and tears filled her eyes. "I don't think she will..."

Mr. Nash slipped back into the room.

"I know." Cali closed her eyes. "This is too much for you alone. Staying here, packing up the apartment... Etta, you can't."

"Let's step outside, please," Etta whispered to Lucy and Mr. Nash.

Cali looked up at them in alarm.

"Be right back." Etta patted Cali to reassure her.

Lucy, Mr. Nash, and Etta stepped out into the hallway. Etta shut the hospital room door. Taking a big breath, she let it out slowly.

"She can't stay here, and she needs bed rest immediately. She also needs care. I can't..." Etta swallowed hard.

"Lucy, if you take Grace and Cali home with you, I can stay with Etta. I'll help her move everything and deal with — well, anything else that comes up," Mr. Nash suggested quietly as if afraid a loud voice might send the women over the edge.

"But staying in the city together?" Lucy gasped at the shocking suggestion of Etta and Mr. Nash in the city for a weekend alone. "What if the board finds out?"

"We aren't staying together." Etta held her hands up.

"I'm not leaving." Mr. Nash straightened up. "You can't do

this alone, and you will need things carried to the car. I'm staying in a hotel; no impropriety here."

"That sounds reasonable." Lucy nodded.

"Cali says that she is… at the end." Etta gulped down her tears at the statement. "As soon as this is over, I am going to Lord Harper, and I will plead my case, privately, and I will send a full report to the Federation. That's all I can do." Etta spoke quietly, defeat stealing her fire. "I can only handle one tragedy at a time. I need you to take Cali."

"I mean no offense, Miss Lynne, but you came to Brandon in your car?" Mr. Nash asked.

"Yes."

"Well, your car has been acting up. I think Lucy, Grace, and Cali should go home in *my* car. We'll take yours; at least if it breaks down there aren't three women in the middle of the prairie on their own."

"That is a very generous offer." Relief settled over Etta as Mr. Nash suggested a good plan for everyone. "Thank you, Mr. Nash. I really appreciate that."

"Of course." Mr. Nash nodded.

Once they agreed on the plan, Lucy, Mr. Nash, and Etta re-entered the room.

Etta straightened up as the doctor entered a few moments later.

"Miss Lynne, Mrs. Tyne. I think someone should stay with your mother tonight." The doctor checked her chart. "The infection is so advanced we can't help her. Her time is very near."

Cali curled into a ball and burst into tears.

"Your sister should not be here. She needs rest. She is exhausted." The doctor snapped the chart shut and hung it at the end of the bed. "I am very sorry. We are doing what we can to keep her comfortable."

"Of course." Etta gathered her last reserves of strength. "Thank you."

The doctor left as swiftly as he entered the room.

"Cali, would you like to say goodbye privately or with me—what would be best?" Etta asked Cali gently. Cali couldn't stop weeping.

Mr. Nash and Lucy left the room to give them privacy.

"I don't know how." Cali put her hands over her face. Etta wrapped her arms around her.

Etta's heart broke to pieces as Cali said goodbye to their mother. Finally, Lucy stepped into the room.

"Cali, darling, you must think of the baby. Come with me."

Mr. Nash hovered nearby with a wheelchair.

They lost track of time as Cali said goodbye and Etta comforted her.

Etta hugged Cali against her to try to share the pain of grief. Lucy rubbed their backs as they wept. "We must think of the baby. Cali, you must come with me now…"

"I can't seem to let go." Etta tried to bring her emotions under control.

Finally, Lucy gently pulled them apart. She kept whispering that Cali needed to think of her baby; she helped Cali get in the wheelchair. Etta tried and failed to blink back tears as Lucy wheeled her down the hallway to Mr. Nash's car.

Mr. Nash gently pulled a chair over by her mother's bedside and settled Etta there.

"Would you prefer if I stay or if I go?" Mr. Nash whispered.

Etta's throat tightened as she looked up at him. "Please, stay."

Mr. Nash brought a chair to the bedside so he could sit beside her. He took her hand in his and said nothing as she wept.

Etta's heart broke as her mother suddenly seemed to regain consciousness. Etta pulled her hand from Mr. Nash's and held her mother's hands in her own.

Etta's eyes locked with her mother's as she struggled to speak.

"Etta." The word dragged out of her with what was surely one of her final breaths. "Sorry…"

"It's all right, Mother. I'm right here. There is no need…" Etta tried to stifle the sob that escaped.

"Et…" Her mother's throat worked as she tried to speak. She gasped and clutched at Etta.

"It's all right. I'm sorry, too… you can go, Mama." Etta's heart shattered as she helped her mother find peace even as the words broke her heart. "We love you, but you can go... you can close your eyes and... Just rest now... Please, just..." Etta's voice cracked as she scrambled for any word that would ease her mother's suffering. "Please rest, Mama." Etta's tears splashed down onto the covers. "I'm right here... you can go."

As her mother drew her last breath, the world stopped moving, the clocks stopped ticking, and the fabric of their life ripped, leaving a hole that would never be mended. This life, her presence, could never be replaced. The truth of that nearly took Etta to her knees.

Mr. Nash gently reached forward and laid his big, broad hand on Etta's shaking shoulder. She turned to him and pressed her face into his shoulder. He shifted in his chair so he could gather her into his arms.

"She was waiting for you, Etta," Mr. Nash murmured. "She's at peace now."

Etta didn't resist as Mr. Nash tightened his arms around her and held her as she shattered.

CHAPTER 19

Once Etta calmed down, she pulled back and wiped her tears away.

As they waited for the doctor to return, Etta turned away from her mother and directed her attention to Mr. Nash. "All these years wasted, being upset that she made me go into teaching. For not telling me the truth about my father until it was too late. I was so hard, so harsh! I am so ashamed of myself."

"It's all right now, Miss Lynne," Mr. Nash whispered. "No one is perfect. People make mistakes."

"Can we step outside?" Etta wiped her eyes.

"Of course." Mr. Nash and Etta left her mother's bedside. He opened the door, and they stood in the hallway together.

"I was supposed to go to the Toronto School of Art. I was accepted, and she stopped me from going. My father was gambling, and she knew she would need me to support her. I was furious, I was awful..."

"Miss Lynne, I am so sorry." Mr. Nash's eyes softened in sympathy.

"You should know how terrible I am. What other choice did she have, really?" Etta's heart broke as she spoke, her eyes dropped in shame. "I was angry that she didn't tell me about my father and all his gambling. Looking back, she was as much a victim as me, as Cali..." Etta paused as the pain of that statement sliced straight through her heart. "I wish I could take it back. All these years, and she is apologizing to me. I…"

"It's all over now." Mr. Nash placed his hand on her shoulder. "Please, just think of the good times, Miss Lynne. Think of the good."

Etta nodded and turned the handle to return to her mother. Down the hall, she saw Dr. McDougall coming toward them.

"Hello." Dr. McDougall's face was a mask of professionalism.

"Dr. McDougall, my mother has passed." Etta opened the door and returned to her mother's side.

"I'm so sorry. Do accept my condolences." Dr. McDougall and Mr. Nash followed her in. "I knew your mother was not well."

Dr. McDougall placed her hand on Etta's shoulder. "Mrs. Hartwell is my dear friend, and she told me of your current situation. She was not gossiping, I promise. The women of Oakland care about you and your situation. One way I can ease your situation is this: I checked your sister's chart, and she is due in late May, early June. If you wish, I can do her checkups and deliver the baby free of charge."

"What?"

"Listen." Dr. McDougall took a deep breath; she let it out slowly. "These are difficult times. I was trained to give where I can, but I take where I can, too." She flashed Etta a quick smile. "Many of my clients are wealthy, and I have a fund they can donate to if they feel their care was exceptional. The fund is for me to give where I want. Your sister fits the criteria. Please, take this gift. I want to ease your worries."

Etta let out a breath she didn't realize she had been holding. "How do I thank you? I don't know what to say."

"Say yes." Dr. McDougall's eyes crinkled at the corners as she smiled at Etta. "I will see Mrs. Tyne when I check on Mrs. Hartwell. My deepest sympathy about your mother. I am so sorry for your loss."

"Thank you. I won't forget this kindness."

Dr. McDougall nodded. "Is Grace here waiting, Mr. Nash?"

"No. Mrs. Lemon brought Miss Lynne to Brandon, so we

sent Mrs. Tyne and Grace home with Mrs. Lemon. I will assist Miss Lynne with any leftover business before we return home to Oakland."

"Very well. Grace's surgery was successful. Please ensure she gets lots of rest. If she has pain or fever, contact me immediately. I think she is on the mend." Dr. McDougall gave Mr. Nash a professional smile.

"Thank you very much, Dr. McDougall." Mr. Nash shook her hand.

Dr. McDougall left them, and the undertaker knocked before entering the room. Etta tamped down her sadness as the undertaker pulled the blanket over her mother's face.

"Can you please let the funeral director know we need the burial to take place tomorrow? I know this is unusual, but the only other family member is my sister, who is on bed rest. We will postpone the service to a graveside service when my sister is able to attend..."

"Which funeral home?" The undertaker cut her off.

"Which one is the most inexpensive?" Etta asked the undertaker.

"Marsh's would be the best bet." The undertaker started wheeling Etta's mother out the door.

"All right. If you would be so kind as to mention that to Mr. Marsh..."

"I will. He will want to square up with you before the burial. What time will I say?"

"Is 11:30 in the morning tomorrow alright?"

"I will let him know. We'll have her ready for burial by say... two pm?"

"Thank you." Etta felt fresh tears gather in her eyes. "This all sounds so crass, but I don't have permission from my school board to be in the city... I need to get back to Oakland..."

"Your mother died." The undertaker shot her a look of confusion.

"Some school boards have no human kindness," Etta said flatly.

"I'm sorry to hear that." The undertaker shook his head and got to work.

Etta's heart broke as they took away her mother. A nurse came in to get the room ready for another patient.

Etta clutched Dr. McDougall's card in her hand and stood in the hallway. Mr. Nash stood by her as she tried to breathe as her heart broke apart from the pain of loss.

CHAPTER 20

When she couldn't see the stretcher with her mother on it any longer, Etta wrestled her emotions under control. Her shoulders slumped in exhaustion at the thought of dealing with Cali's unfinished work and packing up their entire apartment. Her heart ached from loss.

Mr. Nash held his arm out. "I'll take you to your apartment."

"Yes, I have to pack and deliver the laundry." Etta's arms hung at her side. She felt as if someone had reached in and snuffed out her spirit.

"Are you all right?" Mr. Nash asked as he navigated them down the hall to the front desk.

"I knew it was coming, but it's still very hard."

"Of course." Mr. Nash pulled her out of the way of an oncoming wheelchair.

At the front desk, Mr. Nash stopped to speak to the orderly. "Please send Eleanor Lynne's bill to this address. I will handle all the arrangements." Mr. Nash handed the man behind the desk his business card.

Etta's face reddened with shame. Humiliation pulsed through her as she realized that Mr. Nash would pay this bill. No matter how hard Cali and she had worked and slaved to make their own way, the debt of her mother's care was crushing. Their father had left them vulnerable and destitute. They couldn't pay it.

The orderly nodded and made a note on a file. Just like that. Her mother's bill was taken care of, and she had no say in it.

Silently, Etta wanted to protest that she wasn't useless. She had worked hard, agonized over the debt of her mother's care, kept her mouth shut to keep her job, and for what? She couldn't afford basic care for her mother or her sister.

She owed Mr. Nash now.

A lot.

Fury stiffened her back.

She didn't want to owe Mr. Nash, or anyone. It hurt her that Mr. Nash didn't even ask; he just intervened. How long before she had no voice at all? How long before she quit thinking for herself entirely? Hot, salty tears of grief and frustration burned up her throat. Her face crumpled and her head hung as Mr. Nash turned to look at her.

"Miss Lynne, are you all right?" Mr. Nash asked.

In the bottom of her handbag, she found a fresh handkerchief with a sprig of forget-me-nots embroidered along the corner. Her mother's favourite flower. This was the handkerchief her mother had packed for her when she sent her away to Normal School.

Etta looked at the flowers as she pressed the handkerchief against her eyes to dry her tears.

Finally composed enough to speak, her gaze locked with Mr. Nash.

"Etta?" Mr. Nash asked warily.

"I want you to know that having you pay this bill..." Etta's voice caught on a sob she couldn't control. "It's humiliating. I am humiliated."

"What?" Mr. Nash's face fell.

Etta moved away from him. Wild with grief and pain, she lashed out. "I work as hard as any man, and yet I can't even pay for the basic needs of my mother." Her words were sharp with fury. Etta shook her head as he made a move toward her. "This is why I told Grace about her acceptance to university. For this reason, I will fight for her education. So she is never here, where I am today, depending on the charity of others."

Etta put her hand over her mouth.

Mr. Nash didn't move.

Nurses and doctors rushed past them. Patients waiting in the waiting room looked up in alarm as Etta tore into Mr. Nash.

"Etta, there is no shame…" Mr. Nash held his hands out to her.

"There is a tremendous shame in poverty," Etta hissed at him. "You will never know it. You are privileged and educated. You will never know how I feel today relying on you to pay this bill."

"Etta." Mr. Nash reached for her.

"No! You don't understand. I stood there and said goodbye to my mother, knowing I can't afford her funeral!" Etta's voice cracked on the word funeral. "My father gambled everything away. Everything!"

Doctors stopped and then kept moving. A nurse came by and placed her hand on Etta's shoulder. "Would you like a private space?"

"No." Etta jerked away from the nurse.

The nurse looked from Etta to Mr. Nash. Mr. Nash took Etta by the arm and gently but firmly led her to the small room the nurse pointed out. Etta tried to drag her arm out of his embrace but couldn't. His hand was rock hard on her arm, and he couldn't be shaken off.

"Don't fight me. We'll have this conversation in private. Come on." He gently pulled her into the small room and shut the door.

Etta stood in the small room full of Bibles and pamphlets on how to deal with death. She whirled around to face him.

"I want you to listen to me now," Mr. Nash commanded as he pulled a handkerchief from his breast pocket and wiped her tears away.

Etta tried to move away but couldn't. He held her in front of him like a petulant three-year-old.

"There is no shame in letting me pay for this." Mr. Nash finished with her face. He held her by the upper arms. "I would do this for anyone. You won't owe me, personally. I will submit this bill to the municipality. The proceeds of the field will pay for it. Whatever you think is my agenda, there isn't one."

"I feel so abandoned." Etta tried to stop her face from crumbling. "I hate it. You don't *know* this vulnerability, depending on someone to pay your way... What if there was no field or municipal assistance? What then?"

"But there is a field, a municipality that wants to help people in this situation..." Mr. Nash sounded confused.

He doesn't understand how I feel... he never will.

Etta turned from him and cleaned up her face and composed herself before turning back. She took a deep breath.

"I understand this is very difficult," Mr. Nash conceded. The tone of his voice was deep and gentle. "What should I do? Please, tell me what I should do differently."

Etta blinked in surprise.

"I was wrong to just step in; that wasn't respectful of you." Nash acknowledged further.

Etta gasped in surprise. "Really?"

"Yes. Really," Mr. Nash promised. "I am sorry."

Mr. Nash took a deep breath and let it out slowly. "I will start asking for your opinion and consent before I decide and take over your responsibilities. I am very sorry; I wasn't thinking. I am used to a very different sort of woman. Very different."

"Really?" Etta blinked up at him.

"Really," Mr. Nash confirmed. "I never meant to humiliate you or hurt you in any way. I would never hurt you."

Etta wiped her tears away. "I know."

"So, now that's settled. Shall we go?" Mr. Nash asked quietly.

"Yes." Etta nodded. "We have a lot to do."

Mr. Nash opened the door for her. Together, they left the hospital and made their way across the parking lot to Etta's car.

"I'll start it." Mr. Nash opened the passenger side door. "With your permission, I would like to drive."

"If I give you this inch, will you take a mile?" Etta watched him warily.

"I will not." Mr. Nash opened the door for her.

Etta slid into the passenger seat.

Mr. Nash went to the front of the car to start it.

Etta prayed the car would start.

Mr. Nash cranked it again. Nothing. After five tries, the car finally sputtered to life and then died again.

Defeat wore at Etta as the car sparked to life and then died a second time.

Mr. Nash opened the hood, fiddled around with something Etta couldn't see and then cranked it again. The car finally started.

Mr. Nash slammed down the hood, slipped into the driver's seat and, saying nothing, pulled out of the parking lot and drove straight to the nearest mechanic shop.

"Where are we going?" Etta looked at him with alarm.

"This car needs an overhaul." Mr. Nash stopped the car. "It needs to die where someone can fix it."

Etta's car shuddered and gasped — dying completely — half a block from the shop.

Etta's heart sank to her feet. There was no use saying she couldn't afford it.

He knew it.

She knew it.

Mr. Nash got out and walked down the block. Etta watched as he spoke to a mechanic then returned to the car.

"He said he can work on it tonight. This car should be ready tomorrow at some point. Let's go to your apartment."

"Tomorrow?" Etta's eyes widened. "Have you decided where are you staying tonight?"

"A hotel."

"Right." Etta gathered her bag together as they left the mechanic shop and made their way to Pacific Avenue. Her cheeks burned at the thought of him seeing where she lived.

"Are you all right to stay at your old apartment on your own?" Mr. Nash asked as they walked under a bare canopy of maple trees.

"Yes. I am exhausted," Etta said dully.

"I believe it," Mr. Nash's voice was soft with sympathy.

Etta and Mr. Nash walked down into the poorest parts of Brandon quietly. Etta couldn't bring herself to talk anymore.

Exhaustion wore at her. She pressed her fingertips to the blue cameo at her throat, knowing she had to sell it. With a broken-down car and the final rent owed to Santini, there was no choice.

"I have to stop here." Etta hesitated as she pushed open the door into the pawnbroker.

"What is this place?" Mr. Nash looked over the dirty store-front and frowned in concern.

"They exchange money for jewellery and other odds and ends." Etta's heart weighed low in sadness as she unfastened the blue cameo at her throat.

"What are you exchanging?" Mr. Nash's eyebrows rose as he followed Etta into the dark shop.

An old man shuffled to the counter.

Etta placed her grandmother's cameo on the glass display case. "What will you give me for this?"

The old man held the cameo in his tobacco-stained fingers. He turned it over then placed it back down and named a low price.

Etta shook her head and stiffened her spine as she asked for enough money to pay Santini the next day.

The pawnbroker frowned.

"Etta, you don't have to sell this. I can add this—" Mr. Nash sputtered in protest.

"You know it's worth at least double that price." Etta ignored Mr. Nash and held her ground.

The old man scratched at the stubble on his chin, nodding once. He handed her the money. Etta turned to leave when she saw her art supplies still in a display case by the front window. The man running the shop had given her a low price because he couldn't imagine anyone who would want secondhand art supplies. He was right. There they sat, gathering dust.

She caught her breath as she went over to them and picked up her brushes.

"Were those yours?" Mr. Nash asked quietly.

Etta placed her brushes back and stepped away. "Yeah, but I had a set of watercolours that have sold," she said dully. "All the art supplies are... were... mine."

Mr. Nash shot Etta a look of sympathy.

"No need for pity. It's done. This is life. This is post-war new normal, right?" Etta straightened up. "I live a block from here."

Mr. Nash nodded.

Together they left the pawnshop.

"Are you sure it's safe down here for you?" Mr. Nash watched soldiers with hard eyes, grasping bottles in brown paper, stumble down the street. "This looks terrible, Miss Lynne. I don't think I should leave you here."

"I lived here for six months." Etta pulled out the key to her apartment and unlocked the door to the lobby.

* * *

NASH HELD his breath as he walked her through a lobby smelling of cabbage and urine. He grimaced as the screams of children were heard through the door of an apartment. He followed Etta down a dark and dingy hallway to get to a stairway. A soldier stumbled toward them. Nash didn't like the way he looked at Etta; how his eyes travelled over her. Nash moved her so his body partially protected her as he narrowed his eyes at the soldier. The soldier's eyes flicked over Nash as if sizing him up and then shuffled away.

Up the stairs they went to the third floor. Etta placed her key in the lock but didn't turn it. Nash couldn't stand the stench from the hallway. He yearned to pull his collar up over his nose.

How does anyone live like this?

Etta turned to face him.

Nash hoped her apartment didn't smell like the hallway. He couldn't leave her here in this hovel. No woman should live like this. Revulsion crawled around his stomach.

"I'd rather not show you how bad this apartment is." Her eyes flicked up to his and then dropped. "I am deeply ashamed that this is how we live. You've delivered me safe to the door. Please leave me now."

Nash watched as Etta kept her gaze on the floor. Another soldier made his way down the hallway toward them. The hallway was so narrow Nash had to plaster himself against the wall so the man, who also leered at Etta, could pass.

"I don't care what your apartment looks like. You are not staying here alone. This is not safe." A rising panic at leaving her here roared through Nash. Leaving a woman defenseless and helpless against all these men who roamed up and down the hallways was unthinkable.

"As I said before, I lived here for months," Etta said dully. "I'm exhausted, and I just want to wash my face and go to bed. I can't take another step."

"I'll see you safely in. This place is... it is just..." Nash struggled not to offend her.

Etta lifted her chin. She had a hard glint in her eye as she spoke. "It was the best we could do."

"I know." Nash's heart fell to his feet. "Please, let me see you in. There may be someone in there ready to pounce."

"Fine." Etta relented, turning the key in the lock, opening the door to the apartment.

Her shoulders slumped, and her cheeks burned with embarrassment.

"What is it?" Nash asked.

"Cali piled the clothes for delivery with the address pinned to each pile. I will have to iron all this before I drop it off."

"She's not coming back to work. Who cares if it's ironed?" Nash looked at the mountain of laundry in dismay.

Etta slumped down into a rickety old settee that looked like it was on the verge of splitting apart.

He looked from the laundry to the art hanging on the walls of the apartment. "Oh my!" Nash exclaimed. "Did you do... is this artwork yours?"

"Yes."

"Miss Lynne... this is beautiful." Nash stood by a painting of Cali in a field of flowers. Nash tilted his head to the side and studied it. "You are very talented..."

Etta shrugged. "I don't know. I'm not trained. I always feel inferior because of it..."

"You shouldn't. This is really amazing."

"Well, I don't know." Etta shrugged. "I am really tired. I need to sleep… I have so much to do tomorrow."

"We could return it un-ironed with a note of explanation," Nash suggested.

"No, I can't. When we come back here, she'll need these contacts. I'll do it." Etta unbuttoned her jacket.

"It'll take all day." Nash looked over the piles of laundry.

"I don't have to be at the school until Monday morning. I'll finish her work."

Nash sighed. "I'll be back as soon as your car is ready tomorrow. We'll take—" Nash checked the bedroom for more furniture. "Is this furniture yours?"

"No. It was here when we moved in."

"So, just clothes, your artwork, and what else?"

"Cali's clothes and a few other things."

"What about dishes?"

"Nash." Etta pulled off her shoes, lay down on the settee, and let out a weary sigh. "There isn't a thing here I want. The dishes are all secondhand. I'm too tired. I'm just going to leave them. Honestly, I can't think of it right now. I can't take any more today."

Nash stood by Etta. "Come on. Get up and crawl into a bed."

"This is my bed."

"You can't be serious!" Nash gasped.

Etta curled into a ball on the settee.

"The bed in that room smells terrible. I can't bear it. Nash, I can't fight with you." Etta's voice sounded raw with pain.

Nash heard the unmistakable crack in her voice showing that she was trying hard not to cry.

"I am staying here." She pulled pins out of her hair and dropped them on the floor by the settee. "I will sleep now. I am numb and tired."

"This is appalling." Nash couldn't hide the disgust in his tone. He roamed around, making sure all the windows were locked. "The men of your family should have made provisions for you."

"Well, they didn't," Etta mumbled wearily from the settee.

"But they should have," Nash insisted.

Etta's eyes snapped open, and she sat up to face him. She

dragged her fingers through her hair as she spoke. "Men should do a lot of things, like let a woman sleep if she is tired, but they don't!"

"I'm serious, Miss Lynne. This isn't right." Nash turned on his heel to face her.

"I'm serious, too. My parents couldn't cope." Etta dragged her hands through her hair so it settled down around her shoulders, making her look Grace's age.

"What happened?" Nash dragged a chair to sit in front of her and hear the entire tale.

Etta slumped in front of him and launched into the tale. "My father had a drinking and gambling problem all our lives. That's why I was sent to be a teacher. My mother insisted that I would look after her. My brother would float around, he was always shiftless, and my sister would get married. That was the plan. Anyway. The war happened, my brother died, and the gambling flared up. Father lost his mind with grief. My mother pretended everything was all right as he gambled and drank *every penny*. Cali's husband died of the Spanish flu. His family had nothing. Well, one of his brothers is very wealthy, and we asked for help, but no one responded to the letters, so here we are. We are on our own. Cali's war widow's pension is an insult." Etta's tone frosted with ice. "She takes in washing and does repairs on clothes. I was working in a laundry before I came to Oakland."

"What about the proceeds of the house?" Nash rubbed his temple, trying to make sense of this lack of care and concern Etta's father had extended her.

"I sold the house to pay his gambling debts, Mr. Nash." Etta's eyes were dull and flat. "Even good men can turn in the face of insurmountable grief. You do not understand how the world works for women."

The blood drained from Nash's face. "What do you mean?"

"When the bookies came after us, they took everything." Etta's arms dropped at her side.

"Bookies!" Nash gasped, his chest tightening in fear for her.

"There was nothing we could do. They didn't listen to any pleading. They stripped us of everything, including our dignity." Etta shook her head, her hair streaming down around her.

Panic tightened Nash's chest. "Did they hurt you?"

"They would have." Etta kept her gaze steady on his. "If I hadn't made enough on the sale of the house, I don't know how far they would have gone. Thankfully, there was enough, and I haven't seen them since I paid them."

"And now?" Nash could barely get the words out.

"I sold my grandmother's cameo. I have enough for the rent." Etta shrugged.

"Miss Lynne, I have never... I didn't know." Nash stumbled to find something to say that would comfort her, ease her pain.

"So, you great, thick fool, do you see why I am passionate about educating girls? Sometimes men don't do the right thing, and here they are. Left in a hovel like this. I am tired. I have ironing to do tomorrow, and I need to rest. I am on the verge of tears. Please. I don't want to cry in front of you."

Etta lay down, dismissing him.

Nash stood up. He looked around helplessly. "You are not staying here. That is final. I'll take you to a hotel, and we can come back tomorrow."

"Nash, I am not going to a hotel with you," she murmured wearily.

"You would have your own room. In fact, I could stay at a different hotel just in case it looked improper! Please. I can't in good conscience leave you here." Nash was reduced to pleading.

"Where do you think I'll be when my term is up and a soldier takes my place?" Etta shot him a cold look and then closed her eyes again.

Nash's stomach twisted with guilt and anguish at her statement.

Etta was speaking the truth.

A truth he hadn't been aware of.

His heart seized at the thought of her returning here with Cali and a baby.

Quietly, Nash went to the bedroom and brought Etta a pillow to tuck under her head. The pillow had a sour smell. He pulled off his sweater and draped it over the top so she would smell his clean sweater.

"Thank you," she murmured.

IN THE COMPANY OF MEN

Nash draped his coat over her and then a foul-smelling blanket. He tucked her in with great care, promising himself that Etta Lynne was never, ever going to suffer in poverty another day. Not one more day.

He knelt down in front of her. "Miss Lynne, if you won't come with me, let me stay here. I'll sleep on the floor across the threshold of the door in case someone tries to break in."

Etta slid her eyes shut. "I need to cry. Alone. Please, this is nothing new to me. I am exhausted. Tomorrow is a trialsome day. I need to rest."

Nash sighed deeply. A piece of hair had caught in her eyelashes. He gently reached out and smoothed her hair away. She sighed as he stroked her face. Her skin was impossibly soft under his fingertips. "I will be back first thing," Nash promised.

"You'll be cold without your sweater and your coat..." She blinked up at him.

"I'll be just fine. I want to give you..." Nash caught himself. *Everything. Everything I have.*

"Whatever you need to get through this..." Nash finished lamely.

"I'll never get through this." Etta closed her eyes.

She didn't have any hair caught in her eyelashes this time, but Nash smoothed her hair away from her face anyway in an attempt to lend some sympathy and comfort before he left.

Etta didn't open her eyes as he carefully locked the apartment and then made his way down the narrow hallways.

Danger lurked in every shadow; Nash was sure of it. The promise of a threat in the eye of every soldier that passed him made his chest tighten with fear for her. The men looked at him, and their gazes slid away. They noticed his watch, looked for the bulge of a wallet, but then noticed the wide breadth of his shoulders. They knew he wouldn't hand over a penny without a fight. The look he shot at the impoverished men was fierce. He yearned to drag Etta out of this horrific place; to make sure she was safe. Nash knew how to fight, but he didn't know how to be with a woman like Etta, who insisted on fighting her own battles. There, he was at a complete loss. His typical 'take charge and take over' attitude was met with stony, vicious opposition.

The poverty Miss Lynne had endured hadn't broken her; it had made her fierce.

He should not care so much.

But he did.

He thought of leaving her up there on a broken settee with stuffing coming out of the fabric; his stomach turned. The door had only one lock, and anyone could put a shoulder to it and it would collapse.

How do I make her see sense? I want to help! She's impossible!

Nash fumed about that for a minute as he thought about bookies coming after her when her father died. He reflected on the thought of crushing her dream to care for parents who should have cared for themselves — and her. His stomach twisted at the thought of being left destitute because of a stupid gambling addiction.

Slowly, Nash realized with startling clarity that Miss Lynne fought him because she didn't trust him. She had to take care of her father since her father hadn't taken care of her. All men were painted with the same brush.

She hasn't the foggiest idea of how to depend on a man. Miss Lynne thinks if she depends on me, I will let her down. She does not understand that I would protect her with my last breath.

Nash was shocked as that thought bolted through his head.

Why am I thinking like this? She is not the woman for me! She is independent, outspoken, unreasonable, forward thinking! Not like Nell, not like any woman I know!

Yes, she is all those things, but she is tender with Grace. She cares about Grace like she is her mother.

The thought was like a kick straight to Nash's heart. The way Etta cared for Grace during the appendicitis and feminine complaint situation was beyond endearing.

Nash's thoughts turned to Grace, and for the first time in his life, he worried about Grace being let down in a similar manner. He worried his beautiful, bright daughter might end up with a shiftless man and end up in a horrible place like this.

Maybe Miss Lynne had a point.

Maybe men didn't always do the right thing. Maybe they had

good intentions until a war shattered their peace and prosperity and they cracked under the pressure.

Like me, if I'm being honest.

Relying on drink to chase the horrors of war away. To numb the pain of what I saw, what I lost. Am I really any different? Sure, I'm not drinking my money away, but I'm judging her father pretty harshly. I'm not innocent here either. The war changed me, too...

Nash held his breath as he walked by a wet spot on the carpet by the door.

Urine.

Quickly, he pushed open the door to the street and took a deep gulp of fresh air.

Nash leaned against the brick wall and contemplated sleeping at her door, in the hallway to make sure she was safe. He couldn't bear Etta to be up there, alone and vulnerable.

She would hate that. He was certain.

Nash vowed, on the grimy pavement where three men had hats they held out for change and openly drank whiskey from bottles, Etta would never face this vulnerability again. If he had to plant her a field, he would do it.

No.

Etta would hate that. She didn't want a handout. She didn't want charity.

Neither would he.

She didn't want fields and money from him.

The startling thought hit Nash right between the eyes.

Miss Lynne wanted to make her own way.

What was the word for that? Independence? Self reliance? Words he had never associated with a woman, he associated with her. Yes, Miss Lynne wanted to make her own way.

How do I empower her when I can just give her whatever she needs, and it would save us all a lot of time and energy?

Nash wracked his brain, yet nothing came to mind.

Slowly, a gleam of a thought slipped through his mind.

Mrs. Hartwell owns a business, and maybe Mr. Hartwell doesn't allow it. Maybe he *encourages* it.

The thought was a revelation.

I'll talk to Mrs. Hartwell, and I will figure this out. She'll know!

Trust or no trust, Miss Lynne would not live like this one more day. He was stepping in, and he didn't know what the answer was, but he knew there must be one. He was certain Mrs. Hartwell, Mrs. Bennett, and if worse came to worst, Mrs. Holt, could steer him in the right direction. If he had to interview every woman in Oakland to sort this out, he would—forthwith!

CHAPTER 21

*W*eary with sadness and head aching from crying half the night, Etta dragged herself off the settee and stoked the stove so she could make coffee. She stuck her tongue out at Cali's wretched iron. As the coffee percolated on the stove, she put the iron on the hot surface to heat. She looked out over the train tracks that ran by Pacific Avenue. She marvelled at how her heart beat even though it was broken.

For a moment she thought about what life was like before the war. Her throat ached with tears as she remembered happy times before the Great War broke them to pieces.

Etta straightened and shook those thoughts aside. She refused to wallow. There was no time for that.

She poured coffee into her mug and returned to the window. She allowed herself five minutes to weep; then there was a ton of ironing to do. Etta drained the last of her coffee, filled her cup again, and started on the biggest pile of laundry. She placed the other iron on the hot surface of the oven to heat while she worked.

She sipped coffee as she ironed. She wrote a polite note to tuck into each package of clean, ironed laundry. She explained that Cali was indisposed and would be in touch when she could work again. Etta took a break after two piles and eyed the remaining six with derision.

One more pile done, and there was banging on the door.

She checked her watch — nine o'clock in the morning. She'd been working for three hours.

It must be Mr. Nash. Gracious, he's a worrywart.

Mr. Nash had been very kind yesterday, and Etta didn't know how she felt about that. Drawn to him and repelled by his thinking at the very same time. Etta felt confused.

Etta opened the door and gulped when she saw Santini standing on the other side of the door.

"I think you're moving out without paying. I notice no sister, no mother, only you in fancy clothes with a fancy man."

"Mr. Santini, we are leaving today, but I have your money." Etta took a step back to find her purse. She opened her wallet and pulled out the money.

Santini's predatory eyes swept over her before he turned his attention back to the money she handed him. "Miss Lynne, this is not enough."

* * *

NASH, clutching two irons and an ironing board, held his breath as he moved through the terrible lobby and started up the stairs to Miss Lynne's apartment when he heard shouting and screaming. His heart stopped, and he began taking the stairs two at a time.

His gut twisted when he saw Miss Lynne's apartment door hanging open.

Something inside him snapped when he heard Miss Lynne's cry of fear. Dropping his supplies in the hallway, he raced inside.

"That's all the money I have. I..." Nash heard Miss Lynne plead with a huge, sweaty, greasy man.

"I told you last time, there are other ways to pay." The man lunged at Miss Lynne.

Nash watched in horror as he grabbed her.

Nash leaped across the room and dragged the man off of Miss Lynne. He heard roaring in his ears as he defended himself against the big man's attack.

Finally, Nash dragged him out of Miss Lynne's apartment.

"Did he hurt you?" Nash demanded as he slammed the door shut on the vile man.

"No." She shook her head. "You got here just before..."

Nash pulled her against him.

Miss Lynne shook with fear as he tightened his arms around her.

"It's all right now. He can't hurt you now." Nash stroked her face so gently, she blinked in surprise.

As her eyes continued to fill with tears, Nash tenderly pulled her tighter into his embrace.

His heart broke while she cried like a little child.

"He was going to—" Miss Lynne's voice, muffled by his shirt, cracked with emotion.

"I know, darling." Nash pressed his hand against the back of her head to hold her against him.

"I can't stop crying." Her anguish escalated.

He held her so tight he hoped he wasn't hurting her. "I know, and it's all going to be all right. I promise," he whispered against her neck. "I'm going to..." Nash stopped and rephrased his statement. "Miss Lynne, we will figure this out together."

Miss Lynne quieted down in his arms. She pulled back just a little.

Nash settled her against his dry shoulder. She pressed her face into him as she shuddered. Slowly, she regained control. She stopped weeping; she stopped trembling. He heard her take a deep breath and let it out slowly. Finally, she spoke.

"Thank you for pulling the landlord off of me. I was terrified." Her voice, when it wasn't shredding him into ribbons, was very soft.

"Thank you for explaining menstruation to Grace. I was terrified," Nash said to break the tension.

Miss Lynne made a noise that was almost a chuckle. "Are we even, then?" She pulled back a little to look at him. Her eyes were red and wet; she needed a handkerchief. He pulled a fresh one out of his breast pocket and handed it to her.

"I'm not keeping score," Nash said softly.

She pulled back a little farther, cleaned up her face, and then looked up at him.

"I'd drag a hundred men off you, and I wouldn't even think twice." Nash's gaze locked with hers.

Miss Lynne opened her mouth to speak and then clamped it shut.

"Finally! Speechless." Nash grinned.

"Don't get used to it." Miss Lynne smiled back.

Sadness still haunted her eyes.

I never want to see this kind of sadness in your eyes, ever again.

Finally, reluctantly, he released her. "I'll get my supplies. We've got a lot of work to do here."

Miss Lynne looked at him nervously as he opened the door. The landlord was gone. He heard her let out a long sigh of relief. After retrieving his iron and ironing board, he re-entered the apartment.

"Mr. Nash!" Miss Lynne gasped again.

"What?" Nash opened the ironing board.

"What are you doing?" Miss Lynne's eyes widened in surprise.

"Ironing. What does it look like?" Nash placed his irons to heat at the stove beside hers. "What sort of material?"

Miss Lynne stood in the hovel, and her mouth opened, but no words came out.

"Miss Lynne, cotton? Linen? What are we ironing?"

"You are going to… iron?" Miss Lynne could barely get the words out.

"If I knew what sort of material, yes, I will iron. You thought I would leave all this for you?" Nash frowned at her.

"Well… I didn't think… I don't know what to think!" Miss Lynne sputtered

"What kind of man do you think you are dealing with?"

"I don't know, I've never… dealt with… a…" Miss Lynne visibly straightened her shoulders. "I don't know what to say."

"We'll iron and deliver, pack up your things, and then get the details of the funeral settled. I'm taking you home." Nash added more coal to the fire and waited for her reply. "The only variable I'm missing is what sort of fabric. I am guessing cotton, but this really isn't my field of expertise. If it's cotton, it needs to be as hot as possible, right?"

"But you don't know... I'm certain you can't possibly... know... how..." Miss Lynne tried to formulate the sentence and failed.

"Now, that is very narrow-minded, Miss Lynne!" Nash exclaimed. "I expected better than that! I iron my shirts. I had to learn when my wife died! I have a few skills."

"But I thought Grace..."

"No. I do all my ironing. Material identification, please. Darling, we don't have all day."

"Darling!" Miss Lynne's jaw dropped in shock as the word 'darling' hung in the air between them.

"Oops. That slipped out. Miss Lynne, what is the fabric? Please. This will take forever if I have to guess." Nash looked at her expectantly.

"Linen." Miss Lynne shook her head at him. "So, very hot... I never expected you knew what an iron was, never mind how to use one!" She laughed.

Nash liked the sound of her laugh.

"Well, I do." Nash tested the heat of the iron by licking his fingertip and tapping it against the face of the iron. "We can't be here all day. We must get to work."

Miss Lynne picked up a pile of laundry and placed it on a broken chair by his ironing board. "I've never been called darling in my life," she murmured.

"Really." Nash held his breath as Miss Lynne straightened and stood right in front of him.

"Look. We've got some fundamental differences. We disagree on most things—" Miss Lynne took a deep breath and let it out slowly. "But before we go any further here, no matter what happens after today, I will never, ever, in my life, ever forget the kindness you have shown here today."

Nash's heart pounded at the sincerity of her words. He shrugged the emotion away. "Any man would..."

"No, Mr. Nash. I'm fairly certain, in my limited experience, mind you, not all men would." Miss Lynne looked up at him; he saw sincerity in her eyes.

With that, she turned and went to her ironing board. She picked up a lacy unmentionable that made Nash's mouth dry.

He pulled his gaze away from the lace underpinning and concentrated on placing the shoulder of a man's shirt on the narrow end of the ironing board.

"You're doing this with me?" Miss Lynne's eyebrows shot up as he slid the iron across the linen shirt.

"I told you, I will help. I'll do the men's clothes. I don't know how to iron that." Nash nodded at the wisp of lace in her hand.

A few minutes of quiet ironing later, a grin tugged at her lip. "What did it feel like to hit him?"

"It felt very satisfying," Nash admitted as he folded the shirt and then started on another one. "Next time, I'll hold him, and you can take a swing."

"Does it hurt your hand?" Miss Lynne tilted her head to the side as she asked the question.

"Of course not. I hardly felt it at all." Nash grinned as he lied through his teeth.

"It hurts?" Miss Lynne tilted her head to the side.

"A lot. I was pretending to be tough," Nash admitted as he carefully pressed the collar flat before folding the shirt.

Miss Lynne laughed at that. "I'm sorry."

Nash shrugged. "Not the first time, won't be the last."

"I hope it is the last, where I am concerned." Miss Lynne swallowed hard.

Nash's gaze met hers. "You're independent, I get it. But any threat to you, I will deal with it from now on."

Miss Lynne's eyes widened slightly. "What do you want in return?"

"Nothing," Nash said as he dragged another shirt onto the ironing board. "There is no catch. I don't require anything to protect a woman, any woman. So, rest assured, not a thing."

Miss Lynne nodded slightly, a minute bow of her head to acknowledge that she accepted this proposal, this new normal, between them.

They worked together quietly, just the sound of irons sliding over fabric interrupting their thoughts.

"Oh, this is just lovely!" Miss Lynne held a beautiful lace nightgown up against her body.

Nash's eyes locked with hers across the dingy, depressing, terrible room that even her beautiful pieces of art couldn't cheer up. "Miss Lynne, you are not ironing with your grandmother, let's keep this professional. Don't start something you don't mean to finish," he growled.

Miss Lynne's eyes widened in shock as she dropped the nightgown onto the ironing board. She took her cooled iron to the stove and replaced it with a hot one.

Five minutes clicked by, and Miss Lynne finally spoke. "We should talk about this." She finished the nightgown and picked up another one.

"No. We should iron in peace," Nash groaned.

"We are still opposed in so many ways," Miss Lynne reprimanded him. "We should be clear."

"No, we should not. We should iron." Nash frowned at her.

Etta concentrated as she laid a skirt on her board. "Are we... because we can't."

"We are ironing together and dealing with a tragedy. That's all this is," Nash lied to both of them.

"Because if this is something different, I need to be very clear... we disagree about Grace." Miss Lynne stopped ironing and sipped her coffee.

"So noted." Nash's tone was clipped as he dragged another shirt onto his ironing board.

"It means a lot to me that you understand I can't proceed with you if her education... well... Mr. Nash." Miss Lynne stood her iron up on its heel.

Nash gave his iron a moment to cool slightly. "We're ironing. We are not renegotiating the terms of this relationship, such as it is, today."

Miss Lynne picked up the raciest piece of unmentionable either of them had ever seen. She caught a look in his eye and then immediately dropped it on the ironing board. "Right."

Nash pressed the sleeves of a shirt. "Besides, I think you will eventually agree to my thoughts about Grace's education in due time."

She scowled at him. "I won't."

Nash stopped, folded the shirt, and then put his iron down. He moved around the ironing board and stood in front of hers.

Miss Lynne looked up with alarm.

Nash's gaze softened in sympathy. "You don't ever need to look at me with a hint of fear. I will never hurt you."

"I know. It's just you look a bit wild, honestly." Miss Lynne bit her lip.

Nash rubbed the stubble at his jaw. "Look, can we just call a truce today? All this fighting is exhausting. I saved you from your terrible landlord. Can that buy me one day of peace? Please?" Nash begged.

Miss Lynne sighed. "One day of peace. It's a deal."

Nash returned to his ironing board.

She placed a woman's blouse on her board. "I expect to get my way about Grace, though. Just so we're clear."

Nash threw back his head and laughed. "Miss Lynne, Etta... I think you expect your way on most things."

CHAPTER 22

$\mathcal{A}$fter picking up the car and returning the laundry, Etta braced herself to complete the details surrounding her mother's funeral. She hated to bury her alone without Cali. Thankfully Mr. Nash would stand by her. She peeked at him out of the corner of her eye as they waited for the funeral director. His face was covered in stubble as he hadn't anticipated staying the night. He held a newspaper between very broad, strong hands. She noticed his knuckles were bruised from hitting Santini. His nose was a little crooked; she wondered who had hit him. His dark, intelligent eyes skimmed over the news quickly. When the door opened, he looked up at her.

"Everything all right, Miss Lynne?"

Etta nodded.

Together they stepped into Mr. Marsh's cramped office. Etta struggled to figure out the most inexpensive way to bury her mother. After they hammered out a deal, her chest tightened as she picked up the final invoice. The amount, stark in black and white, was impossible to pay without support from the municipality. Her stomach twisted at the final number. Nothing left to sell but the car, and she needed it.

Mr. Marsh looked at her expectantly.

"Could we have a moment before she signs anything?" Mr. Nash asked the funeral director.

He nodded and slipped out of his office, giving them privacy. Mr. Nash turned to Etta. He placed a hand on her shoulder.

"I don't know how to stand back and not intervene. I am doing it wrong. So be it. Let me add this bill to the widow's fund. Please, don't do the most inexpensive things..." Mr. Nash begged her.

"Mr. Nash, what if they decline it?" Etta's face paled with worry. "It will take me years to pay this off. I have to do the best I can with what I have."

"But you have nothing else to sell..." Mr. Nash rubbed his eyebrow and then scrubbed his hands over his face.

"I'm going with the most inexpensive funeral. I am already a huge burden to the municipality as it is." Etta's heart ached with anxiety as she spoke.

"This is your mother's funeral, and I really want to help you..." Mr. Nash begged.

Etta dropped her gaze to the floor. "Mr. Nash, it seems wrong to take it. It makes me feel bad."

Tenderly, Mr. Nash reached out and gently placed his fingertips under her chin to encourage her to look up at him. "I want to do this for you. Please let me. Choose the funeral you want."

"The municipality might decline this bill, and then it is all on you to pay... the least expensive option is the best way." Etta met his sympathetic gaze. "It doesn't matter which coffin. It's going in the ground, and only you and I will see it."

"I don't want you to have any regrets." Mr. Nash took his hand away.

Etta nodded. "Thank you, but I won't regret it."

Etta signed her name at the bottom of the invoice with the most inexpensive funeral plan. "This is good enough."

Etta added a little flourish to the E at the end of her name and then stopped.

Detective Kane was right. Women did often add that little flourish. Even now, devastated from losing her mother and facing a bill she couldn't pay, there it was. A pretty swoop at the end of the E in her last name.

Why do we add that flourish? I always have and never noticed.

She shrugged that off. Who cared about swoops in writing?

Mrs. Ellice must have run away from the dreadful Mr. Spicer, and she would turn up eventually. Likely, she had suffered a breakdown. She had lost her husband so suddenly and then, in desperation, taken the first job she could find. If you added Mr. Spicer and his petticoat inspections to an already fragile situation, who wouldn't run in the night?

Detective Kane had probably found her, and the police would call the search off before they got home to Oakland. Etta had enough on her plate; she couldn't worry about everyone. She placed the pen down beside the invoice and leaned back in her chair.

Mr. Marsh stepped back in. He picked up the invoice and looked at Mr. Nash. "We need to be paid in full before the burial. It's just the two of you? No minister?"

Etta's head snapped up in horror. "What?"

"Miss Lynne, we are burying your mother today; it is very rushed. We need to square this up now." Mr. Marsh sat down and pulled out a tin box containing change.

Etta swallowed hard as she turned to Mr. Nash. "I have the money from Cali's deliveries..."

"We'll sort that out in the car on the way home," Mr. Nash suggested gently.

Etta knew Mr. Nash would not take a penny from her in the car. He was trying to take as much of the sting of humiliation away as possible. His eyes searched hers before he pulled out his wallet, as if asking permission to do what came so naturally to him. Writing a bank note and taking care of this on her behalf.

Etta brushed a tear away as she nodded her consent.

She watched in shame as Mr. Nash wrote the full amount. He knew she couldn't pay any of it.

Her eyes welled with tears as she watched him sign his name.

No flourishes.

Straight black lines promising a number she would have to pay back in installments if the council declined the invoice. Installments that would keep her indebted to him for years. Mentally, she added up the amount of the bill for the hospital and the mechanic and now this. Her shoulders slumped in defeat.

Etta knew Jackson Nash was an old-fashioned man. He was rough around the edges, but he was a good man. If they could ever put their differences aside, she would never be left destitute. Never. He would make provisions for anyone he married, but at what price? Would he expect docile obedience from her? Or would he treat her with dignity? Would he expect her to influence Grace to give up her dreams?

What did men like Jackson Nash really expect in return?

Etta's face burned with humiliation as she watched him hand over the bank note, with a number on it that would cripple her financially, without thinking twice. He stood up and shook the funeral director's hand, indicating the meeting was over.

"You can meet us here." The funeral director handed a map to Mr. Nash. "I suggest you have a bite to eat, and then we will meet at this grave site at two pm."

Etta's throat tightened on a fist of salty tears as Mr. Nash took the paper telling them where to go at two pm.

When the funeral director opened the door to his office, Etta stood up. Mr. Nash immediately placed his hand on her lower back to guide her out of the office and into the car.

"Thank you for paying that bill." Etta swallowed her pride and spoke politely as Mr. Nash navigated them through the city.

"You're welcome." Mr. Nash shot a look at her and spoke cautiously, as if this were a test he might fail. "Where would you like to eat?"

"I don't think I can." Etta closed her eyes and wished she could sleep for an hour.

"Are you sure there is no one you could call to be with you? Friends you used to work with?"

"No. I just want to get this done and get back to town before I'm fired and in a worse situation than I am already."

Mr. Nash nodded sympathetically.

* * *

ETTA STOOD by the graveside as the men lowered her mother into the earth. If the men wondered why there was no one else there, they didn't say anything. Mr. Nash slid his arm around her and held her tight until the burial was over.

Just like that, her mother was put to rest. Etta yearned for Cali to be with her.

As Etta wept, Mr. Nash pulled her tighter.

"We're all done here, miss." One of the men had taken his hat off before he spoke to her.

"Thank you." Etta nodded as she stepped away from the grave.

"Do you want a moment before we finish?"

"No. Thank you. I... we best be going." Etta wiped at her tears and returned to the car with Mr. Nash.

Etta stopped just before getting into the passenger seat. She took a deep breath of icy-cold, early-spring air. She yearned for green grass and leaves on the trees. The ugly landscape was raw and stark. Dirt darkened the melting snow around the grave. Etta wished the day was pretty... but it wasn't.

Crawling into the passenger side of the car, Etta sighed as they left the city. As freezing rain poured down, she worried about getting stuck in mud on the prairie. She fought to keep her eyes open and failed. On the outskirts of the city she nodded off, only to wake up with her head on Mr. Nash's shoulder.

"Oh! I fell asleep!"

"I don't mind." Mr. Nash smiled at her. "That was a long day. I'm glad you could get some rest." Mr. Nash turned his attention back to the muddy road.

"Yes." Etta smoothed her hair back from her face.

"Are you feeling all right?" Mr. Nash looked over at her again.

Etta swept her hair up and into a bun. She poked pins into her hair to put it in place. "I'm glad to be getting home."

"Me, too. I'd like to see Grace and be sure she is all right."

"She's in good hands. Lucy is a natural-born mother and nurturer. She couldn't be with anyone better. I hope she finds someone. She is such a good woman."

"Yes." Mr. Nash thought for a moment. "This is none of my business, but something I've been wondering about... you don't have to answer. Why didn't your mother expect you to get married? You never wanted marriage and family?" Mr. Nash turned to watch her as he asked the question.

"Marriage and children were never on the table. I was too busy looking after everyone who couldn't look after themselves," Etta said wearily. She placed the extra pins into her handbag and then folded her hands on her lap.

"You are a beautiful woman. Someone at some point..." Mr. Nash let the sentence trail away.

"Cali is beautiful. Beside her, I look like a wrung-out dishrag."

"I disagree."

"Well, according to my mother, I guess... at any rate, it is tricky to find a husband when your profession doesn't allow you to court." Etta stiffened as she defended her unmarried state.

"That's true. I keep forgetting about that. It is so ridiculous." Mr. Nash nodded in agreement.

"Well, it's the way it is." Etta shrugged and peered into the darkness. "Since the war, many who got married are widowed, so there was no security in that either."

"True. It's desperate." Mr. Nash navigated around a puddle of water in the road. "I keep worrying about the field. It might not be enough for all the widows, and Mrs. Lemon. What if her cut isn't enough for those taxes? It keeps me up at night, honestly." Mr. Nash rubbed his forehead as he thought. "It really would be the answer if she would consider marrying Lester Lemon. I know he's not everyone's favourite..."

"Jackson Nash!" Etta's jaw dropped open at the suggestion.

"Hear me out! He has a farm that would keep them both, and he is attracted to her."

"She is not attracted to him!" Etta growled at Mr. Nash.

"Maybe you could help her see him as a *sort* of suitor?" Mr. Nash asked hopefully. "Honestly. I worry..."

Etta couldn't believe her ears as the man she had ironed with turned back into an old-fashioned fuddy-duddy right before her eyes.

"You are unbelievable!" Etta squeaked in rage. "You can't figure this out, can you?"

"I am so sorry I brought this up. My apologies. I spoke out of turn... you are distraught about your mother."

"Mr. Nash, please be silent. Let me be clear once and for all."

Mr. Nash groaned.

"Don't you *dare*." Etta hissed. "Mrs. Lemon, and by extension the rest of the women whose lives were demolished from this war, who aren't leaping back into matrimony for various reasons — you don't know what to do with us. You have an ideal we can't fit. I feel sorry for you, Mr. Nash. I really do."

Mr. Nash looked at her, his eyebrows raised.

"You will suffer disappointment if you want things to go back to how they were before the war. Everything has changed. We must change, too." Etta crossed her arms over her chest as her body hummed with indignation.

"The war has changed *enough* things," Mr. Nash grumbled as he looked at her and then back to the road.

"I will fight with my last breath and protest at the top of my lungs if Lucy Lemon is forced into marriage to that creepy Lester. Absolutely not."

"It's just—"

"No. The answer is no."

"Etta, be reasonable. She will get married at some point..."

"To a man she loves! Not one she is *starved* into marrying!" Etta howled at Mr. Nash. "I will not even suggest she entertain the idea! My dear friend Lucy being led like a lamb to the slaughter and you want me to drag her."

"I just want her to think about the possibility..." Mr. Nash sputtered at the vehemence of her words.

"Never! I will never, ever, in this lifetime or the next, suggest Lucy Lemon with her bright spirit and her lovely heart be forced to marry anyone she is not madly in love with! No! And another thing — while we're discussing your wrong decisions — your treatment of Grace's education is a tragedy."

Mr. Nash groaned. "I should have kept my mouth shut!" He

cursed under his breath. "Listen, I've been giving that some thought." Mr. Nash stiffened beside her. "Regarding Grace. I want her to have a fulfilling life. Maybe she could think about being a teacher. I would pay for that."

"You are impossible!" Etta rubbed the tension in her forehead as Mr. Nash so easily dismissed Grace's dream of university.

"I thought you would be glad!" Mr. Nash sputtered. "Since I was in that hovel you were living in and had to defend your honour just hours before, if you remember. I've had a change of heart..." Mr. Nash trailed off as Etta's entire body stiffened in rage beside him.

Etta's fingernails bit into her palm. "She wants to go to university in Toronto, not normal school here!"

Mr. Nash groaned and muttered under his breath.

"I want her to have a normal and happy life!"

"She will be very happy in university!" Etta roared at him.

Mr. Nash opened his mouth to speak and then clamped it shut.

Oakland, late at night, was quiet on every street. Mr. Nash stopped the car at the train tracks so to anyone who was looking on, Etta would appear to be innocently walking home after being brought back by the train from Brandon. A few minutes of icy silence later, finally the train whistle blew. Etta had to walk home now so their scheme looked plausible.

"Thanks for the ride back to Oakland," Etta snapped at him as she fumbled with the door handle of the car. Etta felt her face redden with rage as her petticoats slowed her down. "Whatever we may have felt as we ironed... it's over."

"Etta, be reasonable."

"If you say that again, I will scream!" Etta hissed at him as she grabbed her handbag on the way out of the car.

"Listen. I'll walk you home."

"No. You will not." Etta marched away from him.

Mr. Nash raced to catch up to her. He put his hand on her arm.

"Can we just call a truce for a minute? Hang on. That all

went badly…" Mr. Nash gently took her elbow. Etta jerked away from his touch.

"Take your hand off me." Etta wrenched her arm away from him and kept walking.

"Listen, please, I'm sorry."

"You need not apologize to me. You need to change your thinking and give your daughter some credit. She's brilliant! You must see that! She wants to go to a school of her chosing, and she should. Until you are prepared to see that possibility, we have nothing to say to each other. Leave me alone, and don't you dare think you'll walk me home. I have enough problems. Stay. Away. From. Me!" Etta fumed at him.

Moments later, just before Etta stepped foot on Main Street, she heard Mr. Nash behind her.

Furious, she turned around to face him.

"I told you to stay away from me." She pointed at him.

At that moment, the heavens opened up, and rain poured down in torrents.

"I'm not letting a defenseless woman walk home. Never," Mr. Nash growled at her.

"I don't want you following me."

"You are not walking alone at night by yourself. If something happened, I would never forgive myself. I'll see you safely to the door." Mr. Nash took long strides toward her.

"Do women get any say at all? Do you honestly believe that you are the ultimate authority?" Etta couldn't stop the words from tearing out of her.

"I have never, in my life, let a woman walk alone without protection after dark. I'm not about to start now just because we have had a silly row. There is a teacher still missing, I will remind you."

"Who is going to walk me home and keep me safe when I am back in the slums of Brandon?"

Mr. Nash's face went white.

"Who do you think has protected me until now?" Etta shot at him.

Mr. Nash took a very deep breath. "It scares me to have you

walking in Oakland at night when we still don't know what happened to Mrs. Ellice..."

"She probably saw sense and ran for the hills the first time Mr. Spicer came within five feet of her!" Etta shot at him.

Mr. Nash reached for her arm, and Etta sidestepped out of his reach again.

She walked a few steps before she rounded on him. "Your fundamentals of thought regarding women in society are archaic. Leave me. I'm safe on the streets of Oakland." Etta turned her back on him and kept marching down Main Street toward Willow Avenue.

"Miss Lynne." Mr. Nash boomed at her with a voice that was so commanding she stopped in her tracks. Mr. Nash spoke to her back. "Women require the protection of men at times, and you will have it. As you just saw this morning when I dragged that pig, Santini, off of you."

Etta's back stiffened in anger.

"Mrs. Ellice is still missing. No women out after dark without protection. That is an order."

Etta turned to look at him. Her jaw dropped open.

"You will not walk alone on the streets of Oakland without protection. That is not open for discussion." Mr. Nash's jaw clenched hard. He broadened his stance as he stood by her.

Etta's brain scrambled to formulate a sentence and failed.

"This is what men do. They protect women, and they provide for them. Until we know what happened to Mrs. Ellice, we are taking precautions, and we are well within our rights to do so."

"You are very high handed!" Etta finally gathered her outraged thoughts. "You think you can decide and I will do what I'm told."

"That is how it will go." Mr. Nash crossed his arms over his broad chest.

Etta stomped up to Mr. Nash until they stood toe to toe. She looked up at him. "Think again!"

Headlights swept over the road as a car turned toward them.

Etta's heart pounded in her throat as she took a step back,

worried that it was Mr. Spicer about to catch them in a compromising position.

The headlights illuminated them as the man slid out of the car to face them.

"Well, well, well." Mr. Spicer stood in front of them on the sidewalk.

Etta groaned.

"We can easily explain this." Mr. Nash held his hands up and then grabbed Etta's arm as she tried to bolt toward the Lemon house.

"Miss Lynne, in the company of men — again." Mr. Spicer checked his watch. "It is nearly midnight." Mr. Spicer shook his head. "I thought we would have no further concerns from you."

Etta pulled her arm out of Mr. Nash's grip. "Mr. Spicer, my mother died. I took the train home from Brandon. Mr. Nash is walking me home because he's worried I will face the same fate as Rose Ellice."

Mr. Spicer's face didn't change.

"You left the community without permission, and now here you are, with Mayor Nash... alone. No chaperone." Spicer tisked. "*In the company of men*, past eight o'clock in the evening. So many rules broken, Miss Lynne."

Burning fury made her chest tight and hot. In the company of men past eight o'clock in the evening was a death knell for her career. Etta couldn't stop the frustration as it pulsed through her. She stood toe to toe with Mr. Spicer and threw caution to the wind as she spoke. "Call a meeting, and I will plead my case. We have nothing to say to each other. I know a man who hates women when I see one. You will not intimidate me like Miss Ford, and I will not go running off like Mrs. Ellice. Do your worst. I will fight you every step of the way, and I won't stop until they fire you. I am not afraid of you. I am not afraid of anyone."

Mr. Spicer dropped his head and whispered in her ear. "Oh, Miss Lynne, you should be terrified ... what I could do to you..."

Etta took a step back as she saw the raw fury in his eyes.

He truly hated her, hated everything about her. Etta tried to figure out why. Madness? He despised women who stood up to him?

Etta lifted her chin and looked down her nose at him. Spicer's face twisted in anger.

He hates a show of strength.

"Step away from her, Mr. Spicer." Mr. Nash took a step forward and physically put himself between Etta and Mr. Spicer. "Any accusation should be made in front of the entire board of trustees. This is inappropriate."

Mr. Spicer stepped back. "What are you going to do, Nash? Beat me up? Start throwing punches on behalf of your girl?" Spicer sneered at Mr. Nash. "You're very protective of her. The school board has noticed. We believe that you are courting," Spicer accused him.

Etta's entire body stiffened at the insinuations spilling from Mr. Spicer's lips.

"Mr. Spicer, if you harass this woman, you will answer to me." Mr. Nash's hands balled into fists. He took a step closer to Mr. Spicer.

Mr. Spicer winced as he stepped back.

"Not because we are courting, but because she is in my community, and we do not permit the women of Oakland to be subjected to threats and violence. Go home. Forget this, as we will. You cause trouble from tonight... it will go badly for you."

"Don't you dare threaten me!" Mr. Spicer spat at Mr. Nash.

"I've only just begun," Mr. Nash shot back. "I believe you harassed Miss Ford and Mrs. Ellice by demanding they show you their petticoats. I will find Miss Ford, and I will interview her and have you thrown off the board for indecent behaviour. Won't that be ironic! You have been crowing about indecency, and all along, you have been inappropriate with the teachers of Oakland."

Mr. Spicer's head snapped up, the blood draining from his face. "Someone has to enforce the code!"

"Call that board meeting, and I'll be there, and I will expose you as the threat to these women you are." Mr. Nash faced down Mr. Spicer.

"You are no longer on the board... you can't..." Mr. Spicer sputtered.

"I'll go as a delegate." Mr. Nash took a step closer to Mr. Spicer. "I am well versed in the law, Mr. Spicer. Don't try my patience. I will expose you. So I'm not asking again. Go. Home." Mr. Nash broadened his stance further, battle ready, fists at his side. "Go home right now."

Mr. Spicer shot a furious look at Etta. He stalked to his car, threw open the door, and left them standing in the pouring rain on Main Street.

Etta pressed her lips together.

"I am going to the Manitoba Teachers' Federation about him first thing Monday morning. I am putting an end to this once and for all."

Mr. Nash moved closer to her. "Good. There is no precedent regarding this sort of inappropriate behaviour. Miss Ford likely won't talk; she'll want to save her career."

Etta took a step back; she looked up at him as she wiped rainwater from her face. "I will see myself home. I am in enough trouble."

"No. You will not." Mr. Nash held out his arm, and Etta shook her head.

Mr. Nash shrugged. "You're very independent, Miss Lynne."

"Dangerous quality to have here in Oakland," Etta shot at him as she started walking toward Willow Avenue.

Mr. Nash chuckled.

"What are you doing back there?" Etta finally turned to him.

"You don't want an escort home, but you are getting one." Mr. Nash's eyes burned with intensity in the streetlight.

"What do you think will happen to me?" Etta threw her hands up in the air in frustration.

"One missing teacher is quite enough." Mr. Nash jogged to catch up.

"I bet he threatened her, and she fled to save her career," Etta speculated.

"Maybe." Mr. Nash held his arm out.

Etta frowned up at Mr. Nash, rolled her eyes, and finally conceded and slipped her hand into the crook of his elbow.

"You are tenacious. I will give you that," Etta groaned.

"Is that so hard?" Mr. Nash grumbled under his breath.

"It looks like we are courting, although I was just insubordinate to the secretary treasurer so, whatever, they will have a list as long as their arms."

"It looks like I am seeing a defenseless woman home in a rainstorm," Mr. Nash corrected her again.

"Quit calling me a defenseless woman!"

"Santini— in your apartment— exhibit A!" Mr. Nash crowed.

They walked together in stony silence.

Etta fumed beside him for a moment and then remembered him ironing stacks of laundry, standing by her side as her mother was buried. She held out an olive branch. "Listen, before we get to Willow Avenue, I should say this."

"Yes?" Mr. Nash turned to face her. They stopped walking.

Etta tilted her head back to see him clearly. "I will send a letter to the council making sure they know how much I appreciate the money from the field."

"That would be nice."

"You heard about the pie box social? To raise funds? I am baking a chocolate pie, so be sure to bring cash. A lot of cash, and make sure you purchase it." Etta shivered as the rain soaked through her coat.

"How will I know which pie is yours?" Mr. Nash pulled off his jacket and placed it around her shoulders.

Etta snuggled into his jacket. "It's embarrassing."

"Try me," Mr. Nash said dryly.

Etta frowned up at him. "My pie crusts shrink."

Mr. Nash threw back his head and laughed.

Etta couldn't stop a smile from breaking across her face.

"They shrink?" Mr. Nash howled with laughter.

"Into oblivion." Etta sighed, burrowing deeper into his warm coat. "I have tried different pie plates, weighting the crust with beans, different thicknesses of pastry…"

Mr. Nash laughed so hard Etta couldn't stop herself from laughing with him. His laugh was contagious.

"It's hopeless, and I am certain no one will bid on my pie. It will disgrace me." Etta frowned.

Mr. Nash shook his head and turned to her. "I found that if I rolled my pastry too thin, and I didn't press it into the top of the pie plate firmly enough, my crusts would shrink, too."

"You never made a pie in your life." Etta's jaw dropped open in shock.

Mr. Nash laughed again. "You think so badly of men, Miss Lynne! I'm a widower. I've done many things I never expected to! I've been a soldier and had to assist in the kitchen. You might want to re-evaluate your thoughts about men. About me."

"Maybe that is true," Etta conceded.

"Good, we have an understanding. Now, in my experience, women, like pastry, respond to a firm hand." Mr. Nash grinned as he baited her.

"Firm hand!" Etta sputtered.

Mr. Nash took a step forward and pulled the lapels of his coat together tighter, to protect her from the driving rain. His voice deepened. "Yes. A firm hand is often necessary, in my experience."

"Well, Mr. Nash, since I've come to Oakland, I understand quite a few women are vying for the position of Mrs. Nash, so likely you *do* have lots of experience." Etta spoke imperiously. "You can take your firm hands elsewhere, sir."

"I do *not* have lots of experience." Mr. Nash contradicted her. Again. "That is untrue."

"Well, you better tell Mrs. Delaire because I am certain she has a china pattern picked out, and I have it on good authority that her pie crusts do not shrink. Ever."

"I have no interest in Mrs. Delaire or her perfect pie crusts. I can assure you of that." Mr. Nash's eyes searched hers. Gently, he brushed rainwater from her eyebrows and face. "You are getting soaked straight through. We should have just driven and taken our chances with Mrs. Daindridge and Mrs. Carr. I'm tired of all this nonsense."

"It is irritating. We look guilty even though we aren't," Etta agreed.

Mr. Nash stepped away from her and held out his arm again. Together, they walked in silence for a few moments.

"One other thing, before I forget, you should let Grace stay with us—" Etta stopped speaking as another set of headlights swept over them.

Etta and Mr. Nash leaped apart.

Mr. Nash turned to see who had followed them. He placed her firmly behind him as he waited for the driver to get out of the car. Etta's heart pounded with worry that Mr. Spicer had followed them with two witnesses this time for ironclad proof.

Constable Lark got out of the motorcar and sprinted toward them.

"Mr. Nash?"

"Yes?"

"Mr. Nash, we need a private word."

Etta's eyebrows shot up in surprise as Constable Lark looked from her to Mr. Nash.

"What is going on?" Mr. Nash demanded.

"I don't think we should speak of this in front of a lady." Constable Lark looked pointedly at Etta.

"It is all right. What is it?" Mr. Nash demanded.

"We found Mrs. Ellice's body this afternoon."

CHAPTER 23

$\mathscr{E}$tta felt Mr. Nash freeze beside her. "Body?"

"We are investigating, sir, but as mayor, I thought you should be the first to know. The medical examiner will have to rule on this, but it looks as though Mrs. Ellice was murdered, sir." Constable Lark dropped his tone of voice at the word murdered.

Etta didn't resist as Mr. Nash pulled her closer. "Murdered!"

"We suspect it was murder," Constable Lark confirmed. "There was a nasty gash on her forehead. We pulled her out of the river… it was terrible. With all the flooding…" Constable Lark shook his head. He flicked his gaze to Etta, clearly not comfortable discussing grisly details in front of a woman. "I'm not sure where she would have fallen in. The water is high… the current dragged her… well… we are searching in the morning, and Detective Kane is on his way back. The medical examiner is caught outside of Winnipeg. The main bridge is out, so he's coming on a detour the long way around. He has ordered her body to be left at Dr. Barrett's operating room with a guard. Mr. Holt is there now."

"She was billeted at Barlow's." Mr. Nash started firing orders. "Go straight there tonight to ensure no one enters her room and tampers with evidence. No one in or out of her room."

183

CAROLYN FINCH

"Yes, sir," Constable Lark agreed.

"I will see Miss Lynne safely home." Mr. Nash wiped rain off his forehead before it dripped into his eyes. "Every man will search for the crime scene, starting with the river banks. No women are to walk alone until further notice. Day or night. I'll go to the men tonight. Go now. To Barlow's."

The constable leapt in the police car and sped into the dark and stormy night.

Etta shuddered at the thought of someone murdering Mrs. Ellice.

Mr. Nash turned his attention to her. "You shivered. Are you cold or afraid?"

"Shocked, honestly. All this time, I thought she was just in hiding... this is tragic." Etta's gaze met his. His eyes were hard; he looked distracted.

"Let's get you home," Mr. Nash murmured as he pulled his coat tighter around her.

Etta tucked a wet strand of hair behind her ear and looked up at Mr. Nash. "This is..."

"Terrible," Mr. Nash finished for her. "Come on, it's time for you to be safely tucked into bed. I want you to be very careful."

Mr. Nash held out his arm.

Etta tucked her hand into his elbow, and together they made their way down Main Street to Mrs. Lemon's house. Thoughts of Mrs. Ellice being struck down on the seemingly peaceful streets of Oakland disturbed her. Long shadows cast by the streetlights suddenly didn't seem to shed enough light.

"Let's scoot around the back so we aren't seen." Etta tugged Mr. Nash into the darkness of the wooded path behind Lucy's house.

"Mrs. Daindridge and Mrs. Carr." Mr. Nash pushed a branch away from Etta's side of the path. "Surely they are both fast asleep."

"They never sleep." Etta groaned. "They are watching us constantly. Lucy says they are certain we are entertaining gentlemen callers at all times of day and night."

"They are terrible, aren't they?" Mr. Nash grumbled as he helped Etta sneak around to the back of the house.

184

Etta unlocked the back porch, and they stepped in out of the rain.

"Before I go, I wanted to thank you for your care and concern for Grace. I have a lot to do tonight, or I would stay here. I don't like you all here without protection." Mr. Nash looked out over the river and the creek.

"We'll lock everything," Etta promised.

"Please, tell Grace I will check on her as soon as I can tomorrow." Mr. Nash turned his attention back to her.

"Of course." Etta took his heavy coat off and returned it to him.

Mr. Nash shrugged back into his wet coat. "Whoever did this, did it near the river. Since you live right on the river, none of you are safe. While we look, would you ask Mrs. Lemon if she would consider serving the men who are searching, breakfast and lunch from her dining room?"

"Of course, we'll be happy to help."

"Just so we're clear. Don't even dream of leaving here without me," Nash instructed.

"I heard you the first time." Etta frowned at him.

"See that you remember." Mr. Nash's face hardened with warning. "You should get inside — you will catch a cold." Mr. Nash opened the back door to leave.

Etta bristled at his tone. "I understand your concern for our welfare. I appreciate it, but I am weary of being treated like one of your men. You are used to barking orders. I will not stand for it." Etta could barely get the words past her clenched teeth.

Mr. Nash groaned with frustration. "I don't have time for this."

"I am not a two-year-old, nor a soldier in your command." Etta's lips thinned in frustration.

"I'm keeping you safe. You'll get used to it." Mr. Nash turned to face her. Impatience stamped on his face, he was ready to get to work.

"I. Will. Not." Etta's body stiffened.

Mr. Nash broke the tension with a grin. "You'll come around. I will see you and Mrs. Lemon first thing tomorrow. The search will start here. I'll get Grace—"

185

Etta shivered. "Grace shouldn't be alone when you go to search tomorrow. She needs to be with women. I'm not faulting you. You have done a wonderful job with her, but let us keep her until this all settles down."

"You think I did a wonderful job?" Mr. Nash's eyebrows rose. He stood still, waiting for her answer.

Etta saw a glimmer of truth in Mr. Nash's eyes as he spoke. There was a crack in the façade of confidence. He loved Grace completely, and he worried that he failed her regarding her physical well-being.

"This whole... feminine complaint turned appendicitis attack really threw me." Mr. Nash grimaced. "A few old gossips said it was time to take another wife, I..." Mr. Nash thought about his next sentence. "I think this is the curse of parents; you never think you are doing it right. She could have died."

"She didn't, Mr. Nash. You did the right thing." Etta's heart went out to him; he spoke so sincerely. "You are busy now. Why not let us take care of her? She needs women now."

"Is it very difficult for her? The whole female complaint business?" Mr. Nash's eyes clouded with worry.

"No. It isn't, but she is starved for female attention, and she'll have buckets of it here. Let us keep her for a bit." Etta shivered from cold.

"I appreciate that more than you know," Mr. Nash said sincerely. "I'll bring your car and the clothes tomorrow. I can't believe we have a murderer in Oakland. It is just... I am completely stunned." Mr. Nash shook his head. "In the war, I kept thinking of how it was here, how clean and good and safe. I ran for mayor because I want it to continue to be clean and good and safe. I want things to go back to the way they were before the war. We had such innocence then. I feel as if the whole world was violated by the war."

Etta's teeth chattered. "I wish for the same things, but I fear we can't regain the peace we had before. Nothing will ever be the same. I don't think it's possible to go back to the way things were."

Nash nodded in agreement. "You're freezing. Please, go inside, and check on Grace for me. I'll be here first thing tomorrow." Mr. Nash opened the door to the kitchen for her. "Take a hot water bottle to bed."

"Right." Etta pulled open the door.

Mr. Nash stepped in. "One last thing."

"Yes?" Etta looked up at him.

"If caring for Grace is too much for Mrs. Lemon, let me know. She works very hard. I don't want to add to her burden."

"Grace is a delight. Think of all the books we'll read together." Etta grinned in the dim light of the kitchen.

"Miss Lynne." Mr. Nash's tone sounded a warning. "You will not get your way with this."

"Of course I will. It's just a matter of time." Etta grinned.

Changing the subject, Mr. Nash whispered so the sleeping occupants of the house wouldn't wake up. "The worst part of this tragedy is, it's one of us." Mr. Nash's jaw clenched. "A man of this community did this to a vulnerable woman. I will find him, and I will see him hang."

"You think it's a man?" Etta asked, her eyebrow arched. Memory of a cup of coffee being tossed deliberately on her skirt and blouse jumped into her mind.

"Of course." Mr. Nash's head snapped up in surprise. "Women aren't capable of violence, Miss Lynne. They are much too delicate for such base actions. No. This is a man. No question. Mr. Spicer hated her. Hated her with a passion. I saw it, and I couldn't figure it out. Just as he seems to hate you." Mr. Nash spoke ominously. "I believe you are in danger."

"I agree," Etta said simply.

"You're frozen right through. Your lips are blue, Miss Lynne. Sugar in your tea and then straight to bed with a hot water bottle for you. I mean it. Don't get sick. You remind Mrs. Lemon; the two of you are not to be out after dark. I can't search a crime scene and look after you at the same time. Stay in, stay safe." Mr. Nash repeated his instructions.

"Look after me?" Etta's jaw dropped open.

"Yes." Mr. Nash ignored her outburst, which infuriated her further. "Just this once, please. I beg you. Do as you are told."

Etta's back stiffened in outrage. "Do as you're told? There

you are, right back at it! Treating me like a child! You, sir, have a lot to learn about women," Etta hissed at him.

"I know that you have a lot of enemies!" Mr. Nash shot at her.

Etta opened her mouth to speak and then clamped it shut in outrage.

"I will not see you in danger. Go now. Get some rest." Mr. Nash opened the door to the porch, and just before he stepped out in the pouring rain, he turned. "And another thing—"

Etta grabbed the door and slammed it shut on him mid-sentence.

CHAPTER 24

*D*orothea caught her reflection in the window. Her French-lace nightgown left little to the imagination as it was cut to reveal her delicate physical assets. She gave herself a hard look in the mirror. She remembered the last time she had worn this exact nightgown to get what she wanted. The night her husband had *mysteriously* died of a morphine overdose.

It had been such a simple thing to add another vial of morphine by the bed. To help him fill that syringe and then fill it again... and again until he was out of pain.

Finally.

Permanently.

His last breath of pain was her first breath of freedom.

Dorothea wondered now why she had waited so long. All those endless months of him struggling for breath, gasping, and moaning. She should have done it all much sooner. The doctor would never prove she had put an entire vial of morphine into Ronald's arm.

Standing in the still room and realizing she could finally get on with her life, Dorothea had made a solemn vow that she would let nothing stand in the way of her happiness again.

It wasn't *really* murder.

No.

The war destroyed him. She just *helped along an inevitable death.*

She had taken her time before calling for the doctor. Painted her face, let her black hair fall in waves all the way down her back. She had dressed in this exact same gown. Distracted, the doctor hadn't stood a chance.

Just as Mr. Nash wouldn't stand a chance now.

Meeting a man in a nightgown like this was unheard of.

Scandalous.

Where is he?

Dorothea stepped closer to the mirror and met her own gaze. Her heart sank to her feet.

Desperation looked back at her.

Am I really going to stoop this low? Is this what I am reduced to?

The time to act was now, and it was absolutely an act. But she had to think it through. French lace might cause him to think she wasn't virtuous, or it would entrap him. Dorothea wasn't sure which act to play.

Dorothea grudgingly erred on the side of virtue. Reaching for a robe, she dragged it on. She knew some might think this was wrong, but the Great War had changed everything. A woman did what she had to do to survive. Dorothea's mother's words came back to her. Marry for power and money.

Not love—love doesn't last.

There was no one more powerful in the town than the mayor. She had to ensnare him somehow.

Do I really dare to do this? If he doesn't respond, what then?

Nothing ventured, nothing gained.

Checking her watch, she frowned in frustration.

Past midnight... maybe I should wait until tomorrow night? No... Etta Lynne is entirely too close to him. Mr. Nash needs a reminder I am the best choice. I am more beautiful than her, and I am everything he needs in a wife. Everything.

Finally, his headlights came down the street, and he parked in front of his house. Her eyes flicked over him as he got out of the car and made his way to the front door. His shoulders slumped.

No Grace.

I wonder if something has happened with her.

Mr. Nash would be devastated if Grace was not well, and she would be right there to offer comfort.

It will be much easier if there aren't stepdaughters in the picture when we start our new life together.

Dorothea waited until the light in his bedroom went out. She paced around for another fifteen minutes and then tipped the massive vase over in the back room by an open window.

She tossed her hair over her shoulders and slipped across the street to bang on his door.

Her heart pounded in anticipation as she banged on his door harder.

Mr. Nash came barreling down the stairs, threw open his front door, and took a step back when he saw her.

That isn't good.

"What is it?" Mr. Nash asked; he looked behind her as if someone had chased her across the street.

Mr. Nash took her breath away. Striped pajamas should have looked innocent— they didn't. He was taller and broader up close. His dark hair was tousled; stubble shadowed his hard square jaw. He towered over her, and she loved the feeling of being small beside him. For a moment she forgot her act, and she worried that her mouth dropped open of its own accord as her eyes travelled the length of him.

"Mrs. Delaire, what is it?" Mr. Nash repeated with more than a hint of annoyance.

"Oh!" Dorothea's brain scrambled to form a sentence. "There was a big bang at the back of my house. I am terrified... would you come and see what is going on?"

"Of course." Mr. Nash rubbed his eyes and followed Dorothea across the street to her home. She wrung her hands in the entranceway as Mr. Nash looked through her house and found the vase in the back room.

"It's nothing, Mrs. Delaire, just a vase overturned in the back room here. It looks like you left your back window open a crack, and maybe the wind blew it over." Mr. Nash joined her in the living room.

"Oh! I just panicked. I am so sorry to disturb your rest. I

heard about Mrs. Ellice. I just thought maybe..." Dorothea wanted to weep with disappointment. He wasn't fazed by her French lace— at all.

"Yes, desperate news about Mrs. Ellice." Mr. Nash stood by her front door awkwardly. His eyes stayed level with hers. Frustration built in Dorothea as she expected his eyes to flick over her body.

I should have left this robe off — I blew it!

Mr. Nash stood at the front door, hand on the handle, the perfect gentleman.

"Have you heard anything?" Dorothea deliberately let her eyes fill with tears. She pressed her handkerchief to her eyes.

"We'll know more in the morning. Detective Kane had found an invoice for an apartment in Winnipeg early in his investigation, so he has spent much of his time following that lead. He is back in Oakland tomorrow, so I need to get some rest."

Dorothea wept.

"Now, now." Mr. Nash sighed as he stood by her awkwardly and patted her shoulder. "I locked that window, and I checked all the doors and windows. You are safe."

Patting my shoulder! I want to be swept into your arms and comforted!

"I am just feeling very vulnerable." Dorothea moved closer to him.

He stood still, arms at his side.

"It's so hard to be a woman on your own, with no man to protect you. I am scared all the time now." Dorothea made a final plea for his protection.

"Mrs. Delaire, all is well. I checked every door and lock. This is nothing more than a fright. You are safe." Mr. Nash spoke to her as if she were an invalid aunt.

Dorothea longed to feel his hard arms around her. She took a tentative step forward, deliberately letting the sash of her gown fall to the floor.

Mr. Nash took a step back.

"I will leave you now to get some rest. I have had quite a difficult day. I won't be in to work tomorrow. I have to meet with the constabulary and the detective. All the men of Oakland will be searching. So please get some rest, Mrs. Delaire. We are reminding all the women of Oakland not to be out alone after dark. Please, arrange your affairs so you are home at dusk."

Disappointment winged through Dorothea as Mr. Nash took another step toward her front door. His hand was back on the door handle, and he turned back to face her. "Mrs. Delaire, one last thing. Who told you about Mrs. Ellice?"

"Oh! Everyone is talking about it." Dorothea bit her lip.

"What else do you know, Mrs. Delaire?" Mr. Nash asked pointedly.

Dorothea didn't like the hard edge to his voice. She had been all but draped over him, and he wasn't interested in the least. His eyes didn't drop to her décolletage, not even once. Dorothea felt like a perfect fool. Jackson Nash was not interested in her, her body, nothing. Defeat dragged her spirits down. Her hands trembled as she pressed the handkerchief against her mouth.

He has a woman. He must. It must be that Etta Lynne. I can't believe it! He doesn't like professional women! He wants a woman who will make a home for him. How did Etta sink her clutches into him? How? Or is it someone else? Has pretty Lucy Lemon turned his head?

Dorothea dragged her attention back to the topic at hand. "All I heard was the flood waters crested, the river is receding, her body was found, and the entire town is shocked and appalled." Dorothea spoke dully.

"What does the gossip mill say about potential suspects?" Mr. Nash's eyes narrowed.

Dorothea didn't know which way to jump. Tell him information or pretend she never gossiped a day in her life.

Clinging to her façade of moral and good, she shook her head. "I don't gossip, Mr. Nash. I have no idea..."

"What have you heard about potential suspects? Just say. What is the word in town among the women?" Mr. Nash took a stance that indicated he was ready for any news she could share.

"I'm sure I don't know," Dorothea said demurely.

The women of this town don't like me and wouldn't have me in their confidence under any circumstances. They are all jealous of me. They are threatened by my beauty.

"If you hear of anything, I would like to know," Mr. Nash said curtly.

"Of course. I will tell you anything I hear. How is Grace? I meant to ask." Dorothea scrambled for something to discuss. She was desperate to spark something between them. A mutual concern for his daughter would be good common ground.

"Grace is healing just fine." Mr. Nash checked his watch.

"I'm so relieved." Dorothea was careful to keep her voice slightly breathless.

"Yes, thanks. Good night, Mrs. Delaire." Mr. Nash turned from her, opened the front door and stepped out onto her front verandah.

Dorothea's heart sank to her feet as Mr. Nash left her house.

He isn't interested in me in the slightest! What am I going to do now?

She watched helplessly as he sprinted across the street, and when his bedroom light went out, her chest tightened in fury.

Dorothea tore off her lacy nightgown and hurled it into the corner of the room. She pulled on a comfortable, ugly linen nightgown. Disappointment and discouragement roared through her. She pressed her face into her pillow and wept with frustration.

This is Miss Lynne's fault. I just know it! She will pay for this!

CHAPTER 25

*E*tta woke up to a million realizations in her head. Her heart splintered as her mind ticked through all of them. Her mother had passed away. She owed Nash a fortune for the funeral if the council chose not to add her to the war widow fund. Her sister was here on bed rest. Grace was tucked into the spare room beside Lucy. Mrs. Ellice's body was found, and the men would search today for more clues. The town of Oakland was closed for the search. No school, no business as usual. The investigation would take precedence. She dragged herself out of bed and pulled on a robe so she could warn Lucy that most of the men of Oakland would need breakfast in her dining room.

Drizzle pelted against the windows of the kitchen as Lucy and Etta made their way to the kitchen at the same time. Lucy hugged Etta hard.

"I'm so sorry about your mom. Cali wept most of the night. You are worn out, you poor dear." Lucy squeezed tighter.

"I am," Etta admitted. Exhaustion dragged at her arms and made her shoulders slump.

"I wish I could do more than just say I'm sorry." Lucy spooned coffee into the metal basket of the percolator and started the coffee.

Etta stood at the kitchen sink and looked at the men congregating in their backyard. The rain hadn't let up. The empty

195

branches of the trees were black and charcoal against the grey sky. Etta watched as the hot water and coffee bubbled up inside the glass dome of the coffeepot.

"We are under strict orders to stay inside unless we have male protection, and we need to have breakfast ready for the search crews," Etta said dully.

"How kind of Mr. Nash to include us this way." Lucy poured them both a cup of perfectly brewed coffee and then stirred milk into hers and took a delicate sip.

"I want to be more like you. You are too good. I bristled and told him to stop bossing me around," Etta grumbled.

Lucy smiled and shook her head. "You two fight like cats."

"Yes, we do," Etta agreed. "What a terrible day for a search." Etta looked down the riverbank to her left and the creek bank to her right where the men had searched for a crime scene. Subconsciously she searched the assembled men for Nash.

Why am I looking for him?

Sure enough, he was standing by the detective and Constable Lark, speaking and gesturing, no doubt ordering people around. The difference was, the men didn't mind. She watched him give orders, and the men complied. Her eyes scanned the crowd for Mr. Spicer. He was not there. Etta wondered if he was maybe in a different crew or if they brought him in for questioning.

"What a horrific thing to search for." Lucy pulled her robe tighter around her and refilled Etta's coffee cup. "The worst thing about this time of year is the world can't decide if it's winter or spring. Right now, rain, but it could turn to snow at any minute. Other than the weather, the world has gone mad. Imagine this! Before the war, this sort of thing would be unheard of, and now we face this tragedy."

Their shoulders touched as they stood at the window and watched the men break into groups.

"Do you think someone hurt her? Or is this just an accident?" Etta wondered out loud.

"It *has* to be an accident. There is a trail at the top of the hill, and if she walked there, she may have slipped on ice. Etta, I can't imagine any woman being on that trail this time of year. Still icy and snowy up there, so it would be slippery." Lucy sipped hot coffee. "I feel bad for the men. It is a raw, cold day."

"Yes," Etta said absently.

"You were late coming in with Mr. Nash. I don't suppose…"

"We had a disagreement…"

"Oh, Etta! What now?" Lucy groaned.

"Mr. Nash's tone really gets my back up." Etta spied him again amongst the men on the bank of the river.

"Mr. Nash is old-fashioned, and has a good heart." Lucy grinned at Etta.

"Hmm, I think bossy, domineering, and archaic," Etta contradicted her.

Lucy's laugh filled the kitchen. "I'm used to old-fashioned, and I like it."

Etta looked at her in surprise. "Really?"

"I loved being married and looking after a house and a man. I loved packing a special lunch for him and leaving love notes in his lunch box." Lucy's eyes softened in memory.

Etta rolled her eyes so hard she worried they would fall out of her face.

Lucy ignored her scorn. "I loved making a home for my husband." Lucy smiled warmly. "I wanted children right away, and sadly, that didn't happen. Now, I think maybe that was a good thing. Hard enough keeping a roof over my head, but with a baby that would have been worse. Honestly though, I used to dream about Russ and me getting a nursery ready…" Lucy's face fell a bit. "Sorry. Never mind. I can see by your face that these are foreign thoughts to you. You must think I'm silly." Lucy shrugged. "If I were educated, I wouldn't be such a drain on our community."

"You aren't a drain." Etta shook her head. "You are not. You are the best person I know, who is trying hard to deal with a crisis."

Lucy bit her lip to stop it from wobbling. Every time she spoke of Russ and babies, Etta thought her heart broke again.

Sunshine streaming into a nursery was the furthest thing from what they were facing today— a grey, cold, drizzly day as

197

they searched for a crime scene to make sense of what happened to Rose Ellice.

Etta changed the subject. "Lucy, I hope this is all right with you. I should have asked, but it was sort of spur of the moment. Would you mind if Grace stays with us until we resolve this situation? I think Mr. Nash will seldom be home. I think Grace needs some woman time, and I was hoping we could keep her until all this dies down."

"Of course." Lucy's eyes lit up. "I was hoping she could stay with us."

"Good. I am relieved." Etta cut Lucy's homemade bread to make toast.

A knock at the door startled them.

"Gracious! We are in our unmentionables!" Lucy gasped. "It's Jackson Nash!"

Etta pulled her robe around her tighter. "I'll go," she said grimly. "He's seen me in worse."

Lucy leaped into the pantry.

Etta opened the door.

"Good morning." Mr. Nash looked at Etta warily as if gauging her reaction to his presence. His cheeks were red from cold. His eyes flicked over her.

"Mr. Nash! It's seven in the morning! We aren't dressed," Etta scolded him.

"I used the back door so as not to disturb Mrs. Daindridge and Mrs. Carr. May I step in? It's freezing out here."

"Of course." A blush sneaked up Etta's neck.

"Would you like some hot coffee, Mr. Nash?" Lucy peeked her head around the door of the pantry.

"That's exactly what I'm here for." Mr. Nash shut the door behind him. "Sorry to disturb you, Mrs. Lemon. I know that it's early, but I needed to ask for your assistance. We need breakfast and lunch served here for all the men, and since you are close to the searching, we hoped we could use your house as a base. Would that be all right?" Mr. Nash directed his question to both women.

Etta handed Mr. Nash her coffee. "Here, have this. You look like you are frozen through."

Mr. Nash gratefully sipped Etta's coffee.

"Of course, but I work today…" Lucy bit her lip.

"I will speak to your boss. This investigation takes precedence." Mr. Nash's tone indicated that Simon Treleaven would say yes and there was no need to worry about work.

"But, sir, I need the money." Lucy's eyes widened with concern.

"Council will pay you for your services today. Please, give us a bill of what you need. School is closed. We need all the young men searching. If you could have breakfast for the first shift ready in an hour, that would help." Mr. Nash took another sip of coffee.

"Gracious! I better get to work." Lucy raced up the stairs to get dressed.

Mr. Nash drained the last of Etta's coffee and then handed the mug back to her. "You should get dressed too, miss."

"I said last night you are to stop bossing me around." Etta frowned at him.

"Listen, about that, all the orders and commands…" Mr. Nash started. Embarrassed, he cleared his throat and scratched the back of his neck.

"Yes." Etta poured him more coffee and handed it to him.

"I haven't had a woman in my life for a long time, Miss Lynne." Mr. Nash's tone dropped in case anyone might be listening in. "A really long time, and since that time I have fought a war and then I've worked as the mayor of a town. Since Nell died, I have been in the command and in the company of men only. My authority is never questioned. If it is questioned, it is done so respectfully. I don't stop to weigh out all the feelings of soldiers or council members. I decide, I give orders, men comply."

Etta crossed her arms over her chest. "And?"

"And… I've been thinking…" Mr. Nash cleared his throat. "It occurred to me, it's possible that I need to adjust the way I deal with you. A bit. You're not a man. I shouldn't order you around like you are one. You are not in my employ… I'm sorry. I am not doing this well."

"What are you trying to say?" Etta refused to make this easy for him.

"I'm saying that I realize since we've met, I've been slightly domineering."

"You are *a lot* domineering."

"And I am sorry." Mr. Nash met her gaze and held it. "I really am. I want us to get along. I will be more respectful in how I deal with you. I will try not to infringe on you. If I am overbearing, just say. I will try harder to be... gentle with you." Mr. Nash took a step forward.

Etta's breath caught in her throat.

"Miss Lynne, from now on, things will be different between us."

"Different how?" Etta rasped.

"Just as I said, I will be careful with you and your feelings, but I *will* protect you. This is new ground, so please be patient with me. I don't want to fight with you." Mr. Nash spoke with such sincerity Etta's iron will to defy him softened. A wall inside her crumbled.

Etta grasped at the remaining pieces of the wall around her heart. "What about Grace's education?"

Mr. Nash groaned as he sipped their joint coffee. "I'll get back to you on that. Now, stop glaring at me. I have to get back to the search. Once we find out who did this, we'll discuss Grace. When I get a chance, I'll take your things upstairs for you and Mrs. Tyne. The first shift should be through here in an hour."

"We'll have breakfast ready," Etta conceded slightly. "Have they found anything yet?"

"No. Nothing so far." Mr. Nash's jaw clenched with concern. "The investigator is searching through her personal effects left at Barlow's, and we'll cover the river and creek bank today before sundown. If there is anything out there, we'll find it."

Mr. Nash put their joint coffee cup down and placed his hand on the door handle; he hesitated at the door.

"Before you go." Etta went to him. Grace's education aside, he was trying. Etta worded her peace offering carefully. "Maybe I am a little prickly because of grief. I have been forced to be very independent, Mr. Nash. I have been used to looking after the men of my family. I'm not used to a man looking after me or looking out for me. I am not accustomed to dealing with a man who is putting my best interests or my needs first."

"I'm sorry that has been your experience." Mr. Nash's eyes locked with hers, and he didn't look away.

"It's possible that I may have overreacted — slightly. I will be more respectful in how I deal with you, too." Etta fiddled with the tie of her robe.

"There is no question you overreacted. I was just trying to be the bigger person," Mr. Nash said with deadpan seriousness.

Etta couldn't stop a grin from tugging at her lip. "Best behaviour on both our parts, from now on?"

Mr. Nash held his hand out to shake on it.

Etta slid her hand into his. His grip was warm and firm; hard enough to let her know she was shaking hands and entering into an agreement with a powerful man. The look in his eye reassured her that his power would be used to protect her, never to hurt her.

"Best behaviour from now on." Etta glanced up at him.

A grin broke across Mr. Nash's face. "It's a promise. See you shortly."

With that, he was gone, back to the men, and Etta looked up to see Lucy Lemon in the doorway.

"Well! That was something else altogether. The women of Oakland wondered who would be the next Mrs. Jackson Nash, and honestly, we all thought Dorothea Delaire... but the way he looks at you — he's smitten!" Lucy shook her head.

"He is not." Etta blushed six thousand shades of red.

"He is." Lucy pulled on an apron and grabbed a pound of lard from her pantry. "Anyway. No time for that— we have men to feed."

Lucy shot Etta a broad smile.

"You are thrilled." Etta danced away from the discussion about whether or not Mr. Nash was smitten. She grinned back.

They heard another knock at the front door.

"Hang on." Lucy wiped her hands on her apron to let the

women in. "The cavalry is here. Mrs. Daindridge, Mrs. Carr, and Mrs. Holt are descending upon us."

"Mercy!"

"Good thing Mrs. Daindridge and Mrs. Carr didn't see the world's most scandalous handshake in my humble kitchen," Lucy murmured to Etta as Mrs. Daindridge and Mrs. Carr's canes clattered down the hallway to the kitchen.

Mrs. Holt followed behind with pre-buttered bread pans.

"Good thing." Etta grinned at Lucy and then raced up the stairs to dress.

Back downstairs in record time, Etta smiled as the women of Oakland got to work. Mrs. Holt proofed yeast in a big bowl to make fresh bread. Mrs. Daindridge held out her hand for the flour sifter from Mrs. Lemon.

Etta caught Lucy's eye.

Demanding the flour sifter was a bold move on Mrs. Daindridge's part. "I will do the pastry, my dear."

Lucy frowned, and her grip tightened on the flour sifter.

"Mrs. Lemon, we really must have biscuits that *float*. You are a very good baker, but pastry is my gift." Mrs. Daindridge wrestled the flour sifter from Mrs. Lemon.

Etta couldn't stop a smirk from crossing her face. Her eyes met Grace's over Mrs. Daindridge's head. Grace's eyes danced with mischief as she grinned at the old lady holding the flour sifter in triumph.

Etta's heart swelled. The women of Oakland together — this was Grace's heritage at work. Maybe not in perfect harmony, but what was? Mrs. Carr checked Mrs. Holt's yeast and nodded her head sagely — it was ready to add flour. These dear women dropped everything to ensure the men searching had hot meals. They thought of them as their own sons, brothers, fathers, and husbands. Etta closed her eyes briefly to commit this happy scene to memory.

Grace slipped around the women, slid her arm around Etta's waist, and placed her head on her shoulder. "I'm so sorry about your mother. I know how that feels."

Etta slid her arm around Grace. "Thank you," she murmured. "I am reminded today, as I watch this, that life has a way of replacing what we lose. Remember this, Grace. These women are your community. They will cheer for you and help you every way they can."

"Mr. Nash loves my butter tarts, and he will need hot tarts for his coffee," Mrs. Daindridge declared. "Mrs. Lemon, I will need some walnuts. He prefers walnuts, not just raisins."

Lucy bit her lip. "I was going to make him some..."

"No, dear. I know what he likes." Mrs. Daindridge cut Lucy off.

Mrs. Holt shot Lucy a commiserating look.

Etta choked back a laugh as they fought over how Nash liked his butter tarts and realized the women of this community loved him. They didn't mind his old-fashioned ways. Etta marveled at the thought.

He's spoiled! No wonder he's so difficult to deal with!

Yet another knock at the door interrupted the war of the pastry. Etta hoped no one handed a flour sifter to her by mistake. Her biscuits would sink to the bottom of the river; they would shrink faster than her pie crusts. She sidled up to Mrs. Daindridge and hoped to glean some tips.

"Mr. Spence!" Lucy exclaimed as the man who ran the general store brought in boxes of food.

"I got here as soon as I could! I have eggs, ham, flour; every ingredient you can imagine. Mr. Nash said spare no expense." Mr. Spence took off his hat in the presence of the women. "If you need anything else, just let me know. I'm told whatever you need, I am to supply, no questions asked."

Mrs. Spicer hesitated by the front door.

"Mrs. Spicer hitched a ride with me. She has a pot of soup to contribute," Mr. Spence said to Lucy.

Lucy immediately wiped her hands on her apron and went to welcome Mrs. Spicer into her home.

"Please, come in." Lucy reached for the heavy pot of soup.

"It is very heavy. I carry," Mrs. Spicer said softly in her broken English. She gave Lucy a very shy smile and brought the soup into the kitchen. She placed it on the range.

"Please, stay and have a cup of tea with us," Lucy offered. She pulled out a chair for Mrs. Spicer to sit. "It's such a cold day."

"Oh. I cannot." Mrs. Spicer's eyes widened. "Mr. Spicer is expecting me at home."

"I can run you back after a cup of tea. It's no trouble," Etta offered from the doorway.

Mrs. Spicer looked nervous. Her hands shook at the thought.

"No. I really must get home. Mr. Spicer likes to know where I am." Mrs. Spicer's accent thickened with fear.

What does Mr. Spicer do if his wife isn't home?

Etta couldn't stop herself from moving to her and placing a hand on her shoulder. "Mrs. Spicer, thank you for your generosity. We'll let the men know you supplied this soup. This is very good of you."

Mrs. Spicer's eyes softened as Etta held her gaze. She opened her mouth to speak and then closed it. "I hear she had gash on forehead." Mrs. Spicer's lips pressed together. "Is there chance this is accident?"

"Accident!" Mrs. Daindridge crowed. "No. This is murder. Murder most foul! No question in our minds at all!"

"Mrs. Daindrige!" Etta gasped in alarm. "You are assuming…"

"I know it." Mrs. Daindridge cranked the flour sifter harder with renewed zeal.

"I see." Mrs. Spicer's voice dropped to a whisper; she bit her lip and moved back toward the hallway.

"Please stay, the coffee is almost ready… or tea if you prefer." Lucy held her hands out to take her coat.

"No. I mustn't. He doesn't know I am here…" Mrs. Spicer's eyes darted wildly in fear of being caught in the company of women.

Etta's heart broke for her. Mr. Spicer delighted in humiliating anyone, Etta knew from her own experience. He gained satisfaction from watching someone bend to his will. This poor and vulnerable woman with no friends, no support, would be an easy target. Etta could tell by the faces of the women in the kitchen everyone wanted to help her, to reach out a hand in friendship, but her fear of her husband kept her shackled, separate.

"Mrs. Spicer, maybe you could ask to come back this afternoon for tea and tarts. We would love to have you join us." Lucy stood by Etta and extended the warm invitation.

"Oh, Mr. Spicer would prefer I am home to make him his supper." Mrs. Spicer backed away from the friendship offered to her. "He doesn't like me to get too tired."

Mrs. Holt's lips thinned as Mrs. Spicer made excuses for her husband. It irritated all of them that she was reduced to desperately trying to portray him in a good light when every woman in the room knew the truth.

"Thank you for this very generous pot of soup." Lucy, ever the peacemaker, trailed behind Mrs. Spicer as she followed Mr. Spence out of the house. "I appreciate your kindness."

Mrs. Spicer nodded, and with that she left. Back to the loneliness of her life in Mr. Spicer's home.

The women were silent as they made eye contact with each other. With great force of will, they resisted the urge to gossip. They returned to their work.

Mrs. Daindridge had no such qualms and piped up, saying exactly what was on the minds of all the women in the kitchen. "That poor woman. I don't know how she stands him."

"He's terrible, but what can you expect? With a mother like his…" Mrs. Carr's lips clamped shut when Grace entered the room.

Etta was desperate to find out what sort of mother Mr. Spicer had that would have left him as damaged as he was. Lucy had implied that his mother was promiscuous. Etta wondered if that was why he hated women so much and demanded chastity and virtue as if all immorality was the responsibility of the woman alone.

Mrs. Daindridge cleared her throat; she shot a wild look at Mrs. Carr that they dare not discuss the conduct of Mr. Spicer's mother in front of Grace Nash. Etta itched to get the two old women into a corner and find out everything they knew!

Could he have threatened Mrs. Ellice? Had she been going to the Manitoba Teachers' Federation to report his conduct? Mr. Spicer despised a show of strength. Had her threat gotten her killed? Maybe she had Miss Ford's testimony and together they would have had him fired? Was Miss Winthrop involved? Had the Teachers' Federation been in contact with her, and had she been to Mr. Spicer with that knowledge? Alerting him, sparking rage in him? What happens when you threaten a man like Spicer? Does he go to any length to silence you?

She remembered his voice in her ear when he had caught her with Nash. 'You should be afraid of what I could do to you.' Then he backed right down when Nash stood up to him. He seemed to be a bully who threatened women in a position of subordination, but was clearly terrified of a man like Nash.

Etta shook her head and put those thoughts out of her mind. This was a difficult day, and there was nothing anyone could do for Mrs. Spicer unless she asked for help.

The faces of the women showed that every single one of them was worried about her.

Etta firmly refused to dwell on Mr. and Mrs. Spicer. She turned her attention to the mountain of ingredients Nash had instructed Mr. Spence to bring. Her heart melted as she realized this was more food than they could ever serve to the men searching. This was Nash's sneaky way of filling Mrs. Lemon's pantry in a way that preserved her dignity. Despite her misgivings about his thoughts on Grace's education, Etta's heart soared at the generosity of Jackson Nash.

"Oh, look at this. Coconut!" Mrs. Holt shook her head. "Lucy, this is from Mr. Holt. He requested one of your coconut cakes for afternoon coffee." Mrs. Holt rolled her eyes. "Honestly."

"I will make Mr. Holt a coconut cake, for sure." Lucy smiled at her.

"Don't spoil him!" Mrs. Holt warned. "He's impossible to deal with as it is."

"I'm sure that's not true." Lucy took the bag of coconut from Mrs. Holt. "I will get right on that as soon as the ham is sliced."

Mrs. Holt pulled the bag of flour from the box and started whisking the flour into the warm water and yeast.

Lucy started slicing ham.

"Is there anything I can do?" Etta asked tentatively.

"Would you set the dining room table?" Lucy wiped a strand of hair away from her forehead as she sliced meat. "Grace, I have clear broth for you, and then I think back to bed with you. I don't want you to overexert yourself."

Etta winked at Grace then smoothed the linen tablecloth on the big dining room table. She carefully placed Mrs. Lemon's cream-and-gold china around the table as she listened to Mrs. Carr question Mrs. Holt in the kitchen in an attempt to gather as much information as she could.

Done setting the table, Etta stood at the threshold of the kitchen and watched the women work. This was a terrible day, but as this group of women chattered in the kitchen, Etta's spirits lightened. Losing her mother made her heart ache, but she was reminded that there are mothers everywhere when you need them... not to replace but to fill a void so deep Etta couldn't see to the bottom.

Mrs. Holt met her eye over Mrs. Carr's head. Mrs. Holt, like Mrs. Bennett, had a spine of steel. Mrs. Holt winked at her as she dodged Mrs. Carr's questions.

As the women finished the preparations for the community breakfast, Etta's eyes met Lucy's. They smiled at each other, and for the first time in Etta's life, she felt as though she fit. She felt like one of their own.

CHAPTER 26

*E*tta served coffee and tea to the endless stream of men who quickly ate breakfast in the dining room and then slipped right back out to search, grim lines of worry, concern, and shock etched on their faces. Every man here was horrified by this tragedy befalling a woman in their community. Etta felt reassured by the men intent on seeking justice.

They spoke as though there was a lot of ground to cover.

Mr. Nash caught her eye as she refilled Mr. Holt's coffee cup. "I left Mrs. Tyne's luggage in your room. I didn't want to disturb her."

"Thank you. I haven't checked on her yet." Etta passed Mr. Holt the sugar. "There was a pastry battle I couldn't tear myself away from."

Mr. Nash grinned at her. "Try to keep some order if you can."

"You have a long list of women who want to be sure they make your butter tarts to your specifications. They spoil you." Etta filled Mr. Nash's coffee cup.

Mr. Nash shrugged unrepentantly. "I can't help it if the women of my community love me."

Etta rolled her eyes. "You can rest easy. No one handed a flour sifter to me by accident."

"I think the entire village knows your pie crusts shrink." Mr. Nash winked at her.

"I am sure there is an article in the newspaper about it, with the rest of my shortfalls!" Etta moved down the line of men, filling coffee cups as she went.

"How is Grace?"

"She's been down and fed and sent back to her bed with a book. She is healing well," Etta reassured him.

"What kind of book?" Mr. Nash grinned at her.

"Fiction." Etta grinned back from the end of the table.

Mr. Holt raised his eyebrows at them. Immediately they stopped grinning and carried on with the task at hand. Mr. Nash dug into the ham and eggs left on his plate. Etta returned to the kitchen for a fresh pot of coffee.

Finally, the last man left, and Etta made a tray for her and Cali. She slipped upstairs, away from the sounds of dishes being washed and women chattering in the kitchen.

Etta stood at the threshold of Cali's room, the door open. Cali's eyes, swollen and red from weeping most of the night, made Etta's heart ache. Quietly, she closed the door so she would not disturb her.

Setting her tray with breakfast on her desk, she noticed Cali's luggage near the closet and a box she didn't recognize on her bed.

Tilting her head to the side, she opened the card.

Dear Miss Lynne,

I am so sorry for your loss.

I would like to ease some pain in whatever way I can.

It is my hope that this gift will brighten your spirits.

Sincerely,

Jackson Nash

Etta placed the note on her bed and eyed the box suspiciously. She slid the top off, and her jaw dropped. Her eyes filled with tears as she saw all her old paints, paintbrushes, a new tin of watercolours, and canvases of different sizes. Mr. Nash had returned to the secondhand shop and retrieved everything that they had forced her to sell and added new supplies to her old stock. Pencils, onionskin paper, an eraser she didn't recognize, new brushes in a leather case designed to carry them. The leather case was a pale yellow with a scalloped edge.

A fist of tears tightened in her throat as she noticed, at the bottom, a pretty embroidered handkerchief. She opened it, and tears slid down her face as she saw her grandmother's blue cameo pinned safely inside.

Etta dashed tears from her eyes as she heard a gentle tap at the door.

"Were you in my room?" Cali asked quietly from the doorway.

"I was." Etta stood up and forced a smile on her face, quickly wiping the tears away. "You should be in bed."

"What is all this?" Cali asked, her eyebrow raised.

"Mr. Nash left this for me this morning." Etta cleared her throat as Cali looked into the box.

"Your old art supplies! Where did he find this?" Cali's eyes widened in surprise.

"He was with me when I sold Grandmother's cameo." Etta dashed more tears away.

"Oh, no! Is it gone?" Cali's face fell.

"He bought it back." Etta's heart swelled again as she handed the cameo to Cali.

Cali's eyes filled with tears. "I think this is the most..."

"I think this is the best gift I have ever received in my life," Etta breathed. "I am speechless. I don't know what to say."

"He's sweet on you." Cali's fingertips traced over the cameo. "This is beyond a gift, Etta, this is a promise."

Etta placed her hand on her heart. "A promise of what? Cali, I don't — no one has ever..."

Cali gently cut Etta off. "He's promising that if you are with him, you will never sell a piece of yourself again. That you, and everything that belongs to you, are safe with him." Cali's gaze locked with Etta's.

Etta's eyes filled with more tears. "We have so many differences, Cali! What if we can't sort it out? What then?"

Cali's eyes met Etta's. "You will."

Etta bit her lip. "You sound very sure of yourself."

"I saw the way he looks at you, and I saw the way you respond," Cali said softly.

"Well, I don't know about all that, but this is the kindest thing anyone has ever done." Etta brushed a tear from her eye. "I am stunned."

Cali put her arms around Etta and held on tight. "I'm so happy for you."

"Say nothing," Etta warned. "I can't court anyone while employed as a teacher."

"Etta, every rule is meant to be broken. You are a grown woman. Court if you want, and let the cards fall where they may. You have nothing holding you back now."

Etta bit her lip and let Cali go. "You should eat something before breakfast gets cold."

"Ever the practical!" Cali grinned as she got off the bed and made her way to the breakfast tray. "I thought in the night, E, that now everything has changed. I've been thinking only of myself. With Mother's crippling doctor's bills out of the way, you can breathe. Probably for the first time." Cali poured tea into two teacups and took a delicate sip.

"The guilt is haunting me, Cali. I am grieving for Mother and at the same time feeling relief that she's not suffering and I'm not fretting about paying for her care. Every day I had a tally of the doctor's bills in my head. You are right — I am feeling like I can breathe for the first time. With this new freedom, I have decided, come what may, I will send a letter about Mr. Spicer to the Federation today." Etta joined her at the table near the window.

Together they looked out over the men searching the riverbanks.

"How was the burial?" Cali added sugar to her tea.

"Difficult. I owe Mr. Nash a lot of money. My car broke down, and he had to pay to fix it. They wanted the entire amount before they would bury her. All I had was the money from your laundry." Etta groaned. "So Mr. Nash paid that bill, too."

"How romantic," Cali breathed.

"It was humiliating, actually." Etta shook her head at Cali. "I hate owing him. I hate owing anyone..."

"I think he was likely happy to do it." Cali bit into a piece of toast.

Etta carefully shaped her oatmeal into an island in the center of her bowl and then poured cream around it, like a moat. She sprinkled brown sugar and cinnamon on the top and took a bite.

"I can't believe you still eat your oatmeal like that." Cali shook her head.

"It's the only way."

"You know, there are many ways to eat oatmeal. You need to be open to other ways of doing things, of looking at life," Cali said impertinently.

"No, Cali. There is not. There is one proper way, and I happen to know it." Etta took another bite of oatmeal.

"Oh boy, this should be interesting. I think Mr. Nash has similar convictions." Cali shook her head.

Etta shrugged. "We have yet to come to any *understanding*."

"I see." Cali tried and failed to suppress a grin.

Etta changed the subject. "Since we are likely returning to Pacific Avenue after school is out, we ironed everything and returned it. Once I send this letter to the Federation, I have no idea what will happen. They might not place me anywhere next fall."

"We ironed?" Cali raised her eyebrow in speculation.

"Nash brought two irons and an ironing board and helped me iron every stitch of clothing." Etta finished her oatmeal and leaned back in her chair.

"Really! How kind." Cali gasped.

Etta blushed. "I was surprised, I couldn't believe it."

"He's just full of surprises." Cali looked at Etta with a gleam in her eye.

"Don't even think of it, Cali. I see your very thoughts. There is nothing between us. We are opposed in every direction..."

"I love it!" Cali crowed. "You need a man opposed to you in every direction! Keeps you on your toes. You need someone as tough as you are. I, for one, can't wait to see how this gets sorted out..."

"You'll see us, and by us I mean you and I, back in Pacific Avenue, trying not to starve to death. Don't get your hopes up," Etta warned.

"Such a protest!" Cali finished her tea and reached for the teapot to pour more.

Etta groaned. "Cali. I have been distraught and at the end of my rope. I can't think about the implications of this."

"Stop thinking so much and just go with how you feel," Cali begged.

"That is a recipe for disaster!" Etta shook her head. "No. I must think this through. Far too much on the line here. Cali, put that down. Let me pour it; it's a heavy pot. I don't want you to strain yourself. After tea, back to your bed. I will slip over to the school."

"You are so bossy." Cali smirked at Etta. "I hate that you have to wait on me hand and foot."

"Cali. I love you. I don't mind. Back to bed." Etta pointed to Cali's bedroom. "I mean it."

* * *

ETTA TUCKED Cali in and returned their tray to the kitchen. She rolled her eyes as she noticed Mrs. Daindridge and Mrs. Carr peering out the kitchen window to monitor the men as they searched. She slipped into her coat and scarf and grabbed an umbrella and her keys; she took her car to the school. Really, Mr. Nash was a ninny. No harm would come to her in broad daylight! No killer was waiting to pounce at eleven in the morning!

The high school was closed, and no one should be there. She could slip in and slip out; no one would be the wiser. It was unnecessary to interrupt any of the men. If they didn't find evidence before the snow fell, the investigation would drag on; evidence might be lost.

Racing up the stairs, Etta stopped still at the end of the hall-way. Her breath caught as she watched Miss Winthrop whispering to Mrs. Delaire in front of the open door to her classroom. Their eyes darted around as she walked down the hall toward them.

A hot stab of worry cut through Etta.

What has brought Miss Winthrop and Mrs. Delaire together in front of my classroom? Does she have a key to my classroom? Are they working together? Are they responsible for what happened to Mrs. Ellice?

"Miss Lynne. I am here to find out what pie you are bringing to the pie box social. Miss Winthrop is bringing cherry. What about you?"

Miss Winthrop nodded to Etta as she turned on her heel and went to the staff room.

"Um. I'm not sure. Which kind do you want?"

"Whatever kind you wish. Cherry is Mr. Nash's favourite, but I'm sure you know that." Mrs. Delaire's eyes flashed with jealousy.

"Chocolate pie, Mrs. Delaire. I'll leave the cherry to you and Miss Winthrop." Etta kept her gaze level with Mrs. Delaire's.

Mrs. Delaire's eyes darkened with fury. "Who do you think you are? Do you really think you will waltz off into the sunset with Mr. Nash—?"

Etta held Mrs. Delaire's angry gaze; she didn't back down from the vicious jealousy she saw there.

A noise from inside Etta's classroom cut off Mrs. Delaire's tirade.

"You best run along. I have work to do, and I will not listen to threats from you." Etta moved past her and peeked her head into the classroom.

Mr. Spicer was going through every book in the bookcase.

Etta's heart hammered in her chest.

"Can I help you?" Etta asked politely.

Mr. Spicer's head snapped up. "What are you doing here? School is closed for the search."

"One might wonder what you are doing here when every man is searching for a crime scene." Etta crossed her arms over her chest as she waited for an answer.

"I loaned a book to Mrs. Ellice, and I wanted it back."

Or is there evidence other than the note you must have stolen... did Miss Winthrop steal it for you? Or did you pay a student to go through my handbag?

"Why do you have keys to my classroom?"

"I have keys to every classroom," Mr. Spicer snapped. He replaced the books and swept past her to the hallway.

Relief winged through her as he left her classroom. Hoping that was the end of their altercation, Etta went to her desk. She picked up the assignments that needed grading and frowned at the piece of paper sitting on her day planner.

She had left no scraps of paper on her desk; she was fastidious.

Her stomach clenched in fear as she read the note someone had left behind.

'I know your secret. Stop or your next,' scrawled in black ink.

The blood drained from Etta's face as she picked up the misspelled note and held it in her hand. Her body pulsed with fear. Suddenly feeling very vulnerable in the classroom, she quickly gathered her papers together and then froze as she looked up to see Mr. Spicer standing in the open doorway. She tucked the threatening note deep into her satchel as she braced herself to face him.

Etta cursed herself for her stupidity as her fingers curved around the key to her classroom.

"Miss Lynne, before I go, we should talk about that *performance* last night." Mr. Spicer pulled the door shut on the classroom and locked it behind him.

Etta's heart pounded in fear as he moved toward her. She took a step back.

"Insubordination, in the company of men — you are just racking up the offences, Miss Lynne." Mr. Spicer tisked at her.

"You are very welcome to call a meeting with the school board, and we can discuss this all together. Meeting with me alone is inappropriate, and I will not discuss this privately with you or any board member." Etta scrambled to keep out of his reach, keeping the desk between them.

"It looked to me like you were doing a lot of discussion with

Mr. Nash last night. Looked to me like courting." Mr. Spicer moved as stealthily as a cat. "He's not here. Whatever will you do?"

Etta bolted to the door and tried to wrench open the handle. Locked.

She fumbled to find the metal nub to slide back across the top of the door lock. Her fingertips trembled and slicked with nervous sweat. She couldn't move it.

"One teacher ran. One teacher is murdered. One wonders what your fate will be..." Mr. Spicer tilted his head to the side as Etta struggled with the lock on the door.

"They don't know that it's murder. It could have been an accident." A trickle of terror pooled in Etta's stomach as she turned to face him.

"I think it's safe to assume Mrs. Ellice tangled with the wrong person. Miss Lynne, are you going to make the same mistakes?"

Etta's mouth went dry with fear as he moved closer to her.

"I have a letter here, detailing your list of offences. Such a long list. What I saw last night alone is grounds for dismissal." Mr. Spicer moved closer, like a wolf sizing up a lamb.

"You saw nothing last night." Etta scrambled to slide the nub across the plate to unlock the door.

Mr. Spicer loomed over her. "I saw enough evidence to ruin your career. Do you really think you can get away with immoral conduct in this community and face no consequences?"

"I was being walked home in the dark after my mother died." Etta gave up on the lock. She leaped away from him, careful to keep out of arm's reach. "You know there was nothing immoral going on."

"You don't decide what is indecent. That is not up to you. You are nothing. A worthless, dime-a-dozen teacher." Etta saw the contempt in his eyes as he spoke to her.

"What do you want, Mr. Spicer?" Etta's eyes narrowed.

"I want to see you fired as an example of what happens to women who don't live by the code. The rules in place to protect everyone." Mr. Spicer's face twisted with anger.

"Try it," Etta shot at him.

Mr. Spicer blinked in confusion. His eyes narrowed as he towered over her.

Etta skittered past him and pounced on the door handle again. Finally the little nub slid to the right, unlocking the handle. She threw open the door. "My mother is dead. No more hospital bills. I can quit teaching today. I don't care."

Mr. Spicer followed her into the hallway. "You're lying."

"I don't lie." Etta didn't back down an inch. "Know this." Etta closed her classroom door and put her key in the lock. Turning it, she snapped it off so no one could enter the room.

Just like the desk drawer...

Mr. Spicer's eyes narrowed further. His eye twitched as he saw the broken key in her hand.

"What have you done?" he gasped.

"I just secured a crime scene. Whatever you were searching for in that room is safe until Detective Kane can find it." Etta's eyes narrowed at him, gauging his reaction.

The blood drained from Mr. Spicer's face.

Etta swiftly walked down the hall, away from him.

He followed in close pursuit.

Etta turned to face him. "There will be a letter detailing this altercation to the Federation, but I won't stop there — I am sending correspondence right to the lieutenant governor about how you have harassed me, followed me, threatened my job and my person. In cases such as these, they are never isolated incidents. Your time as secretary treasurer is over. I will expose the truth about you."

"You'll never work again." Mr. Spicer's throat worked in fury.

"I never wanted to be a teacher." Etta fired the statement at him.

"Miss Lynne, the word of a school board secretary will hold much more weight than yours. Especially when they hear of how you have tried to seduce me. My wife saw you show me your ankle in the school parking lot. Such a brazen display. She has made her concerns known to me."

Etta's blood ran cold as Mr. Spicer threatened to lie about her conduct. "Seduce you?"

"Yes." Mr. Spicer blinked twice.

"You produce your evidence, and I will produce mine." Etta refused to back down.

Mr. Spicer's face mottled with rage.

"I see how you look at me, Miss Lynne. I see it all. I know women like you. Desperate women. Women who turn up their noses at civility. Women like Lucy Lemon... you're all the same."

"Keep Lucy Lemon out of this." Etta's tone iced with fury.

Mr. Spicer walked toward her. "You have no proof of anything. I have enforced a code, where I have an eyewitness who will testify that you tried to seduce me. Remember, if you bring forward these ridiculous charges, there won't be a man to protect you. Mr. Nash isn't on the school board now. He can't help you."

Etta stood straight, refusing to take a step back as she felt his breath on her face. "I don't need a man to protect me. I have the truth. I have the contents of a desk drawer no one has seen since Mrs. Ellice broke the key off in the lock."

Mr. Spicer's eyes widened in shock. He raised his hand as if to hit her. Etta held her ground. "Hit me. See what happens if you hit me..." she goaded him. "You leave a mark on a teacher and see what the men of your community are capable of."

Mr. Spicer's face flamed with fury. As reason took over, he dropped his hand. "A silly little girl like you will not threaten me."

"You're right. I'm not going to threaten you, Mr. Spicer. I am going to see that you are brought to justice for whatever you did to Rose Ellice. I noticed you are one of the only men of this community not searching." Etta shredded him with her words. "You can't scare me. I have nothing to lose."

Mr. Spicer grabbed her by the upper arm and dragged her up against him.

"Oh! Gracious!" Miss Winthrop gasped from the end of the hallway. "Is she flirting with you again?"

Hot anger pulsed through Etta as Miss Winthrop immediately took the side of Mr. Spicer.

How many times has she done that before?

Mr. Spicer dropped Etta's arm as fast as he had grabbed it.

Miss Winthrop's hand fluttered at her throat. "Miss Lynne, this is most inappropriate!"

Mr. Spicer rounded on Miss Winthrop. "Move along, Miss Winthrop. Miss Lynne is used to seducing men to get her way. I assure you, I am not under her spell as *some are*."

Miss Winthrop looked from Etta to Mr. Spicer and then back to Etta. "This is outrageous!"

You stole that note and gave it to him. The two of you are working together. I know it.

Etta leaped away from Mr. Spicer and reached down to pick up her satchel. Her hands shook as she dragged the strap over her shoulder.

"Seduce you?" She shook her head as she rubbed her arm where he had grabbed it. "Is that what you accuse women of, women who stand up to you?" Etta lifted her chin and took a step closer to him. "You crossed the wrong woman."

"Gracious!" Miss Winthrop repeated as her jaw dropped.

Mr. Spicer turned on his heel and left them standing in the hallway.

* * *

ETTA STOOD in the silent hallway, her heart beating hard in her ears. Miss Winthrop's lips pursed in disapproval.

"You're no different from Mrs. Ellice. Are you pregnant, too? Is the baby his?" Miss Winthrop's eyes hardened in judgment.

Etta turned on Miss Winthrop. "Do you truly believe that Mrs. Ellice was pregnant with Mr. Spicer's child?" She could barely form the words; they sickened her.

"I am sure of it." Miss Winthrop straightened up in righteous indignation. A flash of jealousy in her eye as she said it.

You're in love with him!

"What if *he* was harassing *her*?" Etta roared at Miss Winthrop.

"Women like you are all the same." Shaking her finger, Miss Winthrop took a step toward Etta. "You're beautiful, and you think all men are panting after you. You make me sick. Life is easy for you. You want something, you just smile at a man until

219

he gives it to you. You're no different than Mrs. Ellice," Miss Winthrop hissed at Etta.

Etta took a step back from the vicious fury in Miss Winthrop's eyes.

You feel passed over, sad and lonely. You were jealous of Mrs. Ellice. How jealous? What did you do to her? Did you kill her and then leave that note on my desk?

"I despise Mr. Spicer. I did not show him my ankle. He wanted to be sure I was wearing two petticoats; he asked to see proof." Etta rubbed her arm where his fingers had bitten into her.

"You could be lying." Miss Winthrop crossed her arms over her chest. "Lying to get what you want."

"Well, Miss Winthrop, I want justice, and I don't have to lie to get it. I will tell the truth, and I will expose him. He won't get away with threats and intimidation anymore." Etta's tone sharpened in warning. "Anyone who supports that behaviour will be exposed, too."

"You don't want justice! You want a man and a meal ticket," Miss Winthrop lashed back. "Find another school…" Miss Winthrop let the sentence die off.

"Or what?" Etta challenged Miss Winthrop.

Miss Winthrop pivoted toward the break room.

Etta pulled the note out of her satchel. "Did you leave this note on my desk?"

Miss Winthrop turned back around to face Etta. Her eyes swept over the note and then narrowed. "It's incorrectly spelled."

"Did you leave this incorrectly spelled note on my desk?" Etta's jaw was tight with fury.

Miss Winthrop sniffed and refused to answer. She let herself into the lunchroom and slammed the door shut.

Etta bolted from the school. Worried that Spicer would pounce on her again when she least suspected it, she quickened her pace. As she drove, a cold finger of terror slid down Etta's spine. Mr. Nash and his men were not looking for the scene of an accident; they were looking for the scene of a crime.

CHAPTER 27

$\mathcal{T}$he men of Oakland hunkered down in their heavy wool coats as they assembled teams to search each bank of the river. The angry April rain punished them, stinging any exposed skin, chapping their hands as they sifted through dead grass and remnants of snow banks. The floodwaters of the creek and the river kept rising each day as the snow melted. The bridges of Oakland were on the verge of disaster if the waters crested any higher. Nash stood on the bank at the back of Mrs. Lemon's house where the river and the creek met and looked down each side.

"We need teams on the creek banks, too," Nash said to Detective Kane. "The current in the creek empties here in the river."

"Right, two teams for the creek banks. There are miles to cover," Detective Kane muttered as he breathed warm air into his bare hands.

"Most of the men from this community are here, and we won't stop until we figure this out." Nash took a broad stance. "I have noticed we're missing two men from the community — Mr. Spicer and Mr. Lemon— I suggest you find out why they didn't show up. This was a community-wide summons."

"We can't make men search." Detective Kane frowned.

"No man from this community would dream of *not* searching." Nash's eyes swept over the men. "I'll start on the creek bank down from the walking trails. I'll take Deputy Mayor Holt."

Mr. Spicer was increasingly becoming a suspect in his mind, which meant nothing. As mayor, he had no authority regarding this investigation, but he would pull out every stop to figure this out, and he would see justice done. A dead woman in their community was the worst thing that had ever happened in Oakland, and it had happened on his watch. Nash shook his head and crossed his arms over his chest. Whoever did this would face swift and brutal justice. He guaranteed it.

Nash crawled up the side of the bank, convinced that if ever there was a place that could cause death because of a struggle it would be here. The bank was so steep that if you fell off the ledge by the path you would never stop yourself. Slippery shale and rocks gave nothing to cling to. Nash, who was born and raised in this community, knew every inch of the riverbank, but like all children raised near a river, he knew every rock under the surface, too. In dry years, rocks and rapids showed up, and he and his comrades had committed the underwater landscape to memory. In and out of the water. The men in the teams had swum here, where the creek met the river for years. He knew only *this* place could cause serious damage if you fell.

Or were pushed.

Deputy Mayor Holt came to his side. They looked at each other as the rain turned to snow.

"If there was a struggle on the path..." Nash said.

"If she fell over the side... maybe hit her head on that rock... the flood water would have taken her downstream," Holt thought out loud.

"We search the walking trail then," Nash said grimly. "Let's focus on that section by the creek."

"Lover's Lane." Holt rubbed the stubble on his chin.

Nash shook his head. "Seems ironic that she might have fallen to her death on a patch of the trail called *Lover's Lane.*"

"I think you and I both know she didn't fall off that cliff face. She was pushed." Holt breathed heavily as he followed Nash up the steep incline.

"I hope you are wrong."

"You're always such an optimist." Holt stopped to catch his breath.

"I've been called worse, and usually by you." Nash took a deep breath at the top of the hill and waited for Holt to catch up.

His eyes swept over the trails. The bare oak boughs brushed the steel-grey sky. Bare red willow was the only colour against the drab grey-and-brown ice-crusted landscape.

Together, Nash and Holt walked the Lover's Lane path. Finally, at the very edge of the trail where it bowed out to the sheer cliff face, they stood still. On top of a piece of snow and ice lay a yarn-covered button.

One button.

Olive green.

Bright against the dirt-covered snow bank.

"A yarn-covered button. Does this suggest a struggle? This is not left from summer and not from fall. It's on top of the ice. This is recent." Nash crouched down to examine it closely.

"This is a woman's button, though." Holt frowned as he looked at it sitting on the snowbank. "Maybe it belonged to Mrs. Ellice?"

"Or another woman? Maybe she saw something, maybe she heard something. But there is nothing else that even indicates a human has been up here. But it's all we have." Nash straightened up. "I'll go for Detective Kane. We'll do a thorough search of this area and see if there is anything else."

"Quickly, this snow is sticking, and we must call off the search soon." Holt stood by the button as Mr. Bennett and Mr. Rood made their way up the incline and stood by him on the trail. They searched the radius around the button, careful not to get too close to the edge of the cliff.

Nash walked swiftly down the path to the men searching the riverbank. Detective Kane stood by the bridge, watching them work.

Nash's heart fell to his feet as he thought how Mrs. Ellice might have met her death on that path on top of the cliff. He knew about being outmaneuvered and overpowered from his time in the war. He couldn't imagine what it would feel like to be a woman overpowered by a man and thrown off a cliff. The thought that someone had harmed her wouldn't leave his mind. That yarn-covered button made his jaw clench with worry, though. Men didn't wear buttons like that. Was a woman with the man?

No.

Women weren't capable of such violence.

Nash shook that thought away. No. This button must belong to Mrs. Ellice herself, or maybe a woman went walking the next day. It was weak evidence. It could have been there from yesterday. But it was all they had to go on.

"We found something," Nash said as Kane turned to look at him. "I think we might need more men to search the top of the hill."

"What did you find?" Kane asked as he followed Nash back up to Lover's Lane.

"It might be nothing." Nash pulled his scarf around his neck closer as the snow clung to his coat. "A yarn-covered button."

Kane stopped walking. "What colour?"

"Kind of an olive-green colour."

Nash turned to look at him.

"There was fiber found in a cut in her fingernail." Kane's voice deepened ominously.

The blood drained from Nash's face. "What colour?"

"Olive green."

Nash muttered a curse under his breath. "Was she wearing an olive-green sweater?"

"No." Kane's face hardened into a mask of professionalism.

Together they joined the men on the trails. The snow drove down heavier, and finally, after half an hour of searching, when they could barely see through the snow, Kane called off the search.

Nash looked up and saw Miss Lynne walking down the path toward them.

He straightened up, and worry winged through him as he recognized fear in her eyes.

Like a moth to a flame, Nash made his way through the men

to reach her side. Wet, sticky snowflakes clung to her long lashes; her cheeks were red from the raw cold. She shivered from cold or terror; he wasn't sure which. Pieces of blonde hair had escaped from her pins and curled against the side of her face.

Nash moved closer to her. With ice everywhere around them, he worried she would slip. Etta's small frame looked vulnerable against the men on the riverbank.

"Is everything all right?" Nash asked her.

"I forgot all the assignments I needed to grade at the school, and I had to prepare for tomorrow," Miss Lynne said, breathless from the incline she had scrambled up.

"I told you not to leave the house alone." Fear tightened Nash's chest, close on the heels of fury at her outright defiance.

"I didn't listen, and believe me, I will never do it again." Miss Lynne's face paled at his tone. "I thought because it was daylight, I was safe. I wasn't."

"What happened?" Nash's heart pounded with worry.

"I have something the investigator needs to see at once." The look she shot him was intense.

"Are you hurt?" Nash ran his hands over her arms to check for damage; he couldn't stop himself.

If someone hurt you, I will kill him.

"No." Miss Lynne fumbled with her handbag. Her hands trembled as she tried to pull out a piece of paper. "This was on my desk when I got to the school."

Nash took the paper from her and read the words in black, angry handwriting. As he read it, his heart pounded in fear for her safety. "Stop or 'your' next."

Acid pooled in his stomach as he imagined her being hurt by Mr. Spicer.

"At the risk of sounding like an English teacher, the spelling is wrong," Miss Lynne pointed out. "'Your' should be 'you're.' It is incorrect." Her blue eyes were wide as she looked up at him.

Nash's lips thinned. "Detective Kane," Nash called out. "You need to see this."

* * *

ETTA STOOD on the trail where the men were convinced Mrs. Ellice had met her death. She shuddered as Detective Kane made his way through the men to her side. His clever eyes skimmed over the note.

Etta crossed her arms over her chest as Detective Kane examined the front and then the back of the note.

"Detective Kane, I found this on my desk at the school this morning." Etta adjusted her scarf as the wind picked up.

"I searched Mrs. Ellice's desk already, but it looks like we need to search your desk and classroom."

"When did you search my desk?" Etta tilted her head to the side.

"No, Mrs. Ellice's desk," Kane corrected her.

"I *have* Mrs. Ellice's desk," Etta insisted.

Kane's head snapped up at her insistence. "You're sure?"

"Yes. I have her desk, and the bottom drawer is stuck. Someone snapped a key off in the lock. Today, when I found Mr. Spicer and this note in my room, once we were in the hallway, I broke the key off in the classroom's door so no one could tamper with anything." Etta hated that fear made her voice sound breathless and weak.

"Let me get this straight." Kane pulled out a notepad. "Miss Winthrop informed me that classroom number 12 was Mrs. Ellice's classroom. The desk in that room was hers and hers alone."

"Detective Kane. I took over her job and her room. Her desk is in room 16," Etta insisted. "Classroom number 12 is a spare room."

Etta shivered harder as the snow fell thicker. It became difficult to see others on the path. "Today, when I got to the school, Miss Winthrop and Mrs. Delaire were just outside my classroom. The door to my classroom was open, and Mr. Spicer was inside, going through books on the bookshelf. If you remember, that is where I found the note with 300 written on it. Same colour of ink as this note."

"You can be sure of that." Kane tucked his notepad away.

The blood drained from Nash's face. "I told you not to go anywhere by yourself! You disobeyed..."

"A direct order. Yes, I know." Etta crossed her arms over her chest as if to protect herself. "It was foolish. No argument there. I thought, eleven in the morning, broad daylight, what could happen? I was utterly wrong, and I will not leave the house without an armed escort again. You have my word."

Mr. Nash blinked in surprise.

"Spicer said he was looking for a book he had lent Mrs. Ellice, but maybe he left that note." Etta pulled her scarf tighter around her neck.

"I will kill him." Mr. Nash's hands balled into fists.

"Careful. I am in earshot here." Detective Kane frowned at Mr. Nash. "We've had enough killing, I'd say."

"Sorry." Mr. Nash stiffened, his face like a thundercloud.

Etta swallowed down her worries about the lecture she would endure later.

"What did he threaten you with?" Kane asked Etta quietly.

"To terminate my career. I'd never work again."

"Then why are you helping?" Kane kept his voice low so no one could overhear.

"A woman is dead. We have to know what happened. No teacher is safe with a man like Mr. Spicer on the school board. This has gone too far," Etta said simply.

"We will go back to the school. The search is off for now, anyway. The snow is covering everything. The men will go home to their suppers." Detective Kane handled the note carefully.

Mr. Nash called to Mr. Holt to say the search was off.

"I'll see you home, and we'll deal with the desk drawer," Mr. Nash ordered Etta.

"I would prefer to come with you. It's my desk." Etta stood her ground.

"I would prefer you listen to me when I ask you to have an escort before leaving the house," Mr. Nash snapped at her.

Etta opened her mouth to speak and then clamped it shut.

"Are you in a relationship with Mr. Nash?" Detective Kane asked Etta.

"No, I am not," Etta responded with clipped tones.

"I assure you our relationship is purely professional," Mr. Nash growled.

"Ah, right. Miss Lynne cannot court or she would lose her job. I realize that." Detective Kane tilted his head to the side as if he were sizing them both up. "I understand you are in the habit of protecting her. Standing up for her at school board meetings. I heard you lost your job as a trustee because of her."

Mr. Nash moved slightly away from Etta. "There is a good explanation for that."

"I look forward to hearing it. All three of us will empty the contents of the drawer with the broken lock," Detective Kane decided.

Mr. Nash's lips thinned. "Am I a suspect because I protected Miss Lynne?"

"I hear you were protective of Mrs. Ellice, too." Detective Kane's tone had a hint of accusation.

"I'm protective of all women. I think that is the job of any man in a position of authority, to be sure the vulnerable of society are taken care of and their needs met if they cannot meet those needs themselves."

"What needs did Mrs. Ellice have that you met?" Detective Kane asked point blank.

Etta caught a look of shock and surprise on Mr. Nash's face as Detective Kane pressed him for the truth.

"Mr. Spicer was accusing her of indecent behaviour, and he had no proof. I refused to let him fire her on such flimsy grounds," Mr. Nash answered.

Detective Kane nodded. "I will meet you at the school in the next fifteen minutes. No one enters the school until I have searched. The classroom is now a crime scene. Try not to kill each other before you get there." Kane frowned at them and made his way down the slippery path to the entrance of the park.

Etta and Mr. Nash nodded their agreement and then made their way off the walking path toward the bridge to the Lemon house.

Etta slipped on the ice on her side of the path, and Mr. Nash grabbed her and righted her.

"You're angry with me." Her jaw clenched.

"I am furious." Mr. Nash let go of her. "I can't believe you would put yourself in danger like that! I was very clear!"

"I know." Etta's shoulders slumped. "I was wrong."

"What was that? I'm not sure I heard correctly," Mr. Nash demanded.

Etta's eyes filled with tears. "I was wrong." Her voice cracked as she apologized.

"Don't. Don't you dare cry, Miss Lynne. That is not fair." Mr. Nash frowned at her.

A tear slid down Etta's cheek as Mr. Nash turned to face her. "Stop that immediately. I can't yell at a crying woman. That is enough."

Two more tears raced down her cheek. She valiantly tried to dash them away.

Mr. Nash sighed and took his glove off.

"Here now, I've had my say. It's all right." Mr. Nash's tone gentled as he wiped her tears away.

Etta blinked, and more tears spilled down her cheeks.

"Tell me what happened." Mr. Nash kept his tone gentle.

"Spicer came into the classroom, and he locked the door." Etta brushed more tears away. She moved and slipped.

Mr. Nash grabbed her by the upper arms, and she winced.

"He hurt you," Mr. Nash gasped.

"He hurt my arm when he held on to it." Etta winced.

Fury flashed in Mr. Nash's eyes as he let go of her upper arms.

"He threatened to tell the board about finding us after eight on the street. I finally unlocked the door, and once I got out of the room and down the hall, he grabbed me. Nothing happened because Miss Winthrop heard the fuss. He only hurt my arm."

"I will kill him."

"You have got to stop saying that! There is already a murder investigation," Etta hissed under her breath.

"I will deal with this." Nash started walking.

Etta grabbed his arm to stop him. "Stop! You mustn't."

"Give me one good reason." Nash turned to face her.

"He wants that!" Etta cried. "He has you off the board. He's

done something. There must be evidence he was looking for…
We have to catch him and ensure that what happened to Mrs.
Ellice doesn't happen to anyone else. We have to keep our
heads…" Etta brushed snow from her eyelashes. She looked
around the landscape, the bare trees, brown grass, and red
willow to try to calm herself.

"Miss Lynne, maybe I haven't been clear." Mr. Nash dropped
his voice to a dangerously ominous level. "I will handle the
threats and intimidation against your person."

"I have a plan. I have a letter to the—"

"Oh, I'm sure he's crying himself to sleep at the thought of a
letter," Nash mocked her.

Etta's tears fled as her spine stiffened. "It is a very detailed
and brutal letter."

"Let me detail the brutality he will face from my fists. Then I
assure you he will cry himself to sleep at night." Mr. Nash's face
was an inch from hers.

Etta shook her head. "I've asked you to step down and let me
handle this. I will not take no for an answer."

"Oh! How interesting. *You* can't take no for an answer, but
you can ignore my requests."

"Demands," Etta corrected primly.

"And I'm supposed to ask how high when you say jump!" Mr.
Nash shot at her.

"Stop." Etta held her hands up.

They stood alone at the bottom of the path. The rest of the
men had dispersed for their homes. Mr. Nash's jaw clenched
hard; Etta could tell he was working to restrain himself from
yelling.

Etta looked around to be sure they could not be seen.

"Can we please call a truce?" Etta held her hands out in
supplication.

"No."

"Mr. Nash, be reasonable," Etta groaned.

Mr. Nash growled in frustration. "I want your word — you
will not leave the house without me."

"Agreed. I want your word you will not play into Mr.
Spicer's nefarious scheme by beating him up and turning the

attention from him to you. He wants a diversion. He wants chaos so he can get away with murder," Etta demanded.

Mr. Nash looked at her. "You are very clever."

Etta shrugged. "Rose Ellice could have been me."

Nash's face went white as she said the words.

"He has to be stopped, and if we're fighting, we can't stop him. It ends here. Truce. Yes or no?"

"Truce," Mr. Nash relented.

Etta and Mr. Nash both sighed with relief.

"Mr. Nash, one last thing." Etta thought of how to say the next sentence without bursting into tears. She placed her hand on his forearm to get his full attention. "Before we go back and have no privacy."

"Yes?" Mr. Nash turned to her.

Etta gathered her thoughts and her emotions as she watched the snow fall against the red willow and white birch trees. She took a deep breath as the emotions of the past few days had left her raw.

"The gift you left me." Etta turned her attention from the beauty of the snowfall to him. "I — I don't know how to say it… that is the nicest and most thoughtful gift I have ever received. Thank you so much. I am so touched by your thoughtfulness."

"You're very welcome." Mr. Nash's face softened as she spoke.

"When I sold those items, I felt like I had sold my dream. It crushed my spirit. When I saw them in my possession, well…" Etta's throat ached from unshed tears.

"Well what, Miss Lynne?" Mr. Nash prompted gently.

"I thought for the first time since I lost my home, since everything happened, I dared to dream again, about art school. I'm not sure how, but maybe someday." A bright smile of hope and joy broke across Etta's face as she spoke of her dream. "You'll think I'm foolish. Pursuing art…"

"No." Mr. Nash stepped closer to her. "That is not foolish at all. I hope you get to go, and you are very welcome. Maybe you can paint me something before you go."

"I would love that." Etta adjusted her mitten. "I'm sorry, again, about going to the school. I won't do that again."

"I could've held my temper better," Mr. Nash conceded.

"You could work on that," Etta suggested slyly.

"Etta, you terrify me." Mr. Nash spoke honestly.

"I do?" Etta's eyebrows rose in surprise.

"What hurts you, hurts me," Mr. Nash whispered.

"Oh." Etta blinked up at him, seeing the sincerity of his words in his eyes.

Mr. Nash moved forward and adjusted her hat so it protected her from the driving snow.

"Other than your arm, did he hurt you? I want to know." Mr. Nash moved a piece of hair that had fallen into her eye.

"He scared me. He didn't really hurt me. But, Nash, I do think he killed Mrs. Ellice." Etta bit her lip.

She watched concern bloom in his eyes.

And fear.

A fear that matched her own.

$\mathcal{M}$rs. Daindrige and Mrs. Carr, from the vantage point of Lucy Lemon's kitchen window, slyly pulled their binoculars out of their handbags.

Alone in the kitchen, they took a break from making biscuits to cast an eye over the men who were searching the riverbanks. As they watched, the men left for their homes. Their binoculars simultaneously landed on Miss Lynne and Mr. Nash.

"What is happening here?" Mrs. Daindridge asked Mrs. Carr out of the corner of her mouth.

"Gracious, he's holding her," Mrs. Carr whispered back. Neither of them wanted Mrs. Holt or Mrs. Lemon to find them spying.

Mrs. Daindridge harrumphed, and Mrs. Carr twisted the wheel to adjust the focus on her binoculars to get a better look. She watched as Mr. Nash stroked Miss Lynne's hair back and adjusted her hat. She gasped as he tenderly tucked a lock of hair behind her ear. Her eyes widened as Miss Lynne looked up at him with a tortured look in her eyes.

Mr. Nash listened to her as if she were the only woman on earth. His entire body was tense, ready to defend her against whatever caused her pain.

Mrs. Daindridge and Mrs. Carr watched with bated breath

as fresh tears gathered in Miss Lynne's eyes. Mr. Nash pulled off his glove and very tenderly wiped them away.

"Do you see what I see?" Mrs. Carr clutched at Mrs. Daindridge.

"I see love's young dream on a path from a crime scene. That's what I see." Mrs. Daindridge's eyes gleamed with anticipation as her binoculars banged into the window as she tried to get as close as she could to the action unraveling in front of them. "I see a teacher about to be fired because she is breaking the code of conduct for teachers."

A throat cleared from the door of the kitchen.

Mrs. Daindridge and Mrs. Carr both jumped, and their binoculars nearly ended up in the sink.

"What you saw in those binoculars was a man comforting a woman who has received bad news, whose mother has died. This is a difficult day. Let's not *infer* anything." Mrs. Holt left the two old women gabbling excuses.

As soon as the door shut behind Mrs. Holt, Mrs. Daindridge and Mrs. Carr grabbed their binoculars and unrepentantly returned to the window.

"What now?" Mrs. Carr put the binoculars back to her eyes.

"He's helping her down the path. It must be slippery," Mrs. Daindridge commented snidely.

"He's got his arm around her waist. She just stopped him to say something," Mrs. Carr whispered in case Mrs. Holt interrupted their surveillance again. "Look at how he looks at her, Mrs. Daindridge." Mrs. Carr's heart hammered, remembering what it felt like to have a man assist you down a slippery path. The way a man ducked his head to listen to you speak. She flushed as memories of Mr. Carr flashed through her mind... a day on that path... away from prying eyes...

Mrs. Carr snapped back to the present when Mrs. Daindridge tisked in disapproval.

They watched the couple walk across the bridge, her hand on his arm. He seemed twice as broad because of his heavy coat, soaked with rain and snow. She seemed tiny beside him as she slipped again and he grabbed her.

"There must be a lot of ice out there." Mrs. Daindridge frowned.

"I know that trick." Mrs. Carr smiled with the memory. Sliding on ice, anything to get Mr. Carr's attention, his hands on her waist.

So long ago.

"Well, it's a scandal. They are smitten." Mrs. Daindridge shot a look of contempt at Mrs. Carr, whose face was soft with dreamy remembrance. Mrs. Daindridge narrowed her eyes. "They're stopping."

"Women teachers should not be caught in compromising positions with mayors, Mrs. Carr. Pay attention! What is wrong with you?"

Mrs. Carr dragged her thoughts back to the scandal in front of them.

"He's cradling her face in his hands," Mrs. Carr whispered to Mrs. Daindridge. She held her breath as she watched Mr. Nash bend down slightly.

"Gracious, he's going to kiss her!" Mrs. Daindridge gasped in outrage.

Mrs. Daindridge and Mrs. Carr held their breath as they watched Mr. Nash's every move through their binoculars.

"He's stroking her cheek," Mrs. Daindridge hissed to Mrs. Carr.

"This is *very* compromising, isn't it?" Mrs. Carr pressed her binoculars right against the glass.

"Yes. It is." Mrs. Daindridge's lips thinned with contempt. "Mrs. Holt or no Mrs. Holt, difficult day or not. This is just plain wrong."

Their hearts plummeted with disappointment as Mr. Nash stepped back and the couple made their way across the bridge. No kiss. No concrete proof that Miss Lynne and Mr. Nash were courting.

Frowning, they lowered their binoculars and hid them away before Mrs. Holt could scold them again.

"In my day"—Mrs. Daindridge put her binoculars away— "younger women didn't scold older women."

"Mrs. Holt went through the change, and now she is a firecracker, and she needs her wings clipped," Mrs. Carr grumbled, secretly disappointed that Mr. Nash *hadn't* kissed Miss Lynne. Life was short. All too soon, your only connection to love was watching it through a pair of binoculars.

Mrs. Holt suddenly appeared at the doorway.

Mrs. Daindridge and Mrs. Carr jumped in guilt.

"I think it's time to serve the soup for the men from out of town. The rest have returned to their homes." Mrs. Holt frowned at them. "The heavy spring snow has stopped the search."

"Oh, that sounds very good. We'll keep working on the dessert," Mrs. Daindridge said to Mrs. Holt.

Mrs. Carr nodded in agreement.

Mrs. Holt left them to their cake batter in the kitchen.

"Did she hear?" Mrs. Daindridge asked Mrs. Carr.

"I don't think so." Mrs. Carr shook her head.

"This relationship between Miss Lynne and Mr. Nash..." Mrs. Daindridge whispered at Mrs. Carr as they kept one eye on the door in case someone could overhear them.

"He didn't kiss her." Mrs. Carr held the cake tin as Mrs. Daindridge poured.

"You must let your son know today, anyway. We cannot have this scandalous behaviour in our community. We must remind the next generation that chastity is a virtue!"

"I'll see. But, really. He didn't kiss her, and she has just lost her mother, Mrs. Daindridge. Maybe this time we can turn a blind eye," Mrs. Carr suggested gently, still thinking of Mr. Carr.

Mrs. Daindridge frowned. "You might have a point. However, I am convinced that these young ones are dragging us to the verge of moral chaos!"

* * *

"I'LL BRING THE CAR AROUND," Mr. Nash said as Etta tucked her hand back into the crook of his arm.

She could feel the power in his arm under her fingertips. "Thank you."

As they got into the car, Etta leaned back in her seat.

"I will stay with you and Mrs. Lemon until this murderer is found and brought to justice. You have nothing to worry about." Mr. Nash pulled the driver's side door shut.

"I'm more worried that we are in this car together. There will be rumours and suspicions, and I can't bear it."

Mr. Nash said nothing.

"Why aren't you speaking?"

"Because all of you are in danger until they bring Mr. Spicer to justice. I'm staying, and I don't care about rumours and suspicions. My mind is made up; there is nothing to discuss."

"You can't just do that. You agreed! You can't decide and expect everyone to just fall into line," Etta growled at him.

"Yes, I can. I'm the mayor— I do it all the time. We called a truce!"

"I un-call it!" Etta snapped.

"You're…"

"If you call me hysterical, it will fare very badly for you," Etta warned Mr. Nash.

"I wouldn't dare."

"Were you in a relationship with Mrs. Ellice? Detective Kane wants to ask questions. Why is he asking you?"

"No, I was not. I had little to do with her, honestly."

"You're sure?" Etta asked. She despised the jealousy that prickled through her heart.

"Positive. She was here only a short time. She started in early January, which is why I was furious when she disappeared. She had hardly even warmed the seat."

"Was Mr. Spicer attracted to her?"

"I don't know, why?"

"Something Miss Winthrop said. She mentioned that she thought Mrs. Ellice flirted with him."

"Really?" Mr. Nash's eyes narrowed.

"I don't know. Miss Winthrop believed she was acting inappropriately."

"He accused *her* of being indecent and insubordinate. All the time. Same as he is doing to you. He was unrelenting. I was sick of him and told him that. We were not in a relationship of any sort. I would have done that for anyone I felt was being dealt with unfairly."

"Very noble," Etta said dryly.

"I'm a gentleman," Mr. Nash said simply.

"She would feel helpless on the path. Facing whoever she faced there. I'm sure you wouldn't understand," Etta said quietly.

"I completely understand." Mr. Nash turned down the street to the school.

Etta shook her head. "I don't believe it. I saw you hit Santini. You weren't afraid at all."

"I was a soldier, Etta." Mr. Nash shrugged. "I've done far worse than what I did to him. However, soldier or not, I know about being powerless."

"When?" Etta's eyes searched his.

"When my wife died in childbirth." Mr. Nash put his car into gear. "I was terrified. Ada told me that Nell had passed and there was nothing they could do. She was crying as she told me. I was numb with shock." Mr. Nash shook his head. "Feminine complaints and childbirth are a closed door to men. We watch the women we love suffer, we hear it on the other side of the door, but there is absolutely nothing we can do. It's awful. I know about being powerless, and I didn't mean to make you feel that way. I'm very sorry you are in the position you are in."

"I am so sorry about your wife." Etta's eyes softened in sympathy.

"Thank you. It's been a long time, but I still feel responsible. I will always feel responsible. I know what that feels like, too."

Etta shivered.

"Are you cold?" Mr. Nash shot her a look of concern.

"No, I am thinking. This is really the first time..." Etta wrapped her arms around herself.

"First time of what?" Mr. Nash took his eyes off the road again to look at her.

"My first time that a man wants to protect and care about me," Etta said quietly.

"Really?" Mr. Nash dragged his attention back to the street.

"Really. I am not used to the impulsiveness, though. You just reacted..."

"I should have been more impulsive when Nell was dying. I regret that every day. I should have broken down the door and held her. They said she bled to death. I regret I wasn't in the room with her. I waited to act. If it were to ever happen again, I wouldn't wait on the other side of the door."

Etta placed her hand on his arm. "Nash..."

"I'm not standing around asking permission in life anymore. Don't wait so long to trust, Miss Lynne. It's not a bad thing to let someone take care of you sometimes."

Etta took a deep breath and let it out very slowly. "It's hard to trust. I trusted my father, but his weaknesses, his vices, left us vulnerable. I am scared." Etta took her hand away. "I'll never forget going to meet with the lawyer and realizing we had nothing after all the debts were paid, it was like the bottom of my world just fell away and I was spiraling into a vulnerability I had never experienced. I didn't know slum housing like Santini runs even existed until I was begging for a roof over my head. It devastated me. I had two family members I was responsible for and another on the way.

"So I am just tired. Honestly. Very tired of holding all this together and equally terrified that if I trust someone to handle things I'll be left open to this vulnerability again. Can you comprehend that at all? Is this too out of your realm?" Etta's voice dropped as she spoke.

A look passed across Nash's face that Etta struggled to read. "I see your point of view, and I'm sorry it happened to you, Miss Lynne. It never should have happened."

Etta swallowed hard. "So, when you decide about Grace, I want you to remember what happened. Santini... all of it."

Nash nodded as he concentrated on the road. "I will."

"Good."

"Is there anything else you want to tell me?" Nash asked as he parked the car in front of the school.

Etta took a deep breath. "Nothing I can't handle."

"You're sure?" Nash asked. "No other threats or concerns? If you need a hand, ask. I can do more ironing if you need it."

Etta smiled. "Very kind of you. I didn't know that about your wife. I never dreamed you knew what it's like to be helpless. You seem completely in control all the time."

Nash shrugged. "We were married for twelve years. I had very little control, actually."

"I don't believe that for a second." Etta rolled her eyes.

Nash grinned at her.

Kane pulled up and parked on the opposite side of the street.

"Who does he suspect at this point?" Etta gathered her handbag before getting out of the motorcar.

"He's being very closed mouth about the entire thing." Nash got out of the driver's seat to jog around his motorcar and help her out.

She put her hand in the crook of his arm. "I'm sure that Mr. Spicer is a suspect, of course, but honestly, there were women in this town who I hear were not nice to Mrs. Ellice either."

"Mr. Spicer didn't show up to search; I pointed it out. Neither did Lester Lemon. I am certain Mr. Spicer is behind this. But, Miss Lynne, to think a woman is behind this is not possible. Women aren't killers." Nash dismissed her suggestion in a way that made Etta's jaw clench in fury. "Women are delicate and fragile. They need protection from men, not other women," Nash reasoned.

"You mean to tell me that you think only men should be investigated?" Etta's eyes widened in shock.

"I told you, women aren't capable." Nash spoke with such finality; Etta's back stiffened in frustration.

"I am telling *you*, Nash. Women are very capable..."

Detective Kane waved them into the school, interrupting Etta in the process. Etta hoped Detective Kane wasn't as naïve as Nash.

Nash placed a hand on the small of her back. Together they made their way up the steps of the school to the classroom and the locked drawer.

CHAPTER 29

$\mathcal{T}$he three of them stood by as the locksmith broke open the door to Etta's classroom. Etta wished someone would speak, but the men remained silent while waiting for the locksmith to do his job. Detective Kane indicated Etta and Nash should sit down while the locksmith worked on the broken lock on the bottom drawer of the desk.

"Did the medical examiner make it here?" Mr. Nash asked Detective Kane.

"Yes, and I have a full report. The only thing left is to search her effects from Barlow's, which I will do as soon as I am done here."

Nash nodded.

"Would you please tell me everything? Starting from when you got to the school. What did you see, Miss Lynne?" Detective Kane leaned against the desk.

"I was standing at the end of the hall. Mrs. Delaire and Miss Winthrop were by the door of the classroom. I can't be sure if they had been in the room or not. They said they were discussing which pies were being supplied for the pie box social. When I entered the classroom, Mr. Spicer was going through the books on the bookshelf. He told me he was searching for a book that he had lent Mrs. Ellice. After he left, I found the note sitting on top of my desk. I don't leave clutter on my desk, so it stood right out to me. He left when he couldn't find what he was looking for. As soon as I found that note, I tucked it in my bag and no longer felt safe. I was leaving my classroom when Mr. Spicer came back."

"Go on."

"Mr. Spicer saw Nash walking me home last night very late. My mother died, as you know, and he didn't think I should be walking alone."

"Very wise."

"So Mr. Spicer saw us, and he had all the evidence he needed to have me fired as I was in the company of men after eight. Anyway, he entered the room and locked the door behind him. Just him and I." Etta swallowed hard.

"And?"

"He said, 'I think it's safe to assume Mrs. Ellice tangled with the wrong person. Miss Lynne, are you going to make the same mistakes?'" Etta quoted word for word.

Detective Kane's eyes squinted. "Did you feel threatened?"

"Of course she felt threatened!" Nash bolted to his feet.

"Sit down, Mr. Nash, it is only a courtesy that you are here." Detective Kane didn't take his eyes off Etta's face.

Nash sat and crossed his arms over his chest.

"As I said, he was looking for something on the bookshelf, and he didn't find it. I think he suspects I found something because he is keen to have me fired immediately. He said he had a letter with a list of offences that he was taking to the board. I told him I was going to the lieutenant governor with a list of *his* offences. I feel like he is pre-emptively making sure my word holds no weight."

"How did he take that, the letter going to the governor?" Kane wrote down 'letter to lieutenant governor' and underlined it.

"He said it was my word against his. No one would listen to me."

Detective Kane scratched down more of Etta's statement.

"I think he was going to go through this desk, but I was here and he didn't want me to know what he was looking for."

Detective Kane shot a look at Nash. "Is it typical for the members of the board to have keys to classrooms?"

"Yes. The board has keys to the school and everything in it."

"So, the teachers working here have no expectation of privacy?" Detective Kane frowned at Nash. "Interesting."

Nash stiffened in his chair. "I think we have all learned that there are flaws in how we have handled things on the school board. I give you my word there will be a change of protocol after this is all sorted out."

"Oh, I hope so. I will be following up, you can be sure." Detective Kane turned his attention back to Etta. "Other than Mr. Spicer, who do you think is capable of leaving this note?"

"Miss Winthrop." Etta answered before Mr. Nash could. She pressed her fingertips against her temple.

"Are you well, Miss Lynne?" Detective Kane asked politely.

"Yes, sir. I am fine." Etta dropped her hand from her temple. "I think Miss Winthrop has a key."

"How does she feel about you?"

Etta cleared her throat. "We don't get along at all, actually."

Nash looked at Etta in surprise. "Why?"

"I thought it was just petty jealousy, but she said Mrs. Ellice was inappropriate. She even accused her of being pregnant. I think she sees all women as a threat."

"Pregnant?" Detective Kane wrote the word on his pad. Etta noticed he underlined it.

"Pregnant!" Nash gasped.

"At the time of death, Mrs. Ellice was twenty weeks pregnant, according to the medical examiner. So she was pregnant when she interviewed for this position," Kane said.

Etta noticed Kane carefully gauging Nash's reaction to the news.

Nash's jaw dropped open in shock.

"We'll return to that. Miss Lynne, who did she think the father was?" Kane directed the question to Etta.

"She thought maybe Mr. Spicer, because Mr. Spicer was here and in her room constantly."

"Did she say Mrs. Ellice knew Mr. Spicer prior to interviewing with the school board?"

"She didn't speak to that at all."

"Continue, please."

"Miss Winthrop said I was like Mrs. Ellice. All beautiful women just use men to get what they want. We have it easy, and on and on."

"What do you mean by 'on and on'?" Kane tilted his head to the side.

"You know, if you are a beautiful woman, maybe life is easier for you." Etta leaned back in her chair.

"You don't think it is?" Detective Kane asked quietly.

"I grew up with a beautiful younger sister, so I never thought of myself as beautiful for a minute. Compared to her, I look like a washed-out dishrag," Etta answered honestly.

"Um, you look nothing like a washed-out dishrag. I have no idea where you came up with that." Nash's eyebrows rose as he contradicted her.

Detective Kane looked from Nash to Etta.

"I have been a target for unwanted male attention, but it has always been my assumption that I was a target because I was in vulnerable situations due to poverty. I don't think the men cared what I looked like, just that I was easy pickings." Etta held Kane's gaze.

Nash turned to her, his mouth dropped open in shock. "Who and where?" Nash's eyes narrowed.

"The laundry on Pacific had a difficult work environment." Etta crossed her arms over her chest. "We banded together as workers; never alone with the boss, ever! We didn't walk alone. We stayed together. Santini, as you remember, took advantage of my vulnerability, financial and physical. Mr. Spicer didn't make a sexual advance, which I find surprising. He craves dominance and control. He just goes about it differently. Essentially though, this is all about power." Etta shifted in her seat, uncomfortable with the intense gaze from both Nash and Detective Kane.

"I didn't invite their attention. None of us needed to. They target us because they can. There is no one to stop them, and now that we've lost our men, our brothers and husbands, the situation has escalated. Sure, you can complain, raise a hue and a cry, but there are fifty women lined up to take your job because at the end of the day, we all need a roof over our heads." Etta shrugged.

Detective Kane and Nash's eyes hardened in outrage at her words.

"Women working in these jobs and factories are vulnerable, sir. They take advantage of that. You are sadly mistaken if you believe the world is made up of gentlemen. I've seen the opposite. A teaching position isn't much different, is it? So, back to Mr. Spicer. First day of school, Mr. Spicer stopped me on the way to the school."

"Why?" Detective Kane asked, pencil poised to write.

The locksmith let out a small cheer as the lock on the drawer finally sprang open.

Detective Kane, Nash, and Etta ignored him.

"He wanted to inspect my petticoats."

Detective Kane's eyes tightened, the only indication that what she was saying bothered him. "Mr. Morris, thank you for opening the drawer. You may leave. Please tell Constable Lark I will be with him at Barlow's shortly."

As the locksmith shut the door to the classroom behind him, Detective Kane returned to his line of questioning.

"Inspect your petticoats?" Detective Kane asked as the door shut behind Mr. Morris.

Nash stood up, hands balled into fists at his side.

"Sit down, Mr. Nash. Let's keep our heads. Miss Lynne, explain how he inspected your petticoats." Detective Kane's tone indicated he would not put up with Nash's outbursts much longer.

"He asked me to lift my skirt above my ankle and show him how many petticoats I was wearing. The code says two."

"So, how far did you lift your skirt?" Detective Kane watched Etta carefully.

"If you are implying that she enticed him—" Nash rounded on Detective Kane.

"Mr. Nash, I am implying nothing of the sort. I just want to be clear about what we are dealing with here." Detective Kane frowned at Nash. "Sit. Down." Detective Kane turned his attention back to Etta.

Etta stood up and lifted her skirt halfway up her shin to show the two petticoats. "Exactly like this."

"Did anyone see this?" Detective Kane kept writing.

"Miss Winthrop. She said I was flirting with him exactly like Mrs. Ellice. I think he does this to teachers to humiliate them and establish his authority over them. I felt like I was being forced to submit to him." Etta shuddered. "It was awful and very upsetting; shameful really. So that is one way the Miss Winthrops of the world have it easier. She has never been asked to show her petticoats." Etta's tone was clipped with fury.

"Did anyone else see this?" Detective Kane waited to write down more of her statement.

Etta frowned.

"Did anyone else need to? This is a gross misuse of power," Nash retorted.

"Mr. Nash, I'm not here to try to take Spicer off the school board. I am here to charge someone with murder."

The word hung suspended between them. Nash's body stiffened. Etta's face paled with fear. Detective Kane jotted a note in the margin in his book.

"Miss Lynne, did anyone else see you show Mr. Spicer your ankle?" Detective Kane rephrased the question.

"Yes." Etta's head snapped up. "Yes, I had forgotten, but Mrs. Spicer was standing at the end of her driveway, and she saw the whole thing. I waved at her, and she turned away."

"I see." Detective Kane wrote the words down.

"She looked very sad, Detective Kane." Etta's tone softened as she spoke of Mrs. Spicer.

"You are sympathetic to her?"

"Of course. I can't imagine being married to a man like Mr. Spicer. She looked sad, and I was sad for her."

"Sad?" Detective Kane repeated the word.

"Yes." Etta pressed her fingertips against her mouth as she thought back. "Mrs. Spicer looked devastated. Should I go to her and explain? Oh my goodness, she might think that I was flirting with him!"

"No, you are not to speak to her. I will handle this. Any other incidents? Anyone else unkind or irritated by you?"

"I feel like a school girl tattling to the teacher." Etta shook her head.

"Please, continue," Detective Kane said kindly.

"When I interviewed for this job, Mrs. Delaire threw an entire cup of coffee on me. On purpose. She said it was an accident, but I am certain it was not."

"Why do you suspect...?"

"I can tell just looking at her. She is in love with Mr. Nash and thought if I got the job, I was a threat." Etta fidgeted with the cameo at her throat as she said the words 'in love with Mr. Nash.' Immediately, she lowered her hand.

"Are you in a relationship with Mrs. Delaire?" Detective Kane asked Nash directly.

"No. She dropped by with a pie, and in the labyrinth of social graces bachelors are suppose to navigate without offending the fairer sex, apparently that means she has spoken for me and is actually making sure other women don't get too close. I think she had some sort of delusion, but no. It is inappropriate. We work together."

"And?"

Mr. Nash sighed. "Recently, after I settled Miss Lynne and Grace at Mrs. Lemon's house, I was on my way home and I was sleeping when she pounded on my door to wake me. She said she had been frightened by a loud bang at the back of her house."

Etta turned to look at Mr. Nash. Her jaw dropped open in shock.

"Miss Lynne, would you please step outside? I will call you right back in."

Etta's throat tightened as she thought about what might have happened between Nash and Mrs. Delaire.

"Nothing happened. She is free to stay," Nash protested.

"Miss Lynne. Please, I am very busy, and I have to get to Barlow's. Please." Detective Kane indicated she should step out of the classroom and stand in the hall.

Etta got up, her face flaming with embarrassment as she

stepped out of the room and closed the door behind her.

* * *

Nash crossed his arms over his chest.

"She called you into her home because someone had broken in?" Detective Kane's pencil was poised to take notes.

"She called me in on the *pretence* that someone had broken in. She was dressed inappropriately, something frilly. I made sure no one had broken in. Her back window was left open, and a vase had fallen over and smashed. She claimed that the sound had woken her—terrified her. I made sure she was safe. She pretended to be terrified and tried to get me to comfort her."

"How do you know she wasn't terrified?" Detective Kane asked, his voice deepened.

"I was married. I know a terrified woman when I see one. She wasn't terrified. There is a calculation about her. She seems to weigh her words. Anyway, she made an unspoken physical offer. I declined and left."

"You declined?" Detective Kane's eyebrows rose. "Mrs. Delaire is stunning. That must have been hard."

"I do not have feelings for her, and I never have," Nash answered honestly.

"Who needs feelings to say yes to a woman?" Detective Kane tilted his head to the side. "A very private, one-night, no-one-needs-to-know sort of affair?"

Nash chuckled. "Detective Kane, this is a village." Nash shook his head. "Everyone would know. Clearly you are from a city! At any rate, I am the mayor, and I have a daughter. I would lose the respect of my community. She is a very new widow. So, no! It would be career suicide. The way she throws herself at me is, quite frankly, embarrassing for both of us. Last but certainly not least, I don't like the way she treats Grace, and my daughter doesn't like her."

"I see." Detective Kane wrote down Nash's words.

"Do you?" Nash demanded.

Detective Kane nodded. "I think you stayed the night

because everybody lies. I'll get Mrs. Delaire's version of the story and go from there."

Nash sighed.

"Anything else you want to add?"

"No."

"Did you meet Mrs. Ellice prior to January 2, 1919?"

"Yes, I did." Nash nodded.

Detective Kane's eyes widened just slightly. "When did you meet her?"

"Her job interview was December 30, 1918. She started work on January 2. I met her December 30."

"That's what my records indicate." Detective Kane's eyes met Nash's. "Good. Did *anyone* on the board know her prior to December 30?" Kane asked the question as if he were weighing every word.

"Not to my knowledge."

"She was twenty weeks pregnant when she was killed or accidentally fell, but all the men of this community would have met her after January 2?" Kane wrote that down.

"Except for the board. They all met her December 30, 1918. She was a recent widow. Is it possible the baby is her husband's? Honestly, we didn't ask if she was pregnant. She was a widow asking for work, but pregnancy would have nullified her contract..." Nash frowned.

"She may not have known." Detective Kane's gaze met Nash's.

"How is that possible?" Nash shook his head in disbelief.

"Apparently it is." Kane spoke with an inflection that indicated that women were the most complicated creatures on earth. "The medical examiner says sometimes cycles aren't regular. It is not uncommon for a woman to believe her menstruation is late, instead of knowing she is pregnant."

"Really?" Nash shifted in his chair.

Detective Kane shrugged. "Whether she knew it or not, she was definitely pregnant at her job interview. The medical examiner says she was in her first month of pregnancy on December 30. When she was found, the pregnancy was clearly in the fourth month, not further."

"So this is a double homicide then? Whoever killed Miss Ellice also killed her unborn child."

"Yes," Detective Kane confirmed. "Did she know a board member prior to being hired here? If the baby belongs to one of the board members or indeed one of the men of the community... was she blackmailing the father? Did you see any men over the week of April 5 who were new to town? Any that might have raised any eyebrows?"

Nash thought carefully and then shook his head. "No. Nothing of the sort."

"Anything you can think of. Any men acting strangely around her."

Nash sighed. "Spicer acts strangely around all women."

"Why?" Kane asked, writing down the name Spicer.

"Well, I think his mother abused him. She was a..."

"Yes?" Detective Kane leaned forward.

"She was promiscuous and a drunk. His father took off and left him with a mother that was half the time drunk in a bar."

"He's done well for himself."

"He's extremely clever," Nash said. "Unusually smart. Something is warped in him about women, though. He puts them down. Always has. He is hard on his wife."

"Is it possible that Mr. Spicer, not her deceased husband, could be the father of Rose Ellice's baby?"

"My first thought is no. Absolutely not! He's a fanatic about morality and virtue and chastity... Also, I wonder who would willingly go to bed with him. I can't even imagine."

"Maybe it wasn't willing." Detective Kane watched Nash's face as he accused Mr. Spicer of a crime.

"Mr. Spicer is a lot of things, but I don't think he would do something like that. As I said, he's obsessed with morality..."

"Worst kind." Detective Kane wrote down the words as Nash spoke.

"She was pregnant, and *if* the baby doesn't belong to her late husband—the medical examiner will be verifying that timeline for sure—that means *someone* is the father." Detective Kane watched Nash's face as he spoke.

Nash nodded and crossed his heavy arms over his broad

chest. "When you find him, let me know. I'd like a few minutes with him."

Detective Kane shook his head. "I understand your anger. Women and children dying at the hand of a man is the hardest thing to investigate. It doesn't bother me as much if men kill men."

"Men killing men is typically an equal playing field." Nash shrugged. "If Spicer killed this woman—"

"Patience. We have to be patient and build a case." Detective Kane's eyes locked with Nash. "In the meantime, I don't have to tell you, but don't let Miss Lynne out of your sight. Whoever did this will not stop until they are caught. Bold move to place a note on her desk the day we are searching for a crime scene. This is someone who has lost touch with reality. Someone who has nothing to lose."

"Mr. Spicer has a lot to lose. He wants to be mayor. He has a reputable business..." Nash shook his head. "I can't think of..."

"What are your feelings for Miss Lynne?" Detective Kane asked Nash abruptly.

"At first, she frustrated me beyond all comprehension," Nash answered honestly.

"What are your feelings for her?" Detective Kane cut through Nash's statement.

"She's safe with me. You picked the right man," Nash replied carefully, guarding Etta's reputation at all costs.

"What are your feelings for her?" Detective Kane repeated the question.

"I care about her a great deal." Nash's gaze met Detective Kane's; he didn't look away.

"Like a brother?"

"No." Nash shook his head. "If how I felt about Miss Lynne was made public, she would lose her job. My feelings for her are nothing like a brother for a sister."

"I appreciate your honesty, Mr. Nash." Detective Kane nodded.

"You'll keep that between us? I don't want her to lose her job. I want her to be placed here next year."

"Oh, Mr. Nash, that is confidential, I assure you. However, I have seen her look at you, and I'd say the feeling is mutual. Miss Lynne, you may return," Detective Kane called out.

* * *

ETTA STEPPED BACK into the classroom and took a seat. She pointedly refused to look at Nash.

Why didn't he tell me about this?

Why would he? We aren't a courting couple. He has no reason to tell me if women are throwing themselves at him morning, noon and night.

Why is this bothering me so much?

"Miss Lynne, nothing happened between Mrs. Delaire and me. I swear it." Nash turned to Etta.

Detective Kane raised his eyebrows.

"Very well." Etta glanced over at him with a look designed to dismiss him.

Nash sighed.

Detective Kane shot Nash a look of sympathy and then turned his attention to the drawer.

"What is it?" Nash asked as he got up to move around the desk to peer inside the drawer.

Kane moved the drawer out of his reach. "This is evidence."

Etta stood up, turning her back on the men as she walked to the window.

"A diary," Detective Kane said as he opened it. "Lots of entries here... I'll read through it later. There are other notes here." Detective Kane leafed through the contents. "Miss Lynne, if Miss Winthrop hadn't interrupted you, how far do you think Mr. Spicer would have gone?"

"He grabbed my arm, and I thought he would hit me." Etta turned back to face the men.

Nash's eyes tightened, his body stiffened, and his hands balled to fists at his sides.

"He didn't hit you?" Detective Kane clarified.

"Miss Winthrop interrupted, so what he would have done if we were alone, I can only guess. I felt unsafe and frightened," Etta responded honestly.

Detective Kane nodded. "I am sorry that you had to deal with that."

Etta nodded.

Detective Kane pulled out another scrap of paper. "Final offer. $300."

Nash's head snapped up. "Three hundred dollars... Mr. Spicer misplaced three hundred dollars when we did a fundraiser for the school."

"Three hundred was on that note that I found." Etta gasped. "The note was stolen from my handbag... remember when Mr. Spicer was in the classroom, and I found that note... he wanted it..."

Mr. Nash's gaze locked with Etta's. "You're sure it's stolen?"

"I can't find it anywhere."

"This is no coincidence. But three hundred dollars for what?" Nash rubbed his forehead as he thought about it.

"The note doesn't say." Detective Kane shook his head. "There is nothing else in the drawer. I am going to take all this to the barracks, and then I am going to Barlow's. Neither of you are suspects, of course, but we would prefer you stay in town until everyone is interviewed. More questions may pop up as the investigation proceeds."

"May I add something?" Etta held her hand out.

"Of course, Miss Lynne. What is it?"

"That note on my desk."

"Yes."

"It's not spelled correctly, sir. It was a 'your' instead of the proper 'you're'. As much as Miss Winthrop is a bit of a pill to deal with, she's a teacher. No teacher would make that mistake."

"Miss Lynne, she may have intentionally made that mistake to make it look like someone else." Detective Kane sighed.

Etta wrapped her arms around herself.

"I never thought of that," Etta whispered in fear.

Nash stood next to her, his arm solid against hers.

"What you have told me indicates that she may be currying favour with Mr. Spicer." Detective Kane kept his gaze level with Etta's. "Does she earn more than you do? Is he the father of Mrs. Ellice's baby, and he was paying her off to stay silent? Mr. and

Mrs. Spicer do not have children. Were they arranging to buy Mrs. Ellice's baby?"

Etta gasped at the suggestion.

"Or are Mr. Spicer and Miss Winthrop together in this crime? Did he harass Mrs. Ellice, all the while depending on Miss Winthrop to lie and say that Mrs. Ellice was asking for it? Misguided affection? Does Miss Winthrop secretly pine for Mr. Spicer? Did he pay her to take that note?"

"Oh my goodness, I had never even dreamed of anything so terrible!" Etta sputtered in horror.

"I am very glad you don't think like this. It is a blessing and a curse. I read people and clues and then piece together the thinking behind it. I've been a detective for ten years, and I have seen every disgusting thing you can imagine. I wish I wasn't able to think like this, but I can, so I use it to bring justice. These are theories only." Detective Kane opened his note pad and wrote something down.

"Is there anything else you want to tell me about? Can you think of anything, no matter how small?" Detective Kane asked.

"I really can't."

"Have you ever seen a button like this?" Detective Kane reached out his hand and handed Etta an olive-green button. "Have you noticed a woman missing a button on her cardigan?"

Etta fidgeted with the collar of her blouse. "Yes, Miss Winthrop is missing a button. The reason I noticed it the first day is because I pointed it out to change the subject."

"What subject?" Detective Kane's eyes flashed at Etta's words.

"Miss Winthrop is a nasty woman who accused Mrs. Ellice of being promiscuous with absolutely no proof. To maintain some peace, I tried to change the subject. I pointed out that Miss Winthrop was missing a button. She said, yes, but it is yarn covered and not replaceable. I said she could remove them all and replace them with new buttons."

"What colour of sweater?" Detective Kane and Nash asked at the same time.

"It had a pattern. I think more than one colour. Ivory, pink and green."

"What colour of green? Were the buttons green?" Detective Kane tilted his head as he wrote down her testimony about the missing button.

"I am so sorry. I can't remember." Etta shook her head.

Detective Kane nodded. "Thank you, Miss Lynne. You have been most helpful. Ensure that she gets home safely, Mr. Nash. Both of you are to stay in town."

"Yes sir."

CHAPTER 30

*E*tta and Nash returned to the motorcar. Etta settled her handbag between them and worried that maybe she had gotten Miss Winthrop into trouble. She was in the company of men in a motorcar in broad daylight, and because of the tragedy, no one would care.

How sad it takes a tragedy like this to shift attention to what really matters...

"I need to stop at the town office before I take you home. Is that all right?" Nash asked.

"Of course." Etta tried and failed to soften the sharp edge of her tone.

"Are you sure? You look exhausted." Nash shot her a look of sympathy. He clearly misunderstood her frosty demeanor. "You must be weary. This has all been very trying."

"I'm getting tired, but we must see this to the end." Etta waved her hand to dismiss his concerns.

They were silent as Nash drove to the town office.

"Nothing happened between me and Mrs. Delaire. I swear it." Nash spoke quietly.

"She's a beautiful woman," Etta said dully.

"So are you, and I've restrained myself." Nash looked over at her.

Etta scowled at him. "That is most inappropriate, Nash."

"Maybe." Nash shrugged as he parked the car in front of the town office. "Come on. I have to find the old statement."

Nash opened her door and then unlocked the front door of the office.

After pulling open the filing cabinet, he began to flick through folders and then lifted out a file marked 'Budget'. His forehead creased as he pushed the drawer closed with his elbow. "There should be two statements here. The old statement is missing. I insisted that we keep a copy of the old quarterly statement for transparency." Nash frowned. "According to this, it was never missing. I put a copy in another file..." Nash opened the filing cabinet again and searched through. He pulled up a file and opened it.

Empty.

The blood drained from Nash's face. "This folder had the old budget in it. I know for sure."

Putting their differences aside, Etta's heart hammered as she watched him search the folder twice. "What does that mean?"

"Someone has been in my office and has gone through my papers. Every single file. I filed the old budget under an obscure name." Nash's jaw clenched.

"What name?"

"Plum Creek School." Nash's gaze met hers.

"What is Plum Creek School?" Etta tilted her head to the side in confusion.

"The name of the town changed in 1900 when we incorporated. Oakland was known as Plum Creek before the incorporation. We finally tossed all the old files when I took over the office. I kept the folders because there was nothing wrong with them. I intended to scratch out the old names and just replace with new."

"That's very thrifty."

"Waste not, want not." Nash shrugged. "I don't squander taxpayers' money."

"Very noble."

"I tucked a copy of the old budget in this file and didn't bother to change the label. I just made a mental note."

"I see." Etta bit her lip as she wondered who would have the audacity to come into a man's office and rifle through his files.

"The only person *working* in this office that would remember the school being Plum Creek is Mr. Spicer." Nash's eyes narrowed. "We were students there together. Good thing I put a budget in my files at home... as long as no one has broken into my study... let's go."

"But why steal a budget? They found the money. The budget is adjusted." Etta frowned at Nash.

"At the time, I thought it was just to protect his reputation. Now, that note about three hundred dollars seems somewhat suspicious." Nash tucked the file away.

Back in the car, as Nash drove around the curve of Crescent Avenue, it was late enough that all the shops were closed. Past Crescent Avenue, Etta watched Oakland through the passenger window. Sunday was a day of rest, and the residents of Oakland were home, preparing supper for families. Plumes of smoke burst out of chimneys. Etta envisioned men piling wood on fireplaces while women prepared supper.

Family supper.

Tonight, Nash and Grace, Cali and Etta would all sit together at Lucy Lemon's table. They would eat together and share their thoughts about the day like a family.

A real family.

Etta's heart, hurting from the loss of her mother, swelled at the thought of being all together at Lucy's.

She watched Nash's strong profile from the corner of her eye. Determination made the lines of his face harden. Whoever killed Mrs. Ellice better hope Detective Kane got to him before Nash did.

Nash switched gears as he turned onto Maple Street.

The sun peeked out of the clouds for a brief moment to shimmer down on the wet and bare branches of mature maple trees. Etta wished the sunshine would chase the worries from her heart.

* * *

DOROTHEA DELAIRE SIPPED whiskey from a cut-glass tumbler in her parlour. The clock ticked on the mantel. She thought she might go mad from boredom. Hearing a car out on the street, she got up and pulled the lace curtain out of the way.

Nash got out of his car and hurried around the front and then opened the passenger door.

Please be Grace. Please be Grace.

Dorothea's body stiffened in rage as Etta Lynne stepped onto the boulevard. Nash held his arm out, and she slid her small hand into his elbow.

He leaned down to listen to something she was saying.

Rage roared through Dorothea as Etta smiled up at Nash. Her knuckles whitened in fury as she gripped her glass.

She is not right for him! He hates forward, independent women! He says it all the time!

Dorothea shoved hair from her eyes as she watched Nash open the door to his home for her.

Nash followed Etta into his house and shut the door firmly behind him.

To Dorothea, as madness darkened her thoughts, it appeared Nash was turning his back *on her.* She couldn't stop a howl of rage that burst out of her as she threw her glass across the parlour. She seethed as the glass smashed to a million pieces.

"She should be fired by now!" Dorothea lunged across the room to the sideboard. "Nash is mine! He just needs some time to see it! If she hadn't interfered, we would be together now. She is stealing my life, my future! We were so close until she showed up!"

Dorothea slammed another glass down and poured three fingers of whiskey into the glass. She stopped herself from taking a gulp.

Not today.

Mrs. Spicer was coming over to bring her a pot of soup and help her organize the pie box social.

Why am I dealing with a stupid fundraiser for women that I don't care about? This should be Miss Lynne's wretched job! What is Mrs. Spicer coming to my home to tell me? Is she trying to be my friend? I don't surround myself with lumps like Mrs. Spicer. No. She would drag me down. She is not connected socially. Why won't Mrs. Holt take an interest? Mrs. Holt is connected to everyone.

Dorothea slammed around her parlour, her movements sharp with anger.

Furthermore, how is that pie box social not cancelled in all this "who murdered Mrs. Ellice" craziness anyway? I'll let Mrs. Spicer deal with all the tedious lists of who is bringing what. That's what I'll do.

Dorothea paused in her ranting as the full weight of what Etta gained by being with Nash sank in. Etta had taken on responsibility for Grace, actually saving her life, if the rumours were true. Etta already lightened his heavy load. Dorothea knew it was Etta who helped him as an intimate partner in his life. A shot of pain stabbed through her heart.

I put extra vials of morphine into Ronald's arm to have a chance at Mayor Jackson Nash. I could have been caught if I hadn't been so clever. I am perfect for him and his life. He needs me, and I want him. How dare Etta Lynne stand in my way?

She better stop...

Dorothea threw herself onto her bed, reached for a pillow, and like a little child, she screamed her rage into it.

CHAPTER 31

*E*tta skimmed her fingertips over the row of law books in Nash's study.

Nash pounced on the file he had tucked away in his desk.

He sat down and compared the statements.

"I have it." Nash let out a long breath as he put the original budget on his desk.

Etta's eyes flicked over the paper, trying to make sense of the numbers upside down.

"Now the question is, what did Mrs. Ellice have that was worth three hundred dollars, do you think?" Nash looked up at Etta. "Not just what did she have, what did she have that he wanted?"

"I believe Mr. Spicer would just take what he wanted." Etta shuddered.

Nash crossed his arms over his chest. "What do you mean?"

"This is something more than a possession," Etta whispered.

"If he stole from her, she could report him." Nash squinted as he thought about that.

"The Spicers don't have children. Maybe Detective Kane is right, maybe he wanted her child." Etta pressed a hand to her heart. "That can't be it. No one would do such a horrific thing. To buy a child."

Nash's eyes widened as he thought of it. "I wouldn't put it

past him." Nash ran his fingers down the two columns of figures on the two sheets of paper.

"How do you put a price on a child?" Etta swallowed hard at the thought. "It's inhuman."

"So is murdering a pregnant woman." Nash's lips thinned. "I'd say we're well past what is normal here. I want you to put this from your mind, Etta. You've had enough to deal with. Let the detective handle it from here. Come on, I'll take you to Mrs. Lemon's."

"You just called me Etta. Again." Etta shot him a look.

"Oh! My apologies. I did!" Nash grinned, breaking the tension in the room. "I'll point out you have started calling me Nash instead of Mr. Nash…"

"My mistake… I let that slip." Etta couldn't stop a smile from brightening her face.

Nash smiled back at her. "I'm glad."

"But we mustn't forget and be so… casual again. You must remember." Etta frowned, having to be serious and wishing it were not so necessary.

"I won't forget. I'm sorry." Nash took a step toward Etta.

Etta looked up at him. "I wasn't going to have a thing to do with you, Nash."

"Oh?" Nash reached out and stroked her face.

Etta's eyes slid closed as desire woke inside her at his touch.

"What changed your mind?" he whispered against her neck as she leaned into him.

His fingertips stroked the side of her face and then under her jaw, making her look up.

"Watching you iron." Her lips parted in anticipation.

"Iron!" Nash sputtered.

"I don't think I've ever seen anything so… incredibly… lovely as watching you iron," Etta whispered.

"Well, I'll have you know, Miss Lynne, I spend hours ironing. It's my passion." Nash smiled so brightly Etta laughed.

She placed her hands on his shoulders as she leaned into him.

"Careful, miss. As I mentioned when we were ironing

together, I'm not your grandmother. Don't start something you don't intend to finish," Nash warned, his voice deepened.

"I think you'll be gentle with me." Etta's breath caught in her throat.

Nash caressed her face with his hands and then pressed his lips to hers tenderly, reverently. "I will be very gentle with you. You can be sure of that."

"Just one kiss." Etta bit her lip as she slid her hands over his shoulders, down his arms and then back up again. "That's all I'm agreeing to here..."

Nash cradled her face in his hands as he gently pressed his lips to hers again, stopping her from speaking any further.

Etta's entire body flooded with desire as he deepened the kiss.

She twisted her fingers in his hair and pulled him closer.

A hard banging on the front door made them break apart like guilty children.

Nash cursed under his breath. "Who would that be?"

Etta pressed her fingertips to her mouth where his stubble had abraded the skin.

"Dorothea Delaire?" Etta suggested as she tried to catch her breath. "Here to finish me off for daring to be here with you— un-chaperoned."

Nash shook his head. "Tempting me against my will?"

"I never!" Etta gasped in outrage.

Nash reached out and touched her reddened skin. "I should have shaved before we left, but I didn't expect... I really didn't expect anything like this."

"No, I didn't either." Etta pressed her fingertips to where her face felt tender. "We can't do this again."

"You dragged me into it!" Nash broke the rule as he very gently pressed his lips against the abraded skin by her mouth.

"Nash you... can't..."

"I'm kissing it better." Nash tilted his head and pressed his lips against the other side of her mouth.

Etta placed her hands on the plane of his chest and pushed. "Mr. Nash!"

"Yes?" Nash unrepentantly kissed her again. Gentle kisses on her lips, cheeks, and neck.

"Please..." Etta stood still as she looked up at him. Her heart pounded as she saw the desire in his eyes. A new power awoke inside her.

Etta understood with sudden clarity that Nash would do anything he agreed with if she needed it. He would never lose every penny because of gambling like her father or work sporadically like her brother. He would ensure she would never be vulnerable. Nash would never let her down; she could see it in his eyes. There would be no poorhouse because of a decision made by Jackson Nash.

The look he gave her now was an unspoken vow that he would put her needs first. A man who cared this deeply for a woman was a powerful thing. A man like Nash wouldn't tolerate threats to her or Grace, either physical or emotional. He would step in swiftly. A heavy weight of responsibility loosened and then floated from Etta's shoulders. If they were together, she would fulfill her role, but he would do his part. Suddenly life seemed brighter with the realization of what it would feel like if the responsibility she staggered under was shared.

"You must answer the door." Etta pressed her fingertips to her lips as she stepped back.

"Right." Nash took a step back, too.

Etta keenly felt the loss of his body heat, his solid strength.

"Please remember, once we leave this room... we can't... we have to pretend this didn't happen. My job depends on it, and if I don't get a placement for next fall... I don't know what Cali and I will do. I was bluffing with Spicer. I can't provide for Cali as a switchboard operator." Etta hated the panic that tinged her voice.

Suddenly, the reality of life piled those burdens back onto her shoulders, and she nearly collapsed from the weight.

"I know." Nash held out his hand to her.

"So. Please, be careful not to..." Etta spoke haltingly as she tried to navigate her way around the delicate subject of her poverty and her deep shame as a result. Her need to secure a position next term rested on his actions as much as her own.

Nash took a step closer and cradled her face in his hands. Etta bit her lip as her gaze met his.

"I will always be careful of you," Nash vowed. He winced as he brushed the pad of his thumb against the abrasion by her mouth and then kissed her gently as if to ease the hurt he had caused.

Etta's heart soared with happiness.

"And I will be careful with you," Etta said reverently.

"Oh, Etta, darling— please don't." Nash's eyes flashed with mischief. "It's much more fun if *you* are not careful at all. Please be as *reckless* as a spinster can possibly be."

Etta rolled her eyes. "The switchboard may not hire me. Just remember, I need this job."

"I need you," Nash said.

Their eyes met, and the spark of desire burst into flames between them.

CHAPTER 32

*T*he pounding on the front door didn't go away.

Sighing, Nash made his way to the front entrance and opened the door to Constable Lark and Detective Kane.

Etta followed Nash to the front door and stood behind him as Detective Kane produced a note.

"Look familiar?"

Etta peeked around Nash's arm to read what the note said.

"Meet Me at Lover's Lane, Friday after school — Nash."

Etta gasped out loud.

"Lark, please escort Miss Lynne home," Detective Kane said. "Mr. Nash, I have a few questions for you. Please come with me."

"That is not my note." Nash's jaw clenched.

"Just a few questions at the barracks. I'm not asking." Kane ignored Nash's defense.

"It's typewritten! It could be sent from anyone..." Nash examined the note.

Etta looked from Nash to Detective Kane.

"Constable Lark, please ensure that Miss Lynne is taken safely to Mrs. Lemon's. Mr. Nash, as soon as I know where you were the night of the disappearance, I can check your alibi, and we can release you. I just have a few questions."

Nash relented. "Let's get this resolved so you can get back to work." Nash locked his house and followed Kane. "Lark, be very careful with her. Whoever did this has threatened Miss Lynne. If anything happens to her—"

"I will, sir," Lark said.

Etta watched helplessly as Detective Kane and Nash drove off.

Constable Lark opened the passenger door on his motorcar. Etta bit her lip as she got in.

"You know Nash couldn't have done this." Etta turned to Constable Lark.

Constable Lark weighed out his reply as if not wanting to give too much away. "The fact is, ma'am, the note says, 'Meet Me at Lover's Lane.' Lots of evidence is pointing at Mr. Nash. He found the button. Detective Kane thinks maybe he planted that evidence. He has been conducting other interviews, and there is some suspicion that he knew her prior to the interview. Detective Kane needs to rule out the rumour that the baby might not have been her husband's. It might be his."

Etta's heart fell to her feet. "What about the fibre?" Etta asked wildly.

"Detective Kane has a theory."

"What theory?" Etta's stomach twisted into a knot of fear.

"Miss Lynne, it's really not for you to worry about. Detective Kane knows what he is doing. You just lost your mother. You should rest."

Etta steamed in fury as Lark stopped the car in front of Lucy Lemon's house.

He escorted her inside. The house smelled like roast chicken, fresh bread, and greens.

"We're just getting ready for supper, Constable Lark. Are you joining us?" Lucy asked. "I'll set another plate."

"No need. Nash is — Lucy, can I see you in the kitchen for a moment?" Etta tried to drag her fear and emotions under control.

"Of course." Lucy raised an eyebrow as she followed her into the kitchen so Grace couldn't overhear them.

"There is no need for another plate." Etta wrung her hands. "They are questioning Nash. A note showed up in the locked drawer. A note that makes it look as though Nash asked Mrs. Ellice to meet him at Lover's Lane. Kane is asking Nash for his alibi."

"No!" Lucy gasped.

Etta's throat tightened as she spoke. "The note says, 'Meet Me at Lover's Lane,' and it is typewritten."

"Gracious!" Lucy sat down in shock.

Etta took a deep breath and let it out very slowly. "This morning I saw a note on my desk at the school. It said, 'you're next,' only 'you're' was spelled wrong. They aren't looking at any women as suspects because Mrs. Ellice was pregnant. They originally thought she was pregnant with her husband's baby, but now they are looking at Nash because of this note! They'll hang him if they can't figure this out, Lucy!" The tone of Etta's voice escalated in terror.

"This won't do." Lucy put down the tea towel in her hands. "What other person could it be?"

"There are three people as suspects. Mrs. Delaire, Miss Winthrop, and Mr. Spicer. I think Mr. Spicer is physically capable, obviously, but the yarn-covered button suggests a woman..."

"The note is typewritten, so who has access to a typewriter?" Lucy interrupted Etta.

"Mrs. Delaire!" Lucy and Etta said at the exact same time.

"I will talk to her myself." Etta straightened.

"But why? Why set up Nash like this?" Lucy tilted her head to the side in question.

"Maybe if she can't have him, no one can." Etta spoke ominously.

"You aren't facing her alone. I'm coming with you." Lucy took off her apron.

"No. You can't." Etta shook her head. "It's too dangerous. I will take Constable Lark. I will say I need to drop off our form for the pie box social."

"I dropped that off earlier." Lucy frowned.

"I know, but he doesn't know that. Once I'm in the house, I will bait her and make her talk." Etta pulled on a coat.

"She won't talk in front of him," Lucy cautioned.

"I'll ask him to wait outside." Etta refused to change her mind.

"I'm coming." Lucy wasn't taking no for an answer.

For a moment, Etta thought about it. "All right. It might not hurt to have two sets of ears."

"Have a sandwich before you go." Lucy's hands shook as she put a layer of cranberry jelly on the bottom half of the bun and then layered chicken on top.

"Lucy," Etta groaned. "I'm about to confront a murderer! I can't think about chicken sandwiches at a time like this! I can't eat a bite."

"You can't take down a killer on an empty stomach," Lucy said ominously.

Their gazes locked across the table.

Etta sighed, obediently gulped down her sandwich, and then went to the front room to confront Constable Lark.

"I forgot to hand in my form for the pie box social. Mrs. Delaire needs to know how many pies to expect, and I have to get this in tonight. I have to go right now." Etta gripped an envelope in her right hand.

"You won't be going alone." Lark stood up and braced himself in case they physically tried to get past him.

"No. Lucy is coming with me. She has a form to drop off, too."

"That's right." Lucy stood behind her.

Lark narrowed his eyes as if suspecting a trick. "We'll pick up Detective Kane on the way. I'm not having the two of you in Mrs. Delaire's parlour as my sole responsibility."

"Listen, Lark." Etta stepped up toe to toe with Constable Lark. He was so tall she yearned to stand on a stool so she could be eye to eye with him. "I am warning you right now, don't get in my way."

Lark held his hands up in surrender. "We get Detective Kane, and then we go."

"Fine," Etta said grudgingly.

Together they got into Constable Lark's car, and he stopped at the barracks at the top of the hill. Etta pounded on the door. Detective Kane came to the door; he frowned at her.

"I have to drop off a form to Mrs. Delaire. I am going with or without police protection. While I am there, I *will* accuse her of killing Mrs. Ellice because, from what I can tell, you don't think a woman committed this crime, and the man in the interrogation room is innocent. So are you coming, or am I doing this alone?" Etta abandoned the pretense.

"I knew it," Constable Lark muttered under his breath.

"Miss Lynne, this is not done. We don't use women as bait to —" Detective Kane sputtered as he looked from Constable Lark to Etta and then frowned at Constable Lark.

"She lied to me, sir." Constable Lark held his hands up as if to ward off an attack.

"You look at Mrs. Delaire and see a gorgeous woman. It's very difficult for men to see women like her as they truly are. You have discounted her from your investigation," Etta accused him.

"I assure you, Miss Lynne, I have discounted no one." Detective Kane rolled up his sleeves.

"Let me talk to her and sort this out."

"Mrs. Ellice was pregnant. Usually, in cases like this, we look at the father as the prime suspect." Detective Kane shook his head. "*Meet Me at Lover's Lane* is very suggestive."

"Yes, it is! Wouldn't a woman know how suggestive that is? I assure you, Mr. Nash didn't do this." Etta shook her head.

"We are checking his calendar to rule him out. I want to know where he was around the time this baby was conceived."

"I'm going now, and I'm questioning her myself." Etta straightened her shoulders. "When she confesses, you can arrest her."

"I'm not in the habit of breaking up a cat fight," Detective Kane said dismissively.

Etta's eyes flashed in fury. "Cat fight! What are you talking about?" Etta demanded.

"Two women fighting is a cat fight, and I don't think I

should have to referee a bunch of women in this town fighting over one man. It's ridiculous!" Detective Kane huffed.

"You found a button, and the button belonged to a woman. How do you know that button isn't Dorothea Delaire's?" Etta put her hands on her hips, waiting for his reply.

"This is my investigation. I will conduct it the way I see fit. You are not going..." Detective Kane protested.

"You can't stop me. I will confront Mrs. Delaire right now. Come or don't. We'll see who is right."

"You will do no such thing." Detective Kane took a step toward her.

"Am I under arrest?" Etta crossed her arms over her chest.

"Of course not."

"Then I don't see how you have any authority to stop me." Etta lifted her chin.

Detective Kane groaned in defeat. "Let's get this over with."

"The only person I know who is obsessed with Mr. Nash and has access to a typewriter is Dorothea Delaire." Etta could hardly get the words out past her clenched teeth. "I happen to know something else. It's gossip. I wouldn't typically repeat such a thing—"

"What gossip?" Detective Kane went very still as he turned his full attention to Etta.

"The source is Mrs. Daindridge and Mrs. Carr, so take this with a grain of salt. An entire salt shaker maybe..."

"What is being said about Mrs. Delaire?" Detective Kane pulled out his notepad.

"There is a rumour that she gave her husband an *overdose of morphine*. It's a vicious rumour if it's not true. But I heard it and couldn't put it from my mind. She thinks of Mr. Nash as hers already, and I know for certain he doesn't feel the same. It is some sort of madness or obsession."

"Why didn't you tell me this before?" Detective Kane hissed under his breath.

"It's vicious gossip! I hate gossip, but now that you are looking at Nash and not at a woman... I think it's time you knew that when the doctor came to pronounce him dead, it's rumoured that she met

271

the doctor in her unmentionables." Etta dropped her voice. "Subsequently, *files were lost*." Etta held her breath as she waited for Detective Kane to decide if he would escort her and protect her or not.

Detective Kane frowned as he picked up his hat and his shackles and followed her from the constabulary. "Let's go."

CHAPTER 33

*D*etective Kane wanted to throttle Constable Lark for not stopping Miss Lynne and forbidding this altercation. He had other people to question and dates and alibis to sort out. But a murder ruled as an accident had to be investigated. Curious, he hid behind a small garden shed that let him see into Dorothea's house but not be seen by her.

Detective Kane, Constable Lark, and Mrs. Lemon huddled together as Etta banged on Mrs. Delaire's front door with every speck of strength she possessed to make it sound like a man was knocking.

Detective Kane's eyes widened as the beautiful Dorothea Delaire threw open the front door. She had tossed a robe over some scandalous underpinnings, but did not tie the robe closed. It appeared that she was dressed for someone...

Who?

Detective Kane watched as Etta pushed her way past Dorothea and let herself into the parlour.

Leaving Lark with Mrs. Lemon at the garden shed, Detective Kane crossed the yard and gently opened the sash window so he could hear and see the altercation between the women in the parlour.

Crouching by the window, Detective Kane watched Etta and Dorothea square off.

Their eyes flashed at each other in anger. He wondered for a moment if they would actually physically fight each other. He leaned in and listened closely.

* * *

"EXPECTING SOMEONE ELSE?" Etta tilted her head to the side.

"You are not welcome here." Dorothea scrambled back to the front door to open it.

"I want to know why you sent this note." Etta pulled the copied note from her satchel. "Enough lies and no more games. Nash has been arrested, and I'm not watching him hang for your petty jealousy." Etta took a step forward.

Dorothea took a big step back, away from the note. "I didn't write that note." Dorothea crossed her arms over her chest.

"Dorothea, do you always open your front door dressed as a strumpet? Who are you waiting for?" Etta's eyes narrowed.

"Well, my nearest neighbour *is* Jackson Nash." Dorothea chuckled. Her wavy black hair shimmered in the low light. "Sometimes he slips over to be sure my house is secure. He is very protective."

"How kind." Etta smiled tightly. "How long have you dreamed about him?" Etta tucked the note away.

"That is none of your concern." Dorothea's back stiffened in outrage.

"He's not interested, though, is he?" Etta took a step forward. "That must be hard for you. Let's see, you get sick of wasting the best years of your life waiting on your husband hand and foot. Rumour has it you gave your husband a morphine overdose to get rid of him."

"I didn't expect you to listen to old women gossiping." Dorothea's eyes tightened.

Etta caught the look in her eyes and knew, down to the ground, that Dorothea would stop at nothing to get what she wanted. What she believed was hers by right.

"He came back from the war broken and useless, and you want a man that is whole." Etta let that statement hang between them. "You killed your husband for a shot at Jackson Nash. You want to be married to a mayor so you will have power through him."

"What a fantastic suggestion." Dorothea tinkled a laugh. She tossed her long wavy hair over her shoulder. "No, Jackson Nash is one of a long line I could have in a minute if I snapped my fingers."

"Why don't you have him then?" Etta challenged. Their gazes locked on each other.

"Rose Ellice was a woman of loose morals. I couldn't compete with that. I'm a lady." Dorothea shrugged.

A glass in the kitchen smashed on the floor. Both women jumped in alarm.

"Who's here?" Etta gasped in fear.

"Just a nobody." Dorothea waved her hand to dismiss the question.

Etta moved closer to the front door in case the person in the kitchen was a threat. She directed the conversation back to the matter at hand. "There was nothing wrong with Rose Ellice's morals. She was married and tragically widowed. The medical examiner says the baby was her husband's because the time of conception was when he was alive."

Dorothea's lips tightened. "Oh, I see, no one has ever in the history of the world been pregnant with another man's baby when married. What a naïve, silly little girl you are. Running around, trying to be the hero." Dorothea picked up her cut glass tumbler and took a sip of whiskey. "You're ridiculous."

Etta said nothing; she waited for Dorothea to elaborate. When Dorothea refused to speak she prompted her further. "Who's the father of the baby then?"

"I don't know. I don't care." Dorothea sipped the whiskey.

"I think you thought that baby belonged to Nash. I think you believed, in your madness, that Rose turned Nash's head, and you burned with jealousy. She had to pay for that." Etta's tone frosted with ice.

Dorothea ran her fingertips around the edge of the cut glass tumbler. "Life has a funny way of evening out the playing field."

"Except we're not playing." Etta took a step closer to

Dorothea. "I will see justice done for the crime you committed. You will confess, and I will be the one to watch you hang."

"What crime are you talking about?" Dorothea frowned as she slid past Etta and went to the sideboard. She refreshed her drink with three fingers of whiskey.

"Word is you killed your husband and flirted your way out of a death sentence." Etta's tone hardened.

Dorothea's back stiffened. "My husband?" Dorothea laughed. "He was a morphine addict! Lots of men are now. The war broke them." Dorothea whirled around to face Etta. "The war killed him. Not me. I came home to him wheezing on the bed. He demanded that I give him a full syringe. So, I did. I did just as he instructed. I had no idea he had already taken a dose. I did as I was told." Dorothea shrugged and smiled over the rim of her whiskey tumbler. "I am a very obedient wife."

"I bet." Etta's jaw clenched at Dorothea's lies.

"So, back to Rose Ellice. She was tough, opinionated; she stood up to corruption. She stood up to Mr. Spicer, and he hated her." Dorothea shrugged and tossed the whiskey back.

"Or did he?" Etta asked pointedly. "Sometimes there is a very fine line between love and hate. Tell me, did Mr. Spicer meet with Rose Ellice alone?"

Dorothea glared at Etta. "Miss Winthrop came into the town office in a huff, wanted to talk to Nash. She said she interrupted Mrs. Ellice trying to *seduce* Mr. Spicer." Dorothea looked hard at Etta; she squinted a bit. "I'd quite forgotten that."

Etta pounced on the detail. "Miss Winthrop accused me of exactly the same thing. It's not true. It is not true of me or Mrs. Ellice, I am quite sure."

"Does Nash know you've been accused of being inappropriate with Mr. Spicer?" Dorothea's eyes gleamed upon hearing the gossip, of knowing a truth about Mr. Spicer she could use against him at a later date.

"It's not true." Etta's eyes narrowed.

Dorothea leaned forward, eyes gleaming with suspicion. "You... and Mr. Spicer!" she hooted.

Etta's gaze burned into Dorothea's as she searched her eyes for the truth. She saw contempt there and an iron will to survive. Etta's stomach twisted with horror as she looked deep into Dorothea's eyes and saw a murderer.

"You tossed coffee on me the first time we met." Etta's voice sounded strangled in her own ears. "You were threatened by me. I know it was you. Admit it. You thought Mrs. Ellice was a threat to your imagined relationship with Nash. Admit it!" Etta roared at her.

Dorothea didn't blink. "As I said, I could have Nash any time I want him." She tossed her hair over her shoulder. "Easy."

"But you don't. He told me how you threw yourself at him and he left." Etta reminded her.

Dorothea took a step closer to Etta. She looked down her nose at her. "He lied."

Etta's eyes bored into Dorothea's.

As Dorothea lied, her lip twitched the slightest little bit.

"You're lying." Etta braced herself for a physical attack from Dorothea.

"You're as naïve as a child." Dorothea smirked.

Etta heard movement in the kitchen and wondered who was in there.

"Listen. If we keep talking, I don't want to see your breasts make any more of an appearance than they already have. That is not a decent or respectable robe." Etta turned and picked up the sweater on the back of her chair. "Can you put that on?"

Dorothea and Etta's eyes locked over the ugly olive-green cardigan with half the yarn-covered buttons missing and the left elbow fraying.

A smirk tugged at Dorothea's pretty lips.

A fist of fear tightened in Etta's chest as she thought about the yarn-covered button on a snowbank, and a fibre stuck in the fingernail of a corpse.

CHAPTER 34

*E*tta backed away from Dorothea as she realized with a certain horror that the murderer was right here in the room with her.

Trembling, she held up the ratty olive-green sweater that was missing many buttons. "Is this your sweater?" Etta demanded.

Dorothea rolled her eyes at Etta.

Etta fought the urge to pounce on her and wring a confession out of her.

"You and I both know that Mr. Spicer must have killed Mrs. Ellice," Dorothea declared as she took a big gulp of whiskey. "Who else could it possibly be? Detective Kane is a smart man, and he will put it together. Did he find the original budget yet? That budget is a nail in the coffin for Mr. Spicer, isn't it? He had me destroy the original budget. He'll hang for this," Dorothea said triumphantly.

Both women turned to hear shrieking from the kitchen at the same time. "No! No! This is mistake! This is all mistake! Not Mr. Spicer." Mrs. Spicer bolted out of the kitchen with a knife in her hand.

"Mrs. Spicer!" Dorothea gasped as Mrs. Spicer moved forward, the knife shaking in her hand as she stood before them with tears in her eyes.

"Mrs. Spicer, what do you mean?" Etta's hands trembled as she held the sweater. The last thing Rose Ellice had clung to before she died.

"It is mistake." Mrs. Spicer's eyes filled with tears as her hand holding the knife shook with fear.

"What do you mean mistake?" Etta gasped in shock. A curl of horror slipped around her stomach as she held up the sweater with the missing buttons. "Mrs. Spicer, is this your sweater?"

"It was mistake." Mrs. Spicer's body trembled.

"Mrs. Spicer... one of these buttons was found at the bank of the creek where they suspected Mrs. Ellice..." Etta watched in horror as Mrs. Spicer shook her head no. As if she could explain.

"You are wrong... I know him. I know you... I know what you did, what she did. He talks about you, Miss Lynne." Mrs. Spicer's tortured eyes swept over Etta. "How you dress to ensnare him. How you refuse to dress modest. He says you are in the company of men after eight at night in motorcar. He said you would run with anyone."

Etta's jaw dropped in shock.

"You want my husband, I know it," Mrs. Spicer accused her.

"Mrs. Spicer, I don't want your husband. I swear it." Shock whipped through Etta at Mrs. Spicer's words. She shuddered at the thought.

"He say you flirt with him. I see you raise your skirt to him. I saw it with own eyes." Mrs. Spicer's eyes were flat. Her accent thickened as she spoke with emotion. "I know you watch him. Don't deny it. I know it!"

"Mrs. Spicer, he made me show him. In the middle of the street, he insisted that I show him and prove that I was wearing two petticoats. He is working hard to have me fired," Etta said, unable to suppress a shudder as she remembered the scene.

Mrs. Spicer blinked twice, and then her eyes filled with tears. "You are young. You can give him children— I can't."

Etta cringed, appalled at the flawed logic that had plunged Mrs. Spicer into this despair.

"Mrs. Spicer, would you put down the knife, please, so we can talk?" Etta suggested gently.

Mrs. Spicer complied immediately; she placed the knife on the sideboard beside the whiskey.

Out of the corner of her eye, Etta noticed Detective Kane had quietly entered the parlour and was listening to every word.

"Would you like children, Mrs. Spicer?" Etta kept her voice very low, working hard to keep her tone gentle.

"I thought I was pregnant." Tears coursed down Mrs. Spicer's cheeks.

"You thought?" Etta prompted softly.

"I knew Mrs. Ellice was pregnant with his child. I knew it! I overheard her with Mrs. Hartwell, saying she wasn't sure what she would do. The pregnancy would get her fired! I couldn't stop the worry that maybe her baby was his. That she could give him something I could not."

"The medical examiner says she was pregnant at the time her husband was still alive, Mrs. Spicer."

Mrs. Spicer stopped crying. She blinked in surprise.

"Do you think Mr. Spicer knew her before she had her job interview?" Etta's heart pounded as she asked the question.

Mrs. Spicer thought about that, and her face fell with sadness. "No. He didn't know her. But, every day, he asks me."

"He asks if you are pregnant every day?" Etta's body shook with horror at the thought of him torturing her like that.

"He wanted his own. When he thought I was pregnant, he was finally happy with me." Mrs. Spicer's hazel eyes filled with fresh tears as she shared her burden. "I couldn't tell him..."

More tears trickled down Mrs. Spicer's cheeks.

"Tell him what?" Etta's breath caught in her throat as she watched Mrs. Spicer's face crumple in pain. "What did you need to tell him?"

Etta's blood ran cold as she finally asked the question. "There is no baby?"

A sob tore out of Mrs. Spicer at Etta's gentle question.

"What I thought was baby is tumour in womb... tumour that has spread." Mrs. Spicer pressed her hands to her lower abdomen. "I will die in a year. No baby." Mrs. Spicer's accent thickened as she spoke her truth. "This was my last... if Mrs. Ellice would have seen sense. She had nothing. No *means* to raise the baby. No husband! No money! We offered her a way to be... respectable..."

Etta listened to the faulty reasoning, and her stomach twisted as she made sense of Mrs. Spicer's words. Tears gathered in Etta's eyes as she watched Mrs. Spicer come apart in grief. "Oh, Mrs. Spicer, I'm so sorry. I am just so desperately sorry that this has happened. Thinking you're pregnant and finding out it is a tumour has to be the cruelest of blows." Etta leaped on the part of her story she could express compassion about.

Etta moved forward and tenderly pulled Mrs. Spicer into her embrace.

"Soon, I am dying." Mrs. Spicer wept into her shoulder. "Mrs. Ellice's baby was my last chance to be mother. I wanted that baby... she wouldn't listen to reason."

Etta's heart broke with sadness for her. "Mrs. Spicer, I am sorry." Tears splashed down Etta's cheeks as she held Mrs. Spicer.

As Mrs. Spicer calmed down, Etta asked Dorothea for a handkerchief.

"Why don't you tell me what happened? Detective Kane has Mr. Nash in custody. I know he didn't kill Mrs. Ellice."

"No one did," Mrs. Spicer responded dully. She pressed the handkerchief to her eye. "She slip on ice. I try to stop her fall. She grab me, and I couldn't stop her. She fell into the river, and the river took her. Right before my eyes."

A silence hushed the room as everyone there wondered if this was the truth. Did she push her? Was she jealous? Or was this a tragic accident?

"That must have been terrible. But, Mrs. Spicer, why not tell someone?" Etta asked gently.

Mrs. Spicer covered her face with her hands.

Etta looked to Detective Kane, who made a motion with his hands that Etta should keep speaking.

"Mrs. Spicer, everyone was frantic... her mother was looking for her..."

"I ask to buy the baby. Three hundred dollars was all I had... It would have been perfect solution." Mrs. Spicer wiped her tears on her skirt. "Mr. Spicer said they would not believe me. No one believes anything I say... I heard what Mrs. Daindridge said about what would happen... how I would hang from a rope if I ... said it was accident."

Etta remembered the exchange at Lucy's house the day they were searching. Inwardly, she groaned at the insensitivity of Mrs. Daindridge.

"Mrs. Spicer, we believe you." Etta held her hand.

"It is a shameful thing. What I did," Mrs. Spicer whispered to Etta. "I saw the money on Mr. Spicer's desk. I knew she would lose her job, I thought I could offer to buy baby, so..." Mrs. Spicer wept from a deep chasm of hurt.

Mrs. Spicer gathered her thoughts. "So I took it. Mr. Spicer was furious with me. He..." Mrs. Spicer stopped speaking. "I deserved it. Such a foolish thing..."

"No one deserves to be hurt this way, Mrs. Spicer."

Mrs. Spicer blinked up at Etta. "But sometimes... he does."

"I know." Etta's lips thinned. "What happened after that?"

"I used Mr. Spicer's typewriter and typed the note."

"The note that said 'Meet Me at Lover's Lane,' signed Nash?" Etta kept her gaze on Mrs. Spicer, knowing that Detective Kane heard every syllable.

"Mr. Spicer said to use Mr. Nash's name. He thought she wouldn't meet with anyone else. He said Mr. Nash had defended her in a meeting and she trusted him. When she refused my money and threatened to tell the Manitoba Teachers' Federation everything, Mr. Spicer said she had to be stopped. She wouldn't listen to any reason! I just wanted to beg her to forget the whole thing, and I *knew* she would meet with Mr. Nash... so I used his name... and she came. Her eyes narrowed when she saw me. She screamed at me. She *ran* from me."

Etta held her breath.

"I ran after her and tried to offer her money, anything she wanted to keep quiet. She wouldn't take the money." Mrs. Spicer's hands shook hard. "She said she would *destroy Mr. Spicer.*"

Etta's heart pounded so hard she could hear it in her ears.

"I beg her not to tell." Mrs. Spicer wiped tears from her eyes.

"What happened then?" Etta whispered.

"She laugh at me. She says she needed good reason to have Mr. Spicer fired, and this was it. It made me think back to the war. I see women like that. They have only one thought, one purpose. They stop at nothing. They only see their own view." Mrs. Spicer's eyes filled with tears. "She said she didn't want money, she wanted justice."

"And then?" Etta's voice was barely above a whisper.

The room was silent as they held their breaths, waiting for her to continue. "I grabbed her arm as she ran. To beg her... I try to stop her from running and talking. She slipped... she struggled out of my grasp, she grabbed me to stay upright... there was ice on the path... she slipped down, down the steep bank of the creek... she hit head on rock and fell into water. The ice swallowed her, the creek took her to river," Mrs. Spicer said dully.

"So, it was an accident then? You wanted to talk, not to harm her." Etta clarified her statement.

"Yes, an accident! But Mr. Spicer said to say nothing, no one would listen..." Mrs. Spicer wiped her tears. "He said I was from another country, no one would believe me... I am so sorry."

Etta's gaze locked with Detective Kane's. "I'm so sorry that you are sick."

"They will not believe me." Mrs. Spicer wept. "They will not..."

Etta pulled her back into a tight embrace to lend her some comfort. She wondered if Mrs. Spicer had ever received any comfort. She thought of what the war might have been like for a Russian woman. Something tragic must have happened to force her to marry that terrible Mr. Spicer. Etta's heart seized with sadness as she imagined a husband hounding her about a pregnancy she longed for. Every month must have been torture, compounded by a man who used that pain to torture her even more.

"I'm so sorry." Etta hugged her tighter. "I'm sorry that you have suffered so much."

Mrs. Spicer wept. Etta smoothed her hair down as she rocked her like a little child.

Detective Kane made a move to intervene.

Etta's eyes met Detective Kane's over Mrs. Spicer's shoulder. Etta shook her head no; she held the other woman in her tight embrace.

Detective Kane nodded.

Etta saw compassion in his gaze. She returned her attention to the broken woman in her arms.

Mrs. Spicer wept into her shoulder and trembled against her.

"I'm so sorry," Etta repeated as she rubbed Mrs. Spicer's back.

In Etta's embrace, Mrs. Spicer began to calm down. She pulled back and wiped her tears on the ratty cardigan.

Olive green.

The same colour as the yarn-covered button sitting on a table full of evidence in the barracks.

The same colour as the fibre in Mrs. Ellice's broken fingernail.

Etta bit her lip as Detective Kane stepped forward and asked them both to accompany him to the barracks for some questions.

Etta noticed that his hand on Mrs. Spicer's upper arm was gentle.

No matter what the courts would do with this information, Mrs. Spicer was a woman already living with a death sentence.

A woman with nothing to lose.

A woman who had already lost everything.

CHAPTER 35

*E*tta slipped down the silent streets to Hillcrest. She took a deep breath, hoping Lord Harper would be able to come with her. She needed the school board to hear and see what she was convinced Mr. Spicer was hiding. He terrorized his own wife; no wonder female teachers were leaving in floods of tears.

After the butler let her in, Etta waited in the parlour. Impatiently, she wandered around the room. The ancestors of the Harper family looked down at her from their oil paintings. One woman wore a cameo on her lacy blouse. Etta stepped forward to look closer to see if it was similar to the one she had sold and Nash had returned.

What would it be like to live like this? To never have to worry about selling your last piece of jewellery?

Lord Harper finally came down the stairs to the parlour.

"Miss Lynne! This is a surprise."

"Lord Harper, I apologize for the lateness of the hour." Etta turned from the painting to face Lord Harper. "You need to be apprised of the latest happenings. Mrs. Spicer has just confessed to killing Rose Ellice. It sounds as though it was involuntary. She has been arrested and is in custody. I need you to hear Mr. Spicer's confession in regards to what happened with Rose Ellice and Miss Ford so that this travesty never happens again.

Mr. Spicer has been threatening these women with losing their careers. He must be stopped. He has used the school board as a way to terrorize women. You need to have rules in place so this never happens again."

Lord Harper's eyebrow arched. "This is most unusual. We should call a meeting."

"Lord Harper, with all due respect, this can't wait. He has a letter full of lies that will destroy my career. I believe there will be evidence against Miss Ford and Mrs. Ellice. I think he was blackmailing them, but I have no evidence of that. This must be dealt with now, before he knows his wife is in custody for murder."

"The whole board should be present." Lord Harper frowned.

"We only want to see what has been written about these teachers, and then that information can be presented to the board. You have all the authority here, I've seen it," Etta countered. "We can pick up members of the board if you want. This is an emergency. If we can't get this truth tonight, he might get away for the role he played in this. To save my career, we have to catch him now. We have no time to spare."

"Right, we'll take my car. I'll pick up Holt, with the two of us to witness whatever this is," Lord Harper conceded.

"May I borrow this leather-bound book?" Etta asked as he pulled on a coat.

"Why?"

"I interrupted Mr. Spicer going through my classroom, and I think he was looking for Mrs. Ellice's diary. If I have something I can claim is her diary, it gives me a bargaining piece."

"This is madness. We don't use women to entrap men. We don't put the lives of women at risk..."

"You put the life of Mrs. Ellice at risk by allowing that madman a place of authority on the school board. It ends now—with me. I have to finish it." Etta gripped the leather journal so tightly her knuckles were white.

Lord Harper's eyes narrowed at her as she pointed out their flaw in keeping a man like Mr. Spicer in office. He frowned as he buttoned his coat.

Together, Lord Harper and Etta drove to Mr. Holt's house.

After they picked up Mr. Holt, they raced to the constabulary. Etta was squished in the back seat between the very broad shoulders of Detective Kane and Nash. The darkness and gloom of the night seeped into her heart at the thought of going up against Mr. Spicer.

"Detective Kane told me..." Nash began as he tried to move his shoulders to give her more room.

"Later. We will talk later." Etta's hands shook with anticipation of what she was going to face at the town office. She gripped the 'journal' with both hands to stop them from shaking.

"Please, all of you stay out of sight. Just listen. If I go alone, he'll think I am vulnerable, and he will be provoked," Etta said to all the men in the car.

Nash looked at Etta in alarm. "We are not in the habit of putting women in danger, Miss Lynne."

"So I've heard. I will say to you what I just said to Lord Harper. You've let this vicious, terrible man stay on the school board, harassing women. You've put plenty of women in danger," Etta countered, her voice rough with emotion.

Lord Harper opened his mouth to speak and then closed it. Mr. Holt turned to look at her from the front seat with a look of apology in his eyes.

"She's got you there," Detective Kane said under his breath.

Together the five got out of the motorcar half a block from the town office. Sure enough, the office Spicer used had a light on. As the men hid in the shadows by the front door of the town office, Etta banged on the door. After what felt like forever, she finally heard footsteps come to the front door.

"Miss Lynne." Mr. Spicer grinned at her as if she were a dish of cream and he was a big cat. "To what do I owe this honour?"

Etta's nerves jangled in fear as she looked up at him. Fear pulsed through her as she smelled smoke coming from the direction of Mr. Spicer's office.

Etta straightened her shoulders and tried to stop the tremor in her voice. "I think you were looking for Mrs. Ellice's journal. So I brought it." Etta's eyes filled with tears, and her lips trembled. She bowed her head in a show of submission. "I spoke out of turn earlier. The truth is, I need the job in September, Mr. Spicer. I will do anything to keep my position here." Etta's voice shook as she baited him. Her heart pounded in her chest so loud she could barely hear over it.

"This is a turn of events." Spicer's eyes narrowed.

Etta's entire body pounded in horror as Spicer grabbed her and dragged her into the town office, bolting the door behind him. After pulling her down the hall into his office, he threw her into a chair and then scrambled through his desk to find a paper.

His metal garbage can contained a small fire.

Has he burned all the evidence?

Etta's entire body shuddered as panic coursed through her.

Her blood ran cold as he turned to face her.

"You must think I am so stupid," Mr. Spicer spat at her. "You must think you are smarter than everyone."

"No, I don't." Etta scrambled to get up out of the chair. Spicer grabbed her and dragged her back.

He waved the paper in front of her.

Etta's heart pounded with fear as he picked up a sharp, long letter opener from his desk.

Spicer held her letter over the flames. "This letter documents the night you were in the company of men past eight at night. Give me Rose Ellice's journal, and I will burn this letter to the Manitoba Teachers' Federation."

Etta's heart pounded as she handed Spicer the journal.

"There is a journal entry about three hundred dollars offered to her for her child." Etta couldn't remove the contempt from her tone.

"Mrs. Spicer is a fool!" Mr. Spicer dropped his letter to the Federation into the flames. "She's an incurable and needs to be sent to an asylum."

Spicer took the journal and tucked it into his breast pocket just as Detective Kane stepped through the door.

"Let's just be calm here." Detective Kane held his hands up as he attempted to negotiate with Mr. Spicer.

Mr. Spicer pounced on Etta and used her as a human shield.

He dragged her through the secondary door of his office toward the back of the building.

The sharp edge of the letter opener tightened against her throat. Terror flooded through Etta as she wondered how Detective Kane would resolve this.

"This isn't going to end well. You know it and I know it. You kill her, you'll be hanged before the end of the week. You let her go, we talk and we'll get to the bottom of this." Detective Kane held his hands out as he spoke as if pleading with him to see reason. "Mr. Spicer, we know you didn't kill Rose Ellice. The evidence points to a woman. You are not a suspect."

Mr. Spicer turned to Detective Kane, still holding Etta tightly in front of him. She tried to claw at the letter opener, to pull it away from her throat, but Mr. Spicer held her in an iron-clad grip.

"She tried to seduce me," Mr. Spicer hissed.

Etta closed her eyes as he spoke.

"She is a tramp, she's like all of them. No respect for men, no respect for authority. She's like every woman. They use their bodies to get what they want with no regard for anyone else. She is a worthless, good for nothing—"

"We believe you. She's tried to entrap all of us. Let's meet as a board, and we will dismiss her," Lord Harper boomed from the end of the hallway. "We've seen her. She is absolutely shameless."

Mr. Spicer dragged Etta toward the back door of the town office.

"Let's just sit down and talk about this." Detective Kane held his hands out as he tried to reason with Mr. Spicer.

"I'm not talking." Mr. Spicer's eyes narrowed. "I've heard enough from you people. You take the side of these women. You don't see them as I do. *The truth about them.*"

Suddenly, a loud clunk came from behind her. She staggered as Mr. Spicer dropped, dragging her down with him.

Nash leaped forward and snatched her out of Mr. Spicer's arms, catching her before she fell.

Detective Kane pounced on Mr. Spicer and flipped him over, putting him in handcuffs.

Etta's eyes widened in shock as she looked around wildly to see who had come up behind Mr. Spicer. All the men had been in the front of the building and near his office. Dorothea Delaire stood in the dim light of the hallway in her French lace underpinnings. She held a coffee pot in her hand, and a slow smile curved her lips as she cast her saucy gaze on Detective Kane.

"Dorothea!" Etta cried.

Dorothea gasped in fake surprise.

Etta knew the men assembled would believe Dorothea's shock was true.

"Gracious! What a spectacle!" Dorothea fiddled with her robe but didn't *actually* close it. She placed the coffee pot she had hit Mr. Spicer with down on the floor beside Mr. Spicer. "I realized my locket had fallen off, and I was so worried that the cleaning staff would sweep it up and discard it. I slipped straight over to fetch it! Imagine my surprise when I stumbled into this!" The strap of Dorothea's nightgown slid off her shoulder.

Etta translated the flimsy excuse in her head.

I knew Etta wouldn't rest until Mr. Spicer was in custody. It made sense he would be at the town office, destroying evidence. I wanted to show Detective Kane my French lace unmentionables and get a new husband. I knew he would be leaving Oakland soon. This was my last chance.

"Mrs. Delaire, hitting Mr. Spicer and knocking him out was very brave." Detective Kane stepped over the prone body of Mr. Spicer. He took off his coat and draped it over her narrow shoulders. "Are you quite all right?"

"Oh, I am fine!" Dorothea simpered.

This is the second time he's been subjected to this scandalous attire!

"Did he have a gun?" Dorothea's eyes widened as she looked up into Detective Kane's eyes.

"Nothing so dramatic. He had a letter opener," Etta said dryly.

Lord Harper cleared his throat. "Mrs. Delaire, what a courageous thing to do! How on earth did you happen to have that coffee pot in your hand?"

"Well. I was in the coffee room, that's where I spend most of my time, you know." Dorothea made a show of lowering her gaze in a false sign of inferiority.

Etta remembered that first day as if it were yesterday. Dorothea did indeed spend much of her time serving coffee, or throwing it on women she felt threatened by.

"I thought I might have lost my locket in there when I heard a commotion." Dorothea tapped on her lips a moment, pretending to think, but Etta knew it was to drag the men's attention there. "So I picked up the coffee pot so I would have some sort of protection, a woman alone... I was very frightened." Dorothea dropped her tone.

Etta worried her eyes might roll out of their sockets.

"Of course you were," Detective Kane murmured as he moved closer to Dorothea.

Dorothea's eyes gleamed under the male attention.

"Well, I am so glad that locket fell off! Imagine if I had taken time to dress!"

Clever, giving a plausible reason to be half dressed in front of all these men!

"Are you all right, Miss Lynne?" Dorothea asked breathlessly.

Etta stepped over Spicer and pulled Dorothea into a tight embrace. "This has been a terrible night. Thank you for saving me with that coffee pot. I really appreciate it."

"Yes... well..." Dorothea untangled herself from Etta, clearly uncomfortable with shows of affection from a woman.

"Well, that settles all that." Lord Harper brought everyone back to the matter at hand. "Thank you, Mrs. Delaire, for your decisive actions."

Dorothea turned her attention from Detective Kane to Lord Harper. Dorothea Delaire wanted one last time to show Detective Kane her underpinnings, Etta realized with a start.

"What happens now?" Etta asked Detective Kane.

"Mr. Spicer will be charged with blackmail. I heard it— we don't need the physical letter as evidence. It is clear that he had letters against other teachers, but the fire in the trash can would have taken care of that. Very unfortunate. Those women were terrified to lose their jobs, and in this current situation, with all these soldiers home, it gave him immense power." Detective

Kane shook his head. "And Miss Lynne. The way you spoke to Mrs. Spicer to get that confession. Your fake care and attention for her was acted out brilliantly."

"It wasn't fake." Etta shook her head. "When I heard her whole story, I was honestly heartbroken for her. Devastated, really. To think you are pregnant and have such brutal and horrible news; to be married to someone who hurts you constantly. I didn't fake my feelings toward her."

"She claims it was an accident, but we have further investigations to complete." Kane dragged Mr. Spicer to his feet.

Mr. Spicer shook his head as he regained consciousness.

"Lord Harper, if you would run us back to the barracks," Detective Kane requested.

"Absolutely. The rest of you can make your way home?" Lord Harper looked from Nash to Etta to Mr. Holt.

"Of course." Nash nodded as the three made to leave.

"Holt, call a meeting first thing. The school board will officially remove Mr. Spicer. We need some by-laws in place for our board to be sure this doesn't happen again. It's getting very late, and I think we have all had enough drama for one night." Lord Harper held the door for Detective Kane to drag Mr. Spicer out of the office.

Detective Kane settled Mr. Spicer in the back seat and then returned for Mrs. Delaire.

"Mrs. Delaire, you can come with us as well. I just have a couple of questions for you. We'll stop at your home to get some suitable clothing." Detective Kane held open the door for her.

Shock flashed across Dorothea's face. Her jaw dropped open.

"Just a few questions this evening." Detective Kane's face was a hard mask of professionalism as he repeated his request.

Detective Kane led Mrs. Delaire out of the town office.

"That fire in his office is out. My apologies, Miss Lynne, we had no idea Mr. Spicer was harassing these teachers, or we would have put a stop to it." Mr. Holt shook his head.

"Thank you." Etta nodded.

"I'll get home to Mrs. Holt. She'll be worried sick. You can ensure Miss Lynne gets home safely?" Mr. Holt asked Nash.

"Yes, of course." Nash stood close to Etta, and his arm around her tightened.

They left the town office, and Holt locked the front door behind him. "Terrible business, isn't it?"

"Ghastly," Nash agreed.

Mr. Holt doffed his cap at Etta and disappeared into the darkness of the night. Nash let out a very long sigh of relief at her side. He held out his arm, and they walked together to Lucy Lemon's house.

Once they were on Crescent Avenue where all the shops and offices were closed, and they were assured of no prying eyes, Nash tugged her under an overhang. Rain started to spatter against the awning they stood under, and Etta wondered if the rain would ever stop.

"Before we get to Mrs. Lemon's and we have no privacy at all, you are all right? Not hurt?" Nash ran his hands over her shoulders as if checking to be sure there was no damage to her person.

"I'm fine. It was all very scary. I feel shaken but physically fine."

"When he grabbed you and slammed that door, my heart stopped, Etta. My heart stopped cold." Nash's jaw tightened.

"As you can see, I am safe and well." Etta smiled up at Nash.

"I promise, you will be safe and well the rest of your life, E. Lynne." Nash pulled her against him.

"I will lose my job if you go around making pronouncements like that!" Etta scolded him as she grinned up at him.

Nash shrugged. "I'll be careful. I assure you," Nash teased her.

Etta rolled her eyes. "I assure you—"

"Yes. I have heard all your assurances, all your demands including the exclamation points. I've battled through all the prickles and stings. Let me have a moment to just have you, Etta. I deserve it."

Etta reached up, and her hands rested on either side of his face.

As he tugged her closer, Etta smiled up at him.

Nash leaned down and kissed Etta.

Etta's heart swelled with desire; she didn't want the kiss to end. Not now, not ever. When Nash pulled back, she protested.

"Not yet," Etta whispered. "We'll have to pretend not to court from now until the end of June. I just saved your life, and I want more."

"You saved *my* life?" Nash's eyes widened. "I was never under arrest. He was just ruling me out..."

"I'm sure your life was on the line a little bit!" Etta teased him as she lifted her chin. "All women to the rescue, as usual!" Etta laughed as he bent his head and kissed her again.

A thought niggled in Etta's mind; she tried to drown it out, but it refused to be silent. She pulled back.

Confusion crossed Nash's face.

"There is still that one thorny issue between us." Etta bit her lip. "You know it—Grace's education."

"Can we just have one moment of passion without fighting?" Nash groaned. "Can we not just have this night, this time, and this present to just be together?"

"No." She stiffened. "Grace is dear to me. We must settle this."

"Dear to you! She is my daughter. I assure you she is more than dear to me! Listen. I'm working on something. Can you just trust me? Just a little bit?" Nash asked against her neck.

Etta bit her lip. "I trust you a lot, Nash. I really do. I won't back down in regard to Grace. This..." Etta waved her hand between them to indicate their budding romance. "This doesn't move forward unless you consider Grace's requests."

Nash pressed his forehead to Etta's. "She's only fifteen."

Etta's heart plummeted as she took a step back.

"Your daughter is brilliant, Nash. They are holding a position for her at university. How can you say no? We have nothing to teach her! Don't make her waste another year..."

"I need you to just trust me. Give me some time." Nash reached for her.

Etta took another step back. "She lost her mother, and she doesn't want to lose Ivy too. She is as close to a sister as she will ever have. Surely you can see that she shouldn't lose out on this chance just because of age. She will be sixteen at the time of enrollment."

"Etta, I can't lose any more... I lost my wife and newborn child. I lost the years I was at war... she is my daughter, and I just want to hold onto her. Plus, she is young and inexperienced —" Nash sighed.

A cold fist of hard realization tightened around Etta's heart, squeezing out any feeling she had for him. In an instant, the similarities between Nash and her mother strangled the feelings for him that bloomed in her heart. Both parents intent on pausing or crushing a dream for their own selfish interests. Her mother needed to be provided for and Nash couldn't endure anymore change. He wanted everything to go back to the way it was before the war. He wanted a world that no longer existed. "Nash. You're holding her back because of your own selfish interests. You can't face more loss. So for that she has to stay." Etta shook her head and stepped back again.

"Etta. She..." Nash frowned at her.

"She has a dream, and you are crushing it, just like my mother crushed mine. Different reasons, same result." Etta's jaw clenched hard. "Instead of thinking of how to help her reach her goals, you are stubbornly holding onto her. Keeping her here with you instead of packing up and going with her."

"Going with her?" Nash's eyebrows shot up.

"Why not? She is wasted here."

"But I'm mayor, and I have clients and..."

Etta shrugged. "You have flexibility she doesn't have."

"She can go when she is older," Nash growled at Etta.

"That's new. You said you were *thinking* of it." Etta crossed her arms over her chest.

"It will happen, just later." Nash scrubbed his hands over his face. "I don't think I should have to uproot my entire life for..."

"For her," Etta finished for him, and all the feelings she felt for him died at her feet.

Nash said nothing.

Etta clamped her mouth shut.

"It's not the same as your mother... I want my daughter to

stay here with me a few more years until she is older and I can feel more comfortable letting her go." Nash finished lamely.

"Well, that's honest." Etta could barely form the words. Her throat was tight with tears of disappointment. "Let's be honest here. Nash, we're adults, and I know things don't change after marriage. You have some decisions to make, and then I have some decisions to make." Etta swallowed hard because in her heart she had already decided they could go no further.

Nash sighed. "I've made my decision, Etta. She will wait until she is at least eighteen, and we'll *see*. At that time we'll look at all her options."

Etta fought the fist of salty tears that made her throat ache. "Well, maybe it's a good thing that the teacher's code doesn't let us court. All I see is you are crushing her dream just as my mother crushed mine."

"It's not like that at all." Nash's face fell as Etta's eyes filled with tears.

"It's exactly the same. She has an invitation to school, and you are refusing on her behalf." Etta could barely get the words out.

"Etta... please." Nash held his hands out in supplication.

"Please take me home. We've hashed over this enough. We will speak of it no more."

"Etta." Nash frowned.

"I need to go home." Etta's eyes filled with tears. "We can go no further with this between us."

"I love her. I really do." Nash stammered.

"Please take me home." Etta stiffened and turned away.

CHAPTER 36

With the Spicers out of the picture, the citizens of Oakland picked up the pieces and carried on. In early May, once baby Josh was safely delivered, Dr. Shannon McDougall said Cali was well enough to attend a graveside service for their mother. Etta, Nash, Cali, Lucy, and the rest of the citizens of Oakland who could attend stood by each other as they stood by the grave of Eleanor Lynne. As the minister spoke of her mother, Etta's eyes locked with Nash's briefly. She held onto Cali, but as much as she loved her sister, she yearned for Nash's solid strength to be at her side on such a terrible day. She wanted him to wipe her tears away. She missed the feel of his strong arms around her. Etta shook those thoughts away.

Stop being so needy!

Days had turned into weeks since they had broken up their courtship under an awning on Crescent Avenue. Nash hadn't presented an option regarding Grace's education. As time went on, Etta hardened her heart; she had suffered too much in life to ignore that sort of hardheadedness. She carefully avoided running into him. As her heart broke apart with loss, she wept in private.

No one knew.

Every time she almost weakened, Etta thought about the daughters she might have had with him. If her daughter wanted to reach for her dream, how could she respect a man who would stifle that? Her mother had dashed her dreams of art school, and here was Nash dashing Grace's dreams. Different reasons, but crushed all the same. She stiffened her spine and meticulously built a wall around her heart, careful to keep Nash out.

After the service, Lucy invited everyone back to her home for tea and refreshments. Etta was relieved that all the men, including Nash, left after they paid their respects. Once the men left them, the women settled into Lucy's parlour. Some pulled out knitting, and others pulled out quilting. Etta and Cali knew they were providing some distraction on this difficult day. Etta's heart warmed to the women of Oakland. She picked up a sketchpad and charcoal to sketch the scene in front of her. Mrs. Daindridge and Mrs. Carr flanked each side of the fireplace. Mrs. Bennett and Mrs. Holt sat on one settee, both quilting with big hoops. Every so often their hoops touched or overlapped, and they laughed. Lucy, Grace, Cali, and Mrs. Rood played a game of cards at the table. Cali excused herself when Josh woke up.

Etta smiled at Lucy.

The friendship in the room began to heal her spirit.

Her healing was interrupted by Mrs. Daindridge, who had waited patiently for the men to leave so she could share her news.

"We heard the verdict is in." Mrs. Daindridge's eyes gleamed with anticipation as she was on the verge of launching into a full report of what the courts had decided regarding the Spicers.

"Mrs. Daindridge, we have just had a graveside service. I'm sure Etta isn't up for a full..." Mrs. Bennett put down her quilting hoop as she frowned at Mrs. Daindridge.

"Mrs. Bennett, I actually would like to know how everything turned out." Etta refilled her teacup and settled in for the whole story. "If you know the truth?"

"It's true. My son has been at every court session, and he has given us a full report." Mrs. Carr kept knitting, content to let her friend tell the news.

"Mr. Spicer got off scot-free!" Mrs. Daindridge sputtered with indignation.

"No!" Etta gasped.

"Yes! His lawyers were very clever, and they placed all the blame on Mrs. Spicer. The blackmail, the whole thing. Her lawyers didn't utter a peep in rebuttal. It seems as though *she* was content to take the entire blame. There was evidence that he was an accomplice, but his lawyers explained it in such a way that he got off. What a sordid affair!" Mrs. Daindridge shook her head. "It's appalling."

"Poor Mrs. Spicer." Etta put down her charcoal pencil— a gift from Nash. A twinge of guilt prickled through her as she thought of how much she used his gift after ending things with him.

"Mrs. Spicer was sentenced to two years for involuntary manslaughter and blackmail," Mrs. Daindridge announced, an inflection of triumph in her tone.

Etta didn't share her sense of justice being served. "I see." Sadness sliced through her at the verdict. "While what happened to Mrs. Ellice is tragic, and it never should have happened, I think that is a very heavy sentence for her. She won't live out her term."

"No." Mrs. Bennett's eyes softened in sympathy. She sipped her tea. "The cancer will take her before the two years is up. I feel as though there was more I could have done. I should have tried harder to befriend her, and I promise you, I won't make that mistake again. We need a welcoming committee for new families to the area. Mrs. Holt, we should add that to the agenda at our next meeting."

Mrs. Holt put down her quilt and wrote the suggestion in a notepad she carried in her handbag. "I feel guilty, too. I should have tried harder."

"She killed an innocent woman who was pregnant!" Mrs. Daindridge's jaw dropped as she listened to the women in the room.

"She accidentally killed an innocent woman. There was a struggle, sure... but there were other circumstances to think about." Etta spoke harshly. At Mrs. Bennett's raised eyebrow she gentled her tone. "Yes. She made a terrible mistake, but her life... living with Mr. Spicer... I believe there should have been some leniency."

Mrs. Daindridge and Mrs. Carr looked at each other in alarm. "Are you saying that she should have gone free?"

"I think in situations like this, there are often grey areas. It's difficult to—" Etta stiffened as she heard the harsh judgment in Mrs. Daindridge's tone.

"Mrs. Ellice wouldn't have been on that path if it hadn't been for the false note from Nash. She wouldn't have been anywhere near that fall without *blatant trickery and outright falsehoods*! No. Two years is not enough." Mrs. Daindridge shook her head.

The women fell silent as they thought of the truth of that comment.

"I see your point, but it still pains me. I heard her confession, and she was a victim, too." Etta picked up her charcoal and continued sketching.

"What about that note you found that was stolen from your handbag?" Mrs. Bennett changed the subject abruptly. She placed her thimble on her third finger and started quilting again.

"Detective Kane suspects it was Miss Winthrop. He believes she was working with Mr. Spicer. She misspelled 'your' to make it look as though *Mrs. Spicer* had left it. With her broken English, that would have been a natural mistake." Etta shaded the sketch. "She has avoided me since everything happened. She eats in her room and hasn't spoken a word to me."

"You haven't heard the news about Miss Winthrop?" Mrs. Carr's eyes lit up as she leaned forward.

"Let me tell it!" Mrs. Daindridge begged.

"No. I heard it firsthand." Mrs. Carr waved at Mrs. Daindridge to be quiet.

The women in the room paused what they were doing and turned their full attention to Mrs. Carr.

Mrs. Carr beamed under their rapt attention.

"I saw Miss Winthrop at school on Friday... what could possibly have happened?" Etta sat up straighter.

"Since Mr. Spicer was acquitted, he has, I heard this on good authority..."

"Care to reveal your source?" Mrs. Bennett asked dryly.

"My son handled the real estate documents," Mrs. Carr snapped at Mrs. Bennett. "Mr. Spicer sold his house, fully furnished, to a young family from Toronto. The papers for the sale of the house were forwarded to an address in... well, you just won't guess where!"

Mrs. Carr smirked at the room full of women desperate for the news.

"Where?" Etta's teeth clenched together with impatience.

"Calgary!" Mrs. Carr burst out with the news. "To the heart of the frontier! I bet he thinks he can just disappear and no one will be the wiser." Mrs. Carr shook her head as if all people on the run from the law could be expected in Calgary sooner or later. "I am so thankful we live in this safe community."

"Safe now." Mrs. Daindridge nodded sagely, as if she had singlehandedly wrapped up the investigation herself.

"But what does Mr. Spicer's whereabouts have to do with crotchety Miss Winthrop?" Etta frowned at Mrs. Carr.

Mrs. Carr picked up a lemon sugar cookie and took a delicate bite while the women held their breaths, waiting for the news.

"Mrs. Carr!" Mrs. Holt exclaimed. "What has happened?"

"Well, I can report, there is a job opening in the Oakland School Division," Mrs. Carr said slyly, revelling in her moment in the spotlight.

Etta put her sketchpad down and sat on her hands so she wouldn't leap across the parlour and shake the rest of the story out of Mrs. Carr. "Miss Winthrop left?"

"She got on a train to Calgary *just this morning.*" Mrs. Carr finished her lemon sugar cookie and picked up her teacup. She frowned at the cool tea.

Lucy, ever the hostess, leaped up to empty her teacup and refill it.

The entire room gasped at the news. "Do you mean... are you saying—?"

"She's in love with him." Mrs. Daindridge stole Mrs. Carr's thunder.

Mrs. Carr's face crumpled with frustration.

"But he's still married... and he's a nut about morality..." Etta's jaw hung open from shock.

Mrs. Carr's eyebrow arched to her hairline. "His wife won't live out the year, according to the doctors. Miss Winthrop is in Calgary to stake her claim as the *next Mrs. Spicer.*"

"I—" Etta looked wildly from Mrs. Carr to Lucy. "I can't believe it! He's terrible!"

Lucy handed Mrs. Carr a fresh cup of tea.

"There is a lid for every pot." Mrs. Daindridge spoke as if she were the final authority.

"Speaking of the next missus..." Mrs. Carr wasn't done. After taking a sip, she leaned forward.

"Oh. Yes. Another piece of scandalous news." Mrs. Daindridge rubbed her hands together.

"What do you know?" Mrs. Holt put down her quilt and demanded they get to the point.

"Mrs. Delaire pranced around in her unmentionables in front of the wrong man. Turns out, she tangled with the wrong detective, let me tell you. Detective Kane had reopened the investigation into Mrs. Delaire's husband's death, and some numbers don't add up." Mrs. Carr stopped to sip, delighting in the gasps of shock in the parlour.

"Reopened the investigation!" Mrs. Bennett's jaw dropped.

"Yes. The coroner rechecked the level of morphine in Mr. Delaire's blood at the time of death... I'm no scientist..."

No one in the room disagreed.

Every woman leaned in closer.

"According to Mr. Carr, she said he had given himself a *full vial* before she entered the bedroom to give him his regular amount. The medical examiner says, if he had taken the amount she claimed, he would have been dead and not able to ask for more. So! She's in jail and awaiting trial."

"Really!" Etta's jaw dropped in shock. Etta marvelled at how Detective Kane had completed this investigation so privately. No one had been gossiping about it until now.

"Really," Mrs. Daindridge confirmed as though her say was final and the only proof needed. "I can assure you there were no

French lace underpinnings there! No! Her days of manipulation are over."

The ladies in the parlour were stunned into silence for a brief moment. "I always thought there was something odd about that woman." Mrs. Holt shook her head as she picked up her quilt.

"Me, too," Mrs. Bennett agreed as she threaded her quilting needle and kept working.

"Any other scandalous news?" Etta asked as she reached for her sketchpad.

"I was thinking, maybe you knew something?" Mrs. Carr's eyebrow arched.

"What would I possibly know, Mrs. Carr?" Etta's jaw clenched as Mrs. Carr looked ready to pounce on her for any information she might have.

"We were wondering about who your new neighbor is?" Mrs. Daindridge looked from Etta to Lucy. "We noticed you have already had a *heated discussion*."

"His name is Liam Tavish, and he has purchased that dilapidated house beside me. He is fixing it up to sell it." Lucy frowned as she spoke of Liam Tavish.

"Is he single or married?" Mrs. Carr asked Lucy.

"He is engaged, Mrs. Carr," Lucy replied, her tone barely civil.

"We noticed you have been..." Mrs. Carr thought about how to word her next sentence.

"We are at odds. Yes." Lucy's tone was clipped.

"What sort of odds?" Mrs. Daindridge leaned forward. Etta wondered if she would fall out of her chair.

"He wants to cut down a tree between our property lines so he can build a fence. I said no." Lucy stiffened in her chair.

"Why not let him cut down the tree?" Mrs. Daindridge asked. "It's a dead tree, isn't it?"

"I have my reasons." Lucy bristled visibly.

"What reasons are those?" Puzzlement splashed across Mrs. Carr's face. "It seems a reasonable request."

"You'll think I'm silly, but Russ carved our initials into that tree... I can't bear to part with it."

"Really. That is all very fanciful…" Mrs. Daindridge shook her head.

Lucy's eyes filled with tears.

Mrs. Holt frowned at Mrs. Daindridge.

A knock at the door interrupted the women.

Etta stood up. "I'll go." Etta shot a look to Mrs. Daindridge.

She opened the front door to the very man they were talking about.

"Is Mrs. Lemon home? I need to ask her about this bit of fence at the edge of the river bank."

Etta caught a slight Scottish accent as he spoke.

Lucy appeared at Etta's side. "Mr. Tavish."

Etta heard the icy frost in Lucy's tone. Lucy, who was lovely to everyone, stood at the entrance of her home, ready to go to battle with Mr. Tavish over her precious dead oak tree.

"I dare not take down a piece of fence without checking with you, miss." Tavish smiled broadly.

Etta heard the sarcasm in his tone.

"I wondered if you would allow me to remove this piece of broken-down fence, or is it precious to you, too?" Tavish looked down at Lucy.

Lucy fumed up at him.

Tavish stood over six feet tall, with shaggy coppery-brown hair and a scruffy beard. He looked as if he had just stepped off the highland, and all he was missing was a kilt and a set of bagpipes. He looked windblown and at the end of his patience with Mrs. Lemon.

Lucy angrily tucked a piece of hair behind her ear and pulled on a coat and shoes. "I better come out with you and see, in case you go too far and take down the tree as well!"

Mr. Tavish shrugged and stepped back so she could lead the way.

Etta's eyes widened as she watched them speak about the fence. Lucy gestured wildly. Tavish threw his hands up in the air at one point.

Mrs. Daindridge and Mrs. Carr crept to Etta's side at the window to spy.

"They say his leg was injured in the war, that's why he limps," Mrs. Carr said out of the side of her mouth.

"He was a sharpshooter," Mrs. Daindridge added as she kept her eyes peeled on Lucy and Mr. Tavish. "He's not hard on the eyes, I can tell you that!"

"He looks like he is ready to strangle Mrs. Lemon." Mrs. Carr squinted to see.

"He's engaged to be married." Mrs. Holt interrupted their gossip.

"Well! Imagine that!" Mrs. Daindridge sounded injured. She was clearly not over the dressing down she received from Mrs. Holt in the kitchen during the search.

"I think that's enough for me." Mrs. Holt finally stood up. "I have supper to get ready."

Mrs. Daindridge and Mrs. Carr regretfully tore themselves away from the window and left when the rest of the ladies filed out of the Lemon home. After seeing them off, Etta and Grace returned to the window to spy on Lucy Lemon and her new neighbour, Mr. Tavish.

"We should have borrowed Mrs. Daindridge's binoculars," Etta joked to Grace.

"What if she doesn't let him cut down that tree?" Grace asked Etta out of the side of her mouth. She couldn't take her eyes from the spectacle in front of them.

Lucy stamped her foot, and Tavish threw back his head in laughter.

Etta watched as Lucy, quiet, lovely, kind Lucy Lemon, lost her temper and shook her finger at Tavish. Etta couldn't tell what she was saying, but the shaggy highlander held his hands up in surrender and grinned at her, which only made her more furious.

"They'll sort it out." Etta shook her head at Grace. "In the meantime, you are so pretty. Can I sketch you? I am getting rusty."

Grace beamed with happiness at the compliment.

CHAPTER 37

*T*he end of the school year loomed before Etta. Every day inched closer to the thirtieth of June, and she wondered if she would be placed in Oakland or not. As the days wore on and there was still no letter, Etta's heart weighed heavy as she began packing up her classroom in her free time. Finally, she received the much-anticipated letter and held her breath as she opened the envelope from the Manitoba Teachers' Federation. She frowned as she read it, the letter from Miss Little requested a meeting in person.

Etta's heart sank with dread. A meeting in person could not be good.

The summer sunshine filtering down through new leaves on the oak trees did nothing to raise Etta's spirits as she made her way to the telegram office to send a message. Bright pink and red geraniums and striped petunias that were intended to brighten Crescent Avenue were lost on her. Worry filled her as she trudged past shiny clean shop windows. She waved half-heartedly at friendly Oakland citizens. Finally, she reached the office and sent a telegram saying she could meet Miss Little on Saturday at two, if that would be acceptable.

* * *

HAPPY, bright sunshine poured into Etta's room as she got ready to meet Miss Little. Cali came in to inspect her clothes.

"Not that dress... no. It washes you out. I have something I've been working on." Cali brought in a pretty dress in deep rose.

"You have a new baby, you aren't supposed to be working," Etta growled at Cali.

"Oh! Such a ray of sunshine!" Cali teased her. "It wouldn't kill you to smile, Etta."

"There is nothing to smile about," Etta grumbled as she pulled on the skirt and lacy top that did look very pretty.

I'll look lovely as I apply for a terrible apartment on Pacific Avenue and go back to the laundry.

The three women and baby Josh piled into Etta's car to go to Brandon, each bearing a list.

Cali and Lucy wouldn't hear of staying in the car while Etta got the news about the teaching position. Etta thought they looked smug, but she knew she had been cranky and difficult to live with lately.

As they waited, Etta remembered, not so long ago, sitting there, trying to hide her obvious poverty. So much had happened since that day. Happiness and loss.

Cali, sensing her fears and worries, reached out and held her hand.

"Whatever this is, we're going to get through this together." Cali gave her hand a squeeze.

A lump in Etta's throat threatened to strangle her. "Thanks."

"Miss Lynne?" Miss Little called her into her office.

Etta pressed her fingers against the blue cameo at her throat and got up.

Together they made their way down the hall to Miss Little's office.

Miss Little stepped aside as Etta entered, eyes widening with surprise as she saw Grace Nash and Ivy Bennett sitting behind the desk.

"What is going on?" Etta looked from Grace to Miss Little.

Cali and Lucy giggled behind her.

"You knew about this?" Etta turned to face them.

"They had to be sure you would come." Cali grinned at Etta.

"Miss Lynne, there *is* a job opening, and I asked Miss Little if I could present it." Grace's eyes danced with excitement.

"I don't understand." Worry sharpened Etta's tone.

Grace grinned at Etta.

"Grace, I assure you. If your father is behind this, we have had a falling out and it is irreparable damage. Whatever scheme..."

"Etta." Cali nudged her sister. "Would you just be quiet for a minute?"

"Grace." Etta ignored Cali. "You are young, but the differences between Mr. Nash and I are so wide... I don't expect you to understand." Etta pressed her lips together as Cali nudged her harder. "If this is a trick—"

"Dad, she's *not* listening to me." Grace's eyes twinkled as she crossed her arms over her chest.

Nash entered the room and stood by his daughter. "I told you she was stubborn and consistently believes she knows better."

"What's going on?" Etta looked from Nash to Grace and then back to Nash.

"You have a choice to make." Miss Little slid a letter across her desk to Etta.

Etta read through the paper swiftly. A position to teach high school English in Appleton, Saskatchewan. One of the highest paid positions in a private school. The people of Appleton were trying to recreate an English settlement. The Harpers' children had been sent there to attend school. Etta swallowed hard. No more apartments on Pacific Avenue if she took this job. She would teach the aristocracy.

Cali moved closer. "This position comes with accommodations for both of us. Lord Harper arranged it."

Etta looked at this gift from the Harpers, and her throat tightened. "This is... this is so amazing. I can't even believe it."

I should want this. I did want this...

In that moment, she knew. Nash had no intention of changing things for Grace. He hadn't pulled strings to make this happen.

Etta's heart sank again.

Why be here to present it, then?

"Or... we have a different offer..." Grace's eyes sparkled with excitement. "Father doesn't want me to go to school..."

Disappointment weighed at Etta's carefully guarded heart.

"Without you." Grace bit her lip.

"What?" Etta looked from Grace to Nash.

"Please, let me finish. Dad asked me to present this because he said you delight in turning him down flat. This is my dream. My *new* dream." Grace's eyes lit up as she handed Etta another piece of paper. "If you go to Toronto, Dad will let me go with you. So, you would go to school, and so would I. You would go to art school during the day while I am at class and be my chaperone, and Ivy's of course, when you are not at class. The university has held my position in the mathematics department. We just need to know what you decide." Grace held her breath.

Etta's hands shook as she picked up the confirmation from the Toronto School of Art with her name on it. Her face creased in confusion.

"It turns out that your application to attend the Toronto School of Art only needed to be renewed, which I have taken the liberty of doing. Miss Lynne, you have been accepted to the Toronto School of Art, to start on September 3rd. All fees are paid in exchange for your careful chaperoning of Grace. I just have to hear a yes or no." Nash's deep voice cut through all her thoughts.

"Is this... I don't know..." Etta stammered as she looked up at Nash. "How much did this cost?"

"Etta! This is the most romantic moment of your life! Just trust! Say yes!" Cali threw her hands up in the air.

Etta's face crumpled at Cali's attack. "All my life, Cali. The cost mattered, and it was too great to pay."

Cali appeared chastised.

Nash took a step closer.

"I thought a lot about this. About how to handle this in a way that would empower you. Not make you feel like you owe me. Mrs. Bennett and Mrs. Holt finally saved me with a suggestion."

Etta locked eyes with Nash as if he were the only person in the room.

"I need Grace to be safe. If she's with you, she'll be safe. My fears about her being in school with older... boys... well. I think you'll protect her and indeed Ivy. So this is the only way it will work. If you prefer to stay and work at Appleton then you can do that and stay with Cali. So it's your choice."

Etta's heart soared with excitement at the thought.

"Grace, are you sure you want me tagging along?" Etta's heart was in her throat.

"I said we are a package deal." Grace slid her hand into Etta's.

Nash took a step closer and took her other hand in his. "I have the possibility of a new job, too."

"You do?" Etta nearly choked on the words.

"If things work out, eventually, once I get things sorted out here, I'll be in Toronto, working as a barrister at a law firm on Bay Street. I don't think I can get things settled by September, so I need you there in Toronto with Grace. Once I'm in Toronto, I will be working long hours until my practice is established, which is why I need a companion for Grace. She and Ivy are too young to be home on their own while I'm working. "

Etta's jaw dropped in shock. "You're going to Toronto?"

"This pesky teacher wouldn't take no for an answer, and when I saw what Grace's future could be, on Pacific Avenue, well, I was engulfed with all-new fears about my precious daughter. So, it turns out that this firm handles delicate cases. They specialize in representing women who are seeking justice." Nash took a step closer to her. "I believe some of them are sleeping on broken-down settees. Some of these women are facing a vulnerability I never dreamed of. Treacherous land-lords, bookies even... because of poor decisions made by their fathers or husbands. I intend to represent those cases to the best of my ability. I intend to work hard to bring to light that we need laws to protect women."

"You are going to work... for women!" Etta couldn't take the surprise out of her tone.

Cali tugged Grace away so Nash could hold both Etta's hands in his.

Nash grinned at her. "I am going to represent women, and men. But I will specialize in cases involving women. Women who have lost everything through no fault of their own."

"Nash, is that why you've been keeping your distance?"

"No. I've just been busy! I have many clients I have to refer on to other barristers. I've been setting my affairs in order. I can hire another companion for Grace, I'm going to Toronto with her regardless... I just hope it's you."

"I don't know what to say!" Etta swallowed hard.

Nash smiled at her. "Say yes."

"Please, Miss Lynne! Would you come to Toronto with us?" The question burst out of Grace before she could hold back.

"Etta, please say yes," Nash begged. "I have worked tirelessly to devise a clever plan that would keep all the women in my life happy. It wasn't easy. I've been worried about this! Terrified that I hadn't done it right and would lose you. What is it going to be? Appleton or Toronto? Grace is supposed to be in school on September 8th... You have some time to think, but we would really like to be able to discuss plans... I need to sell the house and close my law firm here... I want you involved in the decisions so that you are cared for as well. For instance, do you need two bedrooms in your apartment or one?"

"This is all so... shocking... I don't know... what about Cali?" Etta turned to Cali.

"I'm staying with Mrs. Lemon. Mr. Hartwell is insisting I take over Mrs. Hartwell's work as soon as I am able. He doesn't want her overextended." Cali waved Etta's concerns away.

"Are you sure? You want to work and raise a baby..."

"Of course. I knew I would work with a baby, and instead of laundry dripping on our heads, it's dress design and sewing! Much better! It's my baby, my responsibility. I'll handle it. Would you please return to the heart-melting scene in front of you and forget we're here?" Cali waved her objections away.

Etta turned back to Nash.

"I'm not going without you." Grace's eyes shone as she spoke, she was so excited.

Etta took a step back. She picked up the acceptance letter to the Toronto School of Art. A lump in her throat choked her.

"We aren't leaving without you." Grace hovered near both of them. "If you can't go, if you chose to stay here and be a switchboard operator instead of a teacher, then I'll go to school here in Brandon but... Toronto... that is my pick." Grace's eyes silently pleaded with her as she waited for Etta to make a decision.

Nash stepped forward and held his hand out to Etta.

A grin tugged at Etta's lip. "This is coercion at its most disturbing. Using this beautiful child to force me to make a decision! A child I love and want to cheer on to great success."

"A lot is riding on this," Nash said in mock seriousness. "I wasn't about to leave it to chance, so I brought out the heavy hitter."

Etta turned from Nash to speak to Cali. "Cali." Etta didn't need to say a thing to her sister. Cali knew exactly what she meant from the inflection in her tone.

"There has been enough sadness and sacrifice, Etta." Cali's eyes filled with tears. "It's time to live. It's time to choose a path that will make your heart happy. You deserve it."

"But Josh." Etta bit her lip.

"Lucy and I have been talking." Cali brushed her worries away. "I'm staying with Lucy, and we're going to figure it out."

"Where will you live if Lucy..."

"Stop talking about money for once!" Cali finally lost her patience and scolded Etta. "For once in your life, stop all that and just listen to this man. He's offering you everything you have ever dreamed of! Take it, you foolish girl. Either Appleton or Toronto. Your pick."

"This isn't the violin and flower-filled speech I was envisioning," Nash said dryly to all the people in the room waiting to hear Etta's decision.

"Cali." Etta's eyes filled with tears as she searched Cali's eyes to be sure she would be fine if she followed her dream.

Cali's eyes filled with tears, too. "It's all worked out. I am totally fine. You deserve to live your life on your own terms. Have your own baby."

Etta blushed a million shades of red and spluttered at the suggestion.

"You can, you know." Cali reached out and wiped the tears from Etta's eyes.

"Etta, you are only a train ride away. Toronto by rail is not that far." Nash drew her attention back to him.

Lucy, Cali, and Miss Little stood at the doorway and held their collective breaths as Nash took Etta's left hand and Grace clasped her right.

"So!" Grace smiled at Etta as Ivy joined their circle. "Please, I can't wait! Are we going to Toronto? Are we going to be a family? A real one? Am I going to go to school in Toronto? I have to know!"

Etta opened her mouth to speak and then closed it.

"Please. Please, Miss Lynne. Please come with us," Ivy and Grace said at the same time.

"Grace." Etta bit her lip.

Grace's eyes filled with tears.

"All my life, there was only the choice between bad and worse. I've never had this sort of opportunity... I just need a moment to feel this, all of this..."

"Miss Lynne, my dad is good. He will be very good to you. I promise it." Grace's eyes pleaded with Etta.

Etta's heart pounded in her throat as she thought of starting school at the Toronto School of Art, an opportunity she had buried and thought would never happen. She turned her attention back to Grace and then looked up at Nash. He said nothing; he waited patiently.

Miss Little and Cali leaned forward, holding their breaths, waiting for her answer.

Etta held onto Nash and Grace's hands tightly.

"Miss Little, may I take that letter of acceptance to Appleton?"

Disappointment shot across Nash's face. Grace's crumpled in sadness. Cali gasped in outrage. Miss Little's hands shook as she handed her the letter.

"Wait... wait!" The blood drained from Nash's face as he

addressed the women in the room. "Can we have some privacy, please?"

Quickly, the women left Nash and Etta alone in Miss Little's office.

Nash turned to face her. "You don't trust me... I get it. I understand. I had a big talk with Mrs. Bennett and Mrs. Holt. I see exactly what you were talking about... I know, Etta... I know what you have been through and I understand. I promise you will never, ever have one day of uncertainty..."

Etta placed her hand against his cheek. "I know that you know."

"What is it then... what?" Nash pleaded with her.

Etta's gaze locked with Nash's as she stepped closer. "Nash, the school, the accommodations and the work for you... That is all taken care of?"

"Yes." Nash swallowed hard.

She stepped away from him and scratched *Miss Ford* on the Appleton offer and placed the letter on Miss Little's desk. Miss Ford had suffered under the authority of Mr. Spicer too. Etta grinned as Nash peeked over her shoulder, read the name on the offer and sighed with relief. She turned back to face him.

"There is one little thing left." Etta tilted her head to the side.

"There is?" A smile played at his lips. Lips she knew would be pressed against hers right away.

"I want a vow from you. A promise." She reached out to him.

"Oh. Etta!" Nash pounced on her and held her hands in his. "I love you. You know that, right? I think I fell for you the night we dealt with feminine complaints and appendixes and... all that gruesomeness! When you wept, thinking that you made a mistake and Grace could have died, I loved you right then because loving me is loving her, too, and *you do*. I love you with all my heart— there is no other woman for me. When you sent that sketch of Grace, I saw your love for her in every mark on the paper. We have to be together, Etta. Please, come with me to Toronto, please."

Etta's heart soared in happiness as he spoke. "I love you, too."

Nash moved to kiss her, but Etta held her hand against his

chest to stop him. "But first, some conditions, and I want a solemn vow from you."

Nash's eyes searched hers.

Etta detected a hint of wariness in his eyes. "Of course." Nash dropped his hands from her face and straightened; he transformed to a negotiating barrister right on the spot. "What do you need?"

"I want you to promise that you will never..." Etta faltered as she spoke, overcome with emotion at the love she saw in his eyes.

"Never what?" Nash whispered. He brushed a piece of hair from her eyes.

"You will never *iron* with anyone else." Etta caught her breath as he leaned closer.

A grin broke across Nash's face; he chuckled as he vowed solemnly, "I promise to iron only with you, E. Lynne, for the rest of my life." Gently, he cradled her face in his hands. "Are the negotiations over? Can I kiss you now?"

Etta stood up on tiptoes and slid her arms around his neck. "You can kiss me forever."

* * *

The Café on Crescent: mybook.to/Cafeoncrescent
The Great War is over leaving Lucy Lemon a destitute widow
with a tax bill for her dream house that she can't afford.
Worse, her awful brother-in-law wants the house — and her.
Suddenly, an opportunity to open a Cafe lands in Lucy's lap.
As help comes from an unexpected source, Lucy will have to
face a difficult choice. Stay stuck in the past, clinging to a house
she can't afford, or forge ahead with a new dream.
Also, as sparks fly between Lucy and Tavish, do they ever come
to terms over their shared tree?
The Café on Crescent is sweet women's historical fiction with a
sprinkle of romance.
All your favourite tropes: Strength in Sisterhood, small town
romance, and a clean and wholesome love story...

plus gossipy neighbours — Mrs. Daindridge and Mrs. Carr—
will delight you.
The Café on Crescent is available here:
mybook.to/Cafeoncrescent
Stay up to date on new releases here: https://www.facebook.
com/profile.php?id=100071070035219
Join my newsletter here: http://
carolynfinchwrites.com/newsletter/

The End

ACKNOWLEDGMENTS

Thank you to Alex McGilvery of celticfrogediting.com, Nicki Galliers, and Julie Sherwood for your hard work in editing this novel. A big thanks to Red Adept Editing for the first proof reading.

Thank you, Wendy Holmstrom, for final proof before printing. I really appreciate your help and support.

Thank you, Fran Saler, for sending me so much information about war widows from World War 1 and the history of teaching in Manitoba. You are a fantastic research assistant and a huge support!

Also, a big thank you to Mireille Theriault from the Manitoba Teachers' Society. I appreciate that you could verify the code of conduct for me. You also made yourself available for some brainstorming! I couldn't have written this book without your help.

Thank you, Peter. My dream of writing and publishing isn't possible without your support.

Made in the USA
Middletown, DE
14 March 2024

51541075R00191